PRAISE FOR WHAT'S BRED IN THE BONE

What's Bred in the Bone is an exciting, highly imaginative science fiction thriller and police procedural. Whether human or canine, Gephardt knows her characters and breathes life into them. Her writing is taut, the plot intricate and fast-paced. This novel is a dog-lover's dream!

   --Robin Wayne Bailey, author of the *Brothers of the Dragon* Series

There were so many things to love about this book . . . besides from all the animal goodness, there is a good mystery going on. I think this can best be described as a police procedural in space - and with dogs. There's plenty of action and intrigue to keep the reader's attention.

   --Booker T's Farm

Gephardt does a fantastic job of putting us inside of these animals' heads. Every action they take makes sense for an animal, and you get the feeling that she truly understands what makes our canine friends tick. She also has a great sense of humor, with some pages making me giggle as I read them.

--Dogpatch Press

I found the story absorbing and I wanted to keep reading; the day I read it, our dinner was 45 minutes late because I didn't want to put the book down.
    --Amazon Review

I really enjoyed this book. I stayed up way too late several nights as I wanted to read "one more chapter." The story-line was interesting, and I will be looking forward to other books in this trilogy.
    --Goodreads Review

Drawing on deep research into canine behavior, animal cognition, and sustainable environmental design, Gephardt gives us a world full of honor, intrigue, and betrayal, peopled with a cast of believable characters—both human and XK9—we care about, and enjoy spending time with, and filled with problems that are definitely worth talking about.
    --Amazon Review

Please follow **Jan S. Gephardt** on your favorite online platform. She's on Facebook, Twitter, and LinkedIn. Her website https://jansgephardt.com/ includes her regu-larly-updated blog "Artdog Adventures."

Learn more about **Weird Sisters Publishing LLC** at https://weirdsisterspublishing.com/. The website features "The Weird Blog," and information about all of their book and story releases, from **Jan S. Gephardt**, **G. S. Norwood**, and eventually **Warren C. Norwood**.

WHAT'S BRED IN THE BONE

JAN S. GEPHARDT

WEIRD SISTERS
PUBLISHING LLC

What's Bred in the Bone, © 2019 by Jan S. Gephardt

Cover art © 2019 by Jody A. Lee

Excerpt from *A Bone to Pick,* © 2021 by Jan S. Gephardt

A Bone to Pick cover art © 2020 by Jody A. Lee

For permission requests, please use the contact form for Weird Sisters Publishing LLC at:

https://weirdsisterspublishing.com/index.php/about-weird-sisters-publishing/

❀ Created with Vellum

*For **Lucy A. Synk***
Fellow artist, heart-sister, and Rex's first true fan.

"What's bred in the bone will come out in the flesh."

— OLD ENGLISH PROVERB

CONTENTS

1. A WALK IN THE PARK   1
Rana Station Wheel Two, Orangeboro, 9th Precinct,
Terrace Eight, Glen Haven Park   1

2. PLAYOFF MANEUVERS   14
Orangeboro 5th Precinct, Market Garden
Neighborhood, Pam, Balchu, and Shady's
apartment,   14

3. NOTHING GOOD EVER HAPPENS AFTER
MIDNIGHT   25
Corona Tower, an elevator to the Wheel Two Hub,
and Warehouse 226   25

4. SHAKE AND BREAK   35
Wheel Two Hub Docks, Bay 2-18B   35

5. FROM TRIUMPH TO DEFEAT   44
Bay 2-18B, Emergency Bunker 8 and Rescue
Runner *Triumph*   44
Orangeboro 6th Precinct, Orangeboro Medical
Center   50

6. HOW TO CAPTURE AN XK9   54
Orangeboro Medical Center, Central Plaza, and
Orangeboro Police Dept. HQ   54

7. IN QUEST OF CLOUT   62
OPD HQ, Chief Klein's Office   62

8. PERSONNEL ASSISTANCE, DOESN'T   71
Market Garden Neighborhood, Central Plaza, and
OPD HQ   71

9. SCENT FACTORS   82
OPD HQ Briefing Room and Orangeboro Morgue   82

10. SHADY KILLS AN ANGRY MAN   91
Civic Center, Orangeboro Morgue and Social
Services Secured Medical Station   91

11. UNDER RESTRAINTS   101
    5th Precinct, The Sandler Clinic   101
    Civic Center, Social Services Secured Suite 7   106

12. REX FINDS HIS VOICE   113
    Orangeboro Medical Center   113

13. SLAVERY AND FORMWORK   120
    Orangeboro Morgue   120

14. CLARITY OF SCENT   127
    Orangeboro Medical Center   127

15. MORNING MIRACLE   134
    Corona Tower   134

16. DESOLATION AND DOGGIE-BACK RIDES   141
    Corona Tower   141

17. REX TRIES COMMUNITY POLICING   152
    Glen Haven Neighborhood and Park   152

18. CRACKING THE CASE BOOK   162
    Glen Haven Neighborhood and Corona Tower   162

19. REX TAKES A HIKE   171
    Corona Tower   171
    Glen Haven Transit Terminal Station and spinward
    locations   175

20. SHADY SMELLS BAD THINGS   182
    Orangeboro Morgue   182

21. REX FALLS IN LOVE   191
    OPD HQ and Civic Center Sub-Level 3, Corridor 9
    SBI Investigative Center, AKA "S-3-9"   191
    Civic Center Complex, a small courtyard   196

22. REX AND LSA SHIMON GO HUNTING   201
    5th Precinct, OPD HQ and Sub-Level Ten, AKA "the
    Five-Ten"   201

23. ADVENTURESS IN TORO ENCLAVE   211
    The Five-Ten Toro Enclave   211

24. PROBABLE CAUSE   222
    The Five-Ten Toro Enclave, and OPD HQ   222

25. ANSWERS AND NON-ANSWERS   235
Orangeboro Morgue, S-3-9 and S-3-10, and OPD
Detention Suite K   235

26. A COMBINED WEIGHT OF AWFULNESS   243
OPD HQ, Chief Klein's Office   243

27. REX TELLS MORE FORBIDDEN THINGS   251
OPD HQ, Chief Klein's Office   251

28. THE FIRST PACK MEETING   259
Civic Center S-3-9 and OPD Meeting Room Two   259

29. REX COMMUNES WITH THE PALLETS AT DAWN   269
The Sandler Clinic and Civic Center S-3-9   269

30. DOING IT XK9 STYLE   279
S-3-9 Evidence Cavern   279

31. REVELATIONS AND AWAKENINGS   289
S-3-9 Evidence Cavern   289
Orangeboro Medical Center Re-Gen Unit   294
Civic Center Rotunda Elevator and Chief Klein's
Office   297

32. DELAYS, DEVELOPMENTS, AND
DISAGREEMENTS   302
S-3-9 Evidence Cavern, Central Plaza, and LEO's
Grill   302
Central Plaza and S-3-9 Investigative Center   306

33. POLITICS AND POMPOUS INTRUDERS   312
S-3-9 Evidence Cavern   312
OPD HQ, Chief Klein's Office   317

34. REVELATIONS, REORGANIZATION, AND
RECALL   323
S-3-9 Evidence Cavern and Chief Klein's Office   323

35. A WARRANT AGAINST THE UNWARRANTED   335
OPD HQ, Chief Klein's Office   335
6th Precinct, Terrace Four, Teisingas Tower, and the
Sandler Clinic   341

36. POLITICS 347
    S-3-9 Evidence Cavern 347
    Civic Center Rotunda Elevator and Chief Klein's
    Office 352

37. PREEMPTIVE STRIKES 360
    Pam, Balchu, and Shady's apartment, Market
    Garden Neighborhood 360
    Orangeboro Medical Center, Re-Gen Unit 362
    Chief Klein's Office and OPD HQ Entrance 367

38. THE ARREST OF A LIFETIME 370
    OPD HQ Entrance 370
    Orangeboro Medical Center, Re-Gen Unit 373
    Civic Center S-3-9 and OPD HQ 374
    OPD Detention, Interview Suite B 376

39. LEVERAGING INFLUENCE 383
    Orangeboro Medical Center, Re-Gen Unit 383
    Civic Center, OPD Detention and Borough Council
    Members' Office Level 385

40. BUST, BUILDUP, AND BREAKTHROUGH 391
    S-3-9 Evidence Cavern 391
    Orangeboro Civic Center, an antechamber adjacent
    to the Borough Council Meeting Hall 395

41. RETURN OF THE LOST 401
    Orangeboro Council Meeting Hall antechamber 401
    Civic Center S-3-9 405
    Orangeboro Medical Center, Re-Gen Unit 411

42. A FRONT-ROW SEAT ON HISTORY 413
    Orangeboro Medical Center, Re-Gen Unit 413

43. TREACHERY AND REVELATION 423
    Orangeboro Civic Center Auditorium Entrance,
    Rotunda, and Mayor's Office 423
    Orangeboro Civic Center Auditorium 426

44. REQUIEM AND REST 431
    Orangeboro Civic Center Auditorium 431
    Orangeboro Civic Center Auditorium, the
    Orangeboro Medical Center Re-Gen Unit, and
    Corona Tower 434

What happens next? 441
A Bone to Pick-Chapter One 443
Who's Who and What's What 455
Acknowledgments 473
About the Author 477

1

A WALK IN THE PARK

Rana Station Wheel Two, Orangeboro, 9th Precinct, Terrace Eight, Glen Haven Park

Damn it, no horizon should bend upward.

XK9 Rex Dieter-Nell flinched away from the "scenic overlook." He clenched his jaws on a quiet whimper, but the shudder down his back made his hackles prickle.

His human partner, Charlie, met Rex's eyes. *I'm sorry. I know you don't like it.* His words flowed through their brain link on a wave of empathy.

Rex lowered his head, wary of insulting his partner's beloved home. Maybe if he switched to using his collar-mounted vocalizer, he could achieve more emotional distance. "I think perhaps the taste must be acquired."

But is it one you'll ever acquire? Charlie's worry echoed through the link.

Rex looked away. He shared his partner's concern but feared to admit it. "It is getting dark. Perhaps we should move on."

Charlie straightened, stepped away from the guardrail. *I*

know everything's different for you here. It'll take time. Things'll grow less strange. I'm just being impatient.

Rex had hoped to spare his partner's feelings, but the brain link had betrayed him again. *I guess we'll see how things work out.* He hazarded another look. *Ugh.* It was freaky-unnatural for a river to run down the wall at one end of the vista, as Wheel Two's Sirius River did. Even worse for it to run back up the wall at the other. But this weird quirk of Rana Habitat Space Station's toroidal wheel-geography, in itself, was minor compared to all that Rex had lost.

I appreciate your respect for my feelings about my home. Charlie'd followed his thoughts again. He ran a strong brown hand along Rex's neck, then rubbed the base of his ears with soothing strokes.

Rex leaned into his partner's hand, despite his mood. That did feel pretty good. A soft little whimper escaped. He pressed his head against Charlie's sternum and gave in to the ear-rub.

I don't want to belittle your loss. Charlie's fingers kept up their soothing rhythm. *I know how much you miss your Packmates, especially Shady.*

Rex, his mate Shady, and their Packmates, the ten members of the Orangeboro Pack, had spent every day together at their planet-based former home in Solara City. Together for training. Together for meals. Together each night, nestled in the straw bedding on the hard floor in the Unpartnered Kennels. Together was how they'd always hoped to stay. The Pack, together, meant home, meant family. Meant love.

Rex rubbed his head against Charlie, soothed by his partner's empathy and his comforting personal scent. But a burning knot of longing expanded within him whenever he thought about Shady or his Packmates.

None of the Pack had seen each other since the Presentation Ceremony in Orangeboro's Central Plaza. Each XK9 lived at his or her human partner's home now. Rex and Shady spoke secretly on their coms each night, but that was their only contact. It had been almost two entire months.

Charlie had lodged several protests about the Orangeboro Police Department's policy of keeping the dogs apart. Shady said her partner Pam had too. No luck. The XK9 Project had prescribed these handling protocols. The OPD wouldn't budge. The Pack stayed apart, ten lonely exiles in a bizarre foreign place, with only humans around them.

Longing ached from Rex's throat down through his chest, to knot in his gut. A howl swelled from his heart, but he swallowed it unsung. Time to change the subject. _At least we did well today. Even if no one else knows._

Charlie stroked Rex's neck. _We scored a nice win today, and trust me, the right people know._

I guess. Rex flicked his ears, still dissatisfied. Their subject had been an acrobatic burglar who liked to climb up the local residence towers' outer balconies to gain entrance. Rex hadn't needed to climb balconies to chase her, thank goodness. He'd crossed her trail outside a pub she was known to frequent, then tracked her to a storage unit where they'd caught her literally hip-deep in stolen goods. That had been fun.

But then came the rest of the day. They'd spent it in Precinct Nine Station's Evidence Submission Room. That had not been fun. Rex had helped as much as he could with the inventory. But mostly it was Charlie who'd imaged, ID-tagged, bagged, and deposited everything they'd recovered. Meanwhile upstairs DPO Sanchez, the lead detective, received all the congratulations.

Irritation prickled like an itch he couldn't reach. Rex smelled the hot, achey inflammation that lingered in his partner's neck, back, and especially his weaker left arm, although Charlie had not complained. _DPO Sanchez did nothing but tell us a couple of places we might start, and hand us a glove for me to sniff. We took it from there. We followed the scent. We solved the case. It was our victory._

Charlie shook his head. *You know Sanchez has been on that case for months. The glove was crucial, and so was the tip about the pub. Gotta give her that, at least. She deserves the glory.*

Hurt and frustration squeezed Rex's throat. *But I deserve glory, too. Captain Argus had to order her to use us.* He stifled a growl. *Sanchez called me the Chief's new toy. I am not a toy.*

And you proved it today. Charlie scratched behind Rex's ears again. *Do solid work, then don't be obnoxious about it afterward. That's the best way to convince a doubter like Sanchez. And as I said, the right people know what you did. Captain Argus and Chief Klein are both very pleased.*

Rex sighed. He was acting like a puppy, longing for praise. At the mature age of seven, he was old enough to know better. Dogs mustn't snatch admiration away from humans. He did know better. But he loved being at the center of admiration. Having a mature attitude sucked.

They turned away from the overlook, headed up the path toward the steps of the next switchback. All manner of scents flowed down from plants, small creatures, buildings, and humans up-slope: residual odors of what people had eaten, or scent factors that revealed their moods. Rex recognized several human scent-profiles from past encounters, but the nearest was Charlie's neighbor Fatima Smythe. Rex had met her at a neighborhood picnic the week he'd arrived on-Station.

Associated with Fatima's location, other new scents filtered down. Ozzirikkians had a characteristic sweet-organic, almost smoky odor, in contrast to most humans' base-scent, which lay in the musky, mellower mid-ranges. They were Rana Stationers, just like humans, but the higher gravity of human habitat wheels made it unusual for them to visit. *What are two ozzirikkians doing here?*

Charlie gave him a sidelong glance. *Ozzirikkians?*

They're with Fatima and one other human, approaching on the path above us. Rex gazed up the path, but the bushes obscured his view.

The link conveyed Charlie's puzzlement. *To venture into our gravity, these ozzirikkians must be close friends.* Anything higher than 0.823-Terran G taxed ozzirikkian joints and organs if they stayed more than a few hours. Charlie frowned up the path, but then, through the link, Rex felt his realization dawn. *Oh. I bet they're co-workers, here for the Betrothal rehearsal. I wonder if they're part of her Betrothal party.*

Whatever they were doing here, they drew nearer. Rex caught scents similar to those that humans or dogs emitted when in mild-to-moderate pain. Ozzirikkians didn't come into human territory lightly. They had their own habitat wheels, Numbers Five and Six. Those Wheels were a different size, and counter-rotated at a slightly different velocity from the human Wheels, to provide the proper gravity.

Rex froze, nose high. Here was another new scent, an unmistakable combination of human sweat with scent factors spawned by anxiety, hyper-alertness, and ill-intent. There was nothing else in all the scent-spectra quite like the smell of a human preparing to do something bad. And this human was closing in on Fatima and her friends.

A shrill cry cut the air. No mistaking the person's fear.

Rex sprang up the path. He ran into a cloud of malevolent, aggressive male human scent. Mingled with it, Rex caught the human women's and ozzirikkians' scents, sharp with terror.

"Damned click-apes!" the man cried. "What're you doing here?"

Protective fury swept through Rex. He rounded the bend, hackles stiff and teeth bared.

A slender man in dark clothing confronted Fatima and her friends. He leveled an EStee at them.

Rex cranked his vocalizer to top volume. "Police! Halt! Drop your weapon!"

The man swung around. He fired the EStee in Rex's direction, then plunged into the thicket next to the path. With a crackle of dry leaves, he disappeared.

Rex bounded past the human-ozzirikkian group, focused on their assailant. He shoved his head and burly shoulders into the brush. Stiff branches tore at him, but he pushed forward by main force. Being larger than any normal dog had both advantages and drawbacks.

The skinny-hipped subject scrambled through natural tunnels under the bushes. Rex's equipment panniers caught in the stiff twigs.

Rex retreated, shook himself, then stepped back to get a better overview. *My panniers are too wide!*

Charlie reached him in seconds. His hands loosened buckles, released hook-and-loop straps. The panniers lifted off. "Can you get him?"

"Consider him got!" Rex lunged into the brush, the subject's scent hot in his nose. The tunnel twisted. Rex rammed his way through the tough branches.

His quarry's scent went sweaty-cold with terror.

Good. Rex's growl thundered in his chest. He shoved through the bushes.

At the edge of his attention, he sensed Charlie. His partner strove to calm the victims, called for backup. Charlie was covering his end of things. Rex had a different mission.

Rex's quarry doubled back, dodged, evaded. Always stayed beyond Rex's reach. "Give up while you can," Rex warned him.

The man didn't answer. He dodged down another branching tunnel.

Rex halted. This could go on a long while, if he followed the agile young man's route through the brush. He put his nose up, tracked his subject's progress. Then he stepped back through his memory to that overview he'd glimpsed. They were on a narrow section of a flat secondary terrace in Glen Haven Park. The thicket ran along one of the park's terrace walls. At the right end of it lay a muddy drainage groove; at the left end, a flight of steps.

The subject managed to keep his noise-making down to quiet crackles of leaf and twig until at last he stopped deep inside the bushes. By now he'd probably put at least 15 meters of circuitous burrows between himself and Rex. Self-satisfied scent factors drifted out through the branches. He thought he'd escaped.

Rex snorted. Did he think Rex couldn't hear him breathing? Couldn't hear his heartbeat? Couldn't smell his bad self, over there by the terrace wall? Did he believe Rex could only follow his twisted path? Well, screw that. The subject was only four meters away if one took a direct route.

Rex sized up the tough bushes. This'd be doing it the hard way. But only for four meters.

He bunched his haunches, set his hind paws. Breathed in and out, and focused on his subject's location.

Then he launched himself through a blur of breaking branches with a roar.

His quarry screamed. He darted to Rex's left.

Rex rebounded off the wall, lunged after him. Twigs tore at him. He shoved through the brush. He reveled in the sweet taste of his subject's terror. He closed on the heat of his subject's body. Heard the frantic thunder of his subject's heart.

The man struggled free of the bushes. He sprinted upward, three stairs at a time. But no human could outrun an XK9 with a six-meter stride. Rex caught him in two bounds, clamped his jaws around the wrist of the EStee-hand, jerked his head, and laid his subject out on his belly on the landing.

The man gasped for breath. He stared at Rex's teeth on his arm, his scent factors raw with terror. A distinct, pungent odor of soiled pants rose from him. The young man dropped the EStee.

Rex raked it out of reach with a hind paw. Crappy substitute for a real gun, but illegal in civilian hands. Rex didn't fear it, but it could harm a human or an ozzirikkian, so he made sure the subject couldn't grab it.

"Backup's on the way," Charlie called. "Hold him!"

Rex growled. "He is not going anywhere!"

The subject whimpered.

Rex wagged his tail but kept the man's wrist firmly between his teeth.

CRISP, warm satisfaction filled Uniformed Peace Officer Seaton's scent factors. "I have a DNA positive on our subject." She gestured toward the man Rex had flushed from the thicket and caught on the stairs. "Just as I thought! Meet Elmo Smart, AKA 'Thumper.' Got a rap sheet several klicks long. We've been trying to catch him for almost five weeks. He's been working this park and a couple of others, leaping out of hiding to mug unsuspecting passers-by."

Their captive, now cuffed in the back of a prisoner transport, sneered and looked away. But his bravado couldn't conceal the glum, sludgy dread in his scent.

Five weeks? Rex shot another look at the slender young man. That explained his familiarity with the terrain. "How many incidents?"

"In all?" Seaton's brows went up as if the question surprised her, then she frowned. "Oh, dozens. He's a one-man crime wave."

Elmo Smart was more dangerous than he looked. *That's two notorious thieves in one day.* Rex glanced toward Charlie, who'd stayed with Fatima and her friends. *Will we get any credit for that? Will 'the right people' know?* His partner hadn't yet had time even to pull out the traditional squeaky-toy. Rex kept his growl to himself, but that toy'd probably be the extent of the recognition he'd get. The play-reward practice dated back to the earliest days of K-9s on police forces, but the older Rex got, the more it felt like a mockery, not a reward.

Charlie seemed stung by this. *Dr. Ordovich always stressed it was important.*

Rex let a little of his growl out. *If you really want to reward me, let me spend time with Shady.*

Reluctance surged through the link. *I'm sorry.*

Rex knew Charlie's reaction was more than simple disinclination to subvert OPD protocols. Until about seven weeks ago, Charlie and Shady's partner Pam had been lovers. Then she'd dumped him, just a few days before the trip back to Rana Station. She'd left Charlie to take up with a former boyfriend, an OPD detective named Balchu Nowicki. *I can't really blame you for not wanting to see Pam. But Shady and I still love each other.*

Can we discuss this later, please?

Rex sighed. *You always say 'later,' but we never do.*

"Well, well." Seaton had continued perusing Smart's file. "Looks like we have a known human-exclusivist, here. At least, he's made some statements and boosted some posts in support. But an actual assault on an ozzirikkian is new."

Rex snapped his ears flat. "Probably because he never had any ozzirikkians to assault before."

Seaton's partner UPO Wells scowled. "Just needed to find one, I guess." He reached in to fasten Smart's seat belt.

Rex watched with close attention, growled a soft warning.

Smart rolled an eye at Rex. He behaved himself, but the sharp stink of his resentment hung in the air like an invisible fog.

Rex huffed. Resentment was probably Elmo Smart's normal outlook. Charlie said human-exclusivists lived on resentment. They ignored history to justify their bigotry, because without the ozzirikkians Rana Station never would've been financed or built.

Wells slammed the door of the prisoner transport, locking Smart inside. Rex rejoined his partner. They were on call later tonight. Charlie'd want to head home soon.

Paramedics were just finishing their examination of one of the ozzirikkians Smart had targeted. K'ki clicked and whistled to k'kir companion in k'ki'irn home language.

Rex couldn't make sense of what k'ki said. New longing filled him. Shady was the Pack's linguist. She'd studied Pan-

Ozzirikkian when she'd learned the Pack would come to Rana Station. If only he could ask her!

The paramedics gave both ozzirikkians pain-patches. K'ki'i applied them to k'ki'irn foreheads. The blue-black patches blended in with the skin color of one better than the other, whose face was a lighter blue-gray. Soon the achey heat in k'ki'irn scents eased.

"Fatima, you remember my new partner, XK9 Rex Dieter-Nell," Charlie said.

Fatima smiled. She reached out a hand to Rex. "Who could forget? Hello and thank you. You really came to our rescue!"

Rex wagged his tail and offered his paw to shake. He let his tongue loll in a dog-smile. "It is my pleasure to remove someone from our park who would dare to threaten our neighbors and honored guests."

The two ozzirikkians had gone silent at Rex's approach. When he spoke, two pairs of round violet eyes widened. K'ki'irn heavy brows rose, forming wrinkles around k'ki'irn pain patches. K'ki'i emitted sharp, brisk, rising scents that smelled similar to human amazement or surprise.

I'm always astonished by how many people are surprised that we XK9s talk.

He sensed Charlie's agreement through the link. *You're a new thing in k'ki'ir world. They don't know what to expect, so they assume you're a dog, except MUCH bigger.*

Kind of like the human-exclusivists talk as if ozzirikkians are some kind of Terrestrial ape?

Good point. Yes, very much like. Rex glimpsed Charlie's smile from the corner of his eye.

Rex turned toward the ozzirikkians with his ears up, tail waving. Both individuals had pale tufts of fur that partially concealed the half-circle ears high on each side of their round, furry heads. The tufts marked them as kixi, a non-breeding gender. K'ki'i had wrapped k'ki'irn long, furry arms around each other. Like k'ki'irn elongated torsos and short legs, k'ki'irn arms were covered with thick fur, patterned in striking black, gray and yellow spotted markings. One had a vid-recorder on a length of webbing around k'kir neck.

Fatima turned to k'ki'in. "Ter, Jik, this is XK9 Rex. He's Charlie's partner. Don't be afraid of him. He might *look* like a huge black wolf, but he's really very friendly."

The one with the vid-recorder loosened k'kir grasp on the other, lifted k'kir blunt, rounded muzzle and sniffed in short puffs through k'kir flat, triangular nose. K'ki cocked k'kir head at him. K'kir alert violet gaze studied him.

He cocked his head at k'kin in reply. "Hello."

K'kir flexible, gray-blue lips parted to give the fang-flashing gape of greeting the Pack had been taught was a parallel expression to a human smile or a canine ears-relaxed tail-wag. "El-l-l-oh. T-tank you vor-r r-rezzgue us."

K'kir high-pitched voice spoke with studied deliberation, but Rex could follow k'kir words. Shady said many ozzirikkians were able to create the sounds needed to speak Human Commercial Standard. It was much harder for humans to reproduce the clicks and squeaks of Pan-Ozzirikkian. Lucky for XK9s, their vocalizers could do both. Maybe he should learn at least a little Pan-Ozzirikkian from Shady. *If* he ever saw her again.

He wagged his tail, relaxed his ears. "You are most welcome."

"Please meet Terchikni Jochikti, Welder First Class," Fatima said. "K'ki is the leader of my work-group."

Terchikni extended a hand that had six, slate-blue-skinned fingers with black, clawlike nails, an opposable thumb, and yellowish fur to k'kir first knuckles. "My firzzt-t XK9."

Rex went to "parade sit," with head up, ears forward, and tail straight out behind. He offered his paw to shake. "My first ozzirikkian. Hello."

The ozzirikkian emitted high, bright scent factors that

smelled almost like excitement and curiosity in a human. "T-tiz XK9 so big! But-t very smart-t I t-tink!"

Rex let his tongue slide out in a dog-smile. He'd been hasty to think ozzirikkians were bizarre. This one seemed highly perceptive. "It is nice to meet you, Terchikni."

"And this is Jikjikchi Ziktikki, my partner from work," Fatima said.

Apparently emboldened by k'kir work-group leader's example, but still smelling frightened, Jikjikchi also stretched out a hand to shake with Rex. "T-tank you," k'ki said in a soft, high voice.

"And my longtime school friend, Nancy Tibma," Fatima added.

Nancy, a slender blonde human woman, smiled. "Fatima's told us about her XK9 neighbor, but I never imagined you'd come to our rescue." She reached up boldly to stroke his head and neck, then glanced back at Terchikni and Jikjikchi. "His fur is really very soft. You should feel it."

The two ozzirikkians hesitated, looked at Charlie.

Charlie grinned. "Rex loves being petted and admired. He looks fierce, but he's a lover."

Fatima and her friends encircled Rex. They stroked and caressed him, murmuring praise and delight. The ozzirikkians made contented little sounds deep in k'ki'ir throats, like a cross between a coo and a purr. Rex basked in the attention, tail wagging.

Charlie looked on, his brown eyes alight with pleasure. *See? You got to be at the center of admiration after all.*

Rex rolled over to let them rub his belly. *I definitely could get used to this.* All the same, no one had tried to pet Charlie, had they? Not Seaton or Wells, either. Humans were picky about where and when they allowed others to get near them. Yet everyone assumed Rex wouldn't mind if sapient creatures touched him wherever they liked. *Another form of condescension?*

Well, damn. Probably. Then Terchikni's clever fingers found a really good spot. Rex sighed. *I'll worry about whether to be offended later.*

Charlie grinned. *Take your kudos where they come. Just don't expect me to lug your panniers up the switchbacks for you.*

2

PLAYOFF MANEUVERS

Orangeboro 5th Precinct, Market Garden Neighborhood, Pam, Balchu, and Shady's apartment,

Heart pounding with anticipated loneliness, XK9 Shady Jacob-Belle whimpered. She followed Pam into the flat's tiny bedroom, staying close to her warmth and scent. *Please, Pam. Let me go with you.*

Pam checked her reflection in the mirror, fluffed her bangs, then spritzed on a little of that peach-ish-chemical-smelling "perfume." *I haven't been out with my friends since I got back on-Station. I love you, but I don't think you'd be welcome in many shoe boutiques.*

Shady wrinkled her nose at the perfume, but that was minor. Her Pack was gone. Her mate was gone. Now Pam meant to leave, too. Despair loomed. The cramped bedroom seemed to pull in on her. She shifted from foot to foot, toenails clicking on the worn flooring. *I don't want to stay here. I don't care about sports, or Balchu, or his friends. I just want to be with you.*

Pam frowned. *Take a nap here in the bedroom. Leave Balchu and his guests alone.* She bent to make eye-contact in the human way. Her interface through their brain link pleaded, too. *Can you please, please, please just give him this one evening of peace?*

Insubordinate urges to disrupt Balchu's party surged in her mind, her heart. Shady snapped her ears flat and looked away. She'd realized weeks ago that Pam was much gentler and kinder than Dr. Ordovich or Dr. Imre had been. It gave her courage to speak, when once she would have cowered in fear, certain of a beating. But she wasn't sure how far to push, beyond speaking up. *He doesn't want me here. Why should I give Balchu anything?* He'd made his opinion abundantly clear on the evening of the Choosing. *Why did you have to go back to him? Charlie was nicer.*

I know you're lonely. I'm sorry. The melancholy ache of regret washed in on Shady through the link from her partner. Pam hugged her. *I just never realized . . . not any of it. Not till way too late. I still don't know how to apologize to Charlie. But I love Balchu. He doesn't deserve your blame, I do. It's my fault.*

Sharp anguish stabbed. Shady looked away. They'd been through this dozens of times since they'd arrived on-Station. All Pam cared about was Balchu. Even the affair with Charlie had been a "rebound," something Pam herself had only understood *afterward*. Charlie hadn't accounted for the recentness of Pam's breakup with Balchu, either. By the time they realized they'd made a mistake, they were already several months into the relationship.

Pam squeezed between Shady and the end of the bed, then stepped to the doorway. *I'll probably come home before the match ends. Afua, Etsu and Shuri want to go clubbing after shoe-shopping, but Balchu always worries—he's worked too many cases in the Entertainment District. With you so upset, I promise it'll be an early night.* She sighed. *Please be good?*

Shady turned away, lay down on the rug next to the bed. She put her face under the edge of the bedspread and closed her eyes, unwilling to talk anymore.

Pam stood silent for a moment, then her footsteps receded through the doorway. The hollow metal pocket door slid closed with a light scrape against the jamb. Its latch clicked shut. Pam hesitated outside the door. Shady tasted conflicted uncertainty from her, then a flare of angry decision. Next came a sharp smell.

Sealant putty? Bitter betrayal soured Shady's tongue, an echo of the putty-smell. *Pam! What did you do?* Shady scrambled out from under the bed with a snarl, hackles stiff.

Stay put. Be good. Leave Balchu and his guests in peace. Her footsteps moved away, carpet-muffled until she reached the kitchen, and Balchu.

Sadness closed Shady's throat. *Why lock me in?*

Because I don't trust you to leave the guys alone. You know why! Shady sensed not a hint of remorse.

Guilt washed over her. She curled her tail under her belly. *Those were just pranks.*

Pam did not reply. In her place, Shady probably wouldn't have, either. The rhythmic scrape of a spoon stirring something in the kitchen stopped. A pan clunked onto the stovetop. Two steps across the hard kitchen floor, a little muffled sigh from Pam.

Futile weariness sapped Shady. She stood by the door, head down. Those pranks might've gotten her locked in tonight, but they hadn't gotten rid of Balchu.

From the kitchen came the swish of cloth against cloth. That was a hug. And there it was . . . yes, that was kissing.

Shady clamped her ears flat. A little prickle of revulsion rippled through her hackles. No, she was definitely not getting rid of Balchu.

"It'll be all right," Balchu murmured. "She'll be all right."

"I hate to do it." Pam's voice sounded muffled. "I won't be out long."

"You deserve to relax with your friends. You can't be chained to the dog 24-7."

Shady growled. "Chained to the dog"? Typical Balchu-comment.

More kissing.

"The guys will be here soon. I'd better head out."

"It'll be all right," Balchu repeated. "Have fun. Don't worry."

Oh, for pity's sake, more kissing. Pam had never kissed Charlie that much. But then, she'd never really loved Charlie, had she?

Anguish goaded Shady onto her hind legs. She slammed her forepaws against the door. It rattled in its jamb, the thin metal bowing a little. Damn flimsy door! She ought to—

NO! STOP! You'll get us evicted!

Shady had never sensed such alarm in Pam before. It roused her protectiveness, halted her. But her anger still burned. *You locked me in!*

Damn it, what am I supposed to do? Let you destroy Balchu's party? Pam had returned. She stood just outside the bedroom door. From the smells coming through the cracks around the door, Balchu was with her.

Shady dropped to all fours, but her hackles stayed up, her ears stayed clamped to her skull. *What's so special about his stupid old party?*

His sergeant and their lieutenant are both coming tonight. Pam's unease echoed through their link. *It could help him advance at work. Then we could move to a bigger place, but not if you destroy the bedroom door and disrupt everything!*

Shady growled. But she never wanted to feel that kind of fear in her partner again. And certainly never to inspire it with her own actions. *It means that much to you?*

Do YOU like living in this tiny little place? Pam's fear had receded, but her discomfort remained. *It's a crappy dump of an apartment in a not-very-nice neighborhood, but it's all we can afford. It's not as if we have a Chartered Family backing us! We've been trying to save up, but it's hard. Taxes are so high, and there's no place to grow food, here. When Balchu and I are together, sharing expenses, it's better. I make more money now that I'm your partner and a detective. Balchu can make more if he gets Detective Second Level. But we can't make any mistakes.*

Shady's gut took a sickening plunge. *My tearing up the door would be a mistake?*

A big one, yes. The only thing worse would be an eviction while Balchu's bosses are actually here.

"So I have to stay put." Might as well let Balchu hear this too.

She sensed her partner's sigh. "I really can't take you with me to the shoe-boutiques. All the other customers would run away. And I can't just let you wander the streets. You'd terrify the neighborhood."

"I'd be quiet. I'd just go for a walk."

"Shady. Honey. *You* know you're nice. I know you're nice. Even Balchu knows you're nice, by now. Right?"

"Um, yeah. Definitely," Balchu said. From the slight pain and the startlement in his scents that came through the door-cracks, Shady guessed Pam had prodded his response with an elbow to the ribs.

"But you look like an enormous, black-sable wolf," Pam continued. "It's dark out, and the mist is rising. Trust me! If a stranger sees you wandering around in the shadows, they'll have a heart attack."

Shady flicked her ears, lowered her head. They'd had this argument before.

"Dr. Ordovich made you big to be intimidating, and believe me, you are. Whether you want to be or not."

"So I am stuck in here, no matter what."

"I'm afraid so."

Stuck in here, and in every other way, too.

I'm so sorry. But yes, I'm afraid so. At least until we figure out something better.

Nothing would change. There would be no 'better.' That was clear by now. *Go. Shop for shoes. I'll just stay in here and . . . and be a good dog, I guess.*

Her partner's relief surged through the link, echoed by both humans' scents through the door-cracks. "Thank you."

Shady walked away from the door. Despair crushed in on

her, weighed her down like lead in the gut. She thumped onto the floor by the bed and stuck her head back under its edge. There was nothing she could do. Pam would never leave Balchu, and even if she did, Charlie would never take her back. Shady would never see Rex, not ever . . .

A soft whimper escaped. She couldn't bear to think *never*.

Pam and Balchu's footsteps receded into the other end of the apartment. They kissed each other again, then the front door closed. Shady heard Pam's footsteps on the metal stairs to ground-level. She smelled the hot, rancid grease from the Ultra-Fast Tempura place downstairs, heard its squeaky door creak open then slam several different times, as bicycle-delivery riders came and went. They'd do that all night till they closed at midnight, she knew. After a while the motion-triggered bedroom light flicked off overhead. That suited her mood better. Take a nap, Pam had said. Like that was something Shady could just do on command. She lay still and tried to doze. It would make the time go faster. But sleep stayed far away.

Balchu's guests arrived, a few at a time. She kept count: five, total. How could that little-bitty front room hold them all? "Where's your nemesis?" or "What did you do with the dog?" seemed to be first question any of them asked.

"We called a truce," Balchu replied each time. "Shady's being gracious tonight."

Shady gave a soft growl.

The game, match, playoff or whatever it was started with a roar of crowd-noise in the front room. An announcer-voice chattered about the Comets' record. Damned cheap apartment, with its thin walls. Couldn't have napped through that, in any case.

The smell of the men's snacks and companionable scent-reactions reached her, despite the stronger smells from downstairs. Why could Balchu be with his friends, but she couldn't be with hers? Lonely grief swept over her afresh. It gathered in her core, then rose like an irresistible force. She pushed out from under the bed, up to a sit. Then she pointed her muzzle toward the ceiling and poured out her heartache in a howl. She'd meant for it only to be a soft howl, but it gathered force as it rose within her.

Somewhere in the background, men were yelling. Some seemed surprised, but one of them cursed at Balchu, and ordered him to "Shut that damned dog up!"

Shady! Pam cried through their link. *What are you doing?*

"Woah! Shady, calm down." That was Balchu, just outside the door. "Are you okay?"

"Oh, for Chrissake, Nowicki! Just shut the damned mutt up!"

"Gimme a minute, Sarge. Let me talk to her."

This is almost as bad as breaking the door! Pam seemed deeply frustrated. *Don't howl!*

Shady laid back her ears, snarled at the door. "No, I am not okay," she told Balchu. "I am lonely, bored, and far away from my mate and all my Packmates."

"You know Pam will be back in just a couple of hours."

"It is not Pam I miss right now. I can still sense her through the link."

Telling you to be quiet! Pam said.

Go look at shoes. I can't talk to all of you at once.

"What the hell difference does it make?" the grumpy sergeant demanded. "Shut the damned thing up!"

"Shut it yourself, Gorman," another voice said. "Let's see what kinda negotiator Nowicki is."

Shady focused on Balchu. "I miss Rex. I miss the Pack. I want to be with them again."

A swirl of confused scent factors filtered in through the door-cracks from Balchu. "But—you haven't seen Rex or the others in two months. You're only just *now* missing them?"

"I always miss them, but now I have no distractions. It is all I can think about. My mate is gone, and I never see my sister- and brother-Packmates anymore. I am all alone."

"Jee-zus," Gorman muttered.

"I'm sorry you feel so lonesome," Balchu said. "But please don't howl again."

Dispirited discouragement swept through her. "You do not care. You are simply annoyed when I howl."

"Well, I have to admit I don't want you to howl. That's true," Balchu said. "We can't hear the match, and the neighbors will complain. But I don't want you to be sad, either." He actually did smell as if he empathized.

"Yer breaking my heart, Nowicki. Doesn't that thing know 'sit,' 'stay,' and 'shut the fuck up'?" Sgt. Gorman asked.

"Gorman." The lieutenant's voice held a note of warning.

Anger hurt less than the yawning abyss of Shady's loneliness. "What difference does it make to you, if I am sad? You do not want me here."

Balchu gave a soft groan. "I'm never gonna live that down, am I? Look, I'm sorry. I didn't know you then. I didn't realize how good you'd be for Pam."

She stared at the door, ears half-raised. He smelled as if he truly meant that. "Did you just apologize to me?" Humans never did that. What was he thinking?

"Well, yeah. I guess I did." He sounded startled. "I really don't hate you or want you to go away anymore. Not even when you bury my stuff in the planter boxes outside."

"You were pretty mad when I buried your last pair of clean socks."

She heard a couple of stifled chortles from outside the door.

Balchu made a rueful noise. "I did say a few choice words, didn't I? But it made a good story, later. The guys at work have started calling you my nemesis."

She snapped her hears flat. "I heard. That does not seem like a good thing."

He blew out a breath. "Mm, but it gives us a diversion when a case gets bad. Sometimes it's good to have a 'Shady story' to tell. Changes the mood. You're pretty resourceful, you know.

They can't believe some of the stuff you've come up with." Was that . . . admiration she smelled?

She kept her ears down. Balchu worked vice. Some days he came home with nothing at all to say. On those days, he often gave Pam lingering hugs and smelled deeply sad. Perhaps Shady had misjudged him. A little. Maybe. "Thank you for the apology."

"You're welcome. I'm sorry I can't help you with Rex or the Pack." Once again, he smelled as if he really meant that.

"If you continue being nice to me, it might become harder to think of irritating tricks to pull on you. You will not have new stories."

Was that a chuckle? "I don't mind. Being at odds with a housemate takes a toll. Could we maybe have a cease-fire?"

A "housemate"? She'd thought only humans could be "housemates." She sifted through his scent factors but found none of the mockery she'd expected. These Rana Stationers could be unpredictable. Not like the callous Transmondians who'd reared and trained her. "Could you maybe unseal the door?"

"Promise not to lay waste to our playoff party?"

Shady let her tongue slide out. "Promise."

"Détente it is." *Ri-i-i-ip*, off came the sealant putty. The door's latch clicked. Balchu pushed it open. "Better?"

Astonished gratitude welled up within her. "Thank you." It didn't take her loneliness away, but . . . well, he didn't have to do that.

"Will you be okay in there, now?"

Behind him, the others clustered in the archway from the living room. One of them scowled at Balchu, arms crossed: Sgt. Gorman, she presumed. There was impatience in his scent, but also more rising fear than she'd expected. Was he afraid of her? Another man eyed Balchu with rising speculation in his scent. Possibly the lieutenant? The other two men stood back a little, but looked on with concerned scent factors and expressions of worry. Those probably were Balchu's actual friends.

In the empty living room, the crowd on the vid wall roared with excitement. "Comets score!" the announcer cried. "It's all tied up!"

Every man looked toward the living room, then most of their scent factors went wry. The man she'd pegged as Sgt. Gorman growled and pushed his way back to the living room. Yes, his bluster seemed mostly intended to cover his growing fear. Of her.

Chagrin stung her. "You and your guests are supposed to be watching quiddo, not dealing with a lonely dog. I am sorry."

Balchu gave her a wry look. "It feels kind of superficial to think about the game after what you said about being alone. I'll let you be, if you want, but . . ."

She cocked her head at him. Did he almost invite her to join them? "But?"

He shrugged. "I suppose you aren't interested in quiddo, are you?"

Did she want to be alone? She looked at the human faces. Now that Gorman was gone, they all eyed her with expressions of concern. Being near them comforted her. She lifted her ears. "If you—if you do not mind, I would like to . . . to learn about this sport. Can you please tell me about it?"

"Oh, for Chrissake!" Gorman yelled from the living room, but surprised smiles dawned on the other men's faces.

They smelled like pretty nice guys. She might like being around them.

"If . . . if you would not mind?" Shady ducked her head and fluttered her tail.

"Um, sure." A smile curved Balchu's lips. "Care to join us in the living room?"

Shady wagged her tail. "Thank you. Yes, please." She moved forward to peer through the open archway at the 3D projection from the far wall. A swarm of miniature humans and ozzirikkians zoomed around on tiny micro-G sleds, seemingly right above the battered coffee table. Some wore blue on their uniforms, while others wore the muddy brownish color she'd learned was called "orange." Or maybe it was "red." She never could see the difference. "I take it some of those players are 'Comets'?"

Balchu nodded. "They're the ones in orange. Each team has five players . . ."

"Pipe down, I can't hear!" Gorman yelled from the far end of the sofa.

Balchu stifled a sigh. He sat on the floor next to the archway from the bedroom area. Shady stepped back so the other men could return to the living room. The one Shady thought was the lieutenant took the near end of the small sofa, between her and Gorman. The other two sat on folding chairs.

Shady lay down next to Balchu, as far away from Gorman as possible, while still able to see the match. She filled the little archway.

"Can you hear me?" Balchu whispered.

Shady dialed her vocalizer to a parallel level. "Yes. XK9s have excellent hearing."

He smiled. "And a good thing, too. As I was saying . . ."

3

NOTHING GOOD EVER HAPPENS AFTER MIDNIGHT

Corona Tower, an elevator to the Wheel Two Hub, and Warehouse 226

Charlie's com jangled him semi-conscious. He shook off the disquiet of an anxious dream, struggled past the whole-body *ugh* of too little sleep, then lurched up from the sheets. "Light."

The room's illumination began a slow increase.

Charlie blinked, yawned, then blinked several more times, still bleary.

The com rang again.

A tiny light blinked in the lower left of his vision. He triggered the com. "Morgan." He hoped he sounded awake.

"We have a suspicious death in Warehouse 226," the Watch Officer said. "Your lead is Helmer Fujimoto. Report to him on-scene."

Charlie caught his breath. Okay, now he was wider awake. A warehouse meant the Hub. His stomach did a queasy flip-flop. "R-roger that." He clicked off. Hoped he hadn't sounded freaked out. When had the "not rated for microgravity" restriction been removed from his personnel file? How could it have been, without his knowledge? He scowled. Should he have protested? He'd just been given an order. But what if he couldn't make himself follow it? He rubbed his left arm. At least its dull throb had lessened somewhat while he slept.

His neural head-up display said 01:51.

"Did you take a call?" Rex danced with excitement in the doorway.

Charlie drew in a shaky breath. "Cool your jets. We're headed for the Hub." Good, no tremor in his voice. Well, not much of one, but his heart pounded hard. If the brass thought he was ready, then he'd better be ready. God, he hoped he was ready.

Rex stopped mid-pace, one forepaw raised. "Are you all right? You seem frightened of something. Is it the thing that gives you nightmares?"

"I'm fine." Rex's scary-smart eyes reflected a blue glow in the room's low light. Charlie gritted his teeth. "I'm gonna be fine. Leave it, Rex!"

Rex flinched, looked away. "Of course, sir. I apologize. But I am worried. I have not been trained for microgravity."

The brass was really pushing it tonight, that was for sure. But Chief Klein had mandated that an XK9 team must be called for all major cases. That included suspicious deaths. Apparently 'all' meant ALL, whether the dogs were trained or not. At least he had the skills, if he could bring himself to use them. He swung bare legs out of bed with a grimace. "I guess you'll have to learn fast. Go get your gear."

Rex shot him an uncertain look, walked away.

Dread prowled the edges of his mind. Charlie yanked on clothes he'd laid out before bed, determined to focus on the mechanical process of straightening, fastening, smoothing. His regenerated left arm ached, an unwelcome reminder.

He fished a couple of PanaCees out of the bottle on his nightstand and dry-swallowed them. Then he took slow, even breaths. Struggled to envision all stress and fear falling away. Despite years of dutiful practice and other brands of therapy, it only worked somewhat.

Rex dropped his tool panniers in the doorway then disappeared again. He returned dragging his service harness. Charlie pulled it over the dog's head. He cinched down straps, settled the panniers, secured them. By the time he clipped Rex's badge to the band that crossed the dog's broad chest, the pain in his arm had dulled and his hands had stopped shaking.

Outside, Corona Tower's central courtyard lay silent, deep in misty shadow. The only movement followed a little breeze that stirred the vines along the balconies. It rustled the big oak's leaves, slid past Charlie's face in a breath of moist growing things. The only light came from the stars, fog-softened through the sky-windows, and the fuzzy low glimmer of safety lights along the steps and walkways. Corona Tower, the Family, slept secure.

Charlie meant to keep them that way. He and Rex hurried five flights downstairs to the gate, but quietly. Stealth mode, so the Family wouldn't be roused by their departure. Protective mode, to keep them safe. If someone had been killed tonight—if a murderer needed tracking—then he and Rex stood ready.

Even if it meant going back to the Hub.

Charlie mentally accessed his Cybernetically-Assisted Perception implants. Fastest way to Warehouse 226? The CAP mapped it out and displayed it on his neural HUD. As he'd thought, a short jog through the fog-shrouded neighborhood brought them into the Glen Haven Transit Terminal Station's island of bright lights, ranks of benches, and flower-filled planters. Colorful mosaics flanked half-a-dozen elevator door-pairs, their cheerful hues softened by mist. Enormous metal shafts reared to the ceiling and far beyond. In a few hours this place would be packed with dock, warehouse, and space-based-manufacturing workers, but it was empty at 02:09.

Charlie took a hyperbarically-equalizing Emergency Services Express. It could make the fifteen-kilometer climb to the throughway of Rana Station's Central Hub in just under thirty minutes. He and Rex had the elevator car to themselves at this hour. Charlie strapped them in, then accessed the case file. It said alarms at 01:48 had alerted the security staff to movement and a release of biological contaminants: copious blood, as well as feces and urine, in one of the warehouse compartments. Initial DNA scans said the blood belonged to an unidentified female human.

Charlie scowled. He let his anger rise. It helped him focus, helped him keep his resolve. It also kept unhelpful memories at arm's length.

A quiet, internal *ding* alerted him to a new file, uploaded while the elevator continued its climb: a surveillance recording, time-stamped immediately after the contaminant-release alarm. A vid of a tertiary corridor, with basic biometrics on a side channel, showed two unknown male subjects.

They plunged through a hatch as it closed, then darted out of view. Charlie reset the recording to replay in slo-mo. Two burly men emerged, with big muscles and unusual tattoos of intertwining lines on their arms. He frowned. No other sensor had triggered, neither after the men left the warehouse compartment, nor before the alarm. How had they avoided the rest of the surveillance? Sabotage, maybe, but how? By whom? Lucky whoever-it-was had missed this side passage. *Did you get the vid?*

Rex cocked his head. *Vid?*

Impatience welled up. Command never remembered to send essential files to Rex. Irritated, Charlie forwarded it.

Rex alerted, held still for a moment. *Where does that hatch open? Which passage?*

Looks like a branch-corridor on the port side.

I need to go there.

All too soon, the elevator slowed near the top of its climb. Floaty, low-G nausea set in.

Charlie's heart pounded faster. All his years of therapy hadn't yet tamed this reaction. Fear like an icy wave swept over him. His carefully-nurtured resolve shredded before it. His hands shook on the elevator car's railing.

Rex growled. *My nose is swelling up. Soon it will be compromised.*

Charlie couldn't make his hands stop shaking. Fumbling, he managed to clip a two-meter safety tether to his waist, then secure the other end to Rex's harness.

Rex growled again. *I do not need a leash.*

Charlie should be explaining to Rex about what to expect, how to move in the Hub. *In micrograv you'll need that tether.*

I hate micrograv.

Charlie's chest tightened. *Yeah, pal, me too.* Shit. He couldn't think what to tell Rex. Oh, God, let him not devolve into a gibbering wreck. Time for another of Dr. Mariel's breathing patterns.

Rex poked him with a cold, wet nose. *What's wrong?*

Humiliation washed over him, but his partner deserved a straight answer. *It's called a post-traumatic stress reaction.*

Oh. Rex kept his ears up. No sense of judgment or disgust came through the link, only concerned curiosity. *How can I help?*

Just be there. Charlie dragged in another breath. *Work the case. Stay steady.* He gritted his teeth. There'd been a time when the onset of micrograv had given him a thrill of anticipation. He shuddered, and prayed he would not disgrace himself in the Hub this time.

The elevator car stopped. Charlie and Rex kept going. They were strapped in, but Charlie's stomach cramped. He swallowed urgently.

The strap and tether halted Rex's ascent with a snap. He snarled, helpless, but tumbled sideways.

Charlie took a careful breath. He pulled the tether toward himself to stabilize Rex's movement, then released his and Rex's safety restraints. *Micrograv. It'll surprise you. Go carefully. You'll need to use the loops and handholds on the walls like a ladder's rungs. Don't go too fast, or you won't be able to stop.*

The elevator doors opened. Charlie triggered the "Hold Doors 60 Seconds" command via his CAP, then grabbed a wall-mounted handhold with his right hand. He pulled himself out into a three-quarters pipe in the Hub's main corridor. Rex floated, tethered but at an odd angle, behind him.

The Hub never changed: muted lighting, polished metal, almost-cold air. Exactly like *then*.

He pulled up short, his heart pounding triple-time. Stinging shame swept over him, as fresh today as three years ago. He hadn't lost his micrograv rating because of the accident. He'd lost it because he couldn't keep his shit together when he climbed into a MERS-V. The memories played through his head again now, unstoppable. That final day . . . he'd blown his last chance. Disgraced himself in front of Oz, Eli, worst of all, *Hildie*. Afterward, he'd blundered down this passageway to the elevator terminal, barely able to think or see. He'd flung himself into an empty car—any empty car—closed the doors, then wept like a child. It had taken the entire trip down, at normal speed, to get himself under shaky control.

Charlie clenched the handhold. He focused on his breathing, on getting his head right. That was then. Now could be different. The restriction on his file was gone, so somebody must've thought he could do this. Time to prove them right.

Rex floated into him, nudged him with a wet nose. *I have your back. It's okay.*

The tightness in Charlie's chest eased some. He nodded. *Thanks, partner.*

Rex tumbled slowly past him, then managed to hook a forepaw in a loop and caught himself. *When we came through here from the Solara City shuttle, I thought you were upset. Now I know why. But you seemed less bothered then.*

Charlie gulped. He avoided Rex's gaze. *It was easier to pass straight through.* He ran another breathing pattern. His heart rate slowed by gradual degrees.

D'you think you can work this case? Rex's concern echoed through the brain link.

Anxiety hung just out of view, poised to crush him. Charlie drew in a breath. Steeled himself. *I will work it.* He pulled himself forward, Rex in tow.

Rex fumbled along behind him. He bumped against a wall with a growl, scrabbled claws to gain purchase, growled again. Charlie offered pointers. They stopped so Rex could practice going back and forth in one section where there was no other traffic. After a while the big dog moved more smoothly, with fewer growls. Charlie's gut unclenched slightly. They could do this. Just had to take one thing at a time.

The partners came to a junction in a narrow, pipe-like corridor, where an emergency cut-off had been closed. The message-crawl around its center hatch read CRIME SCENE DO NOT CROSS. Charlie braced against it to show his badge to the latch-pad reader.

A few meters on, a cluster of people hovered in the confines of the area near another sealed hatch. Light-blue coveralls and a hand-held imager bristling with sensors marked one woman as a forensic imaging tech. A couple of UPOs flanked a guy in a dark green uniform with the Outworld Distribution Logistics ware-house company logo on it. The burly man in the jacket like Charlie's must be Detective Fujimoto. All five looked up at Charlie and Rex's arrival.

Fujimoto gave a curt nod. "Morgan. Come see what we've got." The detective's once-muscular form had begun a shift to middle-aged fat. His graying black hair was pulled back in a knot. He and the others drew aside to give hatch-window access. Fujimoto tilted his head toward it. "Blood, piss, and some shit floating around in there. Also, probably a body."

The warehouse compartment had gone opaque foggy-pink with a mist of tiny droplets, but the smaller drops had begun to clump together into larger, shiny red spheres of liquid. Charlie stared at the floating droplets. He pitied the CSU crew stuck with that filter-analysis job. *"Probably* a body?"

Fujimoto grunted. "There's enough mass. Blood mist interferes with the sensors." He shook his head. "The filters and air-scrubbers are going full-tilt, but access is gonna take a while."

Rex pushed forward to look, too. "I want to go to the corridor where the subjects came out. I cannot smell as well as normal, but I think I can follow their trail."

Cold anxiety coiled in Charlie's stomach. *On a hunt in this environment, without training?* "Remember, things are different in micro-grav." He spoke aloud, so the others could take warning about Rex's experience level. "You have to go slowly and hang onto the anchors. Be careful, please."

I'll be careful. Rex's tone through the link seemed offended.

I've seen you get tunnel-vision. You could kill me, and maybe also yourself, if you do that here.

I won't. You'll see.

Fujimoto led them down a smaller, tubelike corridor to the hatch they'd seen on the vid.

Rex thrust his muzzle close to it. "Two men. We knew that. Brothers."

Fujimoto shot an eyebrows-up look at Charlie.

Charlie nodded. "Shared genetics make for similar scent profiles. DNA'll confirm. I've never seen him get it wrong."

"Brothers, eh?" Fujimoto shrugged. "Might help narrow down an ID, especially with the tattoos."

"This way." Rex scratched at the handholds to turn, then bunched his haunches and launched down the narrow corridor. He yanked Charlie behind him.

Rex! Watch it! Charlie struggled to right himself and fend off the walls. *This is what I warned you about!*

Are you all right?

You've got to take it slower! Seven-year-old Rex was the XK9 equivalent of an eighteen-year old human: young, brilliant—but impulsive, and he clearly didn't properly respect micrograv yet.

I respect it. I will from now on. Rex stopped at another closed emergency cut-off. "The trail goes farther."

Fujimoto arrived from behind them. He frowned at Rex, then glanced at Charlie. "Is your dog gonna behave itself?"

Charlie grimaced. "He hasn't been trained for micro-grav. He's still figuring it out."

Fujimoto scowled at Rex.

Rex put his ears down. He cringed against one side of the corridor. "I am sorry. I shall do better."

"You're not gonna catch the brothers," Fujimoto said. "They have a forty-five-minute lead on us. But you could kill your partner if you go too fast."

Rex curled in on himself, shot a worried look at Charlie. "I am sorry. I shall go slowly."

"I hope so." Fujimoto frowned at Rex a moment longer, then gave Charlie another eyebrows-up look.

Charlie took a shaky breath. "Let's give him another try."

Fujimoto's frown deepened. "If you say so." He held his badge to the latch-pad reader. "Override. Extend crime scene to where XK9 Rex stops." The emergency cut-off panel retracted.

Rex pulled himself through. Charlie followed, with Fujimoto behind them. They proceeded at a much more sedate pace. Fujimoto kept up easily. Rex's frustration came loud and clear through the link, but the big dog kept his promise.

Charlie's fear ebbed. It became easier to breathe. He relaxed his muscles, unclenched his teeth.

They came to a place where their corridor crossed a slightly wider one.

"The brothers paused here." Rex sniffed along one side of the corridor. "They stayed for quite a while." He moved over to sniff some more. "The older one held on here. See? There is blood from the girl they killed in Warehouse 226. There have been little cast-off droplets all along the way."

Charlie spotted a small rusty smear on the padded surface.

Rex sniffed over the cross-corridor's opening, then continued to the other side. "The younger brother held on here. Both emitted scent factors of fear and anger. I believe they stopped here to argue about something that frightened them."

Fujimoto examined the corridor's metal framework with a scowl. "No sensors or mics here, of course."

"Anything in the cross-corridor?" Charlie asked.

With a gentle push, Rex floated past the opening. He stiffened. "Oh! Here the scent is much hotter! They were just here!"

In the link, Charlie sensed that focus-narrowing reaction the dogs called "hunt joy." Alarm shocked through him. *Rex?*

"Aroo-oo-oo!" Rex's Hound-of-the-Baskervilles hunting cry echoed down the corridor. The big dog bunched his haunches.

Charlie gasped. "Wait! Rex! NO!"

Rex lunged forward. He yanked Charlie after him, dragged by the tether. Hot on the trail, tunnel-focused, Rex dove into a narrow side corridor. Too fast for safety.

Charlie's back smacked a wall. He saw stars, flailed for balance.

Rex gave a wild "Yip!"

A gantry rail whipped by. Charlie grabbed for it. Caught it, then his grip tore loose. He cartwheeled through the air. A metal wall rushed toward him. *Crunch!* He tumbled away, blind with pain. His left arm jerked in spasms of agony.

Powerful jaws grabbed his jacket. They tumbled together. "Charlie!" the mechanical voice of Rex's vocalizer cried. "Charlie! Charlie!"

They whacked against something else. Pain exploded through him. After that, nothing.

4

SHAKE AND BREAK

Wheel Two Hub Docks, Bay 2-18B

Gantry scaffold-bars rushed at Rex. *Wham!* He gasped, knocked breathless, but he caught them in a desperate hug with all four legs, grappling for a better grip. Momentum dragged at him, but he thrust his body sideways to deflect Charlie from a hard, direct hit on the bars.

His effort kept Charlie from a collision, but Charlie's body flopped past like a rag doll, limp and broken. *Oh, Charlie!* What had he done? Terror pounded in his ears. If only he'd listened better!

Rex kept his jaws locked on his partner's jacket. Charlie's momentum wrenched his neck. Sharp pain and raw injury filled his partner's scent, but not the terrible shift in odors that death brought. Not yet.

Rex must think straight now. He must get things right. Where had they landed?

Unlike in the corridors, this was a much wider space. Across from them rose a hill-like cylindrical structure, more than twenty meters long with a conical end. Its shape tugged at his memory . . . *Oh.* That massive cylindrical thing was a berthing cone. He'd seen pictures but hadn't realized they were this enormous. He and Charlie must be inside a docking bay. The berthing cone protruded into the docking area from the Station's outer hull. it created a massive socket into which a ship's grapples locked for docking.

Charlie groaned. He twisted fitfully.

Rex tensed. What if his partner slipped out of his jacket? Would the tether hold? If it did, would it injure his partner?

"Morgan!" Fujimoto's voice on the com was hoarse. "I'm coming. Stay there." He emerged from the end of the corridor several meters away, then skimmed along the gantry like an old spacehand.

Relief washed over Rex. His muscles eased. A paw slipped. *Yikes!* His pulse thundered. He clenched his whole body around the gantry rails in a convulsive grab.

Charlie's right hand fumbled for a grip on a strut at the corner of Rex's vision. The strain on Rex's neck eased. Charlie slowly pulled himself onto the gantry next to Rex. A jumble of pain and confusion came through the brain link.

Beyond his partner's shoulder, Fujimoto floated nearer. "Just stay there. Hang on."

Rex breathed ragged gasps around his mouthful of jacket. Fujimoto knew what to do. Fujimoto would help him and Charlie.

The burly detective grabbed a nearby cross-piece, then crooked a leg over it to steady himself. He slid an arm around Charlie's torso. The pressure on Rex's neck eased. Rex's mouthful of jacket-fabric tugged sideways.

Fujimoto's brows furrowed. "I've got you, Morgan."

Charlie mumbled something incoherent.

Fujimoto nodded to Rex. "Good catch. Let me take him now."

Jaws aching, Rex let go of Charlie's jacket. He clung to the gantry, panting hard. That felt extremely weird in micrograv, with no "downward" for his tongue to loll. A mist of saliva droplets surrounded his mouth.

Something made a hollow *thunk* a few meters away, on the berthing cone.

A new jolt of fear shot though Rex. He looked for the source of the sound, caught a flash and movement. There was a round hatch on the side of the berthing cone near the corridor opening marked "Service Entrance," with the words aligned in four different orientations. Lights pulsed on, then circled the hatch in a repeating cycle. A lighted display panel next to the round hatch read *"Izgubil,"* the name of the ship, and "vacuum locks engaged" in blinking letters.

Rex's body prickled with a sudden chill. He didn't know much about space docks, but he did know that vacuum locks usually engaged before takeoff.

Fujimoto's scent factors shifted to urgent tones. He shouted his ID and his location—to Traffic Control, Rex guessed. "Under no circumstances may *Izgubil* undock!" Fujimoto shouted. "Emergency override on any prior permissions!"

Rex panted harder, worried by the man's reaction. Surely the ship wouldn't . . .

A subtle buzz ran along the gantry.

Queasy foreboding swept through Rex. Every hair and hackle stood straight out. "Why is it vibrating?" Metal parts rattled softly, grew gradually louder.

The strain gauge on the display panel shot up to MAX. It pulsed in one of those colors Rex couldn't distinguish, that humans used for "danger." Every part of him tingled with apprehension.

Fujimoto's scent factors suffused with terror.

Klaxons blared, a painful din. The corridor seal banged shut.

Trapped! Rex didn't know what to do now.

Emergency bunkers popped open. Yellow lights swept the dock.

Fujimoto clutched Charlie tighter, stretched to grab a handhold by the nearest bunker. Rex scrambled along with them across the gantry rails, still tethered to his partner.

The caution lights shifted from yellow to that danger-color.

Fujimoto maneuvered Charlie into the tight shelter of a bunker. "Stay with him. We can't all fit in one." The older detective lunged for the next bunker. Rex pulled himself inside with Charlie. He could barely squeeze in.

All hatches boomed shut. Rex flinched.

The hatch auto-sealed with a grind of gears and a hiss.

Rex lay against Charlie with almost no room to spare. He out-massed Charlie. Didn't want to crush him. But damn! It was a squeeze in here. His partner's injured arm jerked in spasms, jabbed Rex's sore ribs. Rex winced. He shifted away, but he couldn't shift far.

A deep metallic groan vibrated through the bunker. It went on and on and on. Charlie mumbled incoherent things, the brain link a jumble of torment. Rex's pulse fluttered faster. He panted hard, his throat dry.

The bunker rattled harder—harder—bumped and jolted, bounced and banged. Slammed Rex and Charlie back and forth in the narrow space, into each other and into the too-thin wall-pads. Rex tasted blood.

Terror squeezed Rex's throat. He panted in gasps. Tried to brace his feet against one wall, his back against the other. But he couldn't protect Charlie, couldn't defy momentum, couldn't hold himself immobile. The groaning, tearing metal sound ground through his very bones. It seemed to go on a lifetime.

Then all at once the outside noises ended.

Even as the bunker lurched and pitched. Even as Rex heard and felt each helpless thump and smack. Silence outside meant the dock had cracked. It had vented to hard vacuum. If Fujimoto hadn't gotten Charlie in here . . .

Oh no! Fujimoto! New alarm swept through Rex. Had Fujimoto made it into his bunker? Rex could only hope so, even as he and Charlie flopped about. They had just a few hard centimeters' clearance, but it was enough to sting. They flopped into the walls, into each other, into the ceiling, the floor. Each meaty slap stung, each bone against fracture stabbed, each hard thump ached and throbbed. After forever, temblors eased to jolts, calmed to bumps, to rattles, to vibrations. Charlie drifted, limp, his face pinched with agony.

Terrified, Rex sniffed his partner all over. Charlie reeked of injury. His partner's left jacket-sleeve had fattened visibly. He had bruises on his face. It looked as if his nose had bled some, and there was blood in his right ear.

Rex panted, frantic. He had no idea what to do, how to help. This was all his fault! What a stupid! Impetuous! Idiotic puppy he was! If only he hadn't been so tunnel-focused! If only he'd thought before he leaped into the chase!

Charlie opened his eyes a little, then groaned and shut them again.

"Charlie!" Charlie flinched away. Rex dialed his vocalizer down. "Sorry. Is this better?"

Charlie shuddered, then threw up. Tiny droplets of vomit spread everywhere. The air went redolent with gastric acid and the partially-digested beans and spinach from Charlie's late-evening dinner of leftovers. All around the bunker, tiny venti-lator fans kicked on at top speed.

Rex covered his nose with a paw against the bunker's wall, closed his eyes, and clamped his ears flat. His skin burned wher-ever his fur was thinnest.

His com rang. Rex's neural HUD said it was the Emergency Dispatcher. *"What is Morgan's condition?"* a man's sharp voice demanded.

"Semi-conscious. I suspect a concussion and a broken arm at the very least." Rex breathed shallowly. His vocalizer sounded kind of juicy. "He just threw up. I am worried."

"Oh." The dispatcher sighed. "Head trauma? My call to him, um, may have triggered that. The biometrics in those older bunkers don't tell us much. I'll bump you guys higher on the list."

"Thank you."

"And you? Are you injured?"

"XK9s are tough. I am bruised but all right." Rex shifted position. Pain shot through his right side. "I may have cracked a rib or two when I hit a gantry rail."

"I'll pass that along. To confirm, you and Morgan are in Bunker 2-18B-8, correct?"

Rather than open his eyes to the free-floating gastric fluids, Rex stepped back through his enhanced-for-accuracy memory. Yes, he and Charlie had repeatedly lurched into a wall with those numbers printed on it. "Correct."

"Thanks. Hang in there. Rescue runner ETA is about five minutes. Dispatch out."

"Roger that." Five minutes? Thank goodness. That wasn't as long as he'd . . . wait. Rescue runners were small spaceships. They stayed outside in the spacelanes. How could one get inside the docking bay? The ventilator fans still ran at top speed, but the smell had eased up some. Rex half-opened one eye. The air was much clearer. He hugged the wall to protect his nose, shifted with care over to the hatch's small window, then used one paw to clear a patch of it. What was going on, out there?

Woah. An enormous hole in the—from his orientation, it was the "ceiling"—marked where that humongous berthing cone had been. A tangle of conduits, wires, hoses and pipes floated like tentacles around the hole. Beyond them, Rex saw darkness and a dusting of stars. The rescue runner? Getting in would be no problem.

Rex's heart pounded harder. If Fujimoto hadn't helped him and Charlie, they would've . . .

Rex hailed Fujimoto, heart pounding hard.

No answer.

His chest tightened. He took a long, controlled breath, held it, then slowly let it out as he'd seen Charlie do when he was upset.

It helped steady him. He called the dispatcher back. "Detective Fujimoto does not answer his com. I am worried."

"Biometrics say he's alive inside Bunker 2-18B-9, but he may be unconscious."

Relief washed over Rex. "Roger that. Thank you." *Unconscious* was bad, but *alive-inside-a-bunker* definitely beat *sucked-into-space-unprotected.* Better stop bothering the dispatcher.

Rex panted, shaky. At least the ventilators had cleared the air. He and Charlie were still covered with *yuck,* but they could open their eyes and breathe safely. He looked outside again. The damage to the dock boggled him, but nothing had changed since the last . . .

Beyond the hole in the outer hull, the nose of a ship appeared, a ship still connected to the trailing wreck of a berthing cone. *There is the* Izgubil!

Charlie didn't answer, but the warmth of his body floated against Rex in the narrow bunker. Rex glanced sideways. Charlie's bruised, brown face drifted near his own, gray-tinged, pinched with pain.

A surge of affection welled up. Rex flicked his tongue across the ashy cheek, a quick, tender caress.

Oh, my, that left a sour aftertaste.

Charlie, I love you, but you taste terrible. Rex sighed. All the same, it felt good to talk to Charlie. His half-open eyes seemed semi-focused. Impressions through the link were less chaotic. When they got out of this, Rex might be in big trouble. Strike that. Would be in big trouble. But if Charlie would just wake up and be well, Rex was willing to endure any punishment he thought was appropriate.

Meanwhile, however, they had to survive to be rescued. Rex let out a cautious sigh. He returned his attention to the window. Could he still see the *Izgubil?* Could he spot their rescuers?

The *Izgubil* remained in view. It drifted past the hole in the bulkhead. The broken berthing cone slid out of sight. As parts of the ship moved slowly through his view, Rex saw that it had a center core and two slowly rotating globular holds, one on each side. Surely the people at the helm did not imagine they could outrun the Station Defense Force cutters, did they? Certainly not at that speed. Why, then, had they breached?

The nearer hold made a bright flash.

Charlie gasped. He flinched away.

Stunned, Rex blinked through the afterimage. Millions of little pieces flew toward them. The bunker rattled. The lights went out, flickered, then came back on. Next came a thunder of pieces hitting the outer hull and embedding themselves into the walls of the voided dock's yawning wound. Rex flinched away from the window. Vibrations shuddered through the metal structure around the bunker. It reverberated far louder than any hailstorm he'd suffered through in Transmondia. He curled into a ball of terror.

But the thunder slacked off and ended. Rex uncurled, then stared out at the devastation, not quite believing. Through the opening beyond the debris-studded dock, he glimpsed the outline of the second hold on the ship's other side. Then it flashed and blew apart, too. The lights went out again. It was a little longer before they blinked back on this time. The hailstorm clatter crescendoed once more, then trailed off as before. Miraculous: he saw no voided bunkers. But the inner berth, open to the debris, was now even more thickly studded with shrapnel.

Rex struggled to make sense of it. How could this happen? What could anyone possibly gain from blowing up the ship? The crew! Did they get any warning? Rex growled softly. Could Emergency Rescue Teams with MERS-Vs scramble fast enough to save any of them? How could they possibly find anyone in time? *Oh, Charlie. I do not think our rescue-runner will be here in five minutes, after all.*

When they'd first jumped inside, Rex hadn't had time to think about how cramped this bunker was. With all the other things that had happened, Rex hadn't thought about it even once. Until now. But now the walls pressed in. Kind of like the Dark Crate.

Rex's chest constricted. He tried another one of Charlie's breathing patterns. The walls receded . . . a little. Rex panted. This bunker was well-lit. Not dark. Not like the Dark Crate. All the same, Rex panted faster. Charlie was here. Rex was not alone. Not like in the Dark Crate.

He thrust his nose closer to his partner, filled his consciousness with Charlie's comforting personal scent. He was still Charlie, even if he stank pretty badly on the outside. Still warm. Still alive.

But Charlie was clearly in trouble.

Panic fluttered in Rex's chest. He smelled the injuries, the inflammation, the trauma. Charlie could die. Charlie surely would die, if he didn't get help soon. Then Rex would be the worst kind of alone. This was all Rex's fault. He'd been so tunnel-focused! Now Charlie was . . . Charlie was . . . he ran another breathing pattern.

Another.

Then another.

An eternity ticked past, one measured breath at a time. At last came loud bangs. Charlie flinched. So did Rex. But now! At last!

Rex gasped in a breath. Relief swept through him, so powerful it left him trembling.

With a whoosh of air, a vacuum lock sucked snug to the bunker's hatch.

Rex shuddered, whimpered, and wagged his tail at top speed.

5

FROM TRIUMPH TO DEFEAT

Bay 2-18B, Emergency Bunker 8 and Rescue Runner
Triumph

The hatch popped, then swung open. Rex thought he glimpsed a flash of something that rippled across the opening, but almost the instant he'd glimpsed it, it was gone. Beyond the frame of the now-open hatch, Rex saw warm light, the interior of an airlock, and a young woman in a respirator.

He tried to push through the opening, but his nose bumped against something he couldn't see. It gave slightly, but he pulled back, looked again. Wasn't easy to spot, but a clear, flexible membrane had sealed the bunker's open hatch.

"Stop! Stay!" The young woman blocked him. Reflective patches shimmered on her coveralls. A sergeant's chevrons, also reflective, glinted on her shoulder. "Just a sec. Need to get you encapsulated. You're covered with contaminants."

She had a point. No wonder they'd sealed the bunker entrance.

Another young woman appeared, also garbed in a respirator and coveralls. She reached a gloved right hand through the membrane . . . no, the startlingly flexible membrane formed itself around her hand, made it look shiny. How astonishing! The membrane held while she unclipped Rex's tether from Charlie. "Come. Slowly." She squeezed a device in her left hand. The membrane expanded as Rex stepped forward. She pinched off the end once he was out.

In the microgravity, he hung inside a bubble of the clear membrane and stared about. This was unexpected. What would happen next?

The second young woman floated him and his bubble past a gurney, into a vestibule on the other side of the airlock.

Behind him, the sergeant pulled herself halfway inside the bunker. "Here I am, Charlie." Her voice was calm, upbeat. Rex looked back. He couldn't smell her scent factors clearly through the membrane, but the filtered odors smelled like the fragrant warmth of recognition, mixed with even warmer affection. "It's Hildie," the sergeant said. "Can you hear me?"

The second young woman closed the vestibule's hatch. Then she opened the hatch on the other side and towed him into the medical bay of the rescue runner. The inside of the craft was about twice as big as Rex's bedroom, with side compartments. Their design made Rex think they could be sealed away from the other areas. Well, that would make sense.

Rex's paramedic towed him in his bubble toward a tall, boxlike device.

Alarmed, Rex shrank back, inside his bubble. "Wait. What—" Oh, that did *not* look good. It looked like a large, sealable shower stall, with FULL-BODY DECON STATION printed across its thick, transparent wall. Oh, no-*no-no*—!

He tried to scramble backward, but there was nothing to push against but the bubble's wall. It rotated under his feet. "No-no-no, wait! Wait!"

She didn't respond. Simply opened the hatch, pushed both Rex and his bubble firmly inside, then closed the hatch.

Rex's pulse fluttered faster. He stared out at her, imploring.

"Can we talk? Please?" Chest tight, his tongue slid out in a nervous pant.

Pressure seals locked. Jets of water shot from the walls. The membrane-bubble melted. Rex yelped, but there was no escape. Warm water assaulted him from all sides. Water in his mouth. Water in his eyes. Water soaked his coat. He choked. His lungs burned. No air! *No air!* He was drowning! His vision darkened. His ears hissed.

Powerful vacuums roared to life all around him. They sucked the water away. Breathable air flowed in. Rex gasped in a grateful breath, but he was still trapped.

Next moment, the jets sprayed soapy water. *Eww! Ack! Yuck!* He snapped his jaws shut, clamped his eyes closed, then hunched in a miserable, slowly rotating knot of aching ribs and folded legs, his ears clenched flat. Abrasions all over his body burned from the soap and the stinging spray. He bumped from side to side of the Full-Body Decon Station.

Those vacuums felt like they could suck his hair right off. At last the water ran clear again, warm in a soaking spray. The vacuums sucked it all away, then deactivated with a growl. Rex shuddered. He shook himself, but that made him flail even more against the inside walls of the Full-Body Decon Station. He whimpered, shivering, his fur on end every which-way.

The young woman opened the hatch. She'd shed her respirator. Now dark marks creased her light brown face, on her cheeks and around her nose and mouth. "You poor thing. You look miserable. Good dog. Stay."

Rex shuddered. Hot indignation rose within him like lava. He splayed his legs to stop bumping around, braced his paws on opposite walls, and bristled at her. "That was almost worse than the bunker. I get that I needed a bath, but I really would have appreciated a little warning. Could I maybe have had a moment to hold my breath?"

The young paramedic gave a squeak, then stared open-mouthed at Rex. "Oh my God! You really can talk. I—I never met an XK9 before. I didn't think you could understand—I am so, *so* sorry!" The young woman did look and smell properly horrified.

Rex strove to get a grip on his temper. Disrespect would surely earn him a beating. "I am curious why you did not remove my panniers first." He craned his neck cautiously to sniff along the edges his nose could reach. "I do not think most of the equipment will be harmed, although the scent cards are likely ruined. You may need to do some spot-cleaning." The hurricane bath had removed nearly all traces of vomit, dust, loose dog hairs, and other contaminants.

"It all needed cleaning, so I just de-conned everything at once. Also, I wasn't sure how to get it off."

"I am coming out. Then I shall tell you how to remove my equipment." Rex reached paws forward to pull himself through the hatch.

"Wait!"

He did not wait, any more than she'd waited for him. He'd been inside that damned torture-box long enough. He hooked hind paws inside the edge of the Full-Body Decon Station for an anchor, then looked around. In a side compartment to his left, two paramedics worked with intent, precise movements on Detective Fujimoto, who still seemed to be unconscious.

To his right, Hildie had been joined by a partner. They worked on Charlie with an intensity that roused Rex's worst fears. Hildie continued to offer light chatter about what they were doing in a calm, upbeat voice, but the discordant clash in her scent factors signaled both serious worry and that startling depth of affection he'd noted before. As if she knew Charlie. As if she loved him. Who was this woman? Why had Rex never heard of her?

Charlie grimaced and mumbled. The brain link relayed only pain and confusion. His condition continued to deteriorate. Hildie's partner hovered with his back to Rex, intent upon cutting away Charlie's left jacket-sleeve. He and Hildie eased

Charlie out of his bubble-membrane using handheld washer-vacs to clean each newly-exposed part. Charlie's skin looked gray, mottled with stark, ominous bruises.

Bitter shame choked Rex. "Is Charlie going to be all right?"

The young woman who'd put Rex into the Full-Body Decon Station frowned. "I don't know. Sorry. But Hildie and Eli are a top-notch team. They'll give him their absolute best. After all, Charlie's pretty special to all of us." Her scent and expression warmed with admiration, but nowhere near as warm as the scents Hildie exuded.

Rex cocked his head. "I know he is special to me, but why is he special to you?"

Her brows rose. "This is the *Triumph*. Charlie used to be on our MERS-V retrieval team. He's one of ours." She towed Rex over to a medical station in a side compartment.

Confused, gave her a curious look. "I did not know that." Charlie'd never mentioned having been a member of an Emergency Rescue Team. Rex shot another glance at Hildie. What kind of relationship had Charlie had with her? Even Pam had never smelled that way toward his partner.

"Charlie was so good at this job. For things to end so badly . . ." Rex's paramedic bit her lip. One deft arm-twist moved the medical station's bed aside. She grasped Rex's harness, tugged him under her scanner. She attached straps to hold him there, then sighed. "Did you ever hear of the *Asalatu*?"

The name stirred a memory from middle-puppyhood. "A ship. I know it wrecked." Rex hadn't paid much attention to the story back then, but the humans had talked about it. What had they said? Dr. Ordovich had driven him half-crazy testing his freakish memory his whole life, but now he felt grateful to have it. The past reopened for him, fresh and detailed.

Oh. Yikes. Three-hundred-fifty-eight passengers killed. An SDF tug obliterated, with all hands lost. Most of an ERT crew crushed while trying to rescue passengers: one killed, one lost her legs, one lost . . . *his arm*.

Rex gasped. The post-traumatic reaction in micrograv—the weak arm—his partner's reluctance to talk about his personal history . . . *Oh, Charlie.* "He never talks much about the past."

"I guess I can't blame him." The paramedic grimaced. "He was always uncomfortable with the idea that he's a hero. When he couldn't—when he couldn't get back into a MERS-V without a panic attack . . ." Her scent factors shifted to deep distress. She gave a little head-shake, almost a shudder. "Well, we all took that pretty hard."

Rex laid his ears back. "It sounds to me as if there are several stories, here. Please start with the 'idea that he's a hero' thing. What did he do?"

"Oh, you know, the Medal of—" She stopped. Gave him a closer look. "Holy crap. Do you know about Charlie's Medal of Valor?"

Rex's ears went straight up. "Charlie has a Medal of Valor?" He activated his CAP, ran a fast search.

"Oh, that silly man." She shot Rex a rueful look. "Of course he wouldn't bother to bring it up. Why would his dog need to know about that little trifle?"

She hadn't finished talking before his CAP told Rex that the Medal of Valor was the highest heroism award Rana Station's government could bestow. Only fifteen individuals in the Station's history had received it; only one had been awarded in the last decade. That one had gone to a Multipurpose Emergency Response Space-Vehicle driver, an Orangeboro Peace Officer named Charles Morgan, who'd saved the lives of twelve accident victims and a teammate, at great peril to his own life, during the aftermath of the *Asalatu* accident. Charlie really was a hero.

Rex could see it, actually. He cocked his head more carefully, this time. "How did he save all those people?"

Her brows rose. Now she looked and smelled puzzled. "So . . . you do know?"

"You said a Medal of Valor. I looked it up on my CAP."

"You not only talk, they gave you a CAP?"

"How else could I tap into the Station Net or file reports?"

She opened and closed her mouth. "Um, I have no idea."

"But since you know Charlie, I have many more questions," Rex said. "How did he save all those people? When did he start having panic attacks?"

The young woman drew in a breath. "He saved those people because he *didn't* panic. He always had the coolest head in the group, when the pressure was on. I think that's why his problems later were so hard—"

One of Detective Fujimoto's monitors started flashing and beeping.

"Oh!" Rex's paramedic darted over to a supply cart along the wall. She yanked a drawer open, grabbed a package of something, then joined the team already working on the older detective.

Still strapped in place inside the scanner, Rex could only watch from a distance and worry.

Orangeboro 6th Precinct, Orangeboro Medical Center

Sick waves of dread pulsed through Rex. He loped alongside Charlie's mobile med-bed from the Emergency-Services elevator into the ground-level ER of Orangeboro Medical Center. He kept his nose as near to his partner as he could. He meant to stay right beside Charlie, no matter what it took.

ER staff members closed in around them. Rex slowed to give them room. They ran into an area marked RESTRICTED. A pair of doors slammed hard behind them.

Rex collided with the doors.

He staggered back, stunned. His face and chest stung. A sharp stab shot down his right side. "No! Let me in!" *Charlie!* Must stay close! He reared back, body-slammed the unyielding doors, then hunched, blind with agony for a long, awful moment until the pain eased.

"Hey! Get away! Who let that dog in here?"

Rex lifted his head to glare at the speaker. Fury thundered in his ears, his throat, his heart. "My partner is in there. I must go with him!"

The speaker, a chubby man in blue scrubs, scrambled back a couple of steps. "Oh, shit! It's one of those monsters! Shirley! Call the police!"

"I *am* the police! Let me through!" His rage boiled up. With a roar, Rex flung himself at the doors again, then once again recoiled in a spasm of agony. Cold dread dragged at the edges of his thoughts: this was getting him nowhere. Each time he hit the doors it hurt worse. But what else could he do?

"Stop that! How'd you get in here?" Chubby-Scrubs' tone might sound peremptory, but his cold, sweaty fear-reek told a different story. He scowled at the handful of other scrubs-clad humans who stood around nearby, staring at Rex. "Who let him in?"

Charlie! Where are you? A chasm of terror yawned . . . better to hit the doors. "My partner is in there!" Rex backed up—limping, heartsick, desperate—to make another run.

Chubby-Scrubs darted forward. He stopped in front of the doors, arms wide. "Damn it, stop that!" He stank of fear, but also of the bitter heat that came with anger. "You'll hurt yourself. You should go see your vet! You're already bleeding."

Rex's body ached, but the heartsick intensity of his anguish rode him harder. He set his haunches for another run at the doors. "Step aside. I do not care if I am bleeding."

"No!" Chubby-Scrubs stayed put, now sweating freely. "It's a sterile area. D'you want to hurt your partner?"

Desolation clutched him in its talons. "But I must stay with Charlie. I do not know what to do without Charlie."

Chubby-Scrubs shook his head. His anger-smell cooled some-what, shifted to a nose-itching prickle of irritation. "Charlie's getting the care he needs. You'd just contaminate the ER and put him in more danger."

Rex squirmed in the blaze of his own self-condemnation. He was a heedless, stupid, *idiot* puppy, thinking wrong again. This was all his fault! Maybe he should just slink away and die.

"You're making a mess," Chubby-Scrubs said. "Shouldn't you be at your vet's? Why are you here?"

Rex bowed his head. A deep throb permeated his face and chest. The pain in his ribs sharpened to a stab along his right side if he took too deep a breath. He smelled the coppery tang of his own blood. He stared down in despair at the hard, shiny floor, sprinkled with blood-spatter.

Despite the blood in his nose, Rex smelled more than saw a woman approach. "Someone's coming from the police."

"Good." Chubby-Scrubs took a step closer to Rex. "You. Hey, Dog."

Rex lifted his head, heartsick. "I am XK9 Officer Rex Dicter-Nell."

"Whatever." The man grimaced, then pointed to a glass door across the waiting room. "Go wait for your pick-up out *there*."

Rex followed the gesture with his gaze. Out *there* beyond the glass door, it was still dark as midnight. He hesitated, unwilling to leave the last place he'd seen Charlie. What had these people done with him? Would Rex ever see him again?

"Hurry up! Go!"

Charlie wasn't here to tell Rex what was okay to do or not do. Chubby-Scrubs' attitude brought a growl to Rex's throat, but he didn't let it out. His lips itched to snarl, but he resisted. Dogs must always obey humans. Even when they were rude. Even when they were wrong. Even when they told him to do something that made him want to howl in despair.

"Move it! You're supposed to be a smart dog. Prove it!"

The steely glint in Chubby-Scrubs' eyes said he was the kind of human who wouldn't hesitate to use a prod, if disobeyed for much longer. Rex couldn't see a prod anywhere, but there was always a prod.

"Go on! You'll only make things worse. *Get out!*"

Rex didn't want to face the prod. He took a single, reluctant step toward the door. Stopped. Rebellion seethed within him, but it was no use. The human had given an order. He tucked his tail under his belly, then made his way toward the glass door in a low, slow slink.

"Hurry up!" The man's glare cut like a dagger.

Rex turned back, about halfway there.

Chubby-Scrubs shook his head, hands on hips. "Out! *Now!*"

Rex retreated backward until his haunches bumped against the door. It swung open. Rex crouched in the doorway. He whimpered.

The rounded contours of Chubby-Scrubs' face set like concrete. His scowl did not yield.

Rex backed through the door, one slow, reluctant step at a time.

The door thumped closed. The auto-lock snapped shut.

He'd been cast out.

Charlie! Heartbroken, Rex pressed his face against the hard glass. Through the link, he clung to the faint thread of Charlie's consciousness.

Then all at once that faint thread evaporated.

6

HOW TO CAPTURE AN XK9

Orangeboro Medical Center, Central Plaza, and Orangeboro Police Dept. HQ

Rex froze. He couldn't breathe. Couldn't think. Couldn't hear, over the high-speed thunder in his ears. Where did Charlie go? Why couldn't he feel him through the link anymore? What had those people done to him? *Charlie! Charlie!* He called through the link, but deep within him a cold, dreadful voice whispered it was no use. Charlie couldn't hear him. Charlie was . . . Nowhere.

First the Pack and Shady. Now Charlie. Rex shivered, alone in the dark. Despair like a dark, drowning flood overwhelmed him, overflowed into whimpers he couldn't stop. This wasn't right. He needed Charlie. He pressed his face against the locked glass door outside the Orangeboro Medical Center ER and cried. Even in the depths of the Dark Crate, he'd never felt such desolation. Despair rolled up from his very core. He lifted his nose to pour it out in a howl.

Bang-bang-bang came from somewhere beyond the darkness. *Bang-bang-bang,* like hollow thuds on a glass panel. Then again, *Bang-bang-bang.*

Rex pulled back from the abyss. Blinked. Refocused.

Chubby-Scrubs was banging on the glass door. He glared at Rex. "Stop that! Quiet, you stupid mutt!"

Rex snarled at him. A gut-deep, seething rage rose from his heart, but he choked it back. He'd had all too much practice curbing murderous impulses when Dr. Ordovich ruled his life. Now of all times, when he didn't know what had happened to Charlie, was no time to fantasize about ripping humans' throats out. Rex pulled himself back with a sigh that was three-quarters groan, then moved over from the blood-smears he'd just left. He pressed his face against the glass in a new place. He could hold himself back from howling, but his heart and throat and soul ached with stomach-sinking terror of the unknowable. He couldn't keep from crying, but he must constrain himself to cry quietly.

After a while, he caught the fog-fuzzy flash of a headlight in the reflective glass. From across the dark lawn came the hum of a police vehicle.

Uneasy, Rex turned to look.

A UPO rode a motorbike with an empty sidecar up the driveway through the mist toward the ER. He couldn't see where the man had stowed his trank rifle and net.

Rex tensed. He hunched his body, tail tucked but hackles up.

Footsteps approached. Calm, kind scent factors and a faint fragrance of sandalwood, almond, and lavender drew closer. This UPO's clothing also carried smells of coffee, small children, and at least two dogs. "Hey, there, big guy. What's happened to you?" Even his deep voice sounded gentle. "Why are you out here alone, crying in the dark?"

Rex looked up, startled by this approach. The officer held out his hand for Rex to sniff. Rex hesitated, but the man had asked a question. "They made me leave the ER. Took Charlie. I cannot feel Charlie." Rex looked back toward the locked glass door.

The officer still didn't go for a weapon. Didn't tense up or smell nervous, the way the dog wranglers usually did. Instead, he reached out with a slow, calm hand to stroke Rex's neck. His touch was firm but gentle. Nothing about him gave the least hint that he meant to grab Rex's harness or suddenly drop a net over his head. No, he seemed prepared to stand there and simply caress Rex's neck for as long as necessary. "It'll be okay."

Cold, insidious worry slithered in Rex's stomach. He bowed his head. "It is not okay. I cannot feel Charlie. Not at all. Nothing."

"I take it your partner Charlie's in the ER, and they wouldn't let you follow."

If this man had ever been trained in XK9 retrieval by the Project, he hid it well. Rex relaxed a little. "They said I would contaminate things. But I just had a bath! I am clean!"

The officer sighed, his expression and scent factors rueful. "They have rules. Sometimes rules seem stupid, but they exist for a reason." He caressed Rex's neck and shoulder with long, soothing strokes. "Oh, how I wish my daughter Becky was here! She'd know which XK9 you are. She's been so excited about you guys coming to Orangeboro. Now I can tell her that I actually *met* one of you."

This certainly was an unusual way to capture and subdue an XK9. Rex untucked his tail, even wagged it a little, beguiled despite his wariness. "Tell Becky you met Rex Dieter-Nell."

The officer smiled. "And I'm Bill Sloane. Good to meet you, Rex. How about if you tell me what happened to you? Could we start with why Charlie's in the ER?"

Rex yawned a wide stress-release yawn. A tiny bit of his tension fell away. This guy was treating him more like a person than a dog. It was a refreshing change, but how much could he say about the case? Still, a human had asked a question. He'd better give some kind of acceptable answer. "We were at a scene in the Hub, and I chased two murderers—but I went too fast. Charlie got hurt. Then the ship started to leave, while we were still in the docking bay."

Bill drew a quick breath. "You were in the dock breach?"

Rex lifted his ears, relieved. "Yes. Do you know about that?"

"It's the top headline all over the System." Bill smelled amazed, but he continued his soothing, calming strokes. "If you're fresh from the dock breach, why aren't you with a veterinarian?"

Rex's heart rate sped up with remembered agitation. "I would not leave Charlie. But they locked me out."

A whiff of anger like singed cloth slid its tendrils through Bill's scent, but his voice stayed calm. "You're bleeding, you know. Let's go see your vet, okay?"

Rex gave a low growl. "I need to know that Charlie is all right. I need to know for certain that he is—that he is not—"

Bill frowned, but still he did not yell or hit Rex. Instead he seemed to come to a decision. "Tell you what. Let's go to HQ."

Rex put his head down, resistant. "Why would I do that? Charlie is here."

Bill gave him a wry look. "If you want access to the hospital and to Charlie, you're gonna need some clout. That means we go to HQ."

Startled, Rex studied Bill's scent factors. He smelled honest. He even appeared sympathetic to Rex's desire. He seemed to think he had a good idea. Rex wasn't sure what he meant to do, but he'd actually heeded Rex's worries. Rana Stationers were proving to be much more unpredictable than the Transmondians he was used to. Rex straightened, put his ears up. "You think I can find help at HQ?"

Bill nodded. "If you're going to get it anywhere, I'd say Chief Klein's your best bet."

If something could and might be done, Rex must seize the chance. "Okay. Let us go get this . . . clout."

Bill grinned. He called his dispatcher to say that he had Rex and was headed for HQ.

Rex took the moment to run a quick definition-search on his

CAP, but he came up with a confusing mix of definitions. "Bill? What is 'clout'?"

Bill chuckled. "Don't worry. You'll catch on. The trick is to use whatever influence you have or can claim. It gives you leverage to improve your situation or create a better outcome."

Rex cocked his head, startled. "How can I have influence?"

Bill smiled. "First of all, you're an insanely valuable dog. You should not be neglected and shut outside to fend for yourself."

"The hospital staff . . . neglected me?"

"They ordered you outside, when that was a bad place for you to be."

"They were . . . wrong?" No dog was ever supposed to think that humans were wrong, even when they clearly were. That kind of thinking was insubordinate.

To his surprise, Bill nodded. "They were wrong to put you outside alone. Come with me. I'll show you how humans get things done. Would you like to ride in my sidecar?"

Rex's hope rose. He'd been shut out and shoved aside enough. If there was a way to leverage his influence for a better outcome, he meant to learn how to do it. He sniffed the inside of Bill's sidecar, then stepped in gingerly, startled to discover that Bill had no trank rifle or net in there at all. Yet he'd certainly gotten Rex to come away with him. The XK9 Project's typical approach to capturing him seemed needlessly strenuous next to Bill Sloane's method. This was unquestionably an insubordinate thought, but Rex lolled his tongue anyway. Bill's method was faster, too.

They'd traveled only two blocks before Rex caught a distinctive scent in the misty night air. He couldn't see it yet, but the orange-blossom smell of Central Plaza expanded in the misty atmosphere. With it came an avalanche of human scent profiles. Startled, he glanced toward the UPO. "Bill? Why would a crowd of people be in Central Plaza at this hour?"

Bill slowed his motorbike. "Hmm. Probably journalists.

They'll all be eager for a scoop—which means we need to go in the back door." He smiled at Rex. "Good catch. How'd you figure that? We're still several blocks away."

"I can smell the crowd among the orange trees."

"That's quite the schnoz you've got there. Helpful." Bill turned away from the direction of the Plaza, but soon halted his motorbike near a set of cargo-transport-sized elevator doors marked "Official Access Only," set into one end of a long, mosaic-walled, single-level elevator terminal structure.

At the far end Rex saw three sets of public-access elevator doors. These elevators all went down, not up like the commuter trunk to the Hub that he and Charlie had taken. Below ground-level, the Borough was riddled with as many as ten subterranean levels. Most were devoted to an assortment of industrial enterprises and municipal utilities, or storage facilities. Companies or private individuals stored their things there, like the burglar he'd caught yesterday. Some people actually lived down there.

Rex's throat had gone dry with his howling, crying, and nervous panting, but he saw no water here. His stomach growled. Something to eat would be good, too. Stiff already, he stood, which set off a chorus of aching muscles, then yawned. His breath intake gave his ribs a sharp stab.

Bill dismounted. He flashed his badge at the Official Access control panel. A light at the top of the panel blinked twice. The doors opened on an elevator car big enough to hold a bus, or one of the OPD's big Personnel Transport Vehicles. Bill got back on his motorbike. Rex sat again, while Bill drove the motorbike into the cavernous, echoing space.

Rex cocked his head at Bill. "Why is this elevator so big? Do they carry PTVs?"

Bill gave him a startled look. "Um, yes. There's a garage on S-3."

Short ride: they stopped at level S-1. A relatively clean, well-lit but narrow underground driveway led them a considerable distance before they came to another set of elevator doors. Bill parked the motorbike. Rex dismounted gingerly, but his ribs twinged all the same. Another show of Bill's badge, and soon they were headed up, inside a more normal-sized elevator.

"Are we inside the Civic Center now?" Rex asked.

Bill shot him another startled look. "You're a really smart dog, aren't you?" Rex wasn't certain how to read his scent, or how to answer.

Instead, he asked, "Where are we going?"

Bill grimaced. "Probably walking into a madhouse. OPD Admin."

Rex nodded, puzzling out 'madhouse,' and its implications. "Chief Klein is undoubtedly very busy, because the ship breached from an Orangeboro dock." He cocked his head at Bill. "Do you think the Station Bureau of Investigation will come because of the ship blowing up?"

A jolt of astonished apprehension shot through Bill's scent. He stared at Rex. "Um, that's likely, I think. Unless the SDF takes over, instead."

The SDF? Hmm. "Because the ship blew up. I see. The Station Defense Force may know more about exploding spacecraft than the SBI. Which do you think would conduct a better investigation?"

The astonishment in Bill's scent deepened. "A really, really smart dog." He let out a shaky breath. "Um, I'm not sure which would be the better choice for this case. I'm glad I don't have to choose."

Rex didn't have enough information to evaluate the matter. "Will Chief Klein have to choose?"

"I suspect it'll be up to Premier Iskander."

Rex hoped she would choose wisely. Charlie had been disappointed when she was elected. *Charlie.* A surge of longing filled Rex. His partner's absence on the other end of the brain link chilled him. Was Charlie still alive? He yawned a wide stress-yawn, but it didn't relax him. "If Chief Klein is busy with the SBI or the SDF, will he take time for me?"

Bill opened his mouth, closed it, cleared his throat. "Good question. My gut says that sooner or later a scraped-up XK9 in the Chief's waiting room will be noticed."

"Do you think an XK9 in the waiting room could get a drink?"

7

IN QUEST OF CLOUT

OPD HQ, Chief Klein's Office

The final pair of elevator doors opened. Rex had never been inside one this fancy. Normally, he paid little heed to human decorations, but this elevator car even *smelled* different. Cleaner. With little of the dust, paint flakes, body odors, or other grunge that inevitably built up in most elevator cars. The sides had polished strips of real wood that ran from floor to ceiling in between mirror-panels.

Beside him, Bill's scent profile shifted. A little tendril of high, sharp nervousness wove into his calm, pleasant personal blend. He drew in a breath, stepped into the car.

Rex moved beside him. He'd reflexively put himself on "heel." With Charlie, that was just how they normally walked. Rex never had to think about it. But now Rex was more than simply "on heel" to a near-stranger. Bill was the only human in the universe at this moment who seemed well-disposed toward him.

The elevator doors closed them in. Bill punched the top button, then stood at what Rex could only describe as "parade rest." Bill drew in another deep breath, then blew it out all at once. He checked his reflection in one of the mirror panels, made an invisible adjustment to his collar. Squared his shoulders. Resumed parade rest. This well-disposed near-stranger, who'd seemed so confident when they first left the yard outside Orangeboro Medical Center, smelled more and more of tense, jittery worry, the farther the elevator climbed.

Had Bill made a mistake? Was coming here a bad idea, after all? Rex went to "parade sit," next to the man. He couldn't help panting a little, his throat so dry it might crackle if he tried to swallow. His empty stomach growled. The elevator went up and up. Rex became conscious of every stinging abrasion, every cautiously-shallow breath to avoid a sharp stab to his ribs. "Bill?"

"Yes?"

"I apologize, but I am very thirsty. Do you think we might be able to find water?"

"I, um." Bill drew in another breath, swallowed. "I, um, have never been on the Admin level before. I guess we'll have to see what's available."

The elevator continued upward.

"Bill?"

"Yes?" Bill's voice sounded tense.

"Thank you."

Bill held his formal pose, but his eyes shifted toward Rex. His mouth widened to a tight-lipped smile. "You're welcome."

The elevator slowed, then stopped.

"Time to light the fires," Bill muttered.

Rex didn't have time to ask, before the doors rolled open.

A waiting room filled with humans and a few ozzirikkians, most in civilian garb, lay to their left. It was already maxed out— no room for Rex there. Bill stepped out of the elevator, Rex alongside him. Rex kept his focus on Bill: *follow your human's lead* was a maxim he'd learned early. People in the waiting room gasped, exclaimed. Their excited reactions rolled over Rex in a wave of odor. Their babble of words grew louder. Buzzing overhead drew his attention upward. A small swarm of tiny cameras swooped closer.

"Hold up, there! What's this?" A tall man in a captain's uniform strode toward them. Rex remembered him, with his brisk manner, his narrow, pale face, and blue eyes. He'd met him briefly before the Presentation Ceremony. Chief Klein had called him Archy.

Bill stiffened, saluted. "Good morning, Capt. Danvir. I'm Corporal William Goldstein Sloane. This is XK9 Officer Rex Dieter-Nell. He needs to speak with the Chief."

Capt. Danvir—Archy—bent to examine Rex more closely. He frowned. "What the hell happened to him?"

"The dock breach," Rex said. "They took Char—"

Archy held up his hand. Every person in the place had gone silent. All eyes stared at Rex. The swarm of tiny cameras darted closer, dipping and swirling in a buzzing cloud.

"We'll discuss this in my office." Archy pivoted. He marched a short distance past the waiting area, into a hallway lined by sparkling sconces and wall-mounted planters filled with vines or moss. His shoes rapped a quick staccato on the hardwood floor. Rex and Bill followed. Their clicking claws and footsteps tapped a counterpoint. The buzzing cloud followed close behind.

Archy led them into an office the size of Charlie's master bedroom, then hastily slammed the door on the camera-swarm. Their clatter against the door rattled like sleet or pea-sized hail.

"All right, now. What's this about the dock breach?" He turned his scowl on Bill. "And why the hell did you bring him here?"

Bill had brought Rex this far, but the man's scent was shifting like sliding sand into the frazzled, prickly scent of someone overwhelmed by a situation.

"You asked what happened to me," Rex said. "The dock

breach happened. Indirectly, that is why I am here. I want to see my partner."

The door opened. A dark-haired woman with light brown skin stepped inside, then slammed it as Archy had. Rex recognized her, too. She'd been the one who told everyone where to stand, during the Presentation Ceremony: Joslyn Stark, Press Liaison, a civilian. She smelled deeply stressed, but not overwhelmed like Bill. At least one of the little cameras got crushed when she closed the door, but three more entered the room.

Archy took two long strides to his desk, opened a control panel, then hit a button. The three cameras fell to the floor. He and Joslyn Stark took a moment to thoroughly crush each of them. Beyond the door, several voices shouted aggrieved complaints.

Archy and Joslyn stared at Rex.

Joslyn spoke first. "Is it true?"

Archy grimaced. "With Relay One out? How should we know? They're still patching a workaround."

"It is true that Charlie and I were in the dock breach," Rex said. "He is in the hospital. I want to smell him over in person, to make sure he is still alive. That is why I am here."

"Holy shit." Joslyn's scent factors suffused with an even stronger stress-smell. "Only two months along, and an XK9's already involved in a major incident?"

Archy frowned. His eyes took on the vacant, middle-distance "HUD stare" of someone accessing his CAP. Then his eyes refocused. He gave Rex an unhappy look. "Damn. They did deploy that team. Morgan and the lead, Fujimoto, are both in critical condition at Orangeboro Med." He turned to Bill. "How do you fit into this?"

Bill stiffened to attention, gave another salute. "Corporal William Goldstein Sloane, sir. Dispatch sent me to collect XK9 Rex outside the hospital's ER."

Archy shot a glance at Rex. "Has he been to the vet?"

"Negative, sir. He would not budge until—"

"Why didn't you take him to the vet?" Archy glared at Bill.

"We have a more immediate problem," Joslyn said. "An XK9 in the dock breach? That's news. Why didn't I know about this? I should have known this!" She turned to Rex. "Are you all right?"

"I am fine. XK9s are tough. I want to see Charlie, but they ordered me out of the ER." Rex meant to stay on-topic, no matter what might distract the humans.

"Out of—" Joslyn turned to Archy. "This is bad. This is terrible!"

Archy held up his hands. "I know. The—"

A buzzer sounded on Archy's desk. He drew in a breath. "Sir." He went back into the HUD-stare, then nodded vigorously. "Of course, sir." He looked at Rex. "Come with me."

Rex tensed. But he'd come this far. He meant to see Chief Klein. He followed Archy through a side doorway into a bigger office, with Bill and Joslyn right behind him. One wall was all windows. They offered a broad view from twenty-five levels up. Orangeboro's mist-shrouded urban core spread out below them. Lines of tiny lights glowed in minute, misty nimbuses. The first, faint glimmer of dawn shimmered over the tops of the fogbanks.

"Rex." Chief Klein rose from his large desk near the windows. Even from several meters' distance, Klein smelled considerably more stressed than Joslyn or Archy, but his tall, broad-shouldered body relaxed a tiny fraction at the sight of Rex. His scent shifted to a brighter tone, and a smile transformed his dark brown face.

"Hello, sir. It is good to see you again." Rex wagged his tail, encouraged by the Chief's smile. He'd first met Klein in Solara City when the Chief had come to meet the Pack and tour the facility. The whole Pack had agreed he smelled like a much nicer man than many of the others who'd taken Dr. Ordovich's tours. They'd all been relieved to learn they would be sold to Klein.

The Chief approached, then went down on one knee beside

Rex. He ran his hands over Rex's body, hesitating at each of the larger abrasions. "Your injuries seem to be healing. How do you feel?"

"I am worried, sir. I cannot sense Charlie through the brain link."

Klein nodded. "If he's in critical condition, he may be under anesthesia. In that case, you won't be able to sense him for another few hours, at least."

"I want to go to him. I am afraid. I want to smell that he is alive."

Klein grimaced, shook his head. "They won't let you inside the ER, and rightly so. You'd have to gown up in a containment suit—and we don't have any of surgical grade that are made for XK9s."

Rex gave a soft whimper. "But I came all this way. I tried to be good."

Klein stroked his head with a sad smile. "You're wonderful, Rex. But even I couldn't be with Charlie right now. We must allow the doctors to work. For Charlie's sake. They don't need any distractions."

Disappointment stabbed like a knife, but Rex stifled his urge to howl. He recognized the sense in Klein's words. His ears and tail drooped. "I have been frightened that Charlie—that Charlie—"

Klein shook his head. "No, Rex. Charlie isn't dead. Surely if any officer under my command had died, I would know about it." He raised an eyebrow, shot a pointed look at Archy.

Archy stiffened. "You would be notified immediately, sir, but nothing of that sort has happened. I'll make a point of supplying updates about both Morgan and Fujimoto to you frequently."

"While you're at it," now there was a distinct edge to Klein's voice. "Find out how the hell Morgan got sent to the Hub in the first place."

"The Watch Officer called," Rex said. "It was our turn on the rotation."

Klein frowned, shook his head. "Your partner's not rated for Hub duty anymore." The regret in his voice echoed in his scent factors.

"Then why did he go?" Joslyn asked. "Why didn't he protest?"

Klein's expression darkened. "Because he's a brave man who received an order."

"I'll find out what happened, sir," Archy promised. "Meanwhile, what shall we do with Rex?"

"I want to see Charlie as soon as I can," Rex said. "I want to smell him all over from head to foot, as thoroughly as possible. I need to know that he will be all right."

Klein bowed his head. "Here's the thing. If they have to do any re-gen—and they probably will, if he's injured his left arm at all—"

"It is broken." Guilt clutched Rex's throat. "I made a mistake, and—and I hurt him badly enough that the paramedics were worried."

Klein drew in a breath. "There's another reason you shouldn't have been sent to the Hub. None of the Pack has been trained for microgravity yet."

"Charlie tried to give me some quick instructions." Rex flinched away from eye contact with Klein, but he'd better come clean and take his punishment. "I let them slip from my thoughts at the wrong moment. It is my fault he was hurt."

Klein's jaws clenched. He smelled angry, but he did not hit Rex.

Rex lowered his head, tucked his tail. He shivered. Waiting for a beating was hard.

Klein's anger-scents shifted to sadness. He stroked Rex's neck gently. "It is not your fault, Rex. You should never have been sent there untrained." He stood. "Unfortunately, however, the injury to his arm complicates Charlie's prognosis. He'll probably go into re-gen soon. That must also be done in a sterile environment, and it can take days, or, God forbid, weeks. Even his human Family will have to stay out."

Rex whimpered softly.

"This should give you ample time to go see Dr. Sandler," Klein said. "That's an order. Even if you're fine, we need her to certify it."

Rex looked down with a sigh. He did not want to go to the vet, but he understood the need for documentation. "I will do as you say."

"Good." Klein shifted his focus. "Now, then. You are?"

Bill took a step closer. Rex glanced up to see him salute yet again, then rattle off his full name and rank. "Dispatch sent me to collect XK9 Rex from the lawn outside the ER. When he didn't want to go to the vet, I thought it best to bring him here."

Klein gave a slow nod. "Are you willing to act as Rex's Personnel Assistance Liaison? I feel certain the PA office hasn't considered him, if he was expelled that way from the ER."

Rex stared. Personnel Assistance was for humans.

Bill, however, didn't seem surprised. He gave the Chief a broad smile. "It would be my honor, sir."

Klein nodded. "Thank you. After Dr. Sandler finishes with him, I'd take it as a personal favor if you'd connect with Morgan's Family. At Orangeboro Med. With Rex. If there are any updates, Rex can hear them from the most direct source." He strode back over to his desk.

Rex watched him, astonished, ears up but mind reeling with disbelief. Klein's order left him breathless. This was more help than he'd ever imagined possible.

Klein didn't seem to notice. He focused on a case pad he'd picked up from his desk. He typed a few lines, sealed it with a thumbprint, bent to add a retinal scan, then made the special kind of swiping motion that transferred a file from one person to another. "If anyone gives you resistance, present this. In fact, you might want to make a point of showing it to Director Dépoli, *personally*, upon your arrival at the hospital."

After a brief HUD-stare, Bill grinned. "Thank you, sir. That should do the trick."

Rex stared at Klein. Despite Bill's doubts in the elevator, the UPO had been right after all. Chief Klein had just given him "clout"!

8

PERSONNEL ASSISTANCE, DOESN'T

Market Garden Neighborhood, Central Plaza, and OPD HQ

Shady's com rang. *Maybe this time.* She panted fast and shallow, her head fluttery with a panic that circled, taunting, in the back of her mind. Rex had said last night that he and Charlie were on call. What if they'd been in the dock breach? What if—what if they were—

It rang again. Please, answer this time.

Breathe, Pam cautioned through the link. She was still in the bathroom, "putting on her face" and struggling to wake up. *Panic makes nothing better. We'd have heard, if any officers were killed.*

The com rang again. Please, please, answer this time! Shady gasped, swallowed, went back to her fast, shallow panting. *Why won't he answer?*

Maybe he's busy. Or asleep. I'd sure be asleep, if I had a choice. Pam hated to get up early, but when the Watch Officer called, you reported for duty.

The com rang yet again. *Click.* "XK9 Rex Dieter-Nell is not available," the automated voice said. "Please try again later." It clicked off.

Shady leaped up with a growl, then lay down again with a whimper. Frustrated fear squeezed her breathless.

Balchu poked his head out of the kitchen. "Same message?"

"Yes." Shady stood, unable to lie there an instant longer. She paced in restless circles around the tiny living room, but a choked, panicky urgency still clutched her throat. "What can have happened? Do you think Rex is all right?"

"Could be a lot of things." Balchu offered a rueful look. "He could be out on a different call. Or maybe he and Charlie will meet us at the Task Force briefing, and he's not answering because they're busy." Balchu ducked back into the kitchen.

Wouldn't that be nice? But fat chance. "You know they never let Packmates work together." Shady had concluded that no incident would ever be major enough for the brass to assign more than one XK9 team—although this blown-up spaceship was a pretty big deal. The Station Bureau of Investigation was even sending in a team to work with the OPD Task Force. If any incident ever could be big enough, this one might qualify.

Balchu re-emerged from the kitchen. He held three strips of bacon in his square, brown hand. Bacon was an expensive luxury. She'd never tasted it, but it smelled wonderful.

In spite of her worry, Shady's ears went up.

Balchu grinned. "Can you catch?" He tossed a strip of bacon in her direction.

Snap! She intercepted it in midair. It tasted even better than it smelled. "Can I what?"

Balchu laughed. "I asked, 'can you catch?'" He lobbed a second strip to the left.

She had to dive for that one. *Snap!* Damn fine bacon. "Need you ask?"

"Uh-huh. Thought I'd check your reflexes." He threw the last one from behind his back.

Snap! "Consider them checked." She wagged her tail. "Thank you." Pam would fuss, if she knew he'd given her bacon. But what a thoughtful treat!

He walked over to her, stroked her head. "I know how it feels to worry. It's part of being an officer's lover." Empathic concern filled his scent factors.

Shady rubbed her head against him. Their new rapprochement still felt weird to her, but it was acceptable for now. "You have worried about Pam?"

He sighed. "Every time she's called to the Five-Ten, for one." He shot a rueful glance toward the bathroom. "Now whenever she's called there, I know you have her back." A hopeful note rose in his scent. "It helps."

Shady wagged her tail, growled softly. "No one messes with Pam until they get through me."

Balchu grinned. "That's what I'm counting on." He ran his bacon-scented hand along her neck. Much better than that chemical-smelling "perfume" Pam wore.

"Yeah, yeah, blah, blah. Let's get going!" Pam emerged from the bathroom fully dressed, makeup on. "Don't want to keep the SBI waiting!"

Balchu handed her a bacon, cheese and egg biscuit, and a travel mug of coffee.

Pam leaned against him briefly with a smile. "I love you."

"That's what all the girls say when I hand them breakfast." He grinned, kissed her, then pushed the outer door open.

Shady waited for the humans. "I did not."

He leaned close, whispered, "This, after I gave you bacon?"

"I did love the bacon. But love is a strong word." Balchu was still on probation.

Pam led the way down the metal stairs into the predawn mist. She bit into her sandwich. Balchu followed.

Shady tried Rex's com again. It went through another fruitless cycle of unanswered ringing. *Click.* "XK9 Rex Dieter-Nell is not available. Please try again later."

Unease slithered in her gut. Shady shook herself. "I have a bad feeling about this."

"I'm checking the news again," Balchu said. "Maybe there's an update."

Shady cocked her head at him. In school her teachers always said news was little more than gossip about celebrities, but maybe only Transmondian news was worthless. Ranan news had provided several interesting facts about the blown-up ship, so far.

"Did they ever figure out whose ship it was?" Pam asked. "That's usually a pretty basic question. Where was it chartered?"

Balchu's scent factors flushed with sudden, hot outrage. He stopped dead on the foggy walkway. "That bitch!" He glared at the middle-distance in a HUD stare.

Shady growled. "Watch your language."

"Who's a bitch?" Pam asked. "What happened?"

Shady growled again. Both humans ignored her.

"Here, see for yourself." Balchu's eyes twitched toward Pam in a way that meant he was forwarding a file from his HUD to hers.

"HELLO." Definitely still on probation. If turning up her vocalizer didn't do it, Shady planned to bite him next.

"Oh. Sorry." He glanced down as if he'd forgotten she was there. Probably had. Maybe she should bite him anyway. But he had given her bacon. She'd hold off for now.

Shady's HUD pinged with a new file-upload: PREMIER BLASTS ORANGEBORO COPS.

She growled again, then glanced through the article. Rana Station's newly-elected Premier Eliana Iskander . . . wait. Iskander was the Premier? Pam and Charlie had talked about her before absentee-voting from Solara City, but they'd agreed the Transmondians had too much influence over her. Why was she the Premier?

Never mind. What did she do? Shady read on.

The article quoted Iskander as having said stupid things about "lax oversight and shoddy law enforcement practices" on the Orangeboro Docks. Shady's hackles rose. Iskander thought the OPD had "let" a ship explode? That made no sense.

"Holy crap," Pam said. "That bi—" she looked at Shady. "That, um, terrible person!"

Shady flattened her ears. "Thank you. Could not agree more." She read on. Iskander had demanded that Chief Klein resign immediately. She also wanted an apology from Orangeboro Mayor Idris and the Borough Council. Shady's lips drew back in a snarl. An apology was due, all right, but not from—she smelled a stranger's approach, looked back. The new person, a tall, slender woman with dark skin and oddly pale eyes, walked like a cop. Her hair, done up in many beaded braids, swung gently in time with her strides.

"Iskander probably ran her company this way, looking for scapegoats." Balchu remained focused on the news article. "Remember the campaign?"

Pam frowned. "I'd like to forget it."

"Me, too," the new person said.

Balchu turned. His scent factors flared with pleased recognition. "Iruka! Are you on the task force, too?"

"What? They put you on it? Standards, people!" She grinned.

"Admit it. You missed me."

"'Missed' might be putting it too strongly, but you have your uses." She turned to Pam. "You must be the woman who's been driving this guy crazy."

Pam gave Balchu a sidelong look, then extended a hand to the newcomer. "Nothing he didn't bring on himself. Hi. I'm Pamela Gomez. This is my partner, XK9 Shady Jacob-Belle."

Shady wagged her tail. "Pleased to meet you."

The woman nodded. Beaded braids swung. "Iruka Jones."

They resumed their walk toward Central Plaza and OPD Headquarters. The light, citrusy-sweet fragrance of orange blossoms infiltrated the misty, early-morning air. It became more pronounced the farther they walked. At least a hundred humans' scent profiles, as well as those of perhaps a dozen ozzirikkians, mingled with the orange smell. Shady put her ears up. Why would a crowd have gathered in Central Plaza this early?

"Have you heard anything about these SBI hotshots they're sending in?" Balchu asked.

Iruka scowled. "Come to save the investigation from the OPD? Not a lot, except these new Special Investigations Teams are supposed to be the *elite of the elite*."

Pam laughed. "Will there be any space in the briefing, with all the swelled heads?"

Iruka grimaced. "Maybe we lowly flunkies will be of some small use on the task force, in spite of our general ineptitude."

At the far end of the block Shady glimpsed a corner of Orangeboro's Central Plaza, with its many orange trees on concentric crescents of low, mosaic-encrusted retaining walls. She'd been right about the crowd. Better try Rex one more time.

"OPD Personnel Assistance," a woman's kind-sounding voice answered. "How may I—wait, this is the dog's line!" Her voice went muffled. "Is this supposed to route here?"

Shady's world froze. Her pulse thundered in her ears, her neck. Personnel Assistance? That was for officers involved in critical incidents! She cranked up her vocalizer. "I am Rex's mate! What has happened? Is he all right?" Shady could scarcely breathe. Every hackle stood on end.

"Um, actually," the Personnel Assistance woman said. "This is not—"

Shady sucked in a strangled breath. "IS REX ALL RIGHT?" Her damned vocalizer didn't express emotions—just louder or softer, so she cranked it to MAX. "Please, PLEASE tell me! I am his mate! Is he okay?"

The woman's voice went muffled again. "It says it's his mate. It's another dog's line. I swear, these new—"

Shady's mind reeled. She whimpered. "Just tell me! Please tell me!"

Still muffled: "I think it might be upset."

"Yes! Yes, I am upset! I am terrified! IS. REX. ALL. RIGHT?"

Silence on the other end of the line, but the connection stayed live.

Shady couldn't breathe, couldn't move. Pain lanced through her chest.

The line clicked on again. "You are XK9 Officer Shady Jacob-Belle?" this new voice sounded brusque, skeptical.

"Yes! I am Rex's mate!" She trembled, dizzy with dread. "Please tell—"

"Well, I'll be damned." The line went silent again, but still not dead.

"NO! NO!" How could they do that? Rage thundered in her chest, her throat, her jaws. "I think I am on 'hold.' How could she put me on 'hold'?"

"This is insane." Pam's arm curved over Shady's back, her hug taking in the panniers, too. Her other hand stroked Shady's neck. Balchu's arm cradled Shady from the other side. He stroked her chest. Supportive, concerned scents surrounded her. Even the new person, Iruka, smelled worried.

The line clicked on. "This line is for the use of officers' families, XK9 Shady," a third, brusque-sounding woman said.

"I am Rex's family! I am his mate!" Fear choked her. "All the Pack is family, but none closer than me!" She whimpered, terrified. "Please just tell me he is all right!"

The woman sighed. "This is highly irregular, but as far as we know he was not seriously injured. He was retrieved from a bunker with his partner. He is now under medical care. That's all I know." The com clicked off.

Shady's legs collapsed. The hard walkway slammed her breathless.

"Oh, my God!" Pam cried. "What did they say?"

Balchu and Iruka peered down at her from either side of Pam, their faces wrinkled with concern, their scent filled with consternation.

Mind reeling, Shady looked up at Pam and the others. "They

do not think he was seriously injured. He and Charlie were in a bunker. They were rescued. They are 'under medical care.'"

Pam's scent factors filled with alarm. "Where are they now? Was Charlie hurt?"

"I do not know. She hung up."

Iruka scowled. "Damn. That's cold! Now I guess you're just supposed to go on in and report for work, like nothing happened."

Legs still shaky, Shady pushed herself to her feet. She yawned a wide stress-yawn. "I—I guess so. There is not much else I can do." She looked up at Pam, mind reeling, her whole body numb.

"Even a human girlfriend would at least get the morning off to go see him." Balchu smelled outraged. "An Amare, Significant, or other Family member would get Emergency Family Leave, for as long as he needed to recover."

Sadness weighed down on her. Shady bowed her head. "But I am not a human."

"Neither is an ozzirikkian." Balchu's brows knotted in an unsettled frown. "Doesn't mean they're not people."

"No, but they *are* recognized as sapient beings." Pam's rueful tone echoed in her scent. "XK9s aren't."

Balchu gave Shady a troubled look. It was the same expression she'd caught on his face several times last night when she was learning about quiddo while watching the match. "I wonder if that's not a mistake."

Pam sighed. "You and every XK9 partner in Orangeboro, but we're not going to solve that question this morning. Time is passing. The SBI won't care what questions of cosmic justice we've been probing, if we're late for that meeting."

"Your lady has a point," Iruka agreed, but no one moved. Everyone looked at Shady.

She yawned to release stress, then flicked her ears. "What else can we do?" She walked beside Pam, but that floaty, surreal feeling stayed with her. It was as if she was there—but not entirely. Ephemeral, like the fog. Her body walked near the others, but outer things escaped focus.

Rex had been in a bunker. Her mind battered against that fact like a moth against a lighted window. He'd been in the dock breach. The awful implications washed over her, dizzied her like a sudden, sickening drop. What if he'd been killed? What would she do? How could she go on? Her mind balked at the question.

"Oh, man. The press is out in force, today," Iruka said.

Shady looked up, then laid her ears back. They now could see much more Orangeboro's broad, bowl-like Central Plaza. People clustered under the orange grove that gave the Borough its name They sat or leaned on the colorful retaining walls. Swarms of little cameras circled around groups, or individuals who spoke toward them earnestly. Shady's teachers, especially Dr. Ordovich, had always warned the Pack to let the humans do the talking if they ever encountered journalists. Just as well. Shady was in no mood to interact with strangers right now.

The Civic Center stood in the middle of the Plaza, a complex of cylindrical buildings, each housing one or more Borough Government functions. The tall shafts of curving tan masonry, marked with bold white patterns between expanses of glass and steel, rose to the maximum-allowed height of twenty-five levels. A big gold, seven-pointed star-in-a-circle marked the double-door entrance to OPD Central Headquarters. Shady turned toward it dully, head and tail down.

Then a familiar but much-missed personal scent broke into her thoughts.

Shady caught her breath. Her heart thudded faster in startled disbelief. Could it be? "Cinnamon?"

"Shady!" Cinnamon bounded down from a nearby retaining wall, then hurtled toward her. Tail up, mouth wide, she smelled like love-home-Pack.

Joyous relief swept through Shady. She quarter-turned to meet her sister-Packmate, part of her still not daring to believe.

"Shady!" Cinnamon's vocalizer-voice called. "Shady-Shady-

Shady-Shady-Shady-Shady!" Cinnamon dashed in circles around her. "You are here! It is really you!"

Happy but dizzy, Shady lolled her tongue. She soon gave up trying to match Cinnamon's frantic circles. "Yes, it is me."

Cinnamon play-bowed, then froze. She rose, hackles stiff, her nose hard at work. She sniffed Shady's face, neck, and back in urgent detail. "Oh, my! Oh, my! What has happened? What is wrong?" She pressed herself close to Shady. The emotionless, robot-like words of the vocalizer clashed weirdly with her urgent, worried scent.

Joy and sadness warred in Shady's heart. She nuzzled her sister-Packmate's fur. The long, aching weeks of loneliness fell away, left her light-headed, but her fear remained. "It is Rex. He was at the Hub. He was caught in the dock breach."

Cinnamon's eyes showed a little white rim of fear. "Is he all right?"

"Is who all right?" A new vocalizer-voice asked. The light wind brought Razor's scent to them.

Something buzzed overhead, but Shady paid it little heed. Instead, she and Cinnamon turned to greet their brother-Packmate.

Razor moved straight in for a thorough sniff-over of both. He was larger than either female, as big as Rex but tan-colored, with a black saddle and face. His alert amber eyes studied Shady with worry. "Tell us."

"Um," Balchu broke in. "Maybe you should talk about this in a less public place."

"Good idea!" Razor's partner Liz batted at a couple of tiny cameras that darted too close. "Shady and Cinnamon, you've attracted some attention with your greeting!"

A small cloud of cameras circled around them. All over the Plaza, people turned in their direction, moved closer.

The XK9s and their companions pushed past the frontmost of the converging journalists, to hurry across the rest of the Plaza. Up a ramp and into the Atrium they scrambled, but an ever-larger swarm of cameras followed them. The alert desk officer buzzed them in through the "OPD PERSONNEL ONLY" doorway, where cameras weren't allowed.

The corridor beyond the door was only somewhat less crowded. Shady led her Packmates to an alcove outside one of the meeting rooms. There she told them all she could, as quickly as possible. Her nightly talks with Rex on the com, his news that he was on call. Her inability to reach him this morning. The struggle to get information from Personnel Assistance.

Razor rubbed along one side of her, despite the clumsy panniers. Cinnamon pressed close against her from the other side. Razor laid his chin protectively across her back, harness and all, the way Rex sometimes had when they were together. Shady soaked in their love, eyes closed. No need for words. They could smell how she felt.

The Humans stood nearby, their scent factors troubled, their voices low. Balchu spoke in grave tones about the way Personnel Assistance had treated Shady. Liz compared an experience with Razor and a desk officer at their Precinct station. Cinnamon's partner Berwyn sputtered with outrage to Pam about sending Rex to the Hub without proper training.

"I hate to throw a wrench into this little parent-conference, or whatever it is, but it's two till six," Iruka said at last. "We have a meeting to attend."

SCENT FACTORS

OPD HQ Briefing Room and Orangeboro Morgue

Restless worry goaded Shady. Frantic fear destroyed her peace. Nowhere to pace in the crowded Task Force briefing room! She stayed where she was but panted fast and shallow.

Pam sat behind and slightly to one side of her, stroked Shady's neck with a smooth calming touch. Pam tried to soothe her by using the brain link, but she herself wasn't calm enough to help much.

Shady's breath came faster, full of dread.

Shady, get a grip, Pam said through the link. *You're gonna hyperventilate, if you don't settle down.*

Razor and Cinnamon flanked her on either side. Each touched her lightly, their presence a balm. Razor's nose pressed her neck. Shady felt Cinnamon nuzzle her shoulder-blade, lean close, and sigh. Support from her Packmates helped her muscles unclench, but her fear would persist till she knew Rex was safe.

Shady half-stood, then made herself sit again. No place to go. No release. Nothing to do but wait and worry. She couldn't stop panting, yet grew more breathless. Her Packmates leaned against her.

Long, slow breaths. Pam punctuated each word with a stroke of her hand.

Anxiety squeezed her. Her panting sped up. Dizziness gripped her.

You can do this, Pam said. *Long. Slow. Breaths.*

Shady clamped her jaws shut, breathed through her nose. Pam was right. But to gain a better frame of mind, she needed something more. Something to focus on, to distract attention. Where could she find it, when everyone was still?

Behind her, Iruka whispered, "That may come back to haunt us."

What was she talking about? Shady clenched her jaws. She struggled to breathe through her nose, swiveled an ear toward Iruka.

A rustle of cloth, a shift in the scents. Balchu had twisted in his chair to look at Iruka. "Too true. Iskander's not famous for ignoring insults."

Iskander? Why were they talking about the Premier? Shady refocused on her breathing. The fluttery feeling in her tummy slowly calmed. She kept her jaws shut, took another long breath.

Because the Premier just got a pretty direct rebuke from our new boss, Pam said.

"Iskander's the one out of line," Iruka told Balchu.

What new boss? Shady tensed. *Did Chief Klein resign after all?*

"Which makes her all the more dangerous," Balchu answered Iruka.

Certainly not! Shady didn't have to look at Pam to know she was frowning. *I meant Senior Special Agent Adeyeme.*

The SBI leader?

A stir beyond the door of their briefing room brought every head up.

Yes. We'll talk later.

Shady's gut tightened. No choice now but to focus. She,

Cinnamon and Razor straightened to parade sit. They'd positioned themselves near the podium at the front of the room, for better sight lines and clearer smells.

Chief Klein stepped through the doorway, tall and dignified in dress blues. His brown face split with a big smile when he saw the XK9s. "Ah! And here are three of our new secret weapons."

Shady felt a lift of pleasure, despite her worry. She'd liked Chief Klein from the moment she'd first met him. She wagged her tail. Razor and Cinnamon wagged theirs, too.

A small, dark-skinned woman in the blue-black tailored jacket and slacks of an SBI agent followed Klein, but she stopped short at the door, her gaze locked on the XK9s. Her scent factors shifted from determined eagerness to deathly terror, but she paused only a moment. Then she drew in a deep breath and stepped forward to stand by the podium. A meter or so from Shady and her Packmates. As if nothing was wrong.

Shady blinked, astonished. Usually people who smelled like that turned and ran. *I am impressed,* she told Pam through the link. *Can you tell that the small woman is terrified of us?*

Pam leaned forward to look at Shady. *Are you serious?* She lifted a dubious eyebrow, though the link must convey Shady's certainty.

Scent factors do not lie. Shady eyed the small woman, fascinated. Her taut jaw muscles and dilated pupils bespoke an urgent desire to flee, but the rest of her manner seemed alert, even confident. Damn. Had to give her points for bravery.

Two other SBI agents stepped forward to stand on either side of the small woman, a tall, muscular blond man, and a lithe woman with her hair pulled back into a long braid. Those two looked much more like the elite "hotshots" Balchu had predicted than did their diminutive colleague. Their scent factors took on the hot, high tones of protectiveness. They eyed the XK9s warily. Whether or not anyone else in the room knew of the small woman's phobia, the man and woman did. Shady liked their loyalty, even if it boded ill for XK9s staying on the Task Force.

Other dark-clad agents filed in behind them. The already-crowded room became packed.

Klein stepped up to the podium. "Officers, it is my very great pleasure to introduce SBI Senior Special Agent Elaine Adeyeme and her Special Investigations Team Delta." He turned to the small woman. "On behalf of the whole department, I'd like to thank you for your public endorsement at the entrance, just now."

Shady shot a glance toward the row behind her. That was what Balchu and Iruka'd been whispering about.

The diminutive Senior Special Agent nodded to Klein. "I'm looking forward to working with this task force you've gathered." Her alto voice held no hint of a tremor, but Shady spotted a definite shakiness when Adeyeme wove the fingers of her hands together in front of herself.

Pride and delight filled Klein's scent factors. He beamed at her. "I have no doubt you will be both pleased and impressed."

Mm-hmm. Shady cocked her head at Adeyeme. She might not be impressed in the way Klein wanted by all members of the Task Force. But why was Adeyeme so frightened? The XK9s had done nothing but wag their tails. Granted, people sometimes did find large dogs terrifying. Shady and her Packmates must seem even bigger, to a woman as small as Adeyeme. Razor was almost tall enough to look her directly in the eyes while standing on all fours. Adeyeme's fear was distressing, but also a pretty good distraction. Shady's anxiety receded to the middle background, displaced by perplexity.

"I'll let you get started." Klein stepped back.

Adeyeme stayed next to the podium. It was scaled for a human of Klein's height, but no one had brought a box or step stool for her to stand on. "I look forward to meeting you individually as we work together." She was easily audible near the front of the room, but Shady had a sense that she'd pitched her voice to be heard all the way to the back. "For now, we've made an initial division of labor, based on your specialties. Lead Special

Agent Shiva Shimon will head one team. It will focus on the physical facts of the ship, and the initial crime scene."

The tall blond man stepped up to the podium. Powerfully built and dressed in an impeccable blue-black uniform, he carried himself like some of the STAT team members Shady had met. Behind her, Berwyn's scent factors suffused with pleasure.

Shady lolled her tongue, distracted enough to be amused. *I think Berwyn likes him.*

Pam herself was emitting more pleasure-scent than Balchu would have approved, had he been able to smell. *Berwyn's right. He's gorgeous.*

LSA Shimon's alert, light-blue eyes swept the room. "We are operating on the high probability that the *Izgubil* was a Whisper operation."

A ripple of reaction ran through the briefing room.

Shady's ears went straight up. The Whisper Syndicate was the most powerful crime organization on-Station, with influence on two other Chayko System space stations and part of the Asteroid Belt as well. Who would dare to blow up one of their ships?

"We have high confidence that the *Izgubil* was a distribution base for illegal substances, a crooked casino, and a brothel that exploited sapients of several species as slaves, many of them underage." Shimon's cold tone matched the disgust in his scent factors. "The Station Defense Force is currently recovering debris from the spacelanes. It's our job to work with a team of SDF wreckage experts, who should be arriving soon, and analyze what we recover." He read a list of OPD officers assigned to work with his team, including Balchu. But no XK9s.

I can see why he wants Balchu, but why not take Cinnamon? Shady asked Pam through their link. Cinnamon was one of the Pack's top explosives experts. She also had specialized training in detecting certain controlled substances.

Pam shrugged. *You never know what the people in charge will think they want.*

"OPD has given us a big section of Central HQ's subterranean levels, for our center of operations," Shimon said. "We'll set up our war room in S-3-9." He and his team—about half of the officers who'd been called to this meeting—departed.

Shady tensed. Would Adeyeme dismiss the XK9s now?

"LSA Shawnee Kramer will lead the other team, working with the rest of you." Adeyeme nodded to the tall woman with the braid down her back. "Your focus will be the people involved in this. Crucial as the physical evidence is, your team's investigations will be key."

LSA Kramer stepped forward. "I'll need to send several groups of you in different directions today." She called three special agents forward, then assigned a group of OPD officers to each. Behind Kramer and her special agents, Adeyeme moved over to speak quietly with Klein, then the two departed together.

At last, only the XK9s and their partners were left. Kramer regarded them for several long seconds, her brow in a dubious pucker seconded by her scent factors. She sighed. "You'll come with me."

Shady, Pam, and the other two XK9 teams followed Kramer down the main corridor of OPD Central HQ. Shady hadn't actually expected SIT Delta to keep them on the Task Force—but SSA Adeyeme had gone to great effort to conceal her terror of them, and she did seem bent on working well with Klein and the OPD.

All right, then. Shady had better find a way to stay focused.

LSA Kramer led Shady, Cinnamon, Razor, and their partners to the Borough Morgue. Shady's heart skipped a beat at the threshold. The place was all shiny metal, frosted glass, and blue-and-white tile infused with the smell of death. Pulse racing, she searched the scents. Rex was not here. Charlie was not here. *Not here.* Oh, thank goodness. Her gut unclenched a little. They probably were not dead. Probably. *If the* Izgubil *dead are here, Charlie and Rex would be too, if they had died. Right?*

Rex and Charlie didn't die. Pam's mental voice came across firm, certain. *The Personnel Assistance woman said they were rescued. She said Rex wasn't seriously injured. Don't worry so much.*

Shady stress-yawned, then clamped her jaws shut. She took a long, slow breath. She'd already come close enough to hyperventilating today.

Pam stroked her head. *That's better. Hang in there.*

Dr. Anika Chinbat, the Borough Medical Examiner, hurried toward them. "Oh, good! We'll need those XK9s!"

Kramer's brows rose. "The Chief said we'd need them, but I'm unclear why."

"Recovery teams just delivered our first clients, those mostly in one piece. When a client comes in, an XK9 team must complete the first evaluation. Only then can my staff take over." Kramer continued to look puzzled. Chinbat smiled. "I was startled at first, too. But scent evidence will be washed away if it's not documented first." She nodded to Shady, Pam, and the others. "Gown up!"

Once they were gowned, masked, and ready, a morgue tech unzipped a body-bag on the autopsy table nearest to Shady. Inside lay a naked, older-middle-aged human male. His sojourn in space had left him swollen, sunburned, and blue-tinged, but it was still possible to tell he'd had fairly light brown skin and straight black hair.

Kramer frowned. "Did someone take his clothing?"

Chinbat consulted her case pad, then shook her head. "He was recovered like this."

Shady resisted the free-floating anxiety that clutched her throat, took a cleansing breath. She could do this. She knew this routine. Nothing to worry about. She started her examination, but the very first scent factors caught in her throat and sent a frisson of revulsion through her. *Oh. Ugh.* Her hackles rose, but she must remain professional. This man was due a complete, thorough examination, even though he'd been a vile abomination in life. She took a cleansing breath. Centered herself. Then she gave him a full sniff-over, to establish a sort of body-map in her mind.

Kramer watched intently. On an adjacent autopsy table, Cinnamon and Berwyn began work on their client, another human. Razor and Liz waited by the third table. Morgue techs uncovered a young ozzirikkian for them.

Shady used her CAP to open a report form on her HUD. For Kramer's benefit, and because it helped her focus, she vocalized the data as she entered her man's morgue number, the case number with the processing date, and the designation M-001 on the end, into the form.

Preliminary biometrics had already matched him to an Orangeboro citizen, one Hideki Bellamy Moran. Shady stopped. *Oh. That's problematic.* The double last name meant he was married. *Did he have children?* She shuddered.

"Is your dog all right?" Kramer asked.

"I think so." Pam probed gently via the link. *What?*

Nasty pedophile. I'm okay. Shady pulled back, took another cleansing breath. She resumed her data-entry with his species, gender, basic morphology, and approximate age. "Before he died, the subject was relatively healthy. I have residual scent factors indicating sexual pleasure, but it is unkind, hurtful pleasure."

"You can smell that?" Kramer sounded skeptical.

Shady paused the report form with a thought, then looked up at her. "Many creatures exude emotion-linked scent factors involuntarily. Ever since we could communicate verbally, XK9s have documented consistent, emotion-linked patterns in scent factors. Many have parallels across all sentient creatures. Anything that can sense things can feel at least rudimentary reactions. Scent often reflects these reactions. Other, more complex emotions or reactions are more particular to sapient beings."

Kramer's expression remained dubious. "So . . . cruelty has a smell?"

"Simple answer: yes. You humans have an expression about being able to 'smell someone's fear,' which suggests to me that on some level you also are sometimes aware of scent factors."

"That's just an expression . . . I thought." Kramer's own scent factors roiled with discomfort. "What—what kind of emotions?"

Shady let her tongue slid out in silent amusement at Kramer's dismay. "All emotions. Right now your scent factors mirror the doubt in your voice. That is an open emotion. But we also can detect emotions that humans wish to hide. Case in point: SSA Adeyeme's terror of dogs."

Kramer's mouth dropped open. Her scent factors shifted from doubt to alarm.

Shady wagged her tail. "Do not be alarmed. XK9s know not to spread stories about their CO. It was only an example."

Kramer bit her lower lip, then blew out a breath. "I'm . . . not alarmed. Well, maybe a little uncomfortable." She grimaced. "Okay, very uncomfortable."

Pam nodded. "It's an uncomfortable thought. We don't like to be an open book."

"So you're sort of a canine lie-detector?" New speculation dawned in Kramer's expression. Her scent factors brightened. "What an advantage in an interrogation!"

Shady wagged her tail. "Yes, it is. Everyone in the Pack is trained for that."

The high, bright interest-notes in Kramer's scent intensified. She gestured toward the man on the autopsy table. "Please continue. "I confess this is more intriguing than I expected."

10

SHADY KILLS AN ANGRY MAN

Civic Center, Orangeboro Morgue and Social Services
Secured Medical Station

S hady returned her focus to her subject on the autopsy table, but she shuddered at his scent. Dr. Imre, the XK9 Breeding Supervisor, had smelled almost like this on the worst day of Shady's young life. Imre'd stood in the Yearling Kennels with a cruel, taunting smile on her lips and threaded through her scent. She'd ordered the dog wranglers to drag Shady's mother away. Shady's last glimpse of Belle had been her struggles against those men and their nets; the last sound, her grief-stricken howl; the last scent, the sludgy fug of her despair.

Shady clenched her jaws, closed her eyes, breathed in a long, smooth breath through her nose.

Pam stroked her neck, projected love through the link. *I never realized how it happened. I'm sorry you had to feel that.*

Kramer's brows pinched with concern. *"Now* what?"

Pam sighed. "His scent factors triggered a bad memory. Give her a minute."

The sharpness in Kramer's scent factors shifted to surprise. "These XK9s. They have personal memories?"

"Even unmodified dogs remember their experiences." Pam made an effort to keep her voice respectful, but her annoyance simmered through the brain link. "XK9s are extraordinarily intelligent, self-aware, sensitive creatures."

"Hear, hear," Liz murmured.

"Plus, they have enhanced memories," Berwyn added. "Cinnie remembers *everything*."

"They were bred for it," Pam said. "The XK9 Project has a rating scale. The entire Orangeboro Pack tested high in the top range for accuracy of recall."

"So, they're like . . . Biological recorders?" Strong high-tones of interest dominated Kramer's scent by now. "We knew they were supposed to be extraordinary forensic tools, but I didn't really know what to expect." She gave Shady a long, thoughtful look. "I'm sorry about the bad memories."

Shady's chest tightened, this time with loving gratitude toward Pam and the others. She nuzzled Pam's side. Met Kramer's eyes, resolute. "We work with unpleasant realities. I chose law enforcement, not only because I had natural capacities for it, but even more, so I could stop bad people from hurting others. That means I encounter bad memories sometimes."

Kramer nodded. "I respect that."

Feeling stronger, Shady returned her attention to her subject. "This man's body had close contact with that of a young female human, just before he died. The scent transfer is most pronounced on the hands, abdomen, and genitals. The scent factor transfer suggests fear and pain in the girl."

Kramer scowled. "As we expected. Damn it."

"Now that Shady's gotten an overview, or in this case over-scent, it's time to take scent samples, for evidence," Pam said.

Shady showed Pam where to collect samples of everything her training suggested might be forensically germane: chemicals, lingering scent factors, residue from things the person had brushed against, and the location of physical contacts with the girl.

Kramer received a call. She stepped away from watching Shady to reply, her scent a blend of annoyance and disappointment.

Shady and Pam continued to collect and document everything they could find, about the cruel piece of . . . about Hideki Bellamy Moran.

While they worked, little messages popped up from time to time on a side channel.

Ding: The war room's first workstation was operational.

Ding: The first six pallets of debris from . . . oh, for pity's sake, too many meaningless coordinates. Six pallets had arrived in the evidence cavern.

Ding: ERTs had rescued six survivors. No information yet on their conditions.

Ding: Investigators were following up on the morgue's DNA matches with two locals who'd been reported missing.

Ding: Wreckage was now documented as far as some long string of other coordinates on the docks . . .

Why do we need to know all that stuff? Shady pushed aside her irritation and struggled to stay focused. She could retrieve all those info-bits later if she needed them.

Mute your side channel, Pam suggested. *That's what I did.*

Ding: New projections estimated at least fifty more victims remained to be recovered.

Shady's gut took a giddy plunge. Okay, *that* one might be helpful if it wasn't so daunting. Fifty more? Yikes. *I didn't really want to know that.* Definitely time to mute the side channel.

She and Pam finished with the sadistic pedophile after about an hour. Seemed longer.

Shady turned away, took a much-needed cleansing breath, and left him to Dr. Chinbat's techs. Let them chop him up into little pieces, for all she cared. She gave herself a vigorous shake, but the containment gown . . . kind of defeated that. She growled, then took a couple more cleansing breaths. It was good to get him out of her nose.

"Gomez." Kramer stepped toward them. She gave Shady a searching stare, then turned to Pam. "We have a problem. The ERTs have rescued two little human girls. Initial exams say they made it out of the *Izgubil* with minor injuries and some lung trauma, which is damn near miraculous. But so far Protective Services isn't making much progress with them. It's obvious they're terrified, but they don't seem to speak any of the languages the staff knows."

Shady lifted her ears. "What languages have they tried?"

Kramer frowned. "I'm not sure. A bunch." She turned back to Pam. "Anyway, after what you and Shady said about scent factors I wondered . . . I'm not sure bringing Shady in there with them is a good idea, but is there any chance she might be able to give us some insight?"

Pam smiled. "I'd like to give her a try." She pulled off her mask and gown, then did the same for Shady. "Shady is the Pack's expert on scent factors and human psychology."

Kramer nodded. "Good. Let's go."

"She has a comprehensive background in the olfactory and behavioral effects of illnesses, substances such as drugs or poisons." Pam pursued Kramer's retreating back. "Also, symptoms of abuse—"

Kramer nodded, but her pace did not slacken. "Sounds good."

Shady let her tongue slide out in a silent dog-laugh. Pam had practiced that speech for a week before the Presentation Ceremony, in case someone asked. It seemed she was determined to give it.

"*Also—*" Pam half-walked, half-jogged to keep up. "she speaks a lot more languages than I do."

Kramer glanced back, then powered on down the hallway. "What languages?"

Shady pulled her tongue back inside her mouth, picked up the pace. "I have academic literacy and fluency in Human Commercial Standard, American Spanglish, Ullach Gaelic,

Mahusayan, Anglofrankish, and Chaykoan Arabic. Also Pan-Ozzirikkian. I have conversational—"

"Never mind." Kramer stopped to flash her badge at a door-control panel. A pair of doors emblazoned AUTHORIZED ENTRY ONLY unlocked with a *snap* and swung open on a long, white corridor. The usual hospital-mix of scents assaulted Shady: harsh disinfectant odors, with underlying notes of sickly-sweet putrefaction, sour urine, and metallic blood-smells that the humans probably thought they had cleaned away. Above it all, embedded in every surface, hung the pervasive, edgy scent of anxiety.

Shady followed close by Pam's warmth and smell, so she could keep up, and scanned reports about their new subjects. In addition to the two little girls, who'd been sheltered from shrapnel inside a stout-walled box, the available briefings told Shady that there also were four surviving human adults, but they had serious injuries from explosive decompression and shrapnel. One was still in surgery; three more were unconscious in the ICU. The six persons still alive were the only known witnesses from inside the ship.

Shady's heart rate sped up. The little girls were the only ones who could talk right now, *if* investigators could find a way to communicate. Oh, good. No pressure at all.

Kramer stopped near the end of the corridor. She badged this door, too. It clicked, then swung ajar. She frowned into the low light of the room beyond the door. "Hello?"

A wave of terrified scent factors emanated from the doorway. "Go . . . go away," a frightened, breathless voice replied in Oroplanian Urdu. "Leave us alone."

Shady's heart lifted. Oroplanian Urdu was far from her strongest language, but she knew what to say now. She pushed past LSA Kramer and poked her nose through the crack in the doorway. "We want to help you," she told the two frightened little girls inside the room. "Please let us come in."

Beside her Kramer stiffened. "What did she say?"

Pam's amused pride in her flowed through the link. *Show-off.*

Shady wagged her tail, looked up at Kramer. "They speak Oroplanian Urdu."

"Who are you?" asked the little girl.

Kramer stepped back from the door, made a quick call, and spoke in a staccato near-whisper to order an Oroplanian Urdu translator and a child-specialist Listener, stat.

Shady pushed her nose farther in. "My name is Shady. I am a big dog who talks."

A rustle of what sounded like sheets and blankets came from the other side of the room. Curiosity warred with fear in the child's scent factors. "Dogs don't talk."

"Maybe not where you come from, but I do. I can prove it. May I come in?"

Fear-scent boiled up, but curiosity won again. "Okay."

Shady turned to Pam and Kramer. "Please stay here."

"Did your dog just tell us to 'stay'?" Kramer muttered to Pam.

Shady pushed inside and opened her impressions to Pam through their brain link. The second girl smelled younger and more fearful. The girls had pulled covers and pillows from both of the room's beds, dragged them to the far corner of the room, and built themselves a nest behind a chair. They were hidden, except for top of one small, dark-haired head. Pam quietly relayed these impressions to Kramer.

Shady had learned an informal smattering of conversational Oroplanian Urdu from a lonely gardener who'd worked at one of her schools. It was her weakest language. She hoped her vocabulary would suffice. She approached the blanket-nest until she smelled the girls' fear increase. Then she lay down on her belly. "I am a big dog, but not mean. I am friendly." She waited. Neither girl replied. "I told you my name. Please, tell me yours?"

Silence. The fear in their scent factors billowed up. Why was that a scary question?

Beyond the door, Kramer asked Pam, "Do you have any idea what she's saying?"

"Sort of," Pam said. "I'd never even *heard* of Oroplanian Urdu till I met Shady, but I have a sense that she just asked for their names. That seems to scare them."

"How about this?" Shady asked the children. "You can be Brave Girl, and your friend is Thinking Girl. Is that all right?" Must be—their fear receded a little.

"Y-you said you're a big dog," Brave Girl said. "You are a *very* big dog."

"I am a protector. I keep bad people away, so it is good for me to be big."

"You said you are not mean. How can you protect?"

Shady wagged her tail. "Good point. I am only mean to bad people."

There was a short silence. From her scent factors, Brave Girl's internal battle this time raged between fear and dawning hope. "All bad people? Even . . . the angry men?"

Who were "the angry men"? Shady pictured the naked morgue client, and the smell of a different girl. She stifled a growl. "Should I protect you from the angry men? I will, if you want me to."

The girls relaxed a little. They nodded vigorously.

"Please tell me more about them, so I can protect you better."

"They have mean hands," Brave Girl said. "Hit us. Yell at us. Do no-no things. Hurt us."

"Put us in the bad-girl box," Thinking Girl whispered.

Shady snarled silently. She hoped the "angry men" had died as painfully as possible when the ship broke up, although an argument could be made that the box might have saved the girls' lives. "They had better stay away from you, or I will make them very sorry." She smelled the girls' dubiousness. "If I saw one of the angry men, I would growl at him."

Itchy skepticism lingered in Brave Girl's scent factors. "How would growling help?"

"I have a scary growl."

The girls' scent factors brightened with interest.

Shady hesitated. "Would you . . . like to hear me growl?"

The bright, curious tones strengthened. "Yes, please."

Misgivings crowded Shady's mind. *I am about to demonstrate a fierce growl,* she told Pam. *Please DO NOT come inside.*

Consternation came through the link. *You're what?*

Pam would catch on soon enough. Shady stood. "Before I growl, may I come closer?"

Two tiny faces, each rigged with a cannula, peered up from the tangle of bedcovers.

"If I am to protect you, I want to stand closer, to guard you. May I show you?"

Two little heads nodded assent. Piquant scent factors of interest grew stronger. Shady positioned herself so that, between her body and the chair, all access to the girls was blocked. "Does this look good to you?"

Solemn little faces nodded. "Now growl, please," Brave Girl said.

Shady heard Pam outside. "She says she's going to growl, but we shouldn't worry."

"Growl?" Kramer sounded alarmed. "No! The girls are frightened enough!"

Shady looked at Brave Girl and Thinking Girl. A surge of protective affection rose within her. Brave Girl was taller, and likely a bit older than her companion, with straight, silky black hair and dark brown eyes. Thinking Girl was tinier, with light brown hair and blue eyes. They gazed up at Shady from their nest of bedclothes with bright-eyed interest. The curiosity in their scent factors pushed back the fear.

"Growl *real* scary," Brave Girl urged.

Shady faced the doorway, bared her teeth, and uttered a deep, menacing growl.

"No." From beyond the door, Kramer's voice was tense. "I said *don't*."

"They asked her to," Pam said.

"I *really* don't like this." Kramer sounded deeply worried. "I could be up on charges for endangering them."

I appear to be auditioning for a guard-dog job, Shady told Pam through the link. She growled much louder the second time.

Far from acting frightened, both girls smiled. "That was a good growl," Brave Girl said. "Can you go louder?"

"Please give her time," Pam said. "She's proving she can be a guard dog."

"A guard dog?" Kramer sounded dubious.

"Louder! Bark!" Brave Girl cried.

Shady glanced toward the doorway.

"Bark! Bark!" Brave Girl urged. "Growl!"

Hell with it. Shady focused on the girls. They deserved a good effort. She barked till her own ears rang, then snarled as grotesquely as she could.

The girls shrieked with glee.

"No, no, no," Kramer said. "I can't let her—"

"Please," Pam said. "Shady knows what she's doing. Do you hear the girls?"

"Are they laughing or crying?" Kramer asked. "I can't tell!"

"They're laughing," Pam said. "It's okay."

Shady pantomimed grabbing the imaginary "angry man" in her jaws, then took him down far more forcefully than she ever hoped she'd have to with a real person. She even threw in a kill-shake, with another ferocious snarl. It was oddly pleasant, especially when she envisioned Dr. Imre in place of the angry man. "Take that, you angry man!"

Brave Girl clapped her hands. "Oh, yes! Yes!" She and Thinking Girl both laughed out loud. Their fear had mostly flown, replaced by fierce triumph.

"That—that *does* sound more like laughing." Kramer still seemed uncertain.

Shady pranced back to the girls' nest, tail high. "I killed him for you. Now you are safe." Small hands reached out, their touch as sweet as puppy-nuzzles.

"It's okay," Pam said. "They feel safer, now."

Kramer blew out a shaky breath. "I'm not sure why, but you seem to be right."

Shady used her nose to nudge the girls nearer to her, licked their faces, savored their scents. "There, now. It is all right. I am right here."

Brave Girl and Thinking Girl knotted their fists in Shady's fur. They nestled against her tummy like puppies. Thinking Girl cried softly, but it was a good, relieved kind of crying. After a while they stopped trembling. Soon after that, both of them fell asleep.

Shady rested her chin briefly across them, protective. Then she raised her head to face the door. She was on guard duty now. Scary bad guys better stay far away.

11

UNDER RESTRAINTS

5th Precinct, The Sandler Clinic

"I do not wish to wait for test results." Rex met Dr. Sandler's level, brown eyes. His fear of being insubordinate had steadily diminished as the day ground on, yet no one appeared to even *consider* beating him or putting him into a Dark Crate. "This has taken too long already, and I am tired. I wish to go to Charlie."

Dr. Sandler had ordered scans, tests, blood draws, then more tests. Rex had been poked, palpated, and probed. He'd lost track of how long he'd been here. Longer than necessary, for sure. Hours and hours and hours. He checked the time via his CAP, but his sluggish brain failed to make the calculation. He was thirsty, hungry, exhausted, and out of patience.

"This is not up for debate." Dr. Sandler's mouth tightened. Steely resolve rose in her scent, stronger than the diminishing notes of compassion. She pointed to the large dog-bed in the center of the small room where they stood with Bill. "Go over there. Lie down. *Stay* there."

Rex glanced at Bill, but the UPO shook his head. "Can't help you this time, pal."

Rex's mind spun, but he couldn't think of any way to leverage this situation to influence a better outcome. Chief Klein had sent him here; he had no influence that could bypass Dr. Sandler's command. His head, ears, and tail drooped.

Sandler'd lowered the bed to floor-level, so he needn't stress his ribs leaping up. It did look inviting, after the exhausting rounds of tests. His service harness and panniers hung from hooks on the back wall: there wouldn't be any lumps or straps to trouble him.

But he wasn't ready to lie down.

His throat rasped like sandpaper. His cavernously empty belly ached. His heart surged with rebellion. He turned back to Dr. Sandler, tried to widen his eyes while he kept his head and ears low, so he would look as piteous as possible. "But I am so thirsty. Also really, really hungry."

One side of her mouth twitched, but she shook her head. "Not buying it. We'll hook up an IV to replenish your fluids and nutrients, but I want your stomach empty till I go through your results. I may determine you need surgery or re-gen. Now, move."

Fear surged through him. *An IV? Surgery? Re-gen?* No. This was all a mistake. He was stronger than any ordinary dog. He just had scrapes and bruises! XK9s were tough!

Dr. Sandler left the room. Two tall, burly vet techs arrived a few seconds later. One of them reached up to lower equipment from the ceiling above the bed. The other pulled packages of tubes and needles from a cabinet drawer.

Rex stared at them, stiff with horror.

"C'mon, Dog. *Bed!*" the tech with the earrings said.

Rex laid back his ears, stayed where he stood.

"Rex?" Bill reached out a hand to him.

"Move it, Big Boy." The tech with the tattoos pointed at the bed. A loop of tubing dangled from their fingers. "Gotta get you prepped."

"No." Rex bristled at them. He gave a low, warning growl.

"C'mon, Rex," Bill said. "Don't make a scene."

The two techs gave Rex the same kind of look the dog wranglers back in Solara City used to, just before they forced him to do something. "We can't trank you—it'll interfere with anesthesia," the one with the earrings said. "Don't make us get the prod and the muzzle. I really hate that prod."

Revulsion surged through Rex. The tech couldn't possibly hate the prod as much as Rex did. He snarled, then thought better of it: he hated muzzles, too. He looked away, defeated. Heaved a heavy sigh. Then he stepped onto the bed. His toes sank into its soft surface.

"That's right," Bill said. "Thank you."

"Hurry up, now. Lie down," the tech with the tattoos said. "On your side."

Rex growled again, but he kept the growl under his breath. He lowered himself onto the bed. Hesitated, then stretched onto his side. The bed rose with a soft whir of machinery. The tech with the earrings lifted a side-rail, locked it into place at Rex's back.

The tech with the tattoos trundled closer on a stool. They pulled Rex's forelegs out straighter, then rolled a thumb over several areas where the fur was thin and Rex's pulse thumped near the surface. They whipped a small razor out of their lab coat pocket to shave a bare patch. "Big stick coming. Don't make me wish I'd put on that muzzle."

Despairing, Rex laid his head down. He closed his eyes, tried not to whimper when the needle bit. Within a minute they'd gotten him rigged up, complete with a blinking, beeping monitor. A large, fat bag of clear liquid hung overhead, hooked up to drip into his IV. He growled when the techs strapped him down, but he didn't struggle. Way too late for that.

They retreated to the doorway of the little room. "Behave yourself," the tech with the tattoos said.

"We'll be just outside," the tech with the earrings said. "Try to rest."

They closed the door. Good riddance.

Bill dragged up a chair from one corner of the room. He leaned an elbow on Rex's bed. "Well. *That* didn't go the way I thought it would."

Rex slid his tongue out in a frustrated pant. "What can she think is wrong with me? I am fine. XK9s are tough."

"I guess we'll have to be patient a little longer." Bill frowned. "Wonder if this'd be a good time to call the Personnel Assistance office. Ask them what I'm supposed to do now. I've never been anybody's PA Liaison before." He pulled a case pad from an inner pocket, ran his finger across it a couple of times. "I've got the link here somewhere."

"Are you the person who will call Charlie's Family?" Rex raised his head to look at him. "Will you also please tell Shady what has been happening to me?"

Bill nodded. "I imagine Charlie's Family already knows about his injuries, but considering your treatment in the ER, they may not know much about what happened to you." He quirked an eyebrow. "Who else did you say?"

"Shady. My mate. I told her last night that Charlie and I were on call. It is likely she is worried, if she has heard about the dock breach."

"Your mate, eh?" Bill grinned at him. "Way to go, lover-boy. Well, she'd have to be living under a rock not to know about the dock breach, so we'd better call her, too. First things first, though."

His face shifted into a HUD stare. He listened for about half a second, then smiled. "Yes, this is Corporal William Goldstein Sloane. The Chief has assigned me to . . . yes, that's right."

He listened for a while. His smile shifted to a frown. "No, I don't think that's a good idea. No, don't you dare deactivate his —" Frustration rose in his scent factors. "No. Listen, do you have any idea how valuable this—"

Rex snapped his ears flat. "What is wrong?"

Bill folded his arms. Looked up at the ceiling. Listened for a few more seconds.

"No!" He sat forward. "No. The Chief specifically asked me to—" He grimaced. "No. Keep the damned file active. I need—"

Bill stood. His scent flared with anger. "Listen, lady, I have a job to do, and I mean to do it. File the damn formwork, and *don't* make me come over there!" He paused. Scowled harder. "Okay, just do whatever the hell, then. From now on I'll contact your *superiors* through the *Chief's office!*" His eyes refocused on Rex, but it took a while for the anger in his scent factors to cool.

Rex cocked his head, ears up. "What happened?"

Bill ran a hand through his hair. "Let's just say she's about as enlightened as the ER staff was. Can *you* give me com codes for the Family and Shady?"

"Certainly." His brain might be muzzy, but he could make that simple information transfer. He lay his head back down. It hurt less that way.

"Thank you." Bill blew out a breath, looked toward the door. "I'd like to know if your vet found anything, before I call people."

Dread weighed down on Rex. What would Dr. Sandler find? For all his protestations that he felt fine, he couldn't deny to himself that he actually felt pretty crappy. The ribs on his right side ached with a deep, ominous pain that bit harder when he breathed in. Loglike, his legs lay heavy, inert. His head throbbed. Sluggish thoughts dragged, as if through thick mud. Hunger still gnawed, but his throat maybe wasn't so parched. He looked up, startled to see that the formerly-fat IV bag now hung flaccid.

He closed his eyes. Even though hedged in by dread, he slipped with scary ease into the floaty semi-awareness of pre-sleep.

The door opened. Dr. Sandler stepped inside.

Apprehension chilled him; all sleepiness fled.

"Well, Doc, is he gonna live?" Bill asked.

Dr. Sandler frowned. "I have good news and bad news. The good news is that you don't need surgery. The bad news is that you've broken four ribs on your right side—cracked 'em but good, though none are misaligned." She grimaced. "What did you hit? Looks as if you were smacked really hard with a two-by-four. There's a straight line of fractures across all four affected ribs."

His memories resurfaced more sluggishly than usual. Rex stress-yawned. "I fell against a gantry rail, but I did keep Charlie from smashing into it. He had been hurt enough already." Faster now, the memories crowded his mind.

"Yeah, that'd do it," Dr. Sandler said. "You were moving at a fair velocity, right?"

His head hurt. He couldn't estimate it. "I do not know how fast we were going. Pretty fast. Microgravity is weird."

She nodded, but kept her frown. "If you were an ordinary dog and got hit that hard, you'd be dead now. Come to think of it, you probably saved Charlie's life, when you protected him from hitting that rail."

Rex's heart leaped. His ears went up. "I did?" Amid all his mistakes, he'd actually done something right. "Then it is good that XK9s are tough."

"It is, but you pay a price." She gave him a wry look. "For you, that price today includes a couple hours of re-gen."

Civic Center, Social Services Secured Suite 7

Shady crouched on a worn, well-scrubbed rug in a bland, well-scrubbed little room. Brave Girl knelt close by her left side, her fingers twined deeply into Shady's fur, her scent factors drenched in terror and the anguish of remembered pain.

"Can you think anything else?" Lena, an older, medium-height Listener in a professional robe, kept her voice calm, light, neutral. She'd asked all of her questions in that same, unhurried tone, speaking Human Commercial Standard. She sat in a chair at the end of the rug.

Tasbeeh, a short woman with long, straight black hair, repeated the question in Oroplanian Urdu. She sat on a sofa at right angles to Lena's chair, and spoke in a similar, carefully neutral tone, but Shady thought her round brown face and dark eyes looked friendlier. Some of her pronunciations varied from what Shady had been taught, but the girls seemed to understand her.

Brave Girl, who looked enough like Tasbeeh to be a daughter or little sister, kept her gaze locked on the translator's face, her fingers clenched tight in Shady's fur. In a hesitant, breathless voice, she offered a rambling account that gave just enough details to suggest yet another ghastly thing that one of the Angry Men had done to her.

On Shady's right, Thinking Girl curled in a tight ball, her face buried in Shady's fur. She sucked her thumb and held on tight. She did not speak. Earlier efforts to follow standard protocol and "separate the witnesses" . . . Shady's hackles prickled with discomfort at that memory. The humans eventually had managed to cajole the two children into coming a few meters down the hall together, both clutching Shady's fur, to this interview room.

Discretely-placed pickups throughout the room allowed the people in the observation center, including Pam, Kramer, and possibly others, to record the interview while they observed it.

"Is there anything else you'd like to tell me?" Lena was some kind of expert on forensic child-interviews. She'd asked only open-ended questions; she also knew how to use silences to encourage a few more details. For someone who couldn't smell scent factors or speak the girls' language, she'd done pretty well. Shady had provided a long series of texts containing scent factor information, which she sent to her interview log, as well as to Pam, Kramer, and Tasbeeh the translator, but Lena had asked not to be distracted.

Tasbeeh translated Lena's question.

Brave Girl buried her face against Shady's back. She shook her head. Her scent factors confirmed that she'd reached the end of her strength. Shady didn't blame her for not wanting to tell Lena anything else.

Shady's hackles prickled. She hadn't been able to sort out exactly how many Angry Men there had been, possibly because Brave Girl seemed to have little grasp of numbers or know how to count beyond two. But it was abundantly clear that there'd been way too many of them. The child also hadn't made any distinction between *Izgubil* staff and clients. Since nearly all were now dead, it made little practical difference. The interview team's objective had been to learn anything they could glean from the girls' accounts about life on the ship. Brave Girl's life aboard the *Izgubil* clearly had been a living hell, but Shady wasn't sure any of her information could help the investigation. It was early afternoon. They'd been at this since mid-morning, yet what had they gained?

Lena tried a few more questions. She made another effort to get Thinking Girl to talk, but eventually gave up. She smelled weary, wrung-out. "This concludes today's interview with the two child-survivors of the *Izgubil*," she said, then added time, date, participants, and other identification information, including the case number. Not much to Shady's surprise, she left out the fact that an XK9 had been present. Should Shady say something?

The com clicked. Pam's voice came through the general channel, firm and forceful. "The record must identify XK9 Shady Jacob-Belle as a participant, to correlate with the scent-factor log."

"Oh." Lena frowned. "Is that important?"

Through the brain link, Shady caught Pam's flare of fury, the effort needed to throttle it into submission, and the care with which she chose her words. "It's evidence gathered during a forensic interview. Not recording it is a discrepancy."

"Crap." Lena kept that part under her breath, but Shady heard. "All right, if you insist." Her tone implied it was a needless annoyance. "I'll amend it when I get back to my office."

"Thank you." Pam took fewer pains to hide her own annoyance this time. "XK9s are not going away. Better get used to them." Even beyond the implied slight to Pam and Shady, a discrepancy in the evidentiary record tended to make Pam prickly, no matter what. Shady had gathered enough hints during their partnership to infer a traumatizing rookie experience with a wrathful prosecutor. Better not ask.

She turned to Tasbeeh. "What happens to the girls now?" She used the girls' language. They needed to know this answer.

The translator's wise, dark brown eyes studied her. "We must make sure they are safe," she replied in the same language. "But they tell me you are needed elsewhere."

"No, Shady stay." Brave Girl clung to her more tightly.

Shady glanced at the child. "That might become a problem."

Tasbeeh nodded. "At some point they'll have to let go of you. They need thorough physical exams, a better supply of oxygen, probably other medical treatment. They also must eat."

"Am hungry," Brave Girl said.

"Hungry," Thinking Girl echoed.

Tasbeeh beamed at her. "I knew you could talk. You just take your own time, don't you?"

Thinking Girl shrank back against Shady's side, but she smiled at Tasbeeh.

"Her scent says she likes you," Shady told Tasbeeh.

"Beeh is pretty." Brave Girl peered around Shady's shoulder at the translator. "Has nice eyes."

Shady wagged her tail. "Beeh is a nice person. I can smell good from bad people. Beeh is good."

"I do try." Tasbeeh offered Brave Girl a warm smile. "Could you hold my hand?" She reached out.

Lena had moved away to talk by the door with Kramer;

Shady smelled Pam in the hallway behind the LSA. The three humans at the doorway went silent when Tasbeeh reached out.

Brave Girl looked from Tasbeeh's hand to her face, then to Shady.

"She will not hurt you," Shady said.

Tasbeeh said nothing, just continued to hold out her hand.

Shady's com beeped. She flicked her ears, checked the incoming ID. Why would a UPO named Sloane be calling her?

"Do I know you?" she texted. "I'm working now."

Brave Girl kept her death-grip on a big tuft of Shady's fur with her right hand, but very slowly let go with her left. She reached out a small, sweaty, grubby hand covered with black and gray dog hairs. Placed it in Tasbeeh's hand.

"I am Rex's . . . Personnel Assistance Liaison," UPO Sloane texted back. The words appeared a few at a time. Sloane must be typing them into his case pad by hand.

Astonishment swept through Shady, followed by an uprush of relief. Her legs went rubbery. She didn't even feel it when Brave Girl let go with her right hand and took a step toward Tasbeeh. Shady forwarded Sloane's texts to Pam. "Tell me," Shady texted back to Sloane. All her anxieties rushed to the front of her focus.

"Rex is alive," Sloane typed. "Please . . . "

Shady's mind reeled with questions. Somewhere outside of her, Brave Girl snuggled against Tasbeeh, then turned to Thinking Girl. "Tasbeeh will feed us."

". . . do not worry," Sloane's message continued.

"What would you like to eat?" Tasbeeh asked Thinking Girl.

"Was injured . . . dock breach . . ."

"Have sweet potato chaat?" Thinking Girl asked. She continued to cling to Shady, but her scent said this interested her.

". . . now getting . . ." Sloane's excruciatingly slow text continued.

Tasbeeh smiled. "My nani makes the best sweet potato chaat

ever. Will you come with me? We can get you some. I'll ask her to bring it here."

". . . re-gen treatment," Sloane texted.

"Shady come?" Thinking Girl asked.

Kramer watched from the doorway. "What is she saying?"

"He will be okay . . . very soon," Sloane concluded.

Shady let out a long, shaky breath, half relieved, half exhausted. Through the link she sensed Pam's pleasure at Sloane's news.

Tasbeeh turned to Kramer. "The girls are hungry. I've offered a kind of comfort food they remember from back home, but they don't want Shady to leave."

Kramer frowned. "More bodies are being recovered every hour. There's already a backlog of several dozen mostly intact bodies, plus scores of dismembered body parts already collected. They're keeping them in an SDF cold-holding facility at the Hub —but that evidence gives us zero help till it's processed. We need Shady back in the morgue, ASAP."

Tasbeeh returned her focus to Thinking Girl. "I think Shady might have to go away."

"No! No!" Thinking Girl wailed. "Shady stay!" She redoubled her grip on Shady's fur.

Heart pounding, conflicted, Shady texted Sloane: "I can't come now. Working."

"That's OK," Sloane replied. "Treatment not done . . . for an hour or more."

Thinking Girl clung hard to Shady. She cried as if her heart would break. Brave Girl began to cry too. The smell of their distress stirred a howl in Shady's heart, but she kept it quiet.

Kramer looked harried. "That didn't go over too well. How much longer, d'you think?" She had to shout to be heard.

"Let's distract them with food," Tasbeeh shouted back. "If I call my nani—my grandmother—now, she can probably get some over here in half an hour. We're lucky. She just made a big batch."

Kramer sighed. "Whatever you have to do."

"Shh, quiet, never mind," Tasbeeh soothed the children. "It's all right. Shady can stay. It's all right. She said Shady can stay. Now let me call my nani. Very soon, you can eat."

Brave Girl stopped crying but sniffled dolefully. It took a little more time and cajoling to calm Thinking Girl.

"Ma'am," Pam said once she could be heard, "when Shady does get free, we've had confirmation that her mate was in the dock breach. She's been very worried, but she just got a message from his Personnel Assistance Liaison that he's in treatment for his injuries now. Could we take just a few minutes after we finish here, to go see him?"

Kramer massaged her temples with a grimace. "Your dog's mate has a Personnel Assistance Liaison?"

"She's been worried and distracted all day, but she's tried to do her best," Pam said. "Couldn't she go see him for a few minutes?"

Kramer stared at Pam. "There are at least three dozen bodies piled up and waiting for autopsy!"

"LSA Kramer," Lena said, "this might be a good time to remind you that OPD contracts say you have to give Pam a stress break if she requests one." She gave the LSA a sidelong glance. "Might take one yourself, while you're at it. We've all just been through a harrowing interview."

"She's right," Pam said. "It was really hard to listen to that interview. I do need a break. I'd like to take my dog for a walk in the fresh air. Clear my mind, before I leap back into processing a lot of dead bodies."

Kramer closed her eyes, blew out a breath. From her scent, she badly needed that stress break, but didn't plan to take it. "If you can detach the girls from Shady, then go. Take your break. But could you hold it to an hour? Your colleagues in the morgue are probably stressing out like crazy, too."

12

REX FINDS HIS VOICE

Orangeboro Medical Center

Almost blind from his growing fatigue, Rex followed Bill down yet another hospital hallway. Frustration smothered him; it had been that kind of afternoon.

First, he'd been roused from the suspended-in-glue fog of a regeneration treatment, achey in every fiber and shaved bare over the ribs he'd broken. Then he smelled clear evidence that Shady and Pam had recently been here. Right here. In this clinic!

"Shady!" He tried to scramble up, but restraints held him down. "Shady! Shady!"

"I am so sorry!" Bill stroked him, scent and face unhappy. "They were on a time limit. They had to leave, but Shady said to give you her love."

He stared at Bill. "You spoke with her?"

His friend nodded. "She's working with the task force assigned to the SBI team. She was deeply disappointed she couldn't stay, but they needed her back in the morgue."

"What? How could they make her—she was here! Why not let her stay?" Rex's breath wouldn't come. He bristled and twitched and growled. Frantic, he struggled against the restraints.

"Hold on, there, hold on," Bill soothed. "Give us a minute. We'll undo those bindings."

Rex froze. "Please. Thank you."

Dr. Sandler's techs moved in from either side. Soon he was free. They lowered the bed.

Rex sprang up. He paced around the room, sick with despair. Two whole months of nothing but com-calls, and now she wasn't allowed to wait till he woke? No. *No!* Rex threw back his head and howled.

Nobody tried to hush him. Bill, Dr. Sandler, and even the two techs simply watched him with sad faces and sympathetic scent factors. It took a while to cry himself out, but at last he halted, head down, exhausted.

"You should rest," Dr. Sandler said. "You've had a terrible day."

Rex lifted his head, stress-yawned, then lowered his fore-quarters in a long, melancholy body-stretch. His ribs were still tender, but the deeper pain was gone. At least there was that. "Let us go to Orangeboro Med. Even if I cannot see Charlie, I wish to see his Family."

Worry surged in Bill's scent. "Are you sure you don't want to rest, first?"

"I want to finish this."

So they'd come full-circle, back to Orangeboro Medical Center. As Rex had expected after his experiences in the ER, he and Bill moved from one argument to the next, with humans who equated "dog" with "hairy and unhygienic," but weren't eager to tell them where Director Dépoli's office was. Each time, Bill showed the message from Chief Klein. Each time, the person in charge frowned at it, then sent Bill and Rex to a higher rung on the hospital's hierarchy. At last they'd made it to Director Dépoli's office, albeit the hard way.

The Director was a tall, thin woman with short, white hair.

She read quickly, then looked up from Klein's letter with cold gray eyes. She regarded Rex for a long, icy moment, her mouth a narrow, tight line. "Well, I suppose that thing isn't much hairier than an Ozzirikkian." She grimaced, then bent to endorse the order with her signature, thumbprint-sealed.

Rex and Bill went back downstairs. The Post-Op Intensive Care Unit took up part of the level above Emergency. Their waiting room windows overlooked the lawn where Rex had first met Bill. Then, however, it had been dark. Now warm afternoon light made the grass appear to glow.

They stepped inside, turned to the brushed-aluminum reception desk.

"Get that animal out of here." A tall, hard-faced nurse confronted them with folded arms and offended scent factors.

Rex's hackles bristled. Why must they always start with that same line?

Bill pulled out his case pad, with the Chief's order and Dépoli's endorsement. "I am here as the Personnel Assistance Liaison for XK9 Officer Rex Dieter-Nell. His partner recently came out of surgery. Rex needs updates."

"We never allow animals in here." She didn't even look at the case pad he extended.

Bill scowled at her. "Apparently 'never' ends now. Here's the authorization."

The nurse glared at their document, then turned her glare on Rex.

Bill's mouth hardened. "Also, I hope 'never' doesn't extend to service animals."

Rex's ears went up. Denying access to a service animal was a violation of several Borough and Stationwide statutes. Could they arrest her?

She grimaced. "That enormous beast is no service animal!"

Anger flamed up in Rex. That judgment was not hers to make.

Bill kept his voice level. "This enormous being has authorization to be here. From your own hospital director."

Rex reared, placed both forepaws on the metal counter, and jabbed his nose at her. "Is my partner's Family here?"

"Get down! Be quiet!" Her voice scolded, but her scent factors shifted from hot resistance to startled fear.

"Woah, Big Guy. Careful." Bill placed his hand on Rex's shoulder.

Rex laid his ears back. All his life it had been drummed into him that dogs must obey humans—but obedience had so far gained him nothing but an exhausting run-around. Fearful, weary, frustration overwhelmed him. He had a right to be here, damn it. If ever there was a time to be insubordinate, this was it. "I have had enough. Is Corona Family here?"

"Rex?" Bill abruptly smelled worried.

The nurse scowled. "Back off, Dog!"

Rex barked as loudly as he could, three times in a row. "Is Corona Family here?"

"Hush that barking! Get off my—"

"When I get answers." He gave her three more loud barks.

Rex had barely finished his last bark when a UPO burst through the doorway from the ICU's forbidden zone. "Is that Rex?"

Rex's hope leaped up. He did not know this officer. Could he be Charlie's Personnel Assistance Liaison?

"Rex? Is that you?" Charlie's sister Caro followed close behind the UPO.

"Caro!" Rex darted to her, then wagged, squeaked, and wriggled his delight. Her familiar scent warmed and comforted him.

Relief surged through her scent factors. "Rex! Oh, thank God!" She braced herself against his vigorous snuggle and kissed him several times on the top of his head. Caro was five years older than Charlie, but she had similar light brown skin, brown eyes, and wavy black hair. Her hair was much longer, however, and she was a good bit shorter than her "little" brother.

The UPO turned on the nurse. "You knew we were waiting for him!"

"Big hairy dogs have no place here!" She retreated to the inner part of the office. The UPO darted after her. He passed Charlie's parents Mimi and Ted coming out.

Rex's heart filled with new joy to see them.

Mimi's expression relaxed when she saw Rex, but her blue eyes looked puffy. Gray-streaked brown hair frizzed around her pale, worn face. "Oh, thank goodness!"

Ted was taller and a bit older than his wife, with darker skin, worried brown eyes, and short, curly, salt-and-pepper hair. He stroked Rex's head. "We've been watching for you, Big Guy. It's good to see you!"

Rex's tail wouldn't stop wagging. "Is Charlie here? Did they put him in re-gen?"

Caro hugged him. "Oh, sweetheart, yes, Charlie's here. But the re-gen on his arm is going to take several days."

"That's what the Chief guessed," Bill said.

Caro looked up with a smile. "You must be Bill. It's good to meet you in person."

Warm gratitude washed over Rex. "Bill has been amazing." If not for Bill, Rex could still be crying outside the ER. He certainly wouldn't have learned how to leverage his influence for better outcomes.

"Thank you very, very much for taking care of him today, and for bringing him to us," Ted said. "He's only been on-Station two months, but he's already part of the Family."

Rex wondered if his heart might burst from joy. He'd smelled and observed the truth in Ted's words throughout his time here, but it felt good to hear it said.

"It's been an honor to help him, and to get acquainted with him," Bill said. "You should know that Rex has had his own round of re-gen. He saved Charlie's life in the Hub but broke four ribs in the process. Now that he's had his treatment, Dr. Sandler says they're mostly healed."

A new wave of gratitude pulsed through Rex. Bill certainly had found the most positive way to describe his misadventures in the Hub.

Ted gave Rex a sympathetic look. "I'm sure that wasn't much fun. But now you've had a taste of what Charlie's going through. Perhaps it'll help you wait for your chance to smell him over?"

Guilt stabbed Rex. He should confess his part in Charlie's injury. He lowered his ears. "I do not envy him. I am very sorry—"

Mimi straightened with a little gasp and an uprush of pleased scent. "Rex! I just realized. You can receive a vid-feed, can't you?"

Rex's ears went up with curiosity. He cocked his head at her. "Yes."

"They gave us access to one, so we could look in on Charlie. It's better than nothing, since we can't be there in person. Makes me feel a little closer, though I still wish I could hold his hand."

Caro grinned. "Good thought, Mama."

"Let me send it." Mimi closed her eyes, frowned in concentration. "Did you get that?"

A new window blinked in one of his side-channels. Rex's heart filled with grateful amazement. This was a Family privilege. For humans. Yet they'd freely shared it. He really was Family! "Yes. Thank you." He opened it, half-fearful of what he would see.

In the vid-view, Charlie lay deathly still in a crowded space, surrounded by an astonishing profusion of machines. Tubes snaked down from most of them. The tubes all seemed to end in an unimaginable number of needles. They had been inserted all over Charlie's body, but they clustered by far the most densely all over his left arm, shoulder, and hand. Monitor-lights pulsed, flickered, or blinked off-on-off-on at different paces. A bank of readouts that made no sense to Rex glowed with numbers or wavy lines near the bottom of the vid-window.

Chilled, Rex stared at his partner's image. He might want to give Charlie a good smell-over, but he'd never get past all that hardware without causing great harm. Longing pulsed through him, a heartsick stomach-plunge of loneliness. The bare patch over his own ribs now made more sense, but the motionless vid-image gave little solace. His partner lay deathly still on his back with eyes closed, arms by his sides, his skin more gray than brown. Well, that might be a visual effect of the vid. But was he even breathing? Rex's mind reeled. He couldn't tell. Worse, he couldn't *smell*. In the vid Charlie looked more like a corpse than his normal, vibrant living self. Stabbed a thousand times. Cold. Inert.

Charlie stirred.

Rex's heart lifted. It was only a shallow breath, a small, fitful twitch of his partner's face. But that subtle movement meant Charlie really was alive. If Rex could smell him, he'd smell injured, but he'd be warm. He'd be alive. He'd smell like himself, underneath all the medicines.

Rex bowed his head, weak with relief.

13

SLAVERY AND FORMWORK

Orangeboro Morgue

The morgue techs took charge of Shady's last dead person for this long, long day.

She stepped away from the autopsy table, padded out of the immediate area, then stood still while Pam pulled off first Shady's mask and containment garb, then her own.

Oh, thank you! Time for a full-body stretch and a thorough shake. A small cloud of dog hairs flew.

Phew! You need another good brushing! Pam waved a hand in front of her face, then sneezed.

Stress-shed. Shady indulged in another stretch. *I'll feel even better after I ditch the panniers and have a good roll.* Not yet, alas.

No lack of stress, today. Shoulders slumped, Pam stepped into the hall from the morgue. They left the blue-and-white tile behind, but tendrils of underlying death-stench followed them, a throat-clutching, putrid waft that lingered and clung. These *Izgubil* cadavers, at least, had been in the cold of space or under refrigeration most of the time before they showed up on Shady's autopsy table. She and Pam had faced far worse stenches from earlier cases.

They reached a row of data-privacy cubicles in a nearby alcove. Pam slid onto one cubicle's hard bench seat with a sigh. *Ready for this?*

Guess so. Gotta do it. Shady took one last stretch, then hopped up into the next one. She pretty much filled the cubicle. Every law-enforcement teacher she'd ever had, both human and XK9, had stressed the same point over and over. "Keep up with your formwork, or it'll eat you alive," they'd all said. Damn if they weren't right.

She reviewed the morgue forms first. They'd need the fewest changes, because she'd filled them out in detail while she was going over the bodies. She added a minor note here and there, then signed each report with a retinal scan and hit "submit."

There were only three, thanks to her time out of the morgue with Brave Girl and Thinking Girl. Her report on her work with the little girls took longer. She'd already grabbed a few quieter moments to draft parts of it. Now she looked those over, expanded on most of them, then scanned other reports in the girls' file. One in particular caught her eye.

"Shady speaks a country dialect very similar to the girls'," Tasbeeh had written. "This dialect explains why the girls were so afraid to tell their names. In the Jalalpur Valley District, poor families sometimes sell children, so the rest of the family can eat for another season or two. If we send the girls home, their families will be required to return them to their purchaser, or they'll be forced to give back the money they were paid. Children who are sold are therefore coached never to tell their real names."

Shady's hackles prickled. How could humans be so horrible? No wonder Brave Girl and Thinking Girl hadn't wanted to tell her their names!

But Tasbeeh's comment made her uneasy for another reason, too. Shady had learned what she knew of Oroplanian Urdu from a young gardener named Gulnar, whom she'd met at her middle school in Transmondia's Creschen Province. That wasn't far from western Oroplania.

Shady used her HUD and CAP to open a map, heart pounding. She usually had trouble with maps, but there it was. Jalalpur Valley lay less than 60 kilometers east of her old school. Had Gulnar been a slave? Cold certainty filled Shady. She remembered the young woman's quiet sadness, her fearful, furtive ways, her terror of being caught talking with anyone, even a half-grown puppy of three. When Shady had received her transfer to law-enforcement school, Gulnar wept. "You are my only friend," she'd said. "Khuda hafiz! Goodbye!" One last, quick hug, and Shady never saw her again. Shady had never told anyone about Gulnar's linguistic gift to her, but she'd also never forgotten. For well or ill, XK9s weren't built that way.

Enough with the reports. She jumped down from the hard bench.

Shady? You okay? Pam looked and smelled startled.

I'm done. Shady avoided eye contact. *Gonna call Rex.*

Gimme a few more. Stay close.

Her com rang, on Rex's line. Would he be awake this time?

"Hello!" His familiar vocalizer-voice released a flood of joy.

"How are you?"

"I am fine. XK9s are tough." But his mic picked up a yawn.

Worry jabbed her. He needed sleep to heal, but she was glad to hear him. "Where are you now?"

"With the Family at last. They finally allowed me into the ICU waiting room." Another yawn.

Affection and tender protectiveness filled her. "You know you must sleep when you are hurt." Her mother had called it the Healing Sleep. The few times Shady had suffered an injury more significant than a scrape she'd first become parched, then ravenous. As soon as her thirst and hunger were quenched, she'd fallen into a deep sleep for several hours. Her injuries were always healed when she awoke.

"Mimi gave me a vid-feed, so I can see Charlie," Rex said. "I cannot smell him, but I saw him move on the vid. He really is alive." The vocalizer did not render emotions well, but Shady could imagine how worried he must have been. If it had been Pam, and she couldn't sense her partner through their brain link . . . she shuddered. "You cannot spend all your time watching Charlie. You must sleep."

"You sound like Bill." He yawned again. Each time he yawned brought another stab of worry.

"Is she telling you to sleep?" a man's voice in Rex's background asked. "If she is, you should listen."

Shady wagged her tail. She'd met Bill at the Sandler Clinic, and liked him. He'd seemed a sensible man. "I want to see you," she told Rex. "Our watch just ended. Take a nap until I get there."

He growled softly. "They will not let you in. It took a letter from Chief Klein, and permission from Director Dépoli to make them let me in."

"I still want to try. If they let in one dog, why not two?"

"Good luck with that argument," She visualized him giving her a dubious ear-flick, then heard yet another yawn.

Pam gave a little gasp, straightened. Her scent factors bubbled with sudden bright joy. "Hello, you. Is your watch over?"

Shady rolled her eyes. No need to ask who'd called. Only Balchu made Pam light up like that. Poor Charlie'd never had a chance. She sighed.

"Shady?" Rex asked. "Everything all right?"

"Never mind. Pam just got a call from Balchu. This will either mean that she will decide she is done with formwork right now, or it will delay us even longer."

"Oh, no!" The bright joy faded to concern in Pam's scent and body language. "How bad is he? Do they know if he'll be okay?"

Shady cocked one ear in Pam's direction. "Something has happened to someone. Pam seems distressed."

Rex's yawn ended in a snort. "And you seem distracted. Call me back when you figure it out."

"If I cannot go to you, I shall call. Meanwhile, get some sleep."

"If you insist." Yes, that was yet *another* yawn. He ended the call.

She slid her tongue out in an amused loll. Bill wouldn't need to nag him much longer.

"Okay, love," Pam said. "I just have a few last details to scan. See you in ten at the Med Center."

"Orangeboro Med?" Shady asked. "What has happened?"

"One moment." Pam stared into the middle distance, her teeth white against her lower lip. Still working on her reports.

She'd said, "See you in ten," but this might take a while. Shady stretched again, then paced up and down the row of cubicles a couple of times. No, Pam was still working. It probably was best that she and Rex had ended their call, but now what? Unhappy and restless, she paced another lap, then placed a com call to Cinnamon.

"Were all of your dead people drunk, stoned, or high when they died?" her sister-Packmate asked, once they'd greeted each other. "I swear my Client Four was so out of it he did not even smell startled from the ship blowing up around him."

"Mine all had the fear-smell, along with the other scent layers," Shady said. "My Client One was stone-sober, probably so he could enjoy torturing his victim without impairment. Did I smell his victim on your table?"

"Razor had a young human girl of maybe nine or ten, and I think a zhottlo among his. I am not sure how I would react to having a baby on my slab."

Shady shuddered. "I fear we may all have to discover how that feels." A little girl and a zhottlo, a preadolescent ozzirikkian. A zhottlo was parallel in physical maturity to a human preteen, but ozzirikkian society dictated more tender sheltering for a zhottlo by zhir kincircle than human kids typically experienced. Shady's heart constricted in pain at the thought of such innocents enslaved in Whisper's hellish trade.

"My eight today were all adult humans, both genders." Cinnamon snorted. "They had all clearly been drugging themselves senseless with one or more substances."

Shady shook her head, bemused. "I do not understand why anyone would enjoy that. But I also do not understand why anyone would enjoy torturing a child, or how someone could blow up a ship full of people."

Cinnamon sighed. "I guess it is up to the human investigators to figure that last one out. Have you caught up with Rex? Is he out of re-gen?"

Longing to touch and smell her mate swelled within her. Shady told Cinnamon what she'd learned this afternoon from Bill about Rex's experiences in the Hub and afterwards, and that Rex had gained entry to the ICU waiting room at last. "I want to go to him tonight, if I can get into the hospital."

Cinnamon was quiet for a moment, then asked, "How could they stop you?"

Shady's hackles prickled. "What do you mean?"

"I just opened a floor plan of Orangeboro Med Center and checked with Berwyn through our link. He said there are public corridors and an open stairway between the main entrance and the ICU waiting room. If you really wanted to go to Rex, how could the humans stop you?"

Shady tensed. A memory of Pee Wee Pedersen, the XK9 Project's tallest, brawniest dog wrangler, rose in her mind. He'd netted and punished her and various other Packmates several times during her final two years in Solara City. Not one of those episodes was something she wanted to repeat. She shuddered. "Humans have lots of ways to stop XK9s."

"Yes, but have you seen any of them here in Orangeboro? Will they have them at the hospital?"

All of her hackles stiffened upright. "I do not know. Not sure I want to find out, either."

"It occurred to me to wonder, is all," Cinnamon said.

Pam stood abruptly. "There! Done! Shady, let's go!"

"Pam has finished. I guess I shall see you tomorrow."

"Good luck till then." Cinnamon closed her end of the call.

Shady relaxed her hackles, cocked her head at Pam. *Where shall we meet Balchu?*

Orangeboro Med. Remember DPO Fujimoto, the other man in the dock breach with Rex and Charlie? He was a mentor for Balchu—his first Field Training Officer. Balchu's worried. Pam turned to walk down the corridor, away from the data-privacy cubicles.

Shady followed, curious. Balchu was pretty old. It had probably been eight or ten years since he'd been a rookie—longer than she'd been alive. How much older must his first FTO be?

Pam's face pinched with a worry that echoed like smoke in her scent. *Helmer suffered a concussion in the emergency bunker, then had a heart attack on the Rescue Runner.* Shady caught up with Pam in time to see her frown. *Or was it two heart attacks? Can you have two in a row? I'm not sure. Anyway, he's in bad shape.*

I'm sorry he was hurt. Rex saved Charlie's life, but then DPO Fujimoto saved both of them. And after that, the *Triumph* crew had saved all of them. Shady wagged her tail. A lot of saving had gone on, today. Too bad it could not have been extended to more of the *Izgubil's* passengers. That way there would be fewer bodies to process and more witnesses to interview.

Balchu is worried that his friend might die. Also, he said Personnel Assistance is having trouble locating Helmer's daughter Miyu.

Empathic concern rose within Shady. She'd just had her own taste of worry over a loved one. She and Pam hurried up some stairs from their morgue annex blue-and-chrome corridor to a beige-and-chrome utility corridor, then out through an employees-only exit into lowering, late-afternoon light. The long, eventful day was passing at last. What new developments would the night watch bring?

14

CLARITY OF SCENT

Orangeboro Medical Center

The bright mosaics and the jumble of blooms in the planter-boxes could not lift the pall of deepening evening, with its rising mist. Shady's mind raced ahead. Her thoughts flitted, skittish, around the edges of do-they-have-prods and are-there-nets-waiting. *How could the humans stop you?* Cinnamon's vocalizer-voice had asked. Shady repressed a shudder, but longed for Rex's smell and touch.

Pam strode steadily, head down, brow pinched. She did not speak. The sharp, jittery worry in her scent swirled in broken ripples of air that eddied and flowed around her. The orange-grove smells of Central Plaza diminished behind them. The wide glass doors of Orangeboro Medical Center's Main Entrance slid open.

No wrathful guardians emerged from the crowd that milled around the lobby or sat along the edges in rows of chairs. Shady scented Balchu, then saw him.

I'll follow you. From her squint and frown, Pam was still looking. Then her face and scent factors blossomed into joy. She stepped forward into Balchu's arms.

Shady sighed. She made an effort not to roll her eyes again, but she looked away.

Amused expressions or charmed, indulgent scent-reactions told Shady that most who noticed the Amares' passionate kiss thought Pam and Balchu were a cute couple.

Shady swallowed a growl. Ranans had a much higher tolerance for public displays of affection than any Transmondian she'd ever known. "I wish your friend well, Balchu," she said. "I am going to find Rex now."

Neither Pam nor Balchu acknowledged this.

Shady accessed the online map Cinnamon had located earlier and opened it on her HUD. It sort of made sense. She headed toward the main stairway her sister-Packmate had mentioned. That, at least, was plain to see.

A man leaped up from behind the information desk. He hurried to intercept her. "Wait! Miss! You can't let that dog loose in here!"

Pam and Balchu pulled out of their kiss with obvious reluctance. Still in Balchu's arms, Pam frowned at the intruder. "This is a police XK9. She's not 'loose.' She's with me."

"It's too big and hairy. It has to stay outside."

Shady looked the man over. Maybe two-thirds the height of Pee Wee Pedersen, notably without the muscle tone. Without any observable dog-net, prod, or trank-rifle, either. She laid her ears back. "'It' has other plans. My mate is bigger and hairier than I am, and he is upstairs in the ICU Waiting Room. If he can be here, I can be here."

The man's scent flared with surprise, then darkened with determination. "No! You really can't!"

Shady looked him in the eye. Growled softly.

His eyes went round; his scent turned sweaty. He did not fling himself into her path, although his expression and scent factors told her he thought he probably should.

Shady made the stairway's landing in two easy bounds. Yeah. Like he could stop her. She looked back, saw the man gesture Pam over to him. A pang of guilt seized her. What had she done? Now Pam would get chewed out. Her hackles prickled with discomfort.

Dr. Ordovich would have been livid over such insubordination. She quailed at the thought of *his* reaction and hoped desperately that he'd never learn of this. She might be in Orangeboro now, but the Project's protocols still ruled XK9 lives. Should she go back? Perform a submission roll? Beg for forgiveness?

Pam's reaction though the link cut across her guilt with a dash of indignation. *You've had a horrible day. Go see Rex. I'll handle this!*

Could anyone have a better partner? Thanks! Shady turned down the corridor toward the ICU waiting room. Rex's own, beloved scent led her forward. Longing lengthened her strides. She came to a yellow-hued room with a lot of humans and—*yes!*

He galloped to her, ears up, tail pumping.

She squealed with delight and play-bowed, then they launched into a giddy, joyful greeting that quickly took them back out into the wider open space of the corridor. She and Rex circled and pranced, wild with delight. She moved in close to him, breathed his scent hungrily, exhausted and injured though he smelled. She licked his face, rejoicing, and he licked hers. She heard, saw, and smelled only Rex. All was radiant ecstasy.

"One was bad enough, but *two?*" A hard-faced woman in a nurse's uniform stood at the entrance to the waiting room. She glared at Shady and Rex, arms crossed.

Rex whirled on her, bristling. "Do not start!"

Shady gave him a scandalized look. Dr. Ordovich would *never* have stood for this. What had gotten into him?

"Come, Shady." Rex pushed roughly past the woman; she had no choice but to step aside or be knocked over.

Shady's chest went tight. What was he thinking? If Dr. Ordovich were here, Rex would get a beating for sure! Worried, she followed her mate into the waiting room.

The nurse exuded angry scent factors, but she did not call Security. No one else yelled at them, either.

Shady lifted her ears. The tightness in her chest eased. Clearly, this was a new day. Dr. Ordovich, like Pee Wee Pedersen, was nowhere around.

Rex led her to a large hexagonal area where Bill, another UPO, and three civilians stood. It was clear to smell that the three civilians were Charlie's mother, father, and sister. Pam's untimely breakup with Charlie had ended any chance Shady might have had to meet them before now.

The sister smiled at Shady. "Who's your friend, Rex?"

Rex wagged his tail. "This is Shady Jacob-Belle, my mate." He introduced Charlie's Family members. "I believe you know Bill? And this is Pascal Jennings, Charlie's Personnel Assistance Liaison."

They greeted her cordially, but an undertone of wariness lingered in the Family's body language and scent factors.

Caro frowned. "Aren't you . . . Pam's partner?" She glanced toward the corridor. "Where is she?" The parents frowned, too. Clearly, Pam was not popular here. Not that Shady could blame them.

"Yes, I am. But Pam is visiting someone else. I am here on my own."

"Oh." Caro relaxed. "Well. It's nice to meet you." All of the humans took seats on padded chairs in the semi-enclosed hexagon.

Shady settled next to Bill's feet. Rex settled next to her, pressed as close to her as possible, curled against her stomach like an enormous puppy.

Tenderness overwhelmed her. Words failed. He craned his neck back to nuzzle her neck contentedly, and she nuzzled him right back. Her nose detailed his throat, his upper chest, the recently-healed spots, which had a different, fresher smell, and the soap-residue from where someone had recently bathed him.

He was warm, he was real, he was *right here with her*. She closed her eyes, blissful, utterly in the moment.

He rubbed and rubbed his face against her shoulder, more wonderful than the best massage. Then he rested his head on her right-side pannier and fell asleep.

Shady stared at him, her heart full. She burrowed her nose deep into the fur of his neck. She could not drink in enough of his scent, his steady heartbeat, his deep, sleeping breaths. Those two months apart seemed long as years. *You and Balchu may visit with DPO Fujimoto for as long as you like*, she told her partner. *Take lots of time.*

I'm glad you found him, Pam replied.

Caro gave Shady a sympathetic smile. "We've been begging him to take a nap ever since he got here. So of *course* the moment you arrive, he crashes out."

Her relief to be near him filled her, but all the same . . . Shady shifted a little; Rex's head was really heavy. "I did think we might get a little more time to talk before he passed out, but he needs to sleep."

"He's finally at peace," Bill said. "He was so upset when he realized you'd arrived and already left, at the vet clinic!"

Needy from want of his presence, Shady drew in another draught of Rex's comforting personal scent. She nuzzled his cheek, then arched her neck over his. "It is a massive relief to be able to see and smell him. Awake or asleep, I prefer to be with him."

"Now, *that's* love." Ted grinned at her with approval.

Shady snuffled Rex's ear, which twitched at her breath, though he slept on. Surreptitiously, she shifted his weight, seeking a more comfortable position. "It is good that he is asleep. Truly." She explained about Healing Sleep.

A new human stepped near the hexagon, hesitated, then peered inside. She seemed reticent, but Charlie's Family members leaped up when they saw her, their scent factors bright with pleased recognition. Bill and Pascal rose, too.

"Hildie!" Caro advanced, clasped the newcomer's hands warmly. "It's been ages!"

Shady lifted her nose, ears up, to examine this new person. About Charlie's age, and several centimeters taller than Caro, Hildie wore her thick black hair pulled back in a ponytail like Pam's. Her blue Safety Services-issue fatigues bore the shoulder-chevrons of a sergeant, the sweet-metallic odor of transfer-particles from objects that had been in space, and residue of medical-grade disinfectants.

"Rex told us the *Triumph* picked them up," Caro said. "We were all amazed. What are the odds?"

Hildie smiled. "Bran Davis caught the incoming signal. He recognized Charlie's name, and realized we'd all personally crucify him if we found out later that he'd sent some other team." Her expression sobered. Her hands clutched each other. "How is he? I promised the crew I'd find out."

Shady cocked her head. Charlie'd never said much about his past when they'd shared quarters in Solara City. Had he once been part of an ERT crew?

Mimi sighed. "Surgery is over. He's now in the first of several rounds of re-gen treatments on his arm."

Hildie's brow puckered, her shoulders clenched high and tight. "Do you have a prognosis?" The sharp anxiety in her scent factors soared, along with the sweet, poignant high tones of intense longing and deep affection.

Shady's ears went up. Oh! This wasn't a simple checking-up-for-the-crew call. This woman cared about Charlie the way Pam cared about Balchu.

Shady froze, breathless from the sudden clarity that opened for her with one smell.

The way Pam cared about Balchu was special. It dug deep. It went beyond the ordinary. It was startling to smell a response of that sort in anyone, because it was extraordinary. But smelling it in someone else made it impossible to for Shady to deny the truth within her own household. Pam didn't just care about

Balchu, she loved him with all her heart, and he loved her the same way. They were a well-matched pair, a near-perfect fit. They belonged with each other, the way Shady belonged with Rex.

Shady lowered her nose, shoved it deep into the fur of Rex's ruff. His personal scent calmed her, steadied her. But nothing could blunt the terrible rush of realization, the gut-drop, the heartache. The implications echoed through her like shock waves through bedrock.

There never should have been a "Pam-and-Charlie."

And there wouldn't be, there couldn't be, again. Pam was with her mate. She should never go back to Charlie. If Rex was right, Charlie would never take Pam back, in any case. That door was closed.

What, then, would become of Rex-and-Shady?

15

MORNING MIRACLE

Corona Tower

Rex gave a soft growl, twisted away. Someone's insistent tongue anointed his ear with a wet caress. "No. Still sleepy."

"I am sure you are," Shady said. "But you can sleep all day. I cannot."

Warm pleasure filled him. Ahh. He stretched, nuzzled her, breathed in her beloved scent. Such a realistic dream. He'd never had one quite so—

"Come on, Lazybones. Can you be conscious for at least a little while?"

Rex jolted awake. "Shady!" He froze, not even able to breathe. Then his lungs released with a gasp. This was real! She was here! Her tongue on his head. Her personal smell. Her dear presence. This was no dream! "Shady!"

She snorted. "Yes. Still here, but not for much longer. Some of us have to work."

He stared at her in the predawn murk. She was here. Here. IN HIS BEDROOM. He lurched up from the bedclothes. "How are you here?"

She lolled her tongue, her eyes and scent alight with amusement. "Do you remember even the slightest thing from last night?"

Last night!

Last night?

His mind spun. The Hub. The dock breach. The long, weary quest to find Charlie . . . Bill. Where was Bill?

Rex drew in a breath, rattled. Belated memories struggled into consciousness. "I was . . . I was at the ICU Waiting Room. You came." He cocked his head, bemused but overjoyed. Also confused. He'd fought such a battle to be there, but then somehow she'd appeared. He was really fuzzy on how that had happened.

But even that didn't explain the biggest miracle. He couldn't dredge up the faintest memory, nor make any sense of the undeniable fact that she was here in Corona Tower. "How did you come home with me?"

She snapped her ears flat. "I stayed. That is pretty much it. You were using me as a pillow, and Charlie's Family seemed to like me. Pam wanted me to leave, but she did not want to confront Corona Family. Bill offered to escort me home."

He gave her a puzzled look, still confused. "If Bill offered to escort you, why are you here?"

"Pam and Balchu went home. Pam was not happy, but they went. I truly did intend to follow."

Was his head extra-thick? This still didn't make sense. "Something changed?"

"It was very hard to rouse you, and even more difficult to get you into the Family's car." She flicked her ears. "I do not think even Ted, Hector, Pascal, and Bill combined would have been able to get you into it, much less into the elevator from the garage, or from there into your room, if I had not been there to motivate you and help prop you up. You actually were kind of cute, but you also were very, very heavy."

He panted fast and shallow, his heart racing, but his mind a blank. "I do not remember any of that."

Her tail wagged high. Her scent suffused with amusement. "No, I did not think you would." Then her ears went down. "Each step of the way, I had to call Pam again. She is angry with me, but eventually she understood that my staying here was inevitable. She was even less willing to come out here last night to argue about it than she was to face Corona Family in the ICU Waiting Room."

"Will she beat you?"

Shady growled softly. "She never has so far, even when I played tricks on Balchu." She cocked her head at Rex. "Does Charlie ever beat you?"

Charlie? Lay on the strap as Dr. Ordovich had? The image just wouldn't form. Charlie would have to turn into someone else. "No, never. The impression I have formed is that most Ranans would rather de-escalate conflicts than strike out. Even if they are angry with a dog."

Her tongue slid out. "That has been my impression, too." She glanced toward the bedroom doorway and the hall beyond. "Could we maybe talk about this over breakfast?"

Pleasure leaped up within him, strong enough to momentarily push aside his concern that Pam might actually punish Shady this time. Breakfast! "Oh! I have a wonderful thing to show you in the kitchen!"

"The food dispenser?" She glanced back at him over her shoulder. "It is very smooth. I am envious."

Disappointment crushed him. He stopped, stared after her. "You know about that?"

She kept going. "Hector showed me last night. I had not eaten dinner, so I was really hungry. I wish we had one at Pam's."

Peeved, Rex followed her. The food dispenser was Rex's toy! Granted, Charlie's uncle Hector had invented it, but damn. Too late now. He swallowed a growl. "I suppose you also met the gate." Rex had been itching to show it to her since he moved in.

"Sorry, but yes." She nuzzled him. "Both the gate and the door know me now."

Crestfallen, he sighed. The security system was another of Hector's gadgets. "And I guess you also saw the bathroom?"

She gave him a rueful look. "I used it, and I love it. I want one of those, too. Other kinds of facilities made for humans are a terrible pain to use. I am always afraid I will lose my balance, or break the stupid thing."

In the kitchen she stepped on the dispenser's platform to make it fill a large bowl with Master Mix, the optimized XK9 kibble diet. "Good morning, Shady," it said. "This morning you weigh 114.2 kilos. You might need a little extra, to get your weight up to your optimum." More kibbles rattled into the bowl.

Shady wagged her tail. "I definitely want one. Pam never does that!" She snarfed the ration down with ravenous enthusiasm, still talking. "Did you meet Hildie, the woman from the ERT?"

Rex regarded her, ears up with surprise. "How do you know about her?"

"She came to check on Charlie, after her shift. His Family really likes her, but they had not seen her in years. Did you know Charlie used to work on the ERT? Did you know that Hildie loves him?"

"I met her on the *Triumph*, and I have a nose, so yes. I did know that." He flattened his ears, peeved that there seemed to be nothing he could tell her, then he lifted them again. "Do you know that Charlie has a Medal of Valor?"

"A what?" That stopped her.

So she didn't know everything. He wagged his tail. Then he explained about the *Asalatu*, Charlie's heroism, and that his partner had a regenerated left arm.

"Oh, that explains several things." Shady sketched in new facts that she'd learned from listening to the Family tell Hildie about them. Rex hadn't known that Charlie had gone through a terrible depression after he couldn't rejoin the ERT. He'd had no clue that his human partner had developed an unexpected talent for creating Global Reconstructions of crime scenes. And Charlie certainly had never told him that he'd once had an Amare named Felicia, whom the Family detested far worse than Pam. Shady had learned so much! And he'd slept through it all.

Precious time ticked past. Shady used her last several minutes to catch him up on things that she, Razor and Cinnamon had done yesterday for the *Izgubil* investigation. She told him about SSA Adeyeme's irrational fear, and her unusual courage in the face of it. Told him about the three Packmates' morgue analyses, and about the two little girls who were the only conscious witnesses known to have been aboard the *Izgubil*. There were things about cases that one could not tell certain humans, but the Pack exercised fewer restrictions between themselves.

Rex dispensed breakfast for himself. His weight was down, too. But then he stared at it, his appetite weirdly dampened. That never happened! But he was barely up, and already She'd gathered her harness in her jaws. Soon she'd have to drag it to the elevator for the trip downstairs.

He squeezed a question in edgewise from time to time, but mostly he listened with growing envy. He wanted to work the *Izgubil* case, too! To see and smell and talk with Cinnamon and Razor every day. Best of all, to stay near Shady! But even though he now was healed, he was on stand-down. Dr. Sandler had said so yesterday. This was so unfair! He grasped a mouthful of Shady's pannier-webbing, then raised his head as high as he could to keep from tripping on the gear. He followed her out the door.

"Have a good day, Shady," the door-security said. "Have a good day, Rex."

But it was not a good day.

It was a miserable day, a horrible day. Almost before it had begun, Shady was going away.

He dropped the panniers inside the elevator car, stepped closer to his mate, then smelled her all over in the greatest detail he could. He would remember all of this, of course. Would run it through his mind a thousand times, just as he had done with all his memories of her. He'd cherished and reviewed them over and over and over throughout the past two months of aching loneliness. But no amount of detailed touching and looking and smelling could memorize her to the point where she would actually, physically be there when she really wasn't.

He arched his neck over hers, pressed himself hard against her body, and felt her lean into him. Her vocalizer had gone silent. They could only stand as close as possible and wish that somehow time would stop.

The elevator dinged. The doors rolled open. After a while they rolled closed again. A while after that, the bell dinged again, and they rolled back open.

"We should get out," Shady said. "Someone else will want this elevator."

"It is early. Maybe not."

But she was already dragging her harness out.

He didn't have time for a long, procrastinating stretch. Not even for a stress-yawn.

They lugged their burdens through the silent, misty courtyard, then down the main entrance tunnel. The double-door gate swung open for them. "Have a good day, Shady," its voice announced. "Have a good day, Rex. Come back home safely!"

But when could he ever hope for Shady to come back? Rex stifled a whimper. Why couldn't the gate's voice still be muted for nighttime?

Because it was no longer night. The misty air was brightening. The mirrors were turning. He didn't need the safety lights along the steps at any time, but it had grown light enough to tell the tan stones from the gray stones along the steps. Early-dawn mist still blanketed the neighborhood, but it couldn't muffle Rex's despair.

Inexorable morning was here. Each night, fog rose from the Sirius River. Each morning the mirrors shifted, and solar brilliance burned the fog away. The cycle swathed neighborhoods in the fog zone with heavy mist each night. It kept their vegetation lush green with less irrigation than in arid zones above. But the cycle, clocklike, also marked the passing of time.

Rex and Shady stopped at the base of the curving steps by the road. The piercing whine of an approaching civilian motorbike grew louder. Right on time, damn it.

Sadness weighed on him. He cocked an ear toward the sound. "I did not know Pam had a motorbike."

"It is rented. Pam hates to get up in the morning, but she hates being late for work even more. Riding the train, it would be an extra thirty minutes each way. She warned me she is taking the motorbike's hire from my maintenance stipend."

"You will not go hungry, will you?"

Rebellious, hot, rising scent factors surged. "If I do, I shall come to mooch from you again."

He wagged his tail, though the heat of her rebellion worried him. "Please come to mooch from me anytime." Rex focused on savoring her beloved, warm, musky scent for a few, final, precious moments.

All too soon the motorbike arrived. "Hello, Rex." Pam offered him a curt nod. He heard no greeting for Shady. The partners probably had already been using their brain link for a while already.

Shady's ears were down. She eyed her human partner with a smell of smoldering anger.

Pam answered with a smoldering look of her own, then glanced again at Rex. "Shady's been wanting to visit you for two months, so I hope you got good and caught up." She cinched Shady's harness more briskly than necessary, then slapped the panniers onto her back and yanked the straps tight.

Shady appeared to ignore this. She gave Rex one last, lingering nuzzle. "I love you. I shall call when I have a chance." She gave Pam a sidelong glance. Climbed into the sidecar.

Then they were gone.

16

DESOLATION AND DOGGIE-BACK RIDES

Corona Tower

Rex stared after Pam and Shady's motorbike. Sharp, savage pain echoed through the emptiness in his heart.

The motorbike sped away, dimming and reappearing as it whipped through patches of mist on Rim Eight Road. Its departing whine dwindled. Waned. Faded out altogether. Long before it would have turned toward the switchbacks down the terrace wall, it had disappeared from Rex's view into the mist.

He lowered his head, ears and tail down. The fog around him brightened and thinned, but his inner fog grew darker, more dank and dreadful, the more he struggled to find a positive way forward. He'd never seen Pam so angry, so cold. If Pam wanted them separated, he and Shady might never see each other again.

Would Charlie agree with Pam? Would the injuries Rex had caused make him turn away? Rex's insides went cold and liquid-sickly. His pulse fluttered faster. He tucked his tail up under himself till it brushed his belly, then crouched on the stones at the base of the curving steps. He couldn't hold back a soft, terrified whimper. *Oh, Charlie,* he cried into their empty brain link, *I miss you. I need you. Can you forgive me?*

His partner couldn't answer.

Rex shivered. Out of all his seven-plus years of life, Charlie's living presence had only been at the other end of their brain link for a few months. Yet without him there now, Rex felt more alone than he ever remembered. *What should I do?* he called to Charlie through the link. *How can I live without Shady? And how can I function without you?*

Hissing emptiness echoed where the warmth and personality of Charlie should've been.

A howl rose up from Rex's heart. It swelled within him, tightened his throat. He tipped his nose upward . . . But no. Wait! He clamped his jaws tight on it. He couldn't act like an impulsive puppy anymore. Morning might be dawning, but it was too early for a howl. He would wake people. He'd better not.

But the heartsick pain, the ache in his throat, the howl demanded release. What else could he do? What comfort could he find? What would Charlie advise?

What would you do, if you felt this way? He didn't expect an answer, but one came to him anyway. He thought of Charlie, and then he knew what to do. It had helped in the bunker. It had helped on the *Triumph.* It would help him now. *Breathe.* Rex imagined Charlie breathing in, and he breathed in with him. He held the breath, counting mentally. Then he blew out the breath all the way, just as Charlie did, and some of his tension eased.

He breathed in again. Held it. Let it out and tried to go limp, tried to relax, to let his breath carry the fear away. His pulse steadied. He could survive this. He could bide his time. He could wait for Charlie's return.

But his bleak, dreadful loneliness remained. Maybe he'd feel less alone if he checked the vid from the hospital. At least that way he could look at his partner. He could see Charlie's face, see him breathe, and imagine his beloved Charlie-scent.

Rex accessed the vid feed, but . . . what was this?

A slow-crawling, yellow-lettered message slid across a dark gray screen where his wished-for view of Charlie should've been. "Your patient is undergoing a short, previously-announced procedure . . ." Rex froze. His pulse thundered in his ears. *Charlie! I'm supposed to see Charlie!* He snarled, blinked, whimpered. ". . . to make sure your loved one has the best possible wellness outcome." The end of the word "outcome" slid away to the left, disappeared. Then the message started again. "Good morning from the health-care professionals at Orangeboro Medical Center. Your patient is undergoing . . ."

His head hurt. He clicked out of the vid-feed, then climbed the shiny-damp steps with reluctant, heavy legs.

The gate swung wide. "Welcome home, Rex!" Uncle Hector's cheerful voice greeted him.

Head down, he plodded through.

In the courtyard, Ted, along with his parents Steve and Carrie, had settled at a table under the oak tree. They'd draped towels over their dewy chairs to keep from getting wet, and now braced on their elbows over steaming mugs of coffee in relaxed, companionable silence. They smiled when Rex emerged from the tunnel.

He nodded to them, listless but polite.

"You're up earlier than we expected," Ted said. "Seeing Shady off?"

The human had asked a question. Rex should answer. He lifted his head. "Yes. She has to work. Pam came for her."

Ted smiled. "It was good to meet her. I hope she can visit again soon."

Rex bowed his head. His throat ached. "I do not think that is likely. Pam is angry with her."

Ted frowned. "Why? Because she came here? We're damned grateful she did. I don't know how we'd have managed to get you home, without her!"

"Oh, sweetie." Carrie half-pushed herself up from her chair, reached out to Rex, then sat again when he approached the table.

He let her guide his chin to rest in her ample lap. But Dr. Ordovich always said no dog should bother humans by talking about their emotions. Humans didn't care, he said. They would just be annoyed. Rex wasn't sure what Carrie wanted.

Carrie stroked his head and neck with gentle brown hands. She offered a sad smile, and scratched behind his ears. Her dark eyes studied him from beneath pinched gray brows. "I bet you're feeling pretty low right now." Her calm, sweet concern filled his nose with an unfamiliar bouquet . . . but one he could get used to. Rana Stationers. Who could figure them out?

"I am," he admitted. Carrie's empathetic expression and warm, concerned scent encouraged him to speak. "I am unhappy that I slept through most of Shady's visit. I am unhappy that she had to leave so early. I am worried that Pam may not let her visit again."

"*Mm*-mm-mm." Carrie shook her head. Her hands caressed him. "That's just not right."

An unquestionably insubordinate thought rose up in him. Dr. Ordovich had been wrong. Certainly about Carrie. Maybe about others. He rubbed his head against the soft pillow of her stomach and drew in her comforting scent. "I also am worried about Charlie. What procedure are they doing?"

Ted grimaced, then reached over to give him an ear-rub. He looked and smelled as if Dr. Ordovich had been wrong about him, too. "It's supposed to fortify the strength of the bone core matrix in his left arm, so they don't have to replace it with a new one. Exactly what the procedure involves, I'm not sure. They said it'll take about two hours."

Rex pinned his ears back. "I do not remember getting that announcement."

"This was planned yesterday afternoon. Bill told us you'd probably sleep at least till noon today, so we didn't think to warn you."

"I suppose I would be still be sleeping, if Shady had not been forced to leave."

"You probably should go back to sleep. If your vet said till noon, there's undoubtedly a good reason. Shady told us about Healing Sleep."

Rex yawned. He did still feel tired. "Are you going back to the hospital today? I want to go, too."

"A group of us planned to go this morning, actually." Ted frowned. "We thought you'd be asleep, though, so we ordered a pedal-bus. I'm sorry. There won't be any room on it for you." He hesitated. "I suppose we could change the rental order, but there'd be a fee for a last-minute change. It's supposed to arrive in about half an hour." He eyed Rex for a moment, long enough for Rex to yawn again. "What if you fall asleep at the hospital, the way you did yesterday? It took all of us plus Shady to get you home."

Clearly, Ted didn't plan to take him today. He yawned a wide stress-yawn that turned into another sleepy-yawn halfway through. He hated to admit Charlie's father might have a point, but . . . Damn it. He yawned again. "Maybe I should sleep, at that. But next time, I want to ride along."

Ted frowned. "You know there's nothing you can do there."

"I can be closer to Charlie there."

"He's got you there, Teddy." Steve grinned at his son. "Why else would any of us be there?"

Ted stood. "I need breakfast if we're leaving in half an hour."

Rex recognized an exit cue when he heard one. Being sleepy provided a good excuse to take the elevator. He drank his self-refilling water bowl dry a couple of times, discovered he was hungry after all, then curled up on his bed. The bedding still smelled enough like Shady that he could almost fool himself.

He woke sometime after midday, feeling physically stronger. A stretch confirmed there were no tender parts left, no smallest twinge. If only a simple Healing Sleep could help Charlie!

He checked the vid-feed, glad to find it was streaming again. Warm pleasure filled him. He hadn't thought he was tense, but now his throat and chest relaxed so it was easier to breathe.

Charlie bore no outward marks from today's treatment that Rex could see. He looked about the same as yesterday: deathly still, with a distinct gray tinge to his bruised, medium-brown skin. He was still there, still living. Charlie's body twitched. He grimaced, despite his deep sedation. His head jerked, then his arm muscles briefly clenched. His face spasmed again as if in pain.

Unease prickled along Rex's hackles. He eyed his partner's image more intently.

Charlie's body quivered and shuddered. His face scrunched again and again in brief pain-grimaces.

Anxious foreboding slithered in Rex's gut. His throat vibrated with a low growl. What had the doctors done to Charlie?

There was no one to ask. He wished he could talk with Shady about it, but she was busy. Bill probably was, too. Was Bill still supposed to be Rex's PA Liaison today? He reviewed that section of the OPD *Procedural Handbook* from memory, but the rules focused on other aspects. "For as long as help is needed" was pretty vague.

Rex sighed. Now that he was healed, being stuck here at home sucked. With Charlie out of action, Rex had been sidelined as if he was a tool put into storage. As if he wasn't of any use without Charlie.

He could still think. He could still smell as well as ever. He could still analyze the inputs he sensed. He could still work, even without his brain-linked partner, because he could still communicate. Yesterday Bill had made a big deal about Rex being "insanely valuable." The moment returned in a rush of imagery and scent. His chest expanded. His heart warmed, and his head lifted.

But no one was acting as if he was valuable, today. Both the Family and the OPD acted as if without Charlie he was worthless. A frozen fog of melancholy chilled him. Rex's ears and tail drooped. He placed his chin on his forepaws, gave a soft whimper.

But a dog could stand only so much boredom and gloom. He'd had a good rest. There was nothing to do. Yet his muscles itched for action. He paced out onto his and Charlie's inner balcony, the one that overlooked the courtyard. Inner balconies ran around every level, but on the part by Charlie's dining room the decking widened. A pair of louvered dining room doors could fold open. A sturdy table stood near them, but its top was dusty and the chairs that matched it had been stacked along the wall. It was clear Charlie hadn't entertained guests here for a long time.

Planters filled with marigold flowers, cucumber vines, and tomatoes lined the railing. They sparkled in the afternoon light from recent watering and smelled rich with new mulch. From beyond the planters, sounds of children echoed upward.

Rex reared onto his hind legs, found places along the railing where his forepaws wouldn't harm the plants, then peered over. Corona Family's younger children chattered, laughed, and ran about in the play area near the base of the big oak tree. From the look of things, Charlie's sister Caro and cousin-in-law Quinn were on Family Rotation today.

Oh! Of course! Rex's heart lifted. His tail swept into upbeat tempo. His mind leaped ahead to the courtyard. Only a little shorter than a pony, he'd let the children ride him several times since he'd arrived on-Station. Now they asked for rides each time they saw him. He could be useful after all!

Caro's little daughters Lacey and Sophie broke away from the group in the sandbox. They ran to Rex when he arrived, then wrapped him in a pair of chubby-armed hugs.

"Wexie! Wexie!" three-year-old Lacey squealed.

Rex nuzzled her curly baby hair, happier already. "I thought I should come investigate what you are up to."

Five-year-old Sophie pulled back to regard him from beneath her dark lashes. "Maybe give us doggie-back rides?"

Clever girl. Rex wagged his tail. "You read my mind."

Jalani, Kristen, and Hakan all looked up with smiles at the mention of doggie-back rides. From his seat on the far side of the sandbox, Quinn chuckled. He quirked an eyebrow at Rex. "You sure about this?"

They would conspire to wear him out, but how better to spend the time? His heart lightened at the prospect. "I have all day, and nothing to do. Why not?"

The children squealed with delight. "Oh, Mama! Can we?" Lacey cried.

Caro smiled. "Let's go get Rex's gear."

Rex spent a couple of hours in the courtyard with the children riding his panniers like a saddle. He bucked, galloped, walked, or trotted as each rider requested, enforcing equal turns. When at last the children were so tired they could barely hold on, Rex brought them to Quinn and Caro for naps.

Caro gave his ears a scratch, then stripped off his gear. Quinn guided the children inside.

Rex watched them go, tail waving. Lassitude dragged at his muscles. He yawned. Another nap might prove to be a decent plan. He knew just the place for it, too. This time he climbed the stairs, however. The elevator was only for extreme situations.

Like nearly every roof on-Station, Corona Tower's flat roof had a stout guardrail and raised beds for vegetables. Part of the Family's income and much of their food came from here, or from the yards that flanked the tower. Flat decks with sunshades were tucked between the garden beds next to the elevator enclosures, for relaxing and enjoying the stunning port-side view.

A leeward breeze stirred the leaves on the pea and green bean trellises. Charlie's uncle Ralph knelt by one of the beds. He tucked new seedlings into rich, dark soil, his tanned face intent under his straw hat. A Certified Agricultural Technician, gardening was both his passion and his full-time job. He also tended the vineyard, the orchard, and the quinoa patch that flanked the Family's Tower. Ralph looked up to exchange a nod with Rex, then refocused on his work.

Rex wasn't looking for Ralph, however. Charlie's great-grandma Loretta and her son-in-law, Charlie's Gran Pepe, had taken their customary places under a sunshade by the portside guardrail that overlooked the valley. Charlie had told Rex that ninety years ago, when Corona Tower was being built, Loretta insisted it must have elevators on two of its four corners, not just one. She now benefitted daily from her foresight. The Family used the elevators to haul furniture, harvests, and mobility-compromised relatives to any level needed.

Rex padded over to lie down between Loretta and Pepe's deck chairs.

"Here for the view, Rexie?" Loretta reached out a veined hand to stroke his head.

Rex yawned. "Here for a nap. The kids wore me out." He put his head down, then rolled onto his side.

Pepe bent to stroke the partially re-grown patch of fur on his ribs with a gentle hand. "We'll wake you when the hospital expedition gets back."

Rex thumped the decking with his tail. "Much obliged."

The second nap restored him almost as much as the first one had. The "hospital expedition" returned soon after he woke.

Rex bounded down the steps to ground level, eager to inter-rogate Ted about what they'd done to Charlie.

But it was Charlie's mother Mimi, not Ted, at the center of the Family's focus when he arrived in the courtyard. She shook her head, in answer to a question Rex had missed. "No, it makes no sense for me to stay. I spent last night in a noisy place where I couldn't sleep, shut off from Charlie because they have to keep him in isolation to protect him from infections. I wound up sitting in an uncomfortable chair, monitoring him on a vid I could have watched at home."

Rex held back. Several relatives expressed support, then someone asked if she'd eaten, and the "briefing" broke up. Only after Mimi and Ted carried late-lunch trays from the ground-floor kitchen to a table under the oak did Rex approach in a respectful crouch. He fluttered his tail, lifted his nose. "Welcome home."

Mimi smiled. "Thanks. It's good to be back."

Rex lifted his ears, tail wagging. "I am happy to see you. Does this mean Charlie will come home soon, too?"

Her expression went rueful. "I wish. No, it'll be another week at least. But he's in stable condition. Dr. Zuni's still worried about the muscle sheath integrity, but he told me so far it's been a fairly routine second re-gen procedure."

"Still seems kind of like a miracle to me, but the technology's been around for a long time." Ted gave her shoulders a squeeze.

Rex's ears went down. "But Charlie hurts more."

Mimi picked at her salad with a frown, but didn't eat anything. "Dr. Zuni said he's 'experiencing some discomfort,' from that treatment they gave him this morning."

Ted grimaced. "In other words, it would hurt like hell, if he wasn't in a medically-induced coma."

"It appears to hurt a lot, even with the induced coma." Rex gave a soft growl.

"Too true. But at least it's not as bad as last time." Mimi clasped Ted's hand.

Rex lifted his ears, cocked his head. "After the *Asalatu?*"

"This time is definitely better than that, thank God." Ted's brow furrowed. "This time, at least we're not living in daily fear that he'll die." The residual anguish in his and Mimi's scents made it clear how real their fear had been.

Chagrined, Rex lowered his head. "I am sorry to bring up bad memories."

"Eh, comes with the territory." Ted hunched his shoulders. "Even when they don't become cops, you always worry about your kids. We'll get through it."

Getting through it did seem to be the order of the day. Rex let his tongue hang long in an anxious pant. He'd slept for lengthy periods already today, but the afternoon still seemed to stretch out for weeks and years before him. He longed to pace. No. To run.

To run and run and run, till he was through this day and through the night and through Charlie's treatments and back to the work that gave his life meaning. Oh, if only!

He flicked his ears, startled by a subversive urge. Running, or at least jogging, was something he could do, if they'd let him leave Corona Tower. But would they? "Ted? Mimi? I have a question. Pam is always worried that if Shady goes out alone in the neighborhood she will frighten people. But Charlie and I go jogging in Glen Haven Park almost every day. Do you think I would frighten people, if I went jogging there alone?"

Ted chuckled. "Stir-crazy already, eh?"

"Not that we blame you," Mimi added. "After all, what is there for you to do here but sleep?"

Ted's expression shifted to one of speculation. "Maybe you'd scare people, but maybe not. What if you wear your police gear, and stick to the jogging trail?"

They were actually considering it? Rex wagged his tail.

"I guess there's no harm in giving it a try," Ted said. "At least this way you'll know for sure."

Mimi nodded her agreement. "Besides, we're parents. We can recognize a bundle of nervous energy when we see one. There's only one cure for the wiggles."

Rex wagged his tail. "Does this mean I have permission to try?"

Ted grinned. "Sure, why not give it a shot? What can they do, call the police?" He grinned. "Let's go get your gear."

17

REX TRIES COMMUNITY POLICING

Glen Haven Neighborhood and Park

I t was one thing to talk about doing something, quite another to actually . . . DO it.

Kitted out in his full harness, panniers, and badge, Rex looked like a police XK9 on a mission. Perhaps people would think he was patrolling far out ahead of his partner? Much farther out than they'd ever dream, though. Despite his permission from Ted and Mimi, Rex emerged from the Corona Tower gate with a cringing sense of doing something forbidden.

He didn't slink. Whether he felt out-of-bounds or not, he'd be more likely to make people uneasy if he acted suspicious. This excursion was *authorized*. Better "sell it."

So he strode down the curving flagstone steps with his head up and his tail straight behind him, then trotted down Rim Eight Road. He went the same direction Pam and Shady had gone on their motorbike this morning, headed for the same switchbacks.

Nobody seemed to notice. Of course, there was nobody out on Rim Eight Road but him.

Rex moved along at an easy, ground-covering trot, tongue

lolling, nose working. He passed Bonita Tower, where Fatima Smythe lived. How were she and her ozzirikkian friends today?

He passed Fairleigh Tower. Their two German Shepherds ran down to the roadside fence line, barking furiously. Black-and-tan brothers, neutered. He'd never seen one without the other. "Ignore them," Charlie always said, when he and Rex walked or rode past.

But was their barking all bluff and bluster? Rex had always been curious. He probably outweighed the two of them combined. Stood a good ten centimeters taller than the bigger one. Would they face up to him? "You make too much noise," he said with his vocalizer. "Show some respect." He lowered his head to shoulder height, laid his ears back, stiffened his tail. Looked the larger one straight in the eye.

The Shepherd brothers stopped barking. They went still, met his gaze. Their heads went down. The larger one took a step back, but neither broke eye contact. Neither looked away.

Okay, that answered his question. They didn't want to fight him, but they'd defend their territory. Rex snorted. "I'll let it go this time." He turned away, trotted on down the road.

The Shepherd brothers roared after him. Yeah, well, they kind of had a right. They barked him all the way to the leeward end of their hundred-meter-wide front fence line. He smelled triumph in their scent, but also relief.

Rex lolled his tongue, trotted on with his tail high. Those poor suckers had to stop, but *he* had permission to go all the way to the park. Ha! He trotted past Cliffbank Tower, where crops rustled in the breeze that came up from the river, but no dogs patrolled the hundred-meter frontage.

Aurora Tower's harlequin Great Dane bounded down to her fence line with ears up and tail wagging. She stood as tall as Shady, her coat shorter and more piebald than Rex's black-and-white Packmate Tuxedo. She didn't bark at him with the same aggression as the Shepherd brothers. No, she was lonesome and thought Rex looked interesting to play with. She always extended this greeting, but he and Charlie never stopped to play. They always had to be somewhere.

Today Rex stopped, tail waving. He could relate to a lonely dog. The Dane went down into a play-bow, tail up. Rex mirrored her. Then she leaped up, delighted, to spring along the fence with joyous barks. Rex ran along the other side, barking, darting, feinting.

No humans interfered, although they made a lot of noise. But if anyone had, Rex was ready for them. He'd watched training vids of uniformed human patrol officers playing ball games, passing out treats, or busting dance moves with neighborhood children. Surely playing with the Dane fell under the category of "community policing." They danced and barked and played until she faltered and smelled tired. She was older than either Rex or the Shepherd brothers. He'd probably worn her out. But they'd both had fun.

Rex wagged his tail and trotted on. For the first time since the doggie-back rides, he felt almost useful.

The Glen Haven Transit Terminal Station on the lip of Rim Eight, located along the main switchbacks, wasn't exactly *full* of people. Not crowded the way it would be in another hour or two, during shift change rush. But more than a dozen humans waited there for the next train or elevator. Rex's path led through a gap in the safety-barrier berm, past the station, over the bridge that spanned the maglev tracks, then down the switchbacks. He trotted through with a businesslike air, a dog with an objective, who had a right to be there. People looked up, watched him.

"Wow. Is that an XK9?" someone asked.

"Huh. Wonder where that thing came from," someone else said.

No great public panic ensued. Rex trotted on. Another hurdle cleared, with less fuss than he'd feared. Same story on the switchbacks. Same story in the park. There were humans around, even a few dogs. Some kids. He didn't meet many people, but a tall boy from Fairleigh Tower, who'd been practicing football passes with another boy his age, stopped to greet him. "Hi, Rex! I heard about Charlie. How's he doing?"

Rex trotted over. "Hello, Ricardo. Charlie is in stable condition at the hospital."

The other kid's eyes went round. "Ho, Ric, is that a real XK9?"

Ric grinned. "This is my neighbor Rex, from Corona Tower."

"Hello. I am XK9 Officer Rex Dieter-Nell." Rex sat, and offered Ric's friend a paw.

The kid gaped at him, then reached out a hesitant hand to shake his paw. "I'm Jimmy. I live in Trondheim Tower, to leeward of the station."

"Nice to meet you, Jimmy."

"Mama says Charlie and Rex were in the dock breach." Now Ric's eyes were as big as Jimmy's. "They were chasing murderers!"

"That is true," Rex said. "I thought I might be able to catch them, but then the dock breach happened."

"Were you scared?" Jimmy asked.

"The dock breach was frightening, but I was mostly worried about Charlie. I knew he was hurt." Rex hesitated. How much should he say?

"Did you get hurt?" Ric asked.

Rex flicked his ears. "A little. But XK9s are tough. We heal fast. I am fine, now. I came to the park to jog. A police officer has to train all the time, to stay fit."

"Footballers have to stay fit, too," Ric said. "Can we jog with you?"

Rex lolled his tongue. "I am afraid you would not be able to keep up with me. Not even Charlie can do that, and when he is well, he runs very fast for a human. But we could start together."

Rex trotted alongside Ric and Jimmy until they panted and slowed down. Then he wagged his tail. "It was fun to meet you, but now I must do my roadwork. Goodbye!" He bounded forward into a lope. The boys laughed and shouted "Goodbye!" after him. Community policing was fun!

Running felt good. He lengthened his stride. He neared a trio of women joggers on the trail, but there was an empty fútbol pitch to their left. He swung wide, and whooshed past them. Their exclamations sounded more startled or excited than fearful. Being in motion soothed him. He relaxed, uncoiled, extended his stride to the fullest. He flew along the trail, taking the turns, flattening out in the stretches. Oh, yeah. This was the stuff.

Shady called. Pleasure warmed him. "Hello! I am jogging. Hold on a moment." He brought himself down to a gentler lope, panting hard, then a trot, then a walk. It took an uncharacteristically long minute or two to catch his breath. "Oh, that felt so good!"

"Where are you?" Shady asked. "I know Corona is big, but where could you jog?"

His tongue already hung long. He wagged his tail. "Nowhere in Corona Tower is big enough. Ted and Mimi gave me permission to come to Glen Haven Park."

"You went to the park all by yourself?" The vocalizer did not convey emotion well, but he felt certain she was jealous.

"Yes. I am in my work gear. People are surprised to see me, but they do not seem afraid. I met some neighbor boys. They ran with me until I wore them out. Then I really began to run."

"I love you, but right now I am intensely jealous. Pam, did you hear? Rex is jogging by himself in Glen Haven Park and no one is frightened of him."

He couldn't make out how Pam answered, but Shady growled under her breath. "That is what I thought you would say. I am going to talk to Rex now."

Rex stepped off the trail, curled up under a clump of tall bushes. "You are probably having a much more interesting day than I am. I have mostly been useless."

"Not me. Not Razor or Cinnamon, either. SSA Adeyeme may be afraid of us, but she is working us hard in the Morgue."

Rex's irritation flared. "But Cinnamon is an explosives specialist. She should be working with the debris. What are the humans thinking?"

"If SIT Delta received any official information about our specialties, they are not using it. Pam got to give her speech about my skills to Kramer yesterday, but so far all we have done today is pre-autopsies." Shady sighed. "We have done so many, we have filled up the morgue's cooler."

"This is foolish. Why do they not understand?"

"Berwyn tried to suggest changes, but Kramer told him the morgue work comes first."

A new worry rose in his mind. "Are you getting breaks?"

"Our partners have insisted on it, or we probably would not. I checked on my two little Oroplanian girls over Pam's lunch break. They are doing well enough, but the information the investigation can get from children is limited. Two of the adult survivors died last night. The other two are still critical, in the ICU."

"What about our suspicious death from the warehouse?"

"Razor processed her. She was likely a sex slave from the ship, who somehow got away. The men who tried to recapture her broke her neck, maybe by accident. As Kramer pointed out, those slaves were valuable. They would not kill her just from anger. The slashes, bruises, and touch-residue suggest a struggle. She fought hard and suffered injuries to get away."

Rex's hackles prickled. "Who could blame her?" He knew his mate's hot buttons. Sex crimes, especially child abuse and trafficking, infuriated Shady. They shared a moment of silence over the young woman's fate. But a new question nagged. "Why was a sex slave on our dock?"

"The *Izgubil* belonged to the Whisper Syndicate, and part of it was a brothel," Shady said. "It had been parked at that dock for more than a month."

Rex's ears went straight up. "Whisper? In our dock?"

"They never go openly, so they can be anywhere. SIT Alpha's leader is the Chayko System's top law enforcement expert on the Syndicate. Kramer told us he has been tracking this ship for nearly a year. There is no question it belonged to Whisper. I think SIT Alpha will come here to work with Delta soon."

A hot rush of anger made Rex's ears thunder, tightened his throat till it was hard to breathe. He laid back his ears. "That is ridiculous. The case is big enough for two SBI Special Investigations Teams, but they only have three XK9s?"

Shady yawned. "Three very hard-working XK9s. This afternoon we learned we also will be here half the night, tonight. The bodies and body-parts keep coming! I do not know where they will put them all."

"I appreciate your call, especially since you are so busy." Now he felt more useless than ever. His "community policing" efforts paled to irrelevant triviality, next to Shady's work.

She, however, gave a soft whimper. "I miss you. I wanted to —" Rex heard voices in the background. "Sorry! I must go!"

Damn. Rex laid his chin on his forepaws and glared in the direction of a nearby tennis court. He didn't really see it, though. Hot fury surged around inside of him with no release. He was angry with Pam, angry to be sidelined, angry that the humans weren't utilizing their XK9s well. Why didn't they realize what XK9s could really do?

He snapped his ears flat. What was clear to him obviously wasn't clear to the humans in charge. Why not? Well, Chief Klein was following Dr. Ordovich's inefficient protocols. It was as if they'd been designed to hide what XK9s could do. And why expect an outsider from the SBI to know more than Klein could tell her? Shady had said SSA Adeyeme was terrified of dogs. She probably wouldn't have accepted XK9s at all if they hadn't been part of Dr. Chinbat's morgue protocol.

Rex stood with a growl. The investigation needed the whole Pack, and they needed to use them much more effectively. If Rex were in charge—He snorted. Yeah, right. He might be "Pack Leader" to the other XK9s, but that "title" didn't mean anything to the humans.

He lay down again, ears clamped flat and stomach sour. "If I were in charge" was a ridiculous dream. XK9s were just lab equipment on four legs, nothing more. Nobody'd ever put one "in charge" of anything. That was stupid.

Stupid for a dog to daydream at all. Dr. Ordovich always said it would only lead to insubordinate thoughts.

Stupid for a mere, lowly dog to think about how he'd deploy the Pack for better efficiency, if he were in charge. That would never, ever happen.

Stupid, even to imagine how it might feel to go over the evidence, process the bodies, or to make discoveries. That wasn't going to happen for Rex, either. They hadn't called him in, and wouldn't, without Charlie. Chief Klein himself had sent Rex to Dr. Sandler. Dr. Sandler had declared that he was officially on stand-down. And there he'd stay, until Dr. Sandler said he could come back to work.

It didn't matter that he was well now. Didn't matter that he could run and run, with never the slightest rib-twinge. Didn't matter that he might die of boredom before Charlie recovered. *Any* job would be better than this. Even just running scent-discrimination drills—though those were easy-peasy and boring as hell. Why couldn't he walk Bill's patrol beat with him, and practice his community policing?

Because he was on stand-down, rotting into irrelevance, out here *four Precincts away* from the real action. Normally he hated formwork, but he was so desperate for something useful to do, he'd even welcome *that*, right now.

He flicked his ears. Hmm. Come to think of it, he'd never filed his After-Action Report about the events in the Hub. Rather than dreaming stupid daydreams about being in charge, that was one genuinely useful thing he could do. He opened the form. Took the better part of 45 minutes to fill it out in detail.

After he'd hit "file" on his report, he reopened it, to check one little . . .

He tensed. An odd feeling, almost like an earthquake vibrating inside his gut, spread tingling excitement through him.

If . . . if he'd been able to reopen *that* one . . . He held his breath. Slid his gaze to a different file. He wouldn't read anything. He just wanted to know if he could, like, um . . . *open* it.

It opened. His breath wouldn't come for a moment. His heart pounded hard.

He opened another file. The earthquake inside of him made it hard to remember to breathe.

A third.

A fourth.

A rush of joy left him giddy. Rex sprang to his feet. He *had access to the case book. ALL of it.* Here was unanticipated treasure, a relief from his desolation of forced idleness and worry. And ample fodder for his "if I were in charge" dreams. The case book! *The case book!* He did a little dance in the fragrant grass.

Then he stopped, one forepaw raised. He had no business reading SSA Adeyeme's case book. Any puppy in a first-year law enforcement intro class knew that. For him to look at one more bit of it would be a breach of the very security protocols he was sworn to uphold.

Rex lowered his forepaw. Whimpered.

In his mind, the case book shimmered with tantalizing fascination. What he'd glimpsed was the barest hint of a scent he couldn't smell enough of, a fleeting taste of a flavor he never wanted to stop eating.

He shuddered. Every fiber of his being longed to read more. He had no influence to leverage permission to read it . . . but he did not need to ask. There it lay, open to his access through the HUD. He paced in an agitated circle. How long would it continue to be available?

It did not matter. He had no right to read it.

He lay down.

Stood. Whimpered.

Paced another circle.

A wholesale download would surely trigger an alert, as well it should. But SSA Adeyeme was underestimating XK9s, at present. He probably could assume she would continue to do so, and not notice or care if he still had access.

And if she didn't care if he read it, why stand here and dither?

18

CRACKING THE CASE BOOK

Glen Haven Neighborhood and Corona Tower

Rex didn't stop to do any community policing on his way home. The case book weighed literally nothing at all, but knowing he could access it burdened Rex's mind like a heavy load.

Evening rush had swelled the traffic. Glen Haven Transit Terminal Station was packed with people. Rex skirted it, skittish. Dr. Ordovich always claimed he could spot a dog with a guilty secret at fifty paces. Could others?

Rex trotted steadily, head and ears up. Nothing to see, here, folks. This dog has no guilty secrets.

Through the berm-gap, he turned spinward down Rim Eight Road. Traffic had grown heavier. Commuter pedal-buses, motor-bikes, pedestrians, bicycle-riders, even a few auto-nav cars rolled along at a safe and reasonable pace.

Rex felt as if everyone was looking at him.

In fairness, some of them were. Occasionally someone would point or stare. He heard more than one person ask a companion, "Have you ever seen a dog that big?" or "Could that be an XK9?"

The Great Dane didn't greet him, or anyone else. Still sleeping? The Shepherd brothers practiced equal-opportunity barking.

Rex transitioned to the berm-side of Rim Eight Road, farther from Fairleigh property. He passed without undue notoriety. He and his guilty secret returned to the starboard side of the road after he passed Bonita's property line. Food smells wafted through the air. Corona wasn't the only tower where the Family held a communal supper. Rex sniffed, beguiled in spite of his worries.

Mmm. Bonita Family was having Margoog tonight. Someone downslope on Terrace Seven would dine on pulled pork, while someone else was making chili with red beans and habañeros. What was Corona preparing?

Rex walked through evening shadows thickened with the rising mist. A dog with a guilty secret could fade away into such shadows, and not be found till morning, if that was his desire. But Rex smelled . . . Was that tilapia parmesan? Oh, my. The case book might have to wait till after supper. He climbed the curving steps to Corona's gate. Its double sides swung open. "Welcome home, Rex!"

Ted emerged from the kitchen a moment after Rex emerged from the entrance tunnel. He carried a platter of—yes! Tilapia parmesan, with farro pilaf.

Ted grinned. "Right on time for supper! How was your run?"

Rex wagged his tail. "My case of 'the wiggles' has been cured, thank you. No one was afraid of me, I made new friends, and I want to go back again tomorrow."

Ted laughed. "Perfect! Let me set this platter down, and I'll help you out of your gear." Charlie's father gave no sign that he could spot a dog with a guilty secret at fifty paces, or even at arms' length. He hung Rex's gear inside the closet at the courtyard-end of the entrance tunnel, where it would be easy for any Family member to reach. Rex didn't mind leaving it there. It smelled kind of mildewed, anyway.

Rex didn't go upstairs yet. The Master Mix and his guilty secret could wait. The Family was recording greetings to Charlie, for the hospital to play to him during re-gen. "He can't respond," Mimi explained, "but studies have shown people do hear things while they're unconscious. Sometimes those things stick with them. We did this for him the last time, too."

Rex listened to the others speak to the recording. Mostly, they just said their name, "I love you," "I miss you," or that kind of thing.

"I am very grateful you are alive," he told the recording, when it was his turn. "Not being able to sense you through our brain link frightened me. I wish I could share Healing Sleep with you. I miss you more than I can express." Rex couldn't fit everything he wanted to say into just a few short words, but he wanted to include his vocalizer-voice on the Family's audio. He also planned to continue talking with Charlie through the link. Maybe his partner would hear that, too.

Recording finished, he made the rounds to each of the Family's half-dozen courtyard tables. Other times when he and Charlie had been home at suppertime, they'd done this together. Checking in with everyone was part of supper. Tonight, they gave him sad smiles and extra petting. They also slipped him lots more surreptitious leftovers than usual. Maybe he'd be hungry for his own supper of Master Mix later. He burped. Maybe. But it would have to be much later. That tilapia parmesan was really good.

After supper he walked up the stairs, one ear cocked back toward the courtyard. Four of Charlie's cousins, Marilyn, Ari, Kimba, and Luther, covered cleanup duty tonight. The Family shared all kinds of household work, from who cooked to who cleaned up to who was on Family Rotation. All generations, whatever their skills and limitations, had coordinated calendars. Nothing Rex had learned or seen in Transmondia prepared him for this kind of complex Family life. Everybody knew their part, and everybody pitched in. They made it look easy. He stood in awe.

But the case book beckoned, illicit and compelling.

He continued up to fifth floor, then snuggled into Charlie's favorite throw blanket, curled atop Charlie's favorite padded lounge on the inner balcony, near the door to his partner's empty master-bedroom suite. Charlie's scent permeated the blanket. Rex burrowed deeper, comforted to be near his partner in this way, even though the scent had gone stale. *I miss you,* he told his partner through the link. *I want you back!*

Rex couldn't get settled comfortably, however. Surrounded by Charlie's scent, Rex's guilty secret niggled at him with little jabs of shame. Dinner was a reprieve, a moment to relax and distract himself. But now he was face-to-face once again with his intent to do wrong. Would Charlie approve of what he meant to do?

Almost certainly not.

All at once being surrounded by Charlie's scent wasn't so comfortable.

Rex sprang up. He paced onto the unused, leaf-strewn dining-area part of the inner balcony. Crossed it. Crossed back, panting. He didn't have to do this. He could be a good dog. He could try to sleep, try to forget the damned case book. So far, he'd only stretched the rules. Not really broken them.

Oh, but the case book held riches. Answers to certain mysteries. Hours of distraction. Immersion in the professional minutiae that had fascinated him for half his life.

It was a high-level glimpse of a real investigation, in all its messy detail. A high-level glimpse that intrigued and tantalized and seduced him by its very imminent access. The kind of high-level glimpse that dogs never got to see.

This was his one chance.

Probably his one chance ever.

Rex groaned. He'd never forgive himself if he transgressed

tonight. But he'd also never forgive himself if he didn't. *I'm sorry,* he told Charlie through their link. *I have to do this.*

He opened the case book.

Its organizational overview unpacked itself for him, right there on his HUD. Almost like a sign that said *read me.*

Already there were hundreds of files in orderly, logical subdivisions. Rex studied their organization. SSA Adeyeme might not know what to do with XK9s, but her system's elegant structure kept all the information readily available. He opened one. It sucked him right in.

Decisions she'd made about priorities, deployments, and authorizations all seemed well-thought-out. He wagged his tail in frank admiration. He read on with growing respect. So much to learn! New things in each report! If only he could work with Adeyeme's team!

He growled, frustrated. That surely would never happen. Adeyeme might be brave enough to allow XK9s on morgue duty, but she'd have to be legendary to push past her phobia and let Rex in.

Anyway, what could he do for her, without Charlie? He might be able to smell the smells, identify and document them, but he needed Charlie's trained hands to take the samples on scent cards that confirmed the documentation. He might be able to follow a suspect's scent trail, but he needed Charlie to cover the over-watches, secure any needed transportation, take the suspect into custody. Rex couldn't even snap on handcuffs. Without Charlie, what good was he?

None. Melancholy certainty dragged him down. OPD was right. Without Charlie, he was worthless. Stupid to even think about joining in.

But he could read about it. The inexhaustible case book kept growing. Apparently, all parts of the investigation were working late tonight, not just Shady's.

She, Razor and Cinnamon . . . Rex halted. Deep, throat-clutching longing ambushed him. Despair pierced his heart with a physical pang, hung on with a heavy ache. If he could only see them again! For several moments, nothing else existed in his mind. He gasped. His wave of grief slowly ebbed. He panted, ears down. Rode it out. To see them . . . that was a futile wish, too.

He buried himself in the case book, desperate for distraction. For well or ill, his access never faltered.

Late in the evening, Shady called. "I just wanted to say good night. We are released to go home at last."

He was awake tonight. If only she could come back! Better not even speak of it. "How many bodies did you process?"

She yawned. "It is no longer quite accurate to speak of 'bodies,' unfortunately. We had mostly whole ones until mid-afternoon, but since then it has been what Dr. Chinbat's techs called 'meat puzzles.' The shrapnel did terrible things to them. I have identified body parts of twenty-three different individuals, but often there was little more we could discern than simply that this is from a different individual than those other pieces over there. Most were humans. A few ozzirikkians. We also found the leg of a vicurrian."

Rex blinked, startled. "A vicurrian? I did not know they ever came to the Chayko System."

Shady gave a soft growl. "The joint was cut cleanly. Dr. Chinbat speculated that this leg might have come from the kitchen."

A prickle of revulsion ran through Rex, ended in a shudder. "But vicurrians are sapient!"

"Apparently, to some people, that makes them all that much more of a delicacy. The *Izgubil* catered to all manner of perversions, not just the sexual ones."

Rex laid his ears back. "I fear I have begun to lose my compassion for some of those victims."

"I keep my thoughts on the children and the slaves. In any case, we must process them all with equal care. And I am sure we all shall have sweet dreams tonight."

"Of course you will." Rex stress-yawned. "I wish I could be there to distract you."

She sighed. "Do not make it worse. I love you. Good night." She clicked off.

"I love you too," he said into the dead com.

He returned to the case book. He finished his review about 01:20. He sat still for several minutes after that, letting all the information settle. So many inputs already, and yet . . . The data on the debris seemed awfully thin. What kind of analysis were they doing?

He went back over it again. Granted, this was early days, but there was lots more data from the Morgue and the background-information searches than there was on the debris. Shady's commander, LSA Kramer, seemed to be making considerably more progress than her counterpart, the LSA named Shiva Shimon.

Rex found his reports on all the pallets his team had received. Shimon described how loads of debris been coming in by the tonne—more with every shift. His people had laid them out in the evidence cavern, organized by the sector where they were retrieved. A scaffolding stood ready, so evidence could be placed in relative proximity to where it was believed to have originated on the ship. The Station Defense Force was coordinating the retrieval, taking care to record where the debris had been collected.

But where was the analysis?

Shimon's team definitely wasn't doing it. From the tone of some of his reports, he was frustrated to the point of cursing about this. Shimon blamed the SDF.

This helped explain why the investigation wasn't using Cinnamon more effectively. But not doing any analysis at all made no sense. Rex snorted. What were they waiting for?

Apparently it was the SDF. The SDF must be in charge of analyzing the debris. The impression Rex had formed of

Adeyeme made that seem the only possible reason for such a holdup. But why weren't any SDF analysts doing their work?

Rex growled. He knew about debris analysis. He and the rest of the Pack had received specialized training and certification in the analysis of aircraft debris. XK9s could scent-link pieces to aid in the reconstructions of wrecked aircraft parts. The Pack's explosives specialists, Tuxedo, Cinnamon, and Crystal, could identify dozens of different explosive substances. They'd been trained to help deduce from various markers how the substances had been employed. That was for aircraft debris, granted. But how much different could spacecraft debris truly be?

Rex's pulse thumped hard with rising excitement. He pictured how it could be done, down in the evidence cavern among the pallets. He and the Pack's explosives specialists already had done something like this for an aircraft. Of course, that had been on a much smaller scale. It had been unauthorized, a puppy game, but they'd done it. Without human help.

And they'd analyzed it correctly. Their professors hadn't dared tell Dr. Ordovich about it. They'd warned Rex and his Packmates to silence forever. But Rex knew. Tux, Cinnie, and Crys did, too. They had done it.

And they could do it again for the *Izgubil.* But SSA Adeyeme had no reason to listen to Rex. Worse, she had all kinds of reasons not to. No influence existed that Rex could use to leverage this situation. He should put the whole idea out of his mind.

But he couldn't.

He paced back and forth until he was too tired to pace anymore, too worn out to think. Finally, exhausted, he returned to the lounge. To Charlie's blanket

Charlie would not approve of Rex's reading the case book. But Charlie was the only human who'd ever been willing to listen to him. Charlie'd even occasionally agreed that Rex might be right about things Dr. Ordovich said were wrong.

Oh, Charlie! I need to talk with you! You'd know what to do. You could guide me.

But Charlie wasn't there. Charlie couldn't answer. His absence echoed through Rex like a physical ache. Rex buried his face in Charlie's blanket, but it gave him no answers, either. Rex whimpered, empty and alone.

Charlie's scent grew colder and colder, but after a while, in spite of that, Rex slept.

19

REX TAKES A HIKE

Corona Tower

Dark Hub corridor. *Run!* Panic hammered in Rex's pulse. His breath rasped. His chest burned. Something evil grabbed, barely missed.

Rex hurtled away. Tethered, Charlie dragged, bounced, slammed behind him, helpless.

Elmo Smart the mugger sprang out from the shadows. Leveled his EStee.

Rex flinched away. *Smash!* Enormous berthing cone.

Rex tumbled in a bunker.

Charlie! Charlie! What have I done?

Rex landed hard, then hunched where he fell. Tense, dizzy, disoriented, he panted. His breath came in short, strangled gasps. The dream's terror ebbed in time with his pulse, thump by thump, slowing back to normal. He licked his lips. Yawned. What a nightmare!

Must get his bearings. Misty night-smells surrounded him. Corona's distinctive oak tree, the sharp, night-scent of tomatoes, the furled, musky marigolds, the crisp green smell of cucumbers.

Charlie's balcony. He was in Corona Tower, but not in his

bed. He sat up on the decking.

His HUD said 03:48. *Wow.* Almost exactly two days ago, the dock breach had begun. He'd been asleep . . . maybe an hour, so far? Charlie's throw blanket—or what was left of it—twined in shreds around his legs. He struggled free of the dismembered blanket. Retreated inside.

His bed was cold, but it still smelled of Shady.

His chest tightened. He whimpered, then returned to the deck. With care, he gathered the pieces of Charlie's blanket into his mouth, then carried them back to his bed. If he couldn't have his two most-beloved people present with him, he could at least keep their fading scents close by, for as long as those scents lingered. He arranged the shreds of Charlie's blanket across from a spot where Shady must have lain for most of last night. Then he positioned himself between them, turned three times, and lay down.

But not to sleep.

With a growl, he re-ran the dream in his mind. He could make sense of what had inspired most of it. But why dream about Elmo? Everything else belonged in the Hub. Had the mugger somehow been there too?

Rex walked back in his memory through the *real* Hub chase, the one that had ended so disastrously. He slowed it down in his mind, so he could step through each scent and every bit of evidence, to pick up things he hadn't noticed before. Whenever Rex did that, Charlie grumbled that *he* couldn't do that with *his* memories. But the ability came in handy sometimes. Rex had already done a cursory version of this in the park when he wrote his report. Now he looked at even the tiniest details. Why had he dreamed of Elmo?

At last he found it: Elmo's scent on the handholds and wall pads of the corridor outside the *Izgubil's* berthing cone. A few stale whiffs, but a distinct profile. Possible to smell despite micrograv's congestive effects on his nose. Rex's dream was right. Elmo *had* been at the Hub.

But he'd been there days before Rex, and not alone. He'd been part of a larger group. Their outward-bound olfactory traces overlapped a slightly earlier scent-trail of the same group headed toward the ship. There could be no mistake: Elmo and his buddies had used that corridor to go to the *Izgubil*. A few hours later, they'd left the same way. It had happened about eight days before the breach. If Rex could retrieve those corridor pads, he could prove it.

Had the pads and hand-holds been destroyed in the dock breach? A lot of the dock was reportedly wrecked. But DPO Fujimoto *had* expanded the crime scene "to where XK9 Rex stops." Those surfaces should've been preserved as part of the extended crime scene, if they'd survived at all.

Rex laid back his ears. The last remaining *Izgubil* survivors couldn't tell the investigators anything. The Whisper Syndicate wouldn't cooperate with the SBI. Who else could SSA Adeyeme's team interview, who'd been on the ship?

Elmo Smart.

Rex stood up in his bed, hackles stiff. Elmo was likely the only living and conscious adult they could clearly identify who had definitely been on the ship, and whom they could question about it.

SSA Adeyeme needed to know this.

Rex growled. But how to tell her? How to tell her so she would pay attention, that is.

He could ask Shady to tell her, but would any human credit a second-hand account from a dog? No, of course not. All Shady would succeed in doing was get Pam kicked off the Task Force, if she made too much of a fuss.

Frustration tightened Rex's throat. How could he make SSA Adeyeme pay attention to this information?

What if Rex went, himself? What if he made it impossible for her not to listen to him?

But how could he do that?

Well, that part was fuzzy. Worse, he probably would have to

be insubordinate, to manage it. He'd get a beating or spend several long days in a Dark Crate. More likely, both.

His back hunched, his skin crawled and cringed. Those were not small things. He never wanted to face either one, ever again.

But he was a sworn officer. Wasn't it his duty to place himself in harm's way for the good of the investigation and for public safety? He groaned. Of course it was. In dangerous situations, they always sent the dog in first. It was his job.

Rex leaped up. He paced the length of his bedroom and back several times, his gut in a knot. He'd Chosen Charlie, in part, because he'd smelled and acted like a gentle human, less likely to beat his XK9 partner. But Charlie wasn't here. The OPD was definitely following the XK9 Project's protocols. Charlie'd said so, and the Pack's separation was proof. Therefore, the department must be prepared with capture-nets and trank rifles, should the need arise. And also with beating straps and Dark Crates, although Rex had not seen any. So far.

He shuddered, but tried to think logically. Did any part of that change his duty to report what he knew? Did it? Truly? He couldn't see any way that it did. He must find ways to leverage his influence for a better outcome, so he could execute his duty. And try not to think about the consequences.

But what influence could he use? Bill had said he had influence because he was valuable. He was valuable because he was extremely good at his job. Top of his class. Rex blinked. He hadn't thought much about his overall record, but he'd never failed a test in his whole life, except a few times when he'd been over-confident. Re-tests had all been perfect. He'd never scored below Number One in olfaction competitions, in races, in . . . well, in anything he'd ever been asked to do, throughout all of his XK9 Training. Shouldn't that count for something?

He gasped, then opened his jaws to pant. No, that was the wrong way to think. *Asking* was what Dr. Ordovich wanted dogs to do. But if Rex did what Dr. Ordovich wanted, he would fail in this duty. Instead of asking, "shouldn't that count for something?" Rex must say, "That should mean a great deal." Then prove it.

Shady had said SSA Adeyeme had courage. He'd seen for himself that she was an intelligent organizer. Was she brave and bright enough to listen to him? *That* was the question to ask.

He knew only one way to learn the answer.

Glen Haven Transit Terminal Station and spinward locations

Rex stood by the closed platform gate at Rim Eight's Glen Haven Transit Terminal Station. His frustration smoldered. Less welcome was the nagging worry-voice that said maybe he was wrong. But no. He was on an important mission. He must persevere.

As far as the Family knew, Rex was headed back to the park for another jog, so he was kitted out in his full OPD gear. He *looked* official.

Unfortunately, the conductor wasn't buying it. His scent factors smelled like those of the nurse in ICU. "We don't let loose, unaccompanied dogs on our trains."

Rex could walk all the way to Central Plaza, but he'd rather ride. He focused on his mission. "Have you consulted with your Security Officer? It is my understanding that the policy does not apply to the Orangeboro Peace Department's XK9 officers."

The conductor scowled. "Don't need to. The rules are clear. Dogs are dogs."

Rex swallowed, held his temper. An incident from two years ago rose in his memory. He'd planned a prank on Dr. Ordovich, but needed access to a place he shouldn't go. There'd been a civilian contractor on-site. "Kindly accommodate me, sir," he'd said to the man. "My assignment necessitates the acquisition of a supplemental accessory within the confines of this edifice." That fellow'd frozen for a moment, stared at him. But then he'd let him in. Would polysyllabic words also dazzle this conductor? Couldn't hurt to try. "Kindly accommodate me, sir—"

"No." The conductor's bushy white eyebrows did not budge from their forbidding scowl. He stepped back inside the train and closed the door. Metal pedestrian shields rose to lock into place at the edge of the platform. A moment later a shrill whistle and a blaze of flashing lights announced the train's departure.

So much for the magic of polysyllabic words. Rex growled, but he kept it under his breath. Time for Plan B. Well, okay, Plan C or D. No Family "hospital expedition" would make the trek to Orangeboro Medical Center today. It would've been nice to hitch a ride with them, then somehow evade them after that. But he hadn't dared tell Ted or anyone else about his mission, much less risk asking for help getting to OPD Central HQ.

No. Permission could be denied. Rex imagined what Dr. Ordovich would say. Permission *would* be denied. Then Rex would be in the terrible position of having to be *openly* insubordinate. If he didn't ask, they wouldn't forbid him to go, and he wouldn't have to disobey direct orders. His conscience was already guilty enough. Far better to ask forgiveness afterward!

Nor could he ask Bill for help. Even if Bill was still his Personnel Assistance Liaison, Dr. Sandler had put Rex on standdown. Bill had to follow OPD rules, and Rex was skirting those today. It wouldn't be right to ask Bill to help him do that.

In the bright light of day, his mission sounded crazy, even to Rex himself. "I have a tip that is vital to the *Izgubil* investigation. I need to go to OPD Central HQ, to tell SSA Adeyeme about it." He'd practiced that appeal several times in front of the triple mirror across from Charlie's walk-in closet, but he'd never been able to look himself in the eye while saying it. Even though it was true, if he couldn't even face himself, how could he convince anyone else?

The train pulled out. Rex stood on the platform and watched it go.

Damn. Better start walking.

Somewhere in the middle of Seventh Precinct, it occurred to Rex that he'd never actually walked *all the way* from Corona Tower to Central Plaza before, although he'd never doubted until now that he could do it. Getting this far had taken a long time. He was tired already. A kilometer seemed a whole lot farther on foot than in a vehicle. He'd always caught the train or ridden in some other conveyance with Charlie. It was only a twenty-minute ride going straight from Corona to Central HQ in an auto-nav or by motorbike.

He'd set his com to "do not disturb," so no one could interfere while he was en route. The return order he couldn't hear was a return order he didn't have to disobey. He also took pains to avoid OPD patrols, keeping to bushes and side streets or drainage features, although it felt strange and wrong to avoid members of his own agency. But if the Family noticed him missing, they'd call the OPD. A search would ensue. Even if that didn't happen, any patrolling officer who noticed an unaccompanied XK9 would investigate. Rex hadn't dared to leave his badge at home, but it did contain a locator. He must not have been identified as missing, yet, because no search had descended upon him. But the longer his trek dragged on, the likelier that became.

Cold, queasy anxiety filled him. He panted harder. His pulse pounded in his ears, in his throat, in his chest. Rex stumbled. He put his head down. Ran one of Charlie's breathing patterns and kept walking until the dark spots cleared from the edges of his vision.

But his legs shook. His belly felt weird. He slipped behind a clump of bushes next to a wall, to refocus. He stress-yawned. Again. Again. His panting slowed till he no longer feared he'd hyperventilate. His pulse slowed, too. But that sickly-slick, quicksilver fear wreaking havoc with his gut didn't let up so easily.

He had a good reason to talk with SSA Adeyeme.

He was not trying to be bad or insubordinate. So far it had just worked out that way.

All he wanted to do was get information to her that she needed, in a way that couldn't be ignored. He could do this. He must do this. It was his duty as a sworn officer. His limbs gradually stopped shaking. Just keep walking, that's what he must do. He was frightened. That was natural. But the only thing to do now was press on.

By the time he made it to the Precinct Line between Seventh and Sixth, all of him hurt. He really wished he'd been able to ride that train. He wasn't in shape for this. He'd grown soft, despite the roadwork he and Charlie did each day. He took a moment to stretch his aching muscles. The panniers held little besides his basic gear and a few waterlogged scent cards, but he'd never realized they were so heavy.

Head down. Duty beckoned. No turning back.

He figured he surely must've worn the first layer of skin off all his pads by the time he stopped at the top of the shallow half-bowl of concentric terraces outside the OPD Central HQ entrance. He lifted a forefoot: no bloody prints. *Huh.*

But anyway, he'd made it! It hardly seemed possible, but here he was. He lay down under the nearest orange tree with a sigh, careful to keep himself as visually inconspicuous as a 132-kilo dog possibly could be. Seven kilometers was a pretty long hike. He yawned, half stress-yawn, half from fatigue. Lowered his chin onto his forelegs.

Oh, that felt too good. Time to move!

Anxiety bubbled in his gut. He worked his way along the terraces, moving silently behind benches and around planters, wary of the surveillance array. Lucky for him, the crowds were thin at this hour, and most of the people nearby seemed preoccupied. He stopped between a bench and a terrace wall, near the base of the left entrance ramp.

Worry seized him in a harder grip. His pulse pounded in his

ears. This was where it all could fall apart. He'd considered trying to sneak in through the sally port's bustle, but the security there was beefier than at the front desk. Here, he might only have to convince one officer—if his badge didn't simply let him in. He licked his lips, consciously slowed his panting. Hyperventilating wouldn't help.

Don't think, just go.

He entered Central HQ's high-ceilinged, airy atrium, with its reinforced-glass outer walls, inner "green wall" of decorative living plants, and pleasantly gurgling water feature like a minor waterfall. So far, so good. A little hope rose in him. Maybe if he acted as if he belonged here—

"Halt! Where is your partner, XK9?" The desk officer was a middle-aged woman with L. COLLINS on her name-tag.

Crap. Nothing had been easy so far; why expect it now? Rex approached the tall, wall-like desk with his ears up, pulse thudding. His tail waved gently, but each even breath took conscious effort. "Good afternoon, Officer Collins. My partner, Detective Morgan, is unfortunately still in the hospital."

Behind her reinforced-glass shield, Collins's frown deepened. "If Morgan's hospitalized, why are you here?"

No need for lies: he had a legitimate reason. "I have remembered a scent profile I detected just before the dock breach. I wish to speak with one of the SBI agents about a connection I believe I have made."

Collins studied him.

Rex tried to appear open, to hide his dread that she would call for a capture team.

Her gaze shifted to a middle-distance HUD stare. Her mouth tightened. "XK9 Rex Dieter-Nell. You are on stand-down for health leave. You are not authorized to be here."

Rex swallowed a growl, strove to think clearly. "Does this mean I am officially too sick to work, so therefore I should walk another seven kilometers back home, without delivering the very important information I came to share?"

She frowned. "Walk *another* seven kilometers? What are you talking about?"

Rex licked his lips, shifted from one sore foot to another. "You appear to have found my file. Therefore, you know I live in the Ninth Precinct. That is seven kilometers away, and the train has a "no dogs" policy. As you see, I have gone to some effort to get here. I am convinced my information is important. Now, may I please speak to an SBI agent or a member of the Task Force?"

She scowled at him. "Sit. Stay there."

Rex sat with a sigh but tried to keep his hopes up. She hadn't banished him. She hadn't immediately called for a capture team. She was . . . maybe she was actually getting him clearance to enter. His feet hurt all the way up to his hackles, not to mention his pounding head. What he mainly wanted at this point was a nice big drink of water, a snack, and a nap. His "sit" quickly slid into a "down."

He couldn't hear anything she was doing or saying through the shielding and bulk of the desk. She'd disappeared from his view. Where'd she go? What was she up to? Was he being a putz, sitting here waiting for the net?

He lurched to his feet, sniffed around the OPD PERSONNEL ONLY entrance, and just for the heck of it tried his badge on the scanner. It made a *bzzzt* noise and flashed an ACCESS DENIED message.

"Here, now! What are you doing?" Collins reappeared, scowling again.

"It seemed worth a try," Rex said. "You disappeared."

Her mouth twisted with irritation. "I'm *busy*. Don't XK9s know 'sit' and 'stay'?"

Dark fury boiled up from his heart. He snapped his ears flat but struggled to keep his tone civil and his hackles down. "Do most humans respond well to those?"

Then he froze. Holy crap! Had he just said that *out loud?* Cold horror filled him. What an insubordinate thing to say! He was in for a beating now, for sure.

But she only sighed. "*Please,* go sit down and stay put."

He blinked, disbelieving. That was all? 'Please'? He drew in a shaky breath, retreated to sit by the water feature. Ranans. Sometimes he couldn't predict them *at all.* Didn't mean he wasn't in trouble.

Collins looked away, focused on something he couldn't see.

That water smelled good. He was parched from all the walking and panting. He flicked out his tongue to taste the water, unable to resist. Oh, my. Either he was thirstier than he'd thought, or that was really delicious water. He lapped it greedily.

"XK9 Rex!" Officer Collins cried. "That's a water *feature,* not a water *fountain!*"

Who knew when he'd get his next drink? He kept lapping, thankful for the vocalizer. "I apologize, but I am very thirsty after walking seven kilometers."

She grimaced. "You *are* housebroken, right?"

What a great idea. Why hadn't he thought of that? "You are a wise woman. As it happens, there are XK9-adapted toilet facilities just down the main corridor at cross-hallway B." Thirst slaked for the moment, he turned to meet her unamused look.

"Oh, and let me guess—you need the facility."

Rex wagged his tail. "What a perceptive human you are." He cocked his head. Insubordinate impulses filled him, irresistible in the moment. "Unless you'd prefer I use the water feature for that, too?"

"You *wouldn't!*"

Rex sidled up to it, half-panicked at his own audacity. Could this possibly work? He sniffed around a little. Lifted his hind—

"*Don't you DARE!*" Collins was already halfway out through the OPD PERSONNEL ONLY door.

Rex closed the distance in one bound. He made it inside before she could realize she'd been played—then kept going. "Thank you, Officer Collins!"

20

SHADY SMELLS BAD THINGS

Orangeboro Morgue

The putrid smell grew stronger, the nearer they approached. Shady stopped on the top step. Stared down toward the Borough Morgue. This was like confronting a wall of horrid, revolting odor. Their late lunch break hadn't been *remotely* long enough.

"Oh, God, I think it's worse, just since we left." Pam's tone echoed the disgust in her face. "How much longer are they gonna argue?" She seemed in no more hurry to start down the steps than Shady.

Liz groaned. "More to the point, how much longer are they gonna make us work in that?" She stopped next to Pam, glanced at her partner. "Razor, how can you smell anything through that stench?"

"It is becoming increasingly difficult." Razor's hackles rippled.

He sure got that right. A dog could only smell through so much. Shady stifled a growl. Officials had known two days ago that there'd be at least fifty incoming morgue clients. Way too many bodies and meat puzzles for this facility. But the actual count of individuals had since ballooned to seventy, with all the chunks and shreds of formerly-living beings still not collected. The need to move to a larger morgue facility had never been in question.

Except when it came to who'd pay for it.

According to Pam and Balchu's news feeds, SBI, Borough, SDF, Wheel, and Station-government-level officials had all been wrangling over the cost, and who'd pay for what, since the ship first blew up.

SDF recovery teams had slowed deliveries to only what the morgue could process in one day. Unprocessed body-parts in shielded, space-based cold storage would keep better and be more secure than unprocessed body-parts, stacked up in the hallway outside the morgue.

But after processing, they still must be refrigerated. Somewhere.

That's where the problems had arisen. They couldn't be cremated or composted until the investigation released them, but sometimes further tests needed to be run. They'd released all they could to Families, but many of the *Izgubil* dead would likely never be identified, much less claimed. Dr. Chinbat's cooler had been packed floor-to-ceiling until there literally was no more room. Neighboring departments had begun to complain bitterly about the smell coming from the triple-decker carts parked just outside the cooler's door.

Inside the morgue . . . well, even the feeblest human nose had no difficulty detecting the odors. That was true, even *with* the dozen industrial-strength air purifiers cranked to full-throttle that crowded the space between cooler and autopsy area.

Berwyn halted next to Pam and Liz. He made a disgusted noise in his throat. "I hoped if I kept it to a light lunch I wouldn't get so nauseated."

Liz grimaced. "How's that working out for you?"

Berwyn strapped on his respirator. "Aw, nuts. I think the smell's gotten into my filter, too." His voice came out muffled.

"Why wouldn't it? It's gotten into everything else," Pam said. "People avoided me in the street when I went home last night. The minute we got home, Balchu made me put all my clothes in the sanitizer."

If it hadn't increased her ability to smell, Shady would've lolled her tongue. In fairness, Balchu always looked for reasons to encourage Pam to strip down, but there'd been no lack of a plausible excuse last night. They seemed to have fun showering together, but then they insisted on bathing *Shady,* too. This knocked the smell back enough that Pam and Balchu, at least, seemed able to live with it. But Shady could still smell it.

"May I take a fresh air break now?" Cinnamon asked.

"We just got here," Berwyn said.

"Please?"

"You haven't even started working!"

"*Please?*"

"Wuss."

"You call me a wuss?" Cinnamon snapped her ears flat. "Who is wearing a respirator?"

"Not that it's making much difference."

Dr. Chinbat appeared at the doorway. "You're all wusses. Get in here!"

Chastened, they trooped down the steps.

Shady had barely completed her initial over-sniff of a human child's partial torso on her table, however, before voices in the hallway made everyone look up.

"Chief Klein, I really don't think this is called for," a querulous voice protested.

"Oh, no, I absolutely think it is demanded." Good thing Shady didn't need to smell the Chief's scent factors to detect his iron purpose.

Querulous coughed. "I seriously—Chief, I'm begging you, *please.*"

"Oh, hell, no. You don't get off this hook until I get the obvious answer. You and your accursed bean-counter buddies have forced my officers to work in this environment for two straight days. I *insist.*" Klein hauled a slender, older man in a business suit through the morgue's doorway with a firm hand clamped around his upper arm. "Here you go, Darius. Take a nice, deep breath! *Smell* that lovely aroma!"

Darius coughed again, longer and harder. Sounded just short of retching. He groaned.

"Isn't that a *glorious* smell?" Klein cried. "Wouldn't you just *love* to spend the whole day here? Our victims' last hope of justice is us, speaking for them. Do you think this *wonderful aroma* is the best possible environment for analytical, coherent thought?"

Shady fanned the air with her tail, but she resisted a tongue-loll.

Darius clapped a thin, pale hand over his mouth and nose. "You don't understand what we're up against."

"Well, that's true," Klein said. "No police chief has ever needed to worry about turf battles. What was I thinking? Okay. So why don't you tell me all about it?"

Darius shuddered. "If you'll just come with me, back to—"

"What? And leave this glorious smell? Oh, no. I wouldn't dream of it." Klein dragged him closer to the door of Chinbat's cooler. "Let's talk right here, about all the terrible things *you're* up against." He offered a fierce smile to Dr. Chinbat, who strode toward them. "Anika and I are eager to hear all about them."

"Kwame, I'm begging you. I have respiratory issues." There was that half-retching cough again.

"You know, Darius, I do understand." Chief Klein almost sounded sympathetic, if you ignored the look on his face. "It's really not that healthy an environment here, is it?"

More retching coughs racked the older man's slender frame. "No," he managed.

"Imagine working here for days on end." Klein's voice went hard. "Is that healthy, do you think?"

Darius shook his head, unable to speak for coughing.

"Kwame." There was a note of worry in Dr. Chinbat's voice.

"Oh, no. I have to be sure he's going to fund the obvious. Till then, he stays right here."

Darius nodded his head, endured another coughing spasm, then choked out, "okay."

Klein's brows went up. "'Okay,' what, Darius?"

Darius gasped, coughed, gasped. "Funds. You've got—" More coughing.

Dr. Chinbat shook her head. "Kwame, he's—"

"I knew you'd see the light." Klein wrapped an arm around Darius' shoulders, then propelled him rapidly toward the doorway. "You just needed a clear *gasp* of all the facts. Now let's get you into a better atmosphere, so you can document everything you now know needs to be done. Or we'll be back." He glanced toward the M.E. "Come with us, Anika. I'm sure you have some insights I don't."

Dr. Chinbat stared after the two men, then turned. Her frown swept across everyone in the morgue. They all gazed back at her. "Take thirty," she said. "Lock it down and stay close, but clear your lungs. Go to the courtyard. I'll be back." She stripped off her gloves and face mask, shucked out of her lab coat, then hung it on a hook by the door.

Pam put down her scent cards. "That works for me."

"The courtyard" was one of several areas in the Civic Center complex designed to be open to the sky. Benches stood between walls with espaliered fruit trees, or near other walls planted with vertical gardens of salad greens. Gardeners tended the courtyards daily; their harvests helped supply several of the Civic Center's restaurants.

Like most of the Station, most of the courtyard was agricultural as well as decorative, but part of its center was devoted to simple grass. A couple of the morgue techs spread a quilt across one sunny end of it, then lay down with their eyes closed and their arms crossed to form pillows. Other humans sat on benches, chatting quietly. Shady, Cinnamon, and Razor flopped down on the rest of the grass, tongues long, tails waving.

Shady still smelled a distinct undercurrent of morgue, both from the nearby facility and on the fur or clothing of her companions, but the air was fresher here. That warm light felt good, too.

"I already liked Chief Klein," Cinnamon said. "After this afternoon, I like him even more."

Razor lolled his tongue. "Darius, whoever he is, didn't stand a chance."

"He's the Borough Treasurer," one of the techs on the quilt said, without opening her eyes. "He's been holding out for the SBI to cover all the costs to create a morgue annex, even though all the other agencies have agreed to a different division of expenses."

"Oh. Thank you," Cinnamon said. "He really was the problem, then."

The tech's companion propped himself up on one elbow. "Susan, do you realize you just talked politics with a dog?"

Startled astonishment shot through the woman's scent factors. She raised her head. "What?"

"And we appreciate it," Cinnamon said.

Razor wagged his tail. "Usually only our partners tell us how things work."

"Well, I'll be damned." She lay back down.

Shady flicked her ears, grateful neither Dr. Ordovich nor Dr. Imre had been here to catch that exchange. According to them, it was insubordinate for XK9s to talk about the affairs of their betters, even if they were only curious. XK9s—well, Rex, anyway —had been beaten for doing so.

She rested her chin on her forepaws and closed her eyes. Enough thinking about Odious Ordovich. She wanted to enjoy her unexpected break. That morgue stench must be doing strange things to her nose, though. Now she'd almost swear she could smell the man. Good thing she wasn't trying to make forensic distinctions.

Beside her, Cinnamon tensed. She gave a low growl.

Razor's growl rumbled deep and angry, a bass underscore to Cinnamon's.

Shady lifted her head, queasy with misgivings. How was this possible? Her Packmates' reactions ruled out a fluke or a trick of the morgue-stench. She really did smell Dr. Ordovich.

He was still out of sight, somewhere off to their right. But his unmistakable scent drifted past them ever more strongly. A slow, cool current of moving air carried four humans' scents from a colonnade that led to the sally port. Ordovich, two other men, and a woman approached the courtyard. One of the men was Chief Klein's aide Archy. She didn't recognize the others.

"—have seriously begun to think you mean to give us a run-around." Dr. Ordovich sounded almost as querulous as Treasurer Darius.

"I'm sorry you feel that way," Archy replied. "You did arrive with no advance notice, and our XK9s are deployed all over the Borough."

"Good," Ordovich said. "Glad to hear you're following the protocols. We had some problems with our dogs in Neopolis. Very unfortunate. We had to recall them, then put them down because of a late-appearing mutation that affected their behavior."

Shady's heart seemed to stop for an instant. What? *No!* She knew the XK9 pair who'd gone to Neopolis. Fernie and Chaser were mates. Brilliant generalists like Rex, they could do pretty much everything well. *Put down?* Horror dizzied her. *No!* She smelled parallel reactions in Razor and Cinnamon.

"Figured I'd better make spot inspections where our other dogs are working." Ordovich's voice sounded ever-nearer. "Better to head off troubles, you know. Are any of your dogs acting insubordinate?"

Shady exchanged a terrified look with Cinnamon. Her sister-

Packmate's suggestion that the Ranans couldn't stop Shady at the hospital . . . Shady's own bound up the steps past the man who'd tried to stop her . . . was that the kind of thing Fernie and Chaser had been killed for?

"No, ours are all behaving beautifully," Archy said. "We do have three XK9s posted to the morgue right now. Since they're here in the Civic Center, I thought we'd see them first."

Through their link, Shady sensed Pam's deep anger. *They'll have to put ME down first.* Pam hadn't been far away, but now she, Berwyn and Liz converged on their XK9s' patch of grass. Pam's hand slid across Shady's shoulder. Pam's scent flared hot and sharp and fierce.

Berwyn stepped between Cinnamon and Ordovich's direction. He scowled toward the shadowed colonnade from the sally port, crossed his arms. Liz and Pam flanked him, their faces and scent factors resolute, their body stances protective. Shady, Cinnamon and Razor peered out from around their legs, heads low, ears back.

"All in the same place?" Ordovich stepped into the courtyard, his infamous scowl directed at Archy. A cold-eyed woman followed Ordovich. She wore civilian business garb, but her posture and stride paralleled those of the military officers who'd frequented the XK9 Project's facilities for most of Shady's life. The third man had to bend slightly to exit the colonnade. Dressed in Ranan Executive Security black, he stood several centimeters taller than the others.

"It's for the *Izgubil* case," Archy said. "They're pulling overtime shifts, as it is."

"Oh. Well—" Ordovich stopped to stare across the courtyard, zeroed in immediately on Shady, Cinnamon, and Razor. "They don't seem too busy."

Archy stopped too. "Um, I'm not sure what has happened." He strode forward, his face pinched with puzzlement. Ordovich marched alongside as if he were in charge, the woman at his heels. Their large escort in black trailed them in silence.

Assistant Medical Examiner Chin-Hua met them halfway. "We're on temporary stand-down." she directed her words pointedly to Archy. "Chief Klein, Dr. Chinbat, and Treasurer Darius are settling some budget issues."

A knowing grin spread across Archy's face. "Ah."

Ordovich ignored Archy. He'd already turned his scowl on Dr. Chin-Hua. "How *have* the dogs been behaving?"

21

REX FALLS IN LOVE

OPD HQ and Civic Center Sub-Level 3, Corridor 9 SBI Investigative Center, AKA "S-3-9"

Rex bounded down OPD Central HQ's main corridor to cross-hallway B, heart pounding much harder than his exertion demanded. Alert for any sound of a chase, any whiff of an ambush, he hung a sharp left and kept going. His back prickled with dread of capture. One ear cocked backward, one forward, he loped past cubicles, took several turns, then slowed to a wary trot.

Where were his pursuers? They surely must arrive soon. It made no sense for Collins not to have sent anyone after him. He stopped, uneasy. He'd explained what he wanted. Was he walking into a trap?

Trap or no, his duty was clear. The case book had said SIT Delta's war room was on Sub-Level 3, Room 9. Where was that? He reactivated his com, although this might further betray him. At least a dozen message-signals beeped as they downloaded; a little line of blinking lights begged for his attention. Queasy, he minimized that channel. He used his HUD to open a floor plan, with a dot to mark his location. Ah. Even though floor plans rarely helped him much, he could see the access wasn't far.

Too jittery for a potentially long, exposed wait for the elevator to Sub-Level Three, he found stairs nearby. Padded down them as quietly as he could. He met no one, although many humans had come this way in the past few hours. He reached the third sub-level still un-trapped, but jumpy.

He hesitated at the stairway door. The corridor was empty. Distinctive smells beckoned. He followed. His heart pounded harder, the closer he drew to S-3-9. Would they listen to him? He paused at the entrance. Steeled himself to leverage his influence for a better outcome. He did belong here. These humans just didn't know it yet.

He stepped inside. An enormous storage area sprawled to the left, echoing with voices and machinery. He glanced in. Dozens of tall, labeled pallets lay in orderly ranks. They smelled of space-exposure. Must be LSA Shimon's evidence cavern, with the as-yet-unanalyzed tonnes of debris from the *Izgubil*. It was even more enormous and daunting in real life than he'd imagined.

To his right lay a well-lit area populated with intent, focused individuals at workstations, an empty conference table strewn with pads, and several large wall-screens. The war room? He walked in, head and tail half-down. Nothing to look at here, folks. You never saw me. But where was Adeyeme? Surely one small, dark-skinned human with a severe dog-phobia wouldn't be that hard to find. One of the analysts glanced at him, but he kept moving.

"Hold it right there, Dog!" a man ordered.

Rex froze. Mustn't cringe. He was here for a good reason. He drew a careful breath, then turned with ears up and hackles down to face a tall blond man. Three pips and a star on his collar meant only one person. Rex wagged his tail. "Hello, LSA Shimon."

The big blond agent scowled at Rex, his feet slightly apart

and knees flexed, as if prepared to react. His scent spiked hot and fiercely protective. "Where did *you* come from? What the hell are you doing here?"

Panic prickled through him, but Rex kept his ears up. Of course Shimon would be defensive. Shady had said the two LSAs both knew of Adeyeme's phobia, although she strove to hide it from others. Shady had admired the LSAs' loyalty, but he must overcome Shimon's efforts to "protect" his commander from information she needed.

"I am XK9 Officer Rex Dieter-Nell." His vocalizer-voice remained as robotic and emotionless as ever. Gratitude swept through him. He could scarcely breathe, but his robot-voice betrayed none of it. Contact with Shimon meant Rex was near his objective. He must make the man understand. "I have identified a scent profile I detected—"

Shimon shot a worried glance at something behind Rex, then frowned at him. "You are not authorized to be here!"

Rex lowered himself to a submissive crouch and made a conscious effort to breathe. Shimon didn't know he needed Rex's information. "I apologize, LSA Shimon. However—"

"I don't want your apology!" Shimon towered over him, glaring. One muscular arm pointed stiffly toward the main entrance. "Out! Gone! Now!"

Rex pressed his body against the floor. This wasn't working. The man wouldn't listen. He strove not to hyperventilate. How could he convince this guy? What could he do?

He heard a new footstep, smelled a new person's approach. "What's the problem, Shiv?" Her tone sounded mild, but beyond the raw fear in her scent factors Rex caught an acidic frisson of annoyance, and rocklike determination. His heart leaped. Was this SSA Adeyeme?

"This damned dog is not authorized to be here." Shimon placed himself between her and Rex.

Rex kept his chin on the floor, but turned his head to catch a glimpse of her.

The woman's short stature and dark skin contrasted sharply with the tall, blond Shimon, yet Rex would never have mistaken her for the big man's subordinate. "Stop it." She sidestepped Shimon's shielding maneuver, then turned her full attention on Rex. "You're the one whose partner was injured, aren't you? The one who was in the dock breach." Her body was rigid with tension and her scent roiled with terror, but her voice was steady.

Rex stared, entranced. She was every bit as smart and brave as he'd hoped. "Yes, I am." He must reassure her, but absolutely not embarrass her. Throat tight, hoping he'd guessed right, he rolled onto his back at her feet, neck and belly exposed. It was awkward with the panniers on, but maybe she would understand. "SSA Adeyeme, I am incredibly honored to meet you. I have heard of your courage and wisdom." He twisted his head to see her expression.

Her eyes narrowed. The terror in her scent subsided a little, displaced by sharp, jittery surprise and clashing confusion. "You —you know who I am?"

"To the Pack, you are legendary." That was true, at least, for the part of the Pack who'd met her.

Shimon choked. "'Legendary?'" He shot an incredulous look at his boss.

Rex held his position. Focused on Adeyeme. "Please accept my absolute, unconditional submission to your authority. I will do whatever you tell me to do."

"Noted, XK9 Rex." Her voice was cool, even. "Sit."

"E, you're not buying this, are you?" Shimon demanded.

"Yes, ma'am." Rex rolled onto his tummy, then pushed up to a sit. He lifted his ears. "Anything you ask. I am yours to command."

Shimon stared at his commander. "Seriously, E. This is total bullshit."

Adeyeme frowned back. "Forgive me if I prefer it to Iskander's bullshit. Or to Nolan's." She made steady eye contact with Rex. "Tell me why you are here, XK9 Rex."

Better make this good—and fast. "I can positively identify a living adult who entered and exited the *Izgubil,* approximately eight days before it was destroyed."

She pulled back, eyebrows up. Her scent boiled with astonishment. "You are certain?"

Even Shimon stiffened alert. "The hell you say!"

Joy surged through Rex. She'd listened! Finally, someone had listened! "Yes, ma'am. He is a small-time ruffian named Elmo Smart. I smelled his scent in a corridor that connected to the *Izgubil's* service port. I have not previously reported this, because the dock breach, plus my and my partner's injuries, distracted me."

"Just a bit, I imagine." Her mouth quirked.

Shimon went into a HUD-stare. "Holy crap. He might be telling the truth."

"I came here today because I thought you might want to have him questioned while the OPD still has him in custody." Rex accessed Smart's file, now that his HUD was back on . . . *oh, no.* "However, it appears he made bail while I was struggling to see you."

Adeyeme frowned. "He's been released?"

"The file says ten minutes ago." Rex stifled a growl.

"Is there an address?" Shimon's voice held grudging interest.

Rex made eye contact with him. "If he left on foot, I can track him."

"Huh. I guess you could." Shimon's anger-scents faded.

"Shiv, why don't you and XK9 Rex go see if you can find this Elmo Smart." Rex glanced at Adeyeme and saw what almost looked like a smile. Her scent surged with the savage pleasure of the hunt.

Rex gulped. He might be in love. Was there room in an XK9's heart for *two* humans and a mate?

Shimon scowled at Rex. "Um, sure."

Giddy he might be, but he'd be damned if he missed this cue. "Pardon, ma'am, but I am technically not on active duty." Rex's pulse bumped faster. Would she reactivate him?

She arched an eyebrow. "I'm guessing you wouldn't mind being reactivated?"

Joy filled him. Against all the odds—Rex wagged his tail, despite his resolve to stay cool. "I had hoped. Please?"

"I'll speak with Chief Klein. It wouldn't do to have our interview with a person of interest thrown out on a technicality."

The call of the hunt sang in his ears. To hell with his tired feet. "Thank you." The emotionless vocalizer preserved a shred of his dignity, but now his tail fanned at top speed.

She nodded, her face alight with kindred hunting spirit. "Go, then. Fetch me a subject."

Civic Center Complex, a small courtyard

Dr. Chin-Hua turned her frown on Dr. Ordovich, apparently dismissing his companions as less immediate irritations. Shady knew her enough to recognize the tight set of her shoulders, the straight line of her mouth. She gave Ordovich one of her less-than-charmed looks. "I am Assistant Medical Examiner Tanya Chin-Hua. And *you* are?"

At four meters away, Shady clearly saw and smelled that Ordovich missed the warning signs. His scowl deepened. "I am Dr. Gregory Ordovich, Director of the XK9 Project, here to inspect the XK9s." His cold tone and rapid-fire speech left no doubt he considered himself too important and in too much of a hurry for time-wasting courtesies. "How have the dogs been behaving?"

Chin-Hua glanced at Archy; the aide slid his eyes toward the silent Ranan Executive Security officer, gave an almost-imperceptible shrug. Then he took a quiet step backward from

Ordovich's field of vision and began to type on a case-pad. The military woman shot him a sharp look, but soon refocused on Ordovich.

Chin-Hua inclined her head. "The XK9s have added new forensic capabilities. They have uncovered several—"

"They have behaved appropriately?" Ordovich cut in.

Shady searched his scent and body language. He seemed oddly keyed up, but with a sharp new edge of . . . fear? Anxiety? Anger? It was an odd mix. At least part of his agitation seemed inspired by the silent woman's critical gaze. If only Shady dared compare impressions with Cinnamon and Razor!

Dr. Chin-Hua, never patient with time-wasting, gave Ordovich a cold stare. "Yes."

"Yes, they behaved well?" Ordovich scowled at Shady, Cinnamon, and Razor. Without being conscious of it, Shady had straightened to a tense parade sit, as if she were once again a trainee on probation. Razor and Cinnamon had, too. All three panted with quiet anxiety; their partners' coldly furious scents made an odd counterpoint. Pam's hand stroked Shady's shoulder.

Dr. Chin-Hua turned back toward her companions. Shady almost forgot herself and wagged her tail.

"I'm not done with you!" Ordovich cried. "Have you ever worked with the big black one? They call him Rex. Has he ever given you any trouble? And what about the one called Tuxedo?"

Shady's pulse fluttered faster. What did Ordovich want with Rex and Tux? His scent and body language promised nothing good for either dog.

The military woman's scent factors shifted hotter, with strong undertones of contempt.

Chin-Hua stopped, her back spike-straight. She turned her head slightly toward Ordovich. "We've never had *any* problems with *any* of them. On this or other cases." She resumed walking away.

Ordovich glared after her, then confronted Archy. "Where is Rex?"

Archy looked up from his case pad. "Rex is in the Ninth Precinct, on stand-down while his partner is hospitalized." He frowned. "I already told you that. Twice."

"You're certain that's where he is?"

"Yes." The aide's face bore an innocuous, neutral expression, but Shady's nose caught an unexpected note in Archy's scent. He was lying to Dr. Ordovich. A chill swept over her. That meant Rex wasn't at home where he was supposed to be. What was her mate doing? He hadn't called her. Perhaps she shouldn't try to make contact just now.

"We'll see him, of course."

New alarm surged through Shady, but Archy frowned. "The Ninth Precinct is seven kilometers away. Rex is in a private Family tower. The XK9s assigned to his neighboring Precincts, the Eighth and the Tenth, are Razor and Cinnamon, respectively. Since they are here, I had *not* intended to go all that distance to disturb a Family already enduring a personal calamity."

Ordovich gave him a startled look. "Personal calamity?"

Archy drew in a sharp, annoyed breath. "I also have already told you that DPO Morgan was critically injured in the dock breach. I'm not sure what Transmondians may consider a personal calamity, but on Rana Station we take critically injured Family members extremely seriously."

"Oh. Right." Ordovich scowled, waved a dismissive hand. "Of course. Decorum."

The military woman's scent went peppery with frustration. The black-uniformed RES officer's eyes narrowed. Shady would have lolled her tongue if she'd dared. She almost did anyway, when she caught a new scent's approach.

"We'll move along, then." Ordovich took no pains to hide his irritation. "Which dog is next?"

"*None* is 'next,'" Chief Klein said from the opening of the colonnade.

Ordovich's scent spiked hot. He spun to face Klein. "Excuse me?"

The Chief strode over to him, with Dr. Chinbat following. "Hello, Greg. What interesting timing, to find you here. You should have alerted us."

"Your man has been only marginally helpful, and that morgue woman was rude."

Klein gave the military woman a cold stare. His voice hardened. "I'm serious, Greg. You *should* have alerted us."

Ordovich frowned. "I've come to make sure your XK9s are not causing problems. That the protocols are being followed. I have authorization from the Premier herself."

"We do not give on-demand tours of police business."

Ordovich's scowl redoubled. "Premier Iskander authorized it! I must see the dogs."

Klein crossed his arms. "Why?"

Ordovich met his gaze. "Two of our Gen-48 XK9s manifested late-onset behavioral issues. I had to recall them and put them down. Now I'm making sure no others are manifesting this aberration. It is a serious flaw. We can't allow it into the breeding rotation."

Klein's level gaze made him appear untroubled, but Shady caught a surge of dismay in his scent. "Our dogs are completely satisfactory. None has manifested any aberration."

Ordovich crossed his own arms. "I must be the judge of that." Shady drew back. She recognized that scent and voice tone. Always in the past, it had meant a dog was in for a beating.

Klein glanced at the RES officer and the military woman, then returned his gaze to Ordovich. He maintained his outward calm, but Shady smelled his anger. "The Premier's authorization gets you inside my door. No foreigner would make it even that far, otherwise. I'm sorry you've troubled yourself to come all this way on a fruitless errand."

Ordovich drew in an indignant breath, stretched taller. "The contract stipulates appropriate evaluation!"

Shady shivered, but Klein met Ordovich's glare. "I'm satisfied we can do our own 'appropriate evaluation.' After all, it's not wormhole physics, it's the performance of police dogs. Do they do their jobs? Yes. Are we satisfied? Yes, more than satisfied. They are superlative. I think we've got it covered, Greg. Relax. No problems here. You should go home."

"I demand to see the dogs!"

Klein turned to the RES officer. "I shouldn't have to quote the Constitution to you. The Premier cannot overrule a local authority on a Borough matter such as this. Nor can any designated acting agent of the Premier do so. Certainly, no foreign agent may do so. Does this require further debate?"

The RES officer pursed his lips. "Perhaps we should discuss certain issues privately."

Klein's scent shifted to deeper fury. "My office, then. Now."

22

REX AND LSA SHIMON GO HUNTING

5th Precinct, OPD HQ and Sub-Level Ten, AKA "the Five-Ten"

Rex rode the elevator back up to the Main Corridor from S-3-9 with Lead Special Agent Shimon. Rex observed Shimon's critical gaze, smelled distrust in the man's scent.

"You are one fast-talking dog," Shimon said.

Rex cocked his head. "Should I say 'thank you,' or apologize?"

"Huh." That was almost a chuckle, but then the suspicion clamped down again. "Not sure yet. So. Where to?"

"Detention Processing. I should pick up Smart's scent there." Rex led Shimon through the maze of halls. By the time they'd reached their destination, Rex was back on active status. Warm gratitude filled him. SSA Adeyeme was a woman of her word, and Chief Klein had his back. At least, until Rex's latest misdeeds caught up with him.

"That was fast." Shimon gave him a speculative look. "Klein must have a lot riding on you XK9s."

Rex wagged his tail, glad to think of something other than his own postponed-but-inevitable doom. "My partner says it took ten years of campaigning and cost fifteen million novi to bring us here."

Shimon's eyebrows rose. "I didn't remember how much. No wonder there was controversy."

Rex's step faltered. There'd been controversy? His stomach sank. What a naïve puppy he was! Rex had never considered any ramifications of the Pack's purchase beyond its effect on him and his Packmates. But especially if there had been controversy, the Chief's career might depend on how well the XK9s performed. So how was he repaying the Chief's trust? His breath came a little shorter.

They passed the Detention Center elevator. "Ah! Here it is." Rex dipped his head, relieved to focus on the task at hand. Elmo Smart's trail was plain here. The scent cone had mostly collapsed, but it was in the uppermost layer—the one most recently deposited. "We are about twenty minutes behind him." He whisked past the processing desk and out the double doors of Spinward Portal into Central Plaza's fragrant orange grove, Shimon on his heels. Just as well they could avoid the sally port, which lay about twenty meters leeward. There appeared to be an unusual amount of traffic over there.

Shimon squinted through the afternoon glare toward the tail-rotor of a shiny black craft. It protruded from the sally port's main bay portal. "Huh. Wonder what that's all about." He took on a HUD stare. "Yeah, Val. Any clue what's up with the RES flitter in the sally port?" He listened, grimaced, then made an irritated sound. "The payback continues, eh? Well, I wish him luck. Thanks."

Rex cocked his head at Shimon. "May I ask?"

Shimon blew out a breath. "The OPD and Chief Klein are not Premier Iskander's favorites, right now, any more than SIT Delta is. She's been calling Elaine—SSA Adeyeme—every morning since the case began, to harangue her for not solving it yet."

Rex snorted. "But that is unreasonable. It is a massive case."

"Yes, well, you're probably smarter than the Premier to have figured that out." Shimon's disgust with Iskander was clear in every line of him, and redolent in his scent.

Rex stared at him, scandalized by such a blasphemous statement. Wouldn't saying something like that get even a human in trouble?

"Sorry. Politics." Shimon shook his head. "I shouldn't get so wound up."

Rex hesitated, tantalized by a glimpse into an unexplored area of human thought, yet driven by the need to return to the cooling trail. "I can track and listen simultaneously, if you want to talk."

"The Premier is always bad for my blood pressure." Shimon gestured for Rex to move on. "I guess when some Transmondian crackpot with a couple of business connections showed up on-Station, she grabbed the opportunity to plague Chief Klein with him."

Rex followed Elmo's trail across the busy Plaza toward Central Station Terminal, but Shimon's mention of a "Transmondian crackpot" distracted him. There were millions of Transmondians; Rex probably wouldn't know this particular crackpot. But if it was someone from the XK9 Project . . . Rex shook himself, but he couldn't shake that idea's horror. He refocused on Elmo's scent. Even in this high-traffic area, it was fresh and fairly easy to follow. "What did the Transmondian crackpot want?"

"Val wasn't sure. Full access to something, was all he overheard." Shimon shook his head. "As if any PD would grant that to a foreigner! He says Klein's aide Archy was guiding the guy in circles while Klein was in a meeting. They'll send him packing soon enough. Just another case of Iskander being petty and wasting people's time."

Rex hoped so. Shimon kept an eye on the overwatches, just as Charlie always did, so Rex could focus on the scent-trail. A brief pang of loneliness for Charlie clenched his chest, but Rex was working. Better focus on the objective. "Thank you for covering me."

"Of course. For now, we're partners." Shimon's smoky mistrust-smell diminished some. He eyed Rex curiously. "Do I take it you don't bay like a hunting dog when you're on a trail?"

"Only if the situation is appropriate." Rex thought he'd sounded pretty smooth the other night in the Hub corridor. On the other hand, look where that had led. "I am in silent-hunting mode, now. I do not wish to startle the civilians."

"Ah. Good point."

Beyond the Plaza, mixed-use structures stretched for blocks: offices, apartments, or hotel lodging occupied the floors above ground-level commercial spaces. Somewhere among them was Shady's home. Rex crossed a new scent near Central Plaza Terminal. "Elmo met someone. A relative, probably an uncle." The trail led to a table in the terminal's open food court; Rex took a moment to sniff its cleared surface. The scents were smeared around but not removed. "They ate meat-rolls here. Each man had a glass of beer."

"Hey!" A busboy yelled. "I just cleaned that table!"

Rex and Shimon moved away; Rex glanced back. The busboy scowled after them, then gave the table another wipe-down.

"Elmo's meal cost him most of his head start. We are less than five minutes behind." Rex picked up his pace despite his tender feet, then sent a text-only message to Shimon's HUD: "Can you read this?"

"Um." A moment later Shimon's texted reply arrived: "Yes." He switched back to speaking aloud, hurried to catch up. "I have to think it in, letter-by-letter, to reply without using my case pad. Why do you ask?"

Rex resumed vocalizing. "Charlie and I have a dedicated brain link. It is like cybernetic telepathy. We can think words to each other."

"Damn. I want one of those!"

"Our brain-link implants are paired prototypes. Gen-48 is the first generation to get them."

Shimon sighed. "I'm still envious."

Rex wagged his tail. "Perhaps they will be available more widely someday. Before our prototypes, humans had to speak out loud or text to us. XK9s could use their vocalizers or send text messages to the human's HUD. It is an XK9's job to read scent factors and share insights with the human partner, but it often is better to communicate such information silently."

"Texting should work. My colleague Shawnee Kramer has been raving about all the things 'scent factors' can reveal. Sounds like an unfair advantage, to me—and I'm all for any advantage we can get over the criminal element. They have enough of their own."

"Too true." Rex stopped to puzzle out an odd tangle in the trail.

"What is it?"

"Elmo swerved into the path of another pedestrian. They collided right here. I have heavier deposits of scent rafts, hairs, dust—the usual things humans have in their clothing. Also startled scent factors, with minor pain."

"What do you make of that?" Shimon gave him a quizzical look.

Rex growled. "Elmo picked the other guy's pocket. A totally 'Elmo' thing to do. I can't discern what he got, though."

Shimon gave a short laugh. "So you can't smell all details, but nearly all."

Rex lolled his tongue. "Let us say 'many.' I shall take that as a compliment."

"Don't let it go to your head." His expression went wry. "Speaking of which, what was up with all that flattery for Elaine?"

"Do you think that went to her head?"

"She's one tough lady, but she's needed a few kind words,

lately. You really laid it on with a trowel, though." He quirked a pale eyebrow at Rex. "Do you butter up all your COs that way?"

"I, um, kind of surprised myself, there." Rex avoided Shimon's eye. "The fact is that I do intensely admire her. My mate told me how brave she is, and when I encountered her today I . . . Well. You were there."

The uprush of warmth in Shimon's scent explained his loyalty and earlier protectiveness. Rex looked up, caught a fond smile on his face. "Yeah."

"But why do we frighten her so? None of us has threatened her."

Shimon's expression soured. "Military dogs on the Norchellic Frontier, when she was five. Still has physical scars, too."

Rex's mind filled with images of starving, rag-clad refugees, bombed-out tent villages, and huddled lumps of bodies. He'd studied that vicious war in history class. It had dragged on for decades, until a few years before he was born. "I can see how that might instill a phobia." His curiosity about Adeyeme grew stronger. How had she come from that to here?

Elmo's scent cone narrowed. So fresh the scent rafts still hung in the air, it led toward a set of three civilian elevators. Like the terminal Rex and Bill had used Monday, this one included a larger elevator at one end reserved for Emergency Services.

"Getting close now." Rex wagged his tail. Eagerness accelerated his pulse.

"These lead to the sub-levels." Shimon's scent shifted to greater wariness. "With his background, Elmo may be headed for a pretty rough neighborhood."

Rex laid his ears back. This was Fifth Precinct, home to the most infamous neighborhood in Orangeboro. "Let me check." Rex reared up to press the call button. The middle elevator opened on a strong, clear scent of their quarry. Rex stepped inside. His heart sank. Elmo had left a greasy, meat-roll-smelling fingerprint on the lowest one, S-10. "He is headed to the Five-

Ten." Rex backed out of the elevator. "We just lost all that time we made up."

"Bad?"

Impatience goaded Rex, but he mustn't lead Shimon into the Five-Ten unprotected. "My mate is assigned to Precinct Five. She sometimes has to go to the Five-Ten. She and her partner must put on body armor and go in a group of at least four." He growled softly, disappointed.

Shimon grimaced, but called it in. He listened to Dispatch's reply, then sat on a nearby mosaic-encrusted public bench, next to a tree and a soft-looking patch of grass. "You're right. They're sending a pair of UPOs up from Sub-level Ten to meet us, Anthony and Sevencrows. They'll have body armor for us."

Rex settled onto the grass. Nice to get off his feet, although his mind and heart longed for the hunt. "Let us hope the scent does not grow cold before they arrive." He curled a forepaw to lick his sore pads. This grass seemed designed to suck him down into a bone-weary doze.

Shimon unholstered his EStee, checked the charge, then slipped it back under his jacket. The man's tension communicated to Rex through his prickly, peppery scent, the taut muscles in his leg. He sighed. His scent acquired a piquant whiff of curiosity.

Rex looked up to find him staring down at him.

"So. You have a mate?"

Warmth flooded him, mingled with longing. He wagged his tail. "You may have met her. She is assigned to the Task Force."

"Ah." He gave a soft chuckle. "I'm gonna guess it's Shady."

"Got it in one." Rex cocked his head. "How did you guess?"

"Shady's the one Shawnee Kramer's always going on about. Incredible nose, level head, mind of her own. I figured you two would be a good match."

"Thank you. I like to think we are." Gratified, Rex wagged harder. Now that he was officially on the team, maybe he'd see her soon. Longing filled him.

The wait stretched on and on. Shimon alternated between surveying their surroundings, checking his case pad, and eyeing Rex in silence. One foot tapped a soft staccato, the only expression of his growing tension besides his scent. With the LSA on alert, Rex put his chin on his forelegs and closed his eyes. He'd rather be tracking Elmo, but for now his weariness ruled.

The Emergency Services elevator rumbled to the top of its climb after about fifteen minutes. A sleek indigo patrol unit with dark-tinted windows emerged. The car had a large gold seven-pointed star badge logo on its side. The words ORANGEBORO POLICE DEPARTMENT stretched across it in reflective letters with white edges. Two doors swung open.

The Uniformed Peace Officer who stepped forward first was a muscular, middle-aged woman with short, grizzled hair and a stern face. Her tall, younger male partner followed. Their uniforms included the stiff, upright neck-protection collars and the subtle bulk of body armor. The woman gave a curt nod. "Afternoon, gentlemen. I'm Lynn Anthony. My partner is Henry Sevencrows. I understand you need an escort."

Shady had been the last person to wear the armor they offered Rex. He savored her scent but kept his mind on business. "We have to take my panniers off first." Rex coached Sevencrows through the process of putting the armor on and adjusting it for his more ample dimensions. Shimon donned his torso-armor under Anthony's stern gaze. Rex didn't remember armor being this hot. Or this heavy.

At Anthony's insistence, he and Shimon wedged themselves into the cramped back seat of the patrol unit. The car tail-parked inside the elevator. Rex's tongue hung long. He hoped this would be a short ride. The elevator doors closed. The floaty sensation of descending ensued.

Anthony focused on Shimon through the cage divider that ran between the front and back seats. "Where we're going, about two-thirds of the residents'll stay clear of you. The other third'll be happy to jump you or shoot you if you give 'em any provocation. That lot all carry blowguns, everything from homemade outta bamboo to professionally-manufactured. Five-Tenners are proficient blowgun marksmen from about age six. Some have poison-tipped, or even hypodermic darts. Shimon, *pull your visor down*. It could save your eyes. They also sometimes use knives, throwing stars, and some even have EStees." She frowned, her grim scent factors seconded by Sevencrows.

Rex wasn't sure how to respond. Shady had never shared these details . . . maybe so he wouldn't worry. He gave Shimon an apprehensive look, panted harder. However, nothing Anthony'd said made it cooler to sit in the cramped back seat wearing this damned armor.

Shimon frowned. "I'm getting the distinct impression you're trying to frighten me."

She shook her head. "The Five-Ten's been my beat for twenty-five years, LSA Shimon. I've come to appreciate its peculiar charms. But in that time, I've also picked up the bloody pieces of a lot of detectives and agents who didn't take the threats here seriously." She grimaced, met Shimon's eyes. "I really hate doing that. So if I seem rude or grumpy or disrespectful, I'm sorry. It's just 'cause I don't want to have to rescue your broken ass and mop up after you. I try to make an impression beforehand."

"Noted, UPO Anthony," Shimon said.

"I sure hope so." She gave him a dubious look, blew out a long breath. "Toro Enclave's dominated by the Whisper Syndicate, though no one'll acknowledge it. Safest place is inside the unit."

Even if Rex had wanted to stay inside, that made no sense. "How can I follow the scent from in here?"

Anthony kept her focus on Shimon. "If you want Elmo Smart, there's only a few places he'll go. Depends on which girlfriend's speaking to him at the moment." She shrugged. "Since that changes more often than the mirrors adjust, it's anybody's guess."

Insubordinate urges rose within Rex. He gave a soft growl. "I do not intend to guess."

Anthony slewed around to glare at him directly. The cage divider amplified the effect. "Safer just to stake out a girlfriend. Eventually he'll show up."

Rex was too hot to be patient. "Within the half-hour?"

Anthony gave him a pitying look. "Don't be silly."

Rex wanted out. As soon as possible. "I shall do it my way."

"Your funeral." She shrugged, turned to face front.

Rex let his lip curl. A flash of teeth like that would've earned a beating from Ordovich, but he was too overheated to care. He glanced at Shimon, who sat squeezed next to him into the miniscule back seat on the wrong side of the cage divider. The LSA's long legs bent so his knees came to just below his chin. His pale-skinned face was flushed. He, too, smelled excessively warm.

"Think she'll let me out if I insist ?" Rex texted.

Shimon frowned, his mouth in a wry twist. After a moment his text came back. "Maybe."

The elevator stopped, opened. The unit rolled out, into a narrow open area ringed by small, shabby, mechanical-repair and supply shops. They looked doubly grim and grimy in the dingy twilight that passed for "day" around here. Rising above and beyond them, Rex saw the floor-to-ceiling blocks of storage units.

"Let me out," Rex said. "I must find the scent trail."

Anthony turned again, to frown through the cage divider. "I don't advise it."

"Let us out," Shimon said. "It's why we came."

Anthony sighed. "Don't say I didn't warn you. Draw your EStee, Shimon. Keep it in your hand." The locks *chunked.* Both back doors swung open.

Rex sprang from the patrol unit. Freed! He could breathe!

But what was that smell?

23

ADVENTURESS IN TORO ENCLAVE

The Five-Ten Toro Enclave

A gritty layer of dust and machine oil covered everything here. Under it lay smells of dampened rock, mildew, and just a scintilla of old urine. Wafts of moldy basketry and unwashed humans flowed in the odd eddies around Rex. Scent factors of deception, defensiveness, and fear seemed embedded in every surface, but he couldn't detect any particular stranger nearby.

Where was everybody? Rex's neck-hairs prickled in anticipation of blowgun darts, but there was only one thing to do. Head down, he moved toward the graffiti-scrawled, half-lit civilian elevators, where Elmo and his uncle would've emerged at the end of their ride here.

Shimon exited the other side of the patrol unit and followed him. The LSA pulled his helmet's visor down and unholstered his EStee as Anthony had advised. But he kept the weapon pointed down, his finger near the trigger.

The patrol unit's back doors slammed. Just as well. Rex preferred his chances outside.

A couple of lighted shop signs glared. Some of the streetlights that hung twenty-some meters above from the cobweb-shrouded ceiling emitted feeble rays. Good thing Rex needn't depend on his eyes to follow this trail. The closest Transmondian equivalent to this light-level was heavy overcast with an oncoming storm. This place sure didn't smell like rain, though.

The whole enclave seemed to have frozen in place. Nothing moved except Rex, Shimon, and the near-silent patrol unit. It rolled a meter or so behind them with only a soft crunch of gravel under its wheels. Its locked, lurking presence did little to ease Rex's jitters.

Low, distant rumbles could be from anything. Perhaps the massive machinery that kept Wheel Two in motion, or the low hum of ventilator fans. No voices spoke. No creak betrayed shifting weight on bamboo decking. No crunch of footsteps on the pale gray regolith gravel pinpointed someone stalking them. Even Shimon moved near-silently, his muscular body tense but poised.

A chill hung over this place, unexpected after the temperate-to-tropical warmth in most of Rana. The station's centrifugal gravity dragged harder, as well. Not enough to be harmful, but enough to lower the rents significantly. Enough make the body armor even heavier, too. Rex found Elmo's trail within a minute. It veered to their right. The scent rafts had already settled to the decking. The added gravity might mean a shorter interval than twenty minutes, but not much. They'd lost a lot of time waiting.

Shimon stayed close by. He smelled as unsettled and hyper-alert as Rex felt.

An old man stepped out of a doorway onto a narrow, dingy porch. He stared at Rex and Shimon as they passed. Rex sensed no menace from his scent or body language, just curiosity. Shimon acted as if he didn't see him, so Rex didn't wag his tail or acknowledge him, either. During a hunt was no time for community policing.

Rex followed Elmo's trail along the left side of a pale,

regolith-gravel road between silent buildings, with Shimon behind him.

Then a younger, burlier man stepped onto the road from a side alley, about five meters back. He walked with a falsely casual attitude, but dark purpose roiled in his musky scent factors.

Rex's neck hackles rose, prickling. He laid back his ears, gave a soft growl.

Another man joined the first without greeting him, then another. Rex recognized the third man's personal scent. He'd been in Elmo's group at the Hub.

He relayed this to Shimon, via text. "Should we apprehend him?"

"No," Shimon texted back

Their objective was Elmo. Got it. Better not to tangle needlessly with three ruffians who weren't their assigned subjects. All the same, Rex texted Anthony and Sevencrows: "Does your unit have active vid-cams 360? We may need images of the men behind us."

"Recording and uploading," Sevencrows replied on the com.

Elmo's trail abruptly veered left, into a dark, narrow passageway between two ceiling-high, metal-walled buildings. There was room for one person to walk through at a time. It was just wide enough for Rex and his panniers, despite the body armor.

Rex took a cautious step forward. He poked his head into the passageway.

"Do not even *think* about it!" Anthony's voice crackled with irritation on the com.

Rex growled, but stopped. "The trail turns here," he texted.

"Doesn't mean *you* have to," Anthony said. "This is the Five-Ten. You can't know who might be waiting to jump you or shoot at you, just beyond the end of that crack."

Anger prickled all along Rex's back. Blocked beneath the body armor, his hackles itched like fire. *Enough of this.* "UPO

Anthony, it is true that you cannot know," he texted. "But I can smell that Elmo and his uncle are the last persons to have used this passageway for at least ten hours. I smell no lurking attackers at the end of it. I hear no heartbeats or breathing, except for those of LSA Shimon, myself, and the three men who have been following your unit. I can therefore say with reasonable certainty that no one waits to attack us at the end of that crack."

"Nice," Shimon texted to Rex.

Anthony did not reply.

"Since you know Elmo Smart well enough to say where his girlfriends live," Rex added, "perhaps you know where he might go from here."

Shimon's scent factors developed strong notes of amusement, intermixed with his caution and sweat. He stifled a cough.

"Ostra," Sevencrows answered. "Elmo and his uncle Ned will be going to Ostra Import-Export Emporium. It faces the next main road over. Obviously, our unit can't go through your passageway, but we can meet you there, or you can ride with us. If you walk, it's about forty meters ahead, through two alleys to the street."

"Thanks," Shimon said. "See you there."

Rex dragged his panniers through the narrow, metal-walled passage with a scrape of tactical fabric on metal. Urgency goaded him. Those three ruffians they'd picked up might have blowpipes. No way to dodge their darts in this place. Shimon followed.

The passageway jogged right-then-left into an alley. They crossed to another narrow place, still on Elmo's trail. Shimon moved more silently than any human Rex had ever worked with.

Muttered curses and the scrape of fabric echoed from the first passageway.

Rex raised his nose and ears, focused ahead. *Oh good.* "Clear," he texted.

They hurried toward the far end. From there Elmo's path led into a wider space, then ducked to the right, down yet another alley.

This damned warren made his hackles prickle and his gut flutter. It was all narrow passages and tiny alleys. "Bizarre place," he texted Shimon. "Designed for skulking?"

Amused scent threaded through Shimon's personal blend of himself, sweat, and edginess. "If Whisper runs it, who knows?" he kept his voice low.

The one thing he didn't see was the sort of trash and debris found in low-rent Transmondian alleys. "Where is all the rubbish?" Rex sniffed and listened, to make certain no ambush lurked in this next alley.

"No rubbish. Recyclers pay hard currency." Shimon followed him in.

To their right rose the blank metal wall of a storage building that ran the length of what Rex now saw was a box-alley. He growled softly. The flutters in his gut grew stronger.

A few meters down on their left, someone had long ago stenciled the word "Ostra" in now-peeling white paint on a scuffed, dark gray composting receptacle. It reeked of unturned garbage. The Ostra composter half-obscured yet another, even narrower passageway. This one led at right angles to the alley, between a three-level building with a metal fire escape down the back, and one of those closed, windowless metal storage buildings that predominated here.

Rex walked under the fire escape to peek down the narrow side-passage. It was barely wide enough for his panniers. He spotted the patrol unit on the street beyond, and a surge of reassurance rocked him. Well. Hadn't expected that but . . . someone here had their back. That felt good.

Elmo's trail didn't go that way, though. It led straight past the composting receptacle and the storage building to what looked like the back of a narrow shop on the far end, where alley stopped, cut off by another building's ceiling-high, metal-clad wall. The storage building and the shop were painted the same dark gray as the "Ostra" composter. Scent rafts from Elmo and his uncle hung low in the air, just above the shop's back steps. Pale gravel-dust footprints led to the back door.

Rex pointed with his nose. "Back door," he texted.

Shimon mounted the steps with a soft creak of a particle-board plank. EStee pointed at the door, he used his other hand to try the latch. It didn't move. Locked. He shook his head.

At the far end of the alley, footsteps crunched on gravel. Ruffian-scents wafted Rex's way. From the number of footsteps and scent profiles, a couple more had joined in.

"Seven men coming," he texted Shimon. He didn't want to be caught in this box alley.

Shimon frowned. "Side passage." He landed quietly at the base of the steps, then hotfooted it almost silently back to the composter.

Rex moved to the passage, but held back for Shimon. He bristled toward the approaching men.

Shimon slipped into the narrow passage.

Rex followed, but went in backwards, shoving the panniers through with effort. Shimon could shoot an EStee-bolt in either direction, but the space was too narrow for Rex to turn around. He couldn't defend himself with his tail, so he pushed down the passage in reverse, his haunches near Shimon's scent and body-warmth. His eyes and his snarl stayed focused on the receding small gap by the composter in the alley.

Scuffling and muttering rose from that direction, then their first follower shoved himself into the gap. He half-raised his EStee, but then pitched forward, wedged between the walls. His companions shouted dismay. They tugged at his shirt, but his limp, bulky form stayed stuck.

"Good shot." Rex lolled his tongue, startled Shimon could react so fast. "That should slow them down."

"For a minute, maybe. C'mon." Shimon pushed on toward the patrol unit.

Its window lowered. "No one's gone into Ostra or come out," Anthony said.

"That means Elmo is still in there." Rex trotted to the shop's entrance. Shimon told Anthony and Sevencrows about the men in the alley and the one he'd bolted, then followed. Rex pawed the door open, pushed inside. A bell jangled. Shimon stepped through behind him. He closed the door, then holstered his EStee.

Cobwebbed boxes and half-empty shelves cluttered the tiny retail area. What could the air currents tell Rex? A fresh taste of Elmo's scent teased him. Still inside the shop, but Rex didn't see him. Couldn't get a clear sense of his location.

A set of stained brown curtains behind the sales counter parted. A tall, ruddy man with hairy arms, a shaved head, and a disagreeable expression stepped up to the worn, dented-metal countertop. He smelled almost familiar. Another one of Elmo's group from the Hub? No, but related. Father. The gust of air that came with him also told Rex that Elmo and his uncle lurked behind the curtains.

The shopkeeper scowled. "What d'ye want?"

Shimon showed his badge. "Lead Special Agent Shiva Shimon, SBI," he said. "I'd like to speak with Elmo Smart."

"He ain't here."

Hackles up, ears flat, Rex growled. "Yes, he is. He is behind that curtain." He turned up the volume on his vocalizer. "Elmo! Do you remember what I told you Sunday night in Glen Haven Park? Come out quietly. NOW!"

Rex heard the thump of running feet.

"Runner!" He bounded over the counter. The shopkeeper stumbled back with a curse, but Rex was already past.

He leaped into a cloud of his quarry's terror-scent. The back door banged.

Rex plunged through the back room. He burst out, hurtled over the back steps and into a confusion of bodies. Six of the seven men who'd been following him and Shimon remained in the alley. Elmo sprinted through their midst, caromed off a couple of them and pelted on, frantic.

Rex followed, locked on Elmo, at express-train velocity.

Hands grabbed at him. Men shouted.

Rex barreled through.

Elmo checked, panicked, at the now-blocked passageway between Ostra and the three-level building next to it. Then he wheeled and leaped up onto the fire escape.

Rex bounded after his quarry. His claws scrabbled for a hold on the slippery metal bars.

Elmo plunged up the steps to the first level, then darted along a narrow ledge toward the street.

Rex took the steps in one leap, tunnel-focused on his quarry. He scrambled along the tiny, splintery ledge. It buckled under his weight, but he moved fast enough to avoid falling.

Elmo flung himself into a wild wall-volley off the first level onto the side of the dark gray storage building, then *slap* against the ground-level wall and onto the street. He rolled, leaped up, then sprinted past the patrol unit toward a cluster of buildings on the other side of the road.

Rex volleyed off the storage building to the street. He lunged forward, clamped his jaws on Elmo's forearm, then practically sat down, sliding, in an effort to stop.

Too late. They careened into the side of a shed. It exploded in a cascade of bamboo splinters and stored objects. Things clattered and banged and rained down like a thudding hail of metal boxes and cans. The roof groaned, cracked, sagged.

Rex's pulse thudded in his neck, his belly, his ears. His muscles tensed, urgent to run. *Trapped! Buried! Gotta get out!* But he held himself still in the dusty semidarkness, panting hard. He forced down the frantic fear. Must think. Was he hurt? Sore spots, bruises. No searing pain. No woozy head. He could stand. He could breathe. He was okay.

Below his belly, Elmo lay quivering and crying like a child. At least he hadn't soiled himself this time. But he'd behaved just like before, disregarding anyone but himself. Rex growled. "Oh, Elmo. When will you learn?"

Beyond the fallen debris, Anthony yelled at someone about an illegal structure. An angry man suggested where she could shove it.

Rex lowered his head to poke Elmo with his nose. Splintered bamboo, metal containers, and broken pieces of things Rex couldn't identify slid with a crash when he moved. He stopped, tense. Elmo cried out, then curled into a tighter ball under the shelter of Rex's body.

"Rex! Rex!" Shimon sounded frantic. "Rex! Are you okay?"

"Shimon! Get back!" Sevencrows cried.

Something creaked. Next came a sharp crack, then tearing, splintering, sliding. The shed's weight grew heavier, shifted sideways. Rex hunched his body. Braced himself. Was he strong enough to withstand this weight?

All at once the crushing weight lifted. Two dusty, pale-skinned hands thrust upward from dusty, blue-black sleeves, to shove the ceiling beams higher. Other people's hasty hands tore broken bamboo away from the bottom of the gap. Dim light spilled in.

"I can see daylight, such as it is." Rex's hope rose. "You appear to be digging in the right place."

More hands appeared, scrambling to pull away more rubble. Sevencrows and a man Rex didn't recognize kicked, yanked, and tore the hole wider, as fast as they could, while Shimon stood, both arms raised to hold up the roof. How could he lift and hold all that weight?

"Rex, are you stuck?" Sevencrows cried.

"Elmo first." Rex's slightest movement made more things fall. "I dare not move until he is out."

Elmo reached up. "Get me outta here!" He lunged forward, kicked free of the rubble. His heel caught Rex in the ribs, then he and Sevencrows disappeared out through the hole.

"Not so fast, Elmo!" Anthony's voice cried. "Hang onto him, Henry!"

Shimon bowed his head, focused on his task. His upraised arms trembled, but somehow held firm.

Rex rocked forward, urgent to move. He launched himself past sliding debris, leaped clear, then looked back.

"U-u-u-UH!" Shimon gave the roof a hard shove, pushed away, then stumbled backward.

The roof-beams he'd been holding, along with the rest of the shed, thundered down in a deck-shaking avalanche. Debris slid and clattered and rolled. Regolith dust billowed up in choking gray clouds. Caught on a light breeze from an overhead ventilator, it then sifted downward like a strange, dry, silicate fog.

Everyone who'd stayed to watch surged away from it.

Shimon stood bent over, hands on knees, gasping.

Rex ran to him, sniffed up and down his companion's arms, back, legs. He smelled of strain, weariness, some inflammation. But nothing more. The man seemed uninjured, though exhausted.

"I'm all right, Rex." Shimon straightened slowly. His breathing steadied to normal. "How about you? Are you hurt?" He swiped at his sleeve. This raised a small puff of dust but did nothing for the jacket's appearance.

Rex flicked his ears. "XK9s are tough. I am fine." He sneezed. "Although I may be sneezing gray dust for a while. How could you hold such a heavy roof?"

Shimon rolled his shoulders several times, then did a short series of arm stretches before he answered. "Need of the moment, I guess." He looked away toward the remainder of the curious onlookers. His scent factors told Rex that wasn't the whole story, but his body language said that was all Rex would get. *Well, damn.*

The load of dust and grit in his fur irritated him. He moved a few steps away, then braced his legs and shook furiously. Light-gray regolith dust smoked out from his coat, then drifted down.

He moved away from that, let the cloud settle, then shook again. And again. Oh, that felt better!

Back to business. Rex ran a quick smell-check, but the people who lingered around Ostra and the fallen shed did not include Uncle Ned, the shopkeeper, or any of the men who'd followed them earlier. Rex looked down the narrow passageway. Even the guy Shimon had EStee-bolted and left stuck in the gap was gone. "All our suspects but Elmo have fled."

"Big surprise there." Shimon continued making ineffectual swipes at his pantlegs and jacket-sleeves.

Rex sneezed again, then swung his nose toward Ostra. He stepped back through his memories of the flight to the back door. "I noticed something when Elmo and I ran through the work room behind the counter. I believe we have probable cause for a search. That room has recently held explosives."

24

PROBABLE CAUSE

The Five-Ten Toro Enclave, and OPD HQ

"Explosives?" Shimon turned toward the shabby shopfront of Ostra Import-Export Emporium. "When did you have time to smell explosives?"

Rex wagged his tail. A warm little surge of pleasure-in-achievement welled up inside of him. "I noted the explosives-smell in passing, but I reviewed the memory in more detail just now. The scent was easy to smell in the storage area behind the counter. It is a distinctive odor. There can be no mistake. I believe we have probable cause to examine the place with an XK9 team and a CSU crew."

Shimon gave him a startled look. "How is your smelling it probable cause?"

On the other side of the patrol unit UPO Anthony's head came up. Rex caught a whiff of her bright, strong curiosity. She glanced toward Sevencrows and Elmo, then approached Rex and Shimon.

Rex took a few steps toward Ostra. "The Project worked for decades to convince the Transmondian courts, but at last they extended the 'in plain sight' standard for probable cause to 'plainly smelled' by a sworn XK9 officer. After that, it was only a few years before System legal codes accepted it too."

Shimon's expression morphed from dubious to astonished. "Is that right?"

"I caught a clear scent, while engaged in a legal pursuit." Rex lolled his tongue. This was how to prove his worth!

"I remember that." Anthony gave Rex a look of respect. "We had to review a whole bunch of statutes when OPD was getting ready to bring you XK9s here. Hell of a memory you've got there."

Shimon had already acquired a middle-distance HUD stare. "E." He paused, then smiled. "Yes, Elmo Smart's in custody. Better yet, Rex found explosives. We have probable cause for a search warrant." His explanation paralleled Rex and Anthony's.

Rex's com rang a few seconds later. "Good work, XK9 Rex!" Adeyeme's praise filled his heart with bubbly, radiant joy. "Shiv tells me you suggested an XK9 team. Can't you and he handle it?"

Rex's pulse sped up. She'd listened again! *Oh, Charlie, I miss you, but you're opening a door for me.* "LSA Shimon has not been trained in the forensic standards. We need an XK9 whose trained partner is not in the ICU."

"Ah." She let out a small breath. "Fair enough. Which team do you recommend?"

Elation ballooned in his chest, along with astonishment that she'd ask a dog's opinion. He hoped Cinnamon would forgive him for what he said next, but this was an opportunity to expand the team. "Tuxedo is the top explosives expert in the Pack. However, he and his partner Georgia Volkov have not been assigned to this case."

"Oh." Adeyeme hesitated.

Excitement made his pulse thunder. His tail couldn't go any faster. She was thinking about it! Rex stress-yawned.

"I wonder if Klein . . . Hmm." Silence, then a quiet exhalation. "Maybe he'd give me a specialist team."

Yes! Yes! She'd listened to him! She would ask! Oh, what a pleasure to work with this woman! "Thank you, SSA Adeyeme. I know they will do an excellent job." The emotionless robot-voice of the vocalizer saved his dignity again. Rex did not dance, but he couldn't keep from wriggling a little.

What a great opportunity! If Klein agreed to assign Tuxedo, Rex would be halfway to his rapidly-forming goal of getting all ten Orangeboro Pack members on this case. It wasn't until after she'd closed the communication that another thought bubbled up through his delight. She'd treated him like a trusted expert. Like a Pack Leader!

Jubilation made him lighter than any exhaustion, even after the call ended. Anthony and Shimon set up crime scene lasers. Sevencrows kept an eye on Elmo in the patrol unit. Once the ambulance arrived, Rex struggled to hold still so the paramedic team could run a handheld scanner over him. But when they declared him fit for duty and turned their attention to Elmo's glum, slumped form, he couldn't keep himself from bounding around in the street.

Shimon gave him a quizzical look. "You seem happy all of a sudden."

Rex wriggled and squeaked and wagged with delight. "Yes. I am happy. SSA Adeyeme is considering my suggestion. I love working with her. She is so wise and reasonable."

"She has her moments." Shimon's expression mirrored his dubious scent. "Celebrate after Elmo spills his guts in the interview room and Adeyeme follows your advice."

A Personnel Transport Vehicle rolled around the corner a short while later. It halted near the ambulance. Four UPOs and a couple of SBI agents emerged, followed by a CSU crew, but Rex looked in vain for Tuxedo and Georgia. Worry darkened his excitement. His ears drooped. Maybe Tux and Georgia couldn't get here this fast. Maybe they'd be here later. Mustn't give up yet.

"Shimon! Rex!" Anthony called. "A word?"

Two of the newly-arrived UPOs stood with Elmo by the ambulance. One of the paramedics spoke to them earnestly. The other two flanked Anthony. Rex nodded to them as he and Shimon approached. He put his ears back up.

"Change of orders, Rex." Anthony's scent and voice seemed more puzzled than upset. "Chief Klein just ordered you, me, and Henry to report to him ASAP."

What? No! Cold terror swept over Rex. He struggled to breathe. Just when he'd started to make progress. Just when SSA Adeyeme had been willing to listen. All for nothing, now. The jig was up. This summons to the Chief's office could only mean one thing. His misdeeds had caught up with him at last. He'd been fooling himself, to think he'd get away with any of today's insubordination.

Shimon smelled confused and upset. He stared at Anthony. "But Rex was only just assigned to us."

"Sorry. No idea what's up, but ours is not to question, Shimon." Anthony shook her head. "Good luck with your investigation!"

Sevencrows stepped forward to unstrap Rex's armor, and lift it off. Rex had hated the armor, but stripping it off left him chilled and undefended.

Anthony popped open the back door of the patrol unit. "Looks like you're riding with us again."

Rex froze. The hard, painful throb of his heartbeat shook him. Until this moment, he hadn't realized how much that back seat looked like the Dark Crate.

Anthony grimaced. "C'mon! If we miss the elevator, we'll have to wait for the next cycle."

He'd long ago learned that resistance simply earned him a worse beating. Numb, he staggered forward on wobbly legs. He tucked his tail, closed his eyes, held his breath.

Stepped up into the unit behind the cage divider.

Doors *chunked* shut. Locks cycled.

He was trapped. Crated. Doomed.

Rex squeezed onto the floorboards. He pressed his face against the carpet. The trip back to OPD Central took little time. Two blocks to the elevator, up to ground-level, less than a kilometer back through the Central District to HQ. He and Shimon had, after all, never left Precinct Five, and they'd tracked Elmo on foot. All too soon, the unit slowed, then halted.

Rex raised his head enough to look past the cage divider. A black tail rotor loomed in front of the patrol unit.

The Transmondian was still here. Rex tensed. His worst fears rose up to gnaw at his gut, but he snarled them back into their shadows. It couldn't be Ordovich. Not—No. NO. A Transmondian was here, but there were lots of Transmondians. He didn't have to be *that* Transmondian.

Sevencrows opened his door, stood. "How much longer?" He got out, walked away, but soon returned to sit back down. "Let's take the underground route. They said it still may be a while."

The unit reversed. The rotor slid out of view. "What's with the RES?" Anthony asked.

Sevencrows shook his head. "Damn flitter takes up five bays. Some Transmondian blowhard. Thinks he ought to run the place, just 'cause the Premier smiled at him."

"Geez, what next? We get annexed as a colony?" Anthony smelled as angry as she sounded.

"Klein'll handle him."

"If they let him."

"Pandra might roll over, but Idris won't." Sevencrows didn't sound entirely confident. Rex lifted his ears, grateful for even a fleeting distraction. He sorted through the names. "Pandra" was Secretary of Public Safety Oma Pandra, Chief Klein's boss. "Idris" was Ailani Idris, Mayor of Orangeboro, and *Pandra's* boss. Rex had met both briefly at the Presentation Ceremony.

The unit went through more maneuvers before Anthony killed the engine at last. "Let's go see if Klein's gotten shed of the pesky foreigner."

Rex walked with the two UPOs. On the main level, they

entered a round foyer, the Civic Center Rotunda. Dozens of scent trails crisscrossed its polished floor. Some so fresh they were still airborne, others barely discernible, overlain by multiple others. Across the rotunda stood a bank of elevators Rex remembered well. He'd been here on Monday with Bill.

He'd been worried then, too, but not like now. He panted, sick with dread. *How did I come to this? Why must it be this way?* This was the worst thing that had happened to him since he'd arrived on Rana Station.

But then they walked into a new scent trail.

A trail so fresh the scent rafts still hung in the air.

A scent so detestable it closed his throat.

Rex couldn't breathe. Couldn't think. Couldn't move. His ears roared. All he smelled was that hated scent. For a long, horrible moment he lived his worst fear.

Someone far away was shouting his name.

"Rex!"

"Rex!"

"Rex! What's wrong?"

He became aware that Anthony and Sevencrows knelt on either side of him. Their scents roiled with frantic worry.

"Rex! Rex! What's wrong? What's happened?" On his left, Anthony stroked his side with rhythmic, gentle hands.

On his right, Sevencrows patted his shoulder, adding a counterpoint of encouragement. "Steady up there, Big Guy. C'mon now—"

Rex shuddered. His mind shrieked terror, but he must think straight. His nose was full of Ordovich. Rex gasped, began panting too fast. *No. Stop. Get a grip.* He licked his lips. *Was Ordovich coming in, or did the trail overlay itself with another layer, going out?*

Coming, or coming-then-going?

Rex stress-yawned. He dipped his nose. Forced himself to sniff. *One scent-layer? Two?*

He pushed through hate and panic. *One or two?*

There . . . were two.

He shuddered again, re-checked it. The timing was close, but there definitely were two scent trails. One went toward the elevator with Archy and some other people. The other, made only by Ordovich and the strangers, departed toward the sally port. Better yet, the more recent layer contained massive anger-scent, mingled with harsh frustration.

Rex drew in a long, shaky breath. Held it. Let it out slowly. *Good. That was good.*

Ordovich had come, but then he had gone again.

The anger and frustration in his outward-bound scent meant he had not gotten what he wanted. That was good news, too. Maybe the Pack was safe. Dizzy with relief, Rex breathed more freely.

Ordovich is not here. Rex repeated it to himself like a mantra. Must get a grip. *He is not here. He left. He will NOT be waiting in Klein's office. NOT be ready to put a bullet in Rex's head. NOT be ready to lay on the strap in person.*

Oh, but that led him back to their errand. Just because Ordovich wasn't there, that didn't mean Rex wasn't in for a beating. There probably was no help for that, at this point. But he might live to see evening. He might be able to stay in Orangeboro, where he could at least talk to Shady. Relief swept over him, left him trembling.

"He's shaking again," Sevencrows said.

"Rex, you're scaring us, " Anthony cried. "What's wrong?"

Time to get this over with. It took all his focus and courage to step into the elevator. The tiny car still reeked of Ordovich, hot with fury, stinking of frustration. Rex focused on the smell of the man's frustration. That was where his hope lay.

Too soon, the doors slid open. The waiting room, the hallway with the wall-plantings and sparkling light-sconces . . . Rex walked between Anthony and Sevencrows, able to keep moving but still trembling. He focused on putting one foot in front of the other. *Useless to run.* Even when he'd had a whole planet to run away on, Ordovich and his dog wranglers had embedded some kind of locator in his body. He could never get away. Ordovich himself might have left, but the OPD followed the project's protocols. All he could do now was face what was coming with as much bravery as he could manage.

Scent layers told him that Bill also had walked down this hallway within recent minutes. So had Dr. Sandler, Ted, Caro, and Charlie's Uncle Hector, as well as Desk Officer Collins. *Why all of them? How many accusations are they bringing against me?*

His heart constricted with pain at this betrayal. How many times had he confided in a teacher, only for them to tell Ordovich about it? *Why do I keep trusting humans? Why can't I realize that none of them are—*

No. Not Ted and Caro. Not Bill! And surely Charlie would stand with me, if he wasn't . . . Rex winced. Charlie was in the ICU as a direct result of Rex's hubris. *Would even Charlie side with me, after that?*

Behind Klein's door . . . Rex tried to blank his mind, to just go away mentally, so he wouldn't think about what waited there. Experience had taught him it helped. A little, anyway. He, Anthony, and Sevencrows arrived at Klein's office door. Its latch made a quiet click. It swung open.

The three members of Corona Family rose from their seats on his left. They'd been sitting with Bill. Dr. Sandler and Officer Collins had been sitting on the right. They, too, stood when he arrived.

Chief Klein waited, dead ahead. "Thank you. Please join us."

Rex kept his head down. Anthony walked toward Dr. Sandler and Officer Collins. Sevencrows patted Rex's shoulder before he followed her. "Chin up. It'll be okay."

He clearly had never seen what would come next. Rex stifled a whimper.

Chief Klein strode toward him. "You've been a busy dog today."

Rex braced himself. He crouched, tail tucked under his belly. Couldn't keep from cringing, but he didn't retreat.

"Rex?" Klein knelt in front of him, reached out.

Rex flinched away.

"Rex?" Klein smelled . . . that was weird. He didn't smell angry at all, but worried. Even sad. He sighed, ran his hand very gently along Rex's neck. "Guys, has something happened to him?"

"We reported on the chase, and the shed." Anthony sounded worried.

"I don't have a good picture of what happened with the shed." Dr. Sandler knelt beside Klein. "Odd behaviors can result from frightening injuries."

Rex kept his gaze focused on the carpet's pattern. Sandler bent to make eye contact, but he avoided her gaze.

"Were you hurt?" She ran her hands over his head, his neck, across shoulders, then down his forelegs. She worked around the panniers, testing. Probing. "Tell me about the shed."

"An illegal structure built against the side of a storage building," Anthony said. "I've issued several citations, but the owner's right that you can't get building permits in the Five . . ." She hesitated. "It collapsed."

Now Sandler's fingers explored his hips, haunches, hind legs. She found a lot more bruises than Rex anticipated. "Were you near it when it fell?"

The next-to-last thing Rex wanted was a return trip to Dr. Sandler's clinic, but the human had asked him a question. *Better answer honestly.* There were too many witnesses, and he was already in enough trouble. "Elmo and I knocked it down. Part of it fell on us."

"Part of it? How much of it?"

Anthony made an impatient sound. "The part underneath all the rest of it. Rex had just collared LSA Shimon's person of interest when they slid into the side of the shed. It was a flimsy piece of—um, it was not well built, so it caved in on them."

Rex lifted his head, urgent to stave off more vet-clinic time if he could. "But I am all right. XK9s are—"

"Tough. Yes, you've told me that already." Dr. Sandler's brows, mouth and scent made her displeasure clear. "I still mean to give you another exam." She turned to Anthony. "When did these odd behaviors begin?"

"He acted fine, till I told him we were supposed to report here. After that, you'd have thought we were hauling him away to the pits of Hell. He got even more upset by the elevator in the foyer."

Klein gave a little grunt of dismay. "Ah. I suspect he smelled Dr. Ordovich by the elevator. He was just here. I'm sorry, Rex. I forgot you'd cross his scent-trail there."

"I've seen a lot of panic attacks in my day," Anthony said. "I've rarely seen anyone or anything react like Rex did."

"Most of the partners have told me how little the dogs liked Dr. Ordovich," Klein said. "After hearing Jill's report on Rex' bone-scans—well, it seems they had good reason."

Rex wasn't sure how to interpret the Chief's reaction. His scent factors signaled dismay, anger, deep unhappiness . . . But he did not smell or act like a man intent on beating a dog. He kept his focus on Anthony. "Was the person of interest injured?"

Anthony shook her head. "Paramedics said he sustained only minor scratches and bruises. Rex was standing over him. The shed mostly hit Rex. I don't know how LSA Shimon did it, but he lifted up part of the wreckage, so Rex and Elmo could escape."

Dr. Sandler's scent hardened with determination. "Definitely need another exam."

Klein smiled at Rex. "I knew you'd find him once you'd picked up his trail. Good work!"

A pale ray of hope brightened Rex's spirit, brought his head up again. "Thank you, sir." He untucked his tail and fluttered it, but kept it low, ready to go back into a submissive crouch. It might be possible that he wasn't in for a beating after all, but he couldn't fathom why not.

"But that brings us back to the reason we're here." Klein crossed his arms and tilted his head. He eyed Rex as if he was a challenging enigma. "You should know that you have been a great source of ongoing curiosity, not to mention considerable speculation, today. From the time your Family reported you missing this morning, we've been tracking you via your badge, wondering where you were going, and what you meant to do."

Rex's ears went up. He cocked his head, then realized Klein might see that as mimicry, and shrank back. "You have? But . . . you did not stop me. May I ask why not?"

"We wanted to see what you'd do." Klein gave him a quizzical look. "You weren't running amok or causing trouble. You clearly had a plan. I suspect Archy and Joslyn had an office pool going for a while, until we realized you must be headed for HQ. But we still had no notion of what you meant to do, until you got here."

Rex bowed his head, tingling with chagrin. "I guess my stealth attempts looked pretty silly."

"Oh, no. They were fascinating." Klein's half-smile came paired with a puzzled brow-pucker. "Quite a marvelous demonstration of your skills. If we hadn't had your badge to track, we frequently wouldn't have been able to spot you at all."

Rex flicked his ears, unexpectedly gratified, but unwilling to relax just yet. He could still be in trouble. Scratch that: likely *was* still in trouble.

"Several of the people you've encountered have alerted me to your surprising level of initiative," Klein continued. "Even before SSA Adeyeme called me this afternoon, I was planning to ask most of them here for a discussion. When we were considering our purchase of the Pack, I was never led to expect this kind of behavior from an XK9. But then when—"

Rex cowered low again, his face averted. "I am sorry. Sometimes I get so full of ideas I . . . I become insubordinate." He shrank in on himself. Sick fear pulsed through him.

The worry returned to Chief Klein's scent. "Rex, what are you afraid of? Why do you cringe like that?"

Rex kept his head bowed, tail clamped firmly under his belly again. "I do not like beatings, sir, even when I know I deserve them."

Klein's scent suffused with revulsion. "You think I plan to beat you?"

Rex hazarded a glance up at the Chief. *Could this be?* "Do you not?"

Chief Klein stood with a groan. Angry dismay filled his scent. "What have I ever done to make you think I would beat you?"

Rex hunched his back, lowered his head. "You separated the Pack. Charlie said the OPD follows XK9 Project protocols. Dr. Sandler's techs have a prod, so we have always assumed you also must have trank rifles, nets, dark crates, and beating straps."

Klein stared at him, his face and scent redolent with dark dismay. After a while he drew in a long breath. "Who are 'we'? You said, 'we always assumed.' Who are 'we'?"

Rex kept his tail tucked, his head low. "Shady and I talk on our coms. No one expressly forbade us, and we miss each other very much. It is not like touching and smelling, but it is contact of a sort." He hesitated. "Please do not be angry."

Klein scrubbed his hands over his face, then dropped his hands to his sides and stared at Rex with sad eyes. "I'm not angry at you. I'm not going to forbid you to talk on the com, and I'm not going to beat you."

Heart pounding hard, still disbelieving, Rex dared to uncurl a bit more. "The Dark Crate, then?"

The sadness in Klein's scent redoubled. He shook his head. "No. No 'dark crate,' either. Is that what Ordovich would do?"

Fear stabbed Rex. He cringed again. "I am not supposed to talk about it."

Now Klein smelled angry. "The rules have changed, Rex."

His voice rang like steel on stone. "It's okay to talk about it to me. In fact, I insist."

Rex froze, but a tiny tendril of hope arose. It warmed, strengthened, pushed upward through icy despair. Klein was Rex's new owner. *Ordovich had sold him.*

Klein makes the rules here.

It even appeared that Klein had chased Ordovich away—and he'd done it in spite of Ordovich's Ranan Executive Security detail and the Premier's personal approval.

Rex lifted his head. If Chief Klein said it was okay . . . maybe it really was okay.

So Rex told him.

25

ANSWERS AND NON-ANSWERS

Orangeboro Morgue, S-3-9 and S-3-10, and OPD Detention Suite K

Shady took shallow breaths of fetid air, but the rotting death-smell overpowered everything. She stood rock-still while Pam's hands flew, filling her panniers with morgue supplies as fast as possible. Berwyn and Liz filled Cinnamon and Razor's panniers at breakneck speed, too.

Morgue techs scurried about, their hands full of things that needed packing. Industrial-size exhaust fans roared, too loud for chit-chat. They'd needed special venting and filters, to maintain Central District's air quality. The news feeds said there was a movement afoot to sue Treasurer Darius for those extra costs.

Workers had almost finished clearing a section of storage cubicles adjacent to Adeyeme's war room in S-3-9. They'd been installing refrigeration units as soon as space opened up. Once the entire area was repurposed and all morgue equipment placed, the accesses to the S-3-10 corridor would be secured, sealed and alarmed. After that, the only morgue access would be through SBI-controlled areas. Shady looked forward to being in a facility where their evidence could be handled properly.

That's all I can stuff in. Pam hoisted a pack onto her own back and grabbed the handle of a trolley. *Let's get out of here!*

With pleasure. Shady headed for S-3-9 at a heavy walk. Her panniers weighed considerably more than twice their usual. She labored up a ramp, then crossed the courtyard where they'd taken their break earlier. The scent trails of Archy, Dr. Ordovich, the military woman, and the large RES officer still lay in an upper layer by the colonnade entrance. Where had Chief Klein taken Dr. Ordovich? *Someplace far, far away,* she hoped. Neither Klein nor Archy had seemed happy to see Ordovich. She hoped that was a good sign.

And what was Rex up to? Why in all of space wasn't he at Corona Tower? Why did Archy lie to Dr. Ordovich and say he was? She'd texted Rex a warning about Ordovich, but the com said he hadn't read her message yet. She'd walked out of the worst morgue-stench, but her stomach clenched and rolled with anxiety. *What if he'd met Dr. Ordovich? What if Ordovich wanted to put him down, the way he'd killed Fernie and Chaser?*

What if? What if? We don't know, and you're making yourself crazy, Pam said through the link. *Yourself, and me too. Why don't you go to your happy place and try not to think about it for a while?*

But my happy place is curled up with Rex.

That's not helping.

Neither are you. Quit eavesdropping on my thoughts.

I don't mean to eavesdrop. You're not distancing yourself from the link too well. Probably too tired and worried. And I'm sorry.

Shady stress-yawned. *Me too.* Head down to balance the load better, she entered a cross-hallway and Rex's beloved scent suddenly was all around her. Rex had passed this way, no more than three hours ago!

Well. Damn if you weren't right. Pam had been dubious about her judgment that Archy was lying to Ordovich. *I wonder what he's up to.*

Shady moved a couple meters down, stopped again. *He went*

toward Detention . . . with LSA Shimon? She raised her head to share a puzzled look with Pam.

Bet we'll find answers in the war room.

Unload panniers first.

Definitely!

They rode down to S-3-10, deposited their loads, then both partners stretched weary muscles. After hauling all that weight, Shady had the odd sensation of semi-floating into the war room.

"There's one!" SA Emshwiller leaned over her workstation to wave an arm at someone out of view. "Hey, Frankie! Shady's right here!"

Wiry SA Freas poked his head around the corner. "Perfect! You two do interviews, don't you?"

"Sure," Pam said.

"Great! Shimon's in Detention with a subject of interest, but he needs an XK9 team to cover the interview. He even asked for Shady."

"What happened to that enormous black dog that was in here earlier?" Emshwiller asked. "Can't he do interviews?"

Startled, Shady wondered the same thing. "Of course, he can."

"All I know is, Shimon needs an XK9, ASAP, preferably Shady." Freas beckoned to Shady and Pam. "C'mon, let's go!"

Pam frowned at Shady. *This can't be just so Rex can touch noses with you.*

Once back in the elevator, Shady turned to SA Freas. "Why was Rex in the war room?"

Freas gave a sharp laugh. "Rex is his name? Huh. I'm still not sure why he was there. He just showed up out of nowhere. Shimon about had a fit, as you might imagine. Everybody came to see who he was yelling at, including Adeyeme."

"I'm surprised she went anywhere near Rex," Pam said.

"You and everybody else." Freas gave her a bemused head shake. "That big ol' dog just rolled over at her feet and started babbling about what an incredible honor it was to meet her, and how legendary she was among XK9s, and how she was so smart and brave."

Shady's mind spun. *What was Rex thinking? What was he up to?*

The elevator doors rolled open. "Next thing I know, the dog's sitting at her feet, staring up at her like she's God's gift to the Universe, and she's telling him and Shimon to go 'fetch her a subject.'" Freas offered Pam an amazed smile. "Looks like they went and did it."

I'm trying to imagine Adeyeme getting anywhere near Rex. Pam's amused astonishment resounded through the link. *He'd be almost as tall as she is!*

Shady flicked her ears. *I'm interested to get his impressions of The Icicle.* In the time they'd worked with SIT Delta, Kramer was the LSA who dealt with the XK9s. Tall, pale, immaculate Shimon had kept the team's three XK9s at a distinctly frosty distance.

They arrived in Detention.

"Suite K," the desk officer said.

Disappointment stabbed Shady. *Rex isn't here.* Her ears and tail drooped. Would they ever catch a break? *Can't smell him anywhere. Should've guessed, I suppose, when they needed an XK9.*

Shimon'll know where he is.

The door to Interview K was closed, with the OCCUPIED blinker on.

LSA Shimon stood at the threshold of Observation K, focused inside. "Check," he said. "Check. Check. Sounds good." His normally impeccable blue-black jacket and trousers bore large streaks of light-gray regolith dust.

Pam chuckled. *Oh, yes, he definitely met Rex.*

Shimon turned to greet them. Dust streaked his face and made his pale hair look almost white. From the smell of him, he'd gotten overly warm during his outing. His face lit up with a grin at the sight of Shady, Pam, and SA Freas. It was an expression Shady had never seen on his face before.

"Adventuresome afternoon?" Freas asked.

"You could say that." Shimon's blue eyes crinkled at the corners, fierce and eager. "We got him, though."

Pam sighed quietly. *Oh, God, I thought he looked adorable BEFORE.*

Shady stifled a snort. *You're as bad as Berwyn. What would Balchu say?*

Do not breathe a WORD of this to Balchu!

Shady wagged her tail. *I could be persuaded to keep quiet.*

Pam scowled at her. *Anyway, Berwyn's WAY worse.*

Shady gave her a dubious look. *If you say so.*

"Shady! Excellent!" Now Shimon was smiling at *her*. What magic had Rex wrought, to change his attitude so? "Our subject today is Elmo Smart."

Shady's ears went up. "The mugger?"

"Good. You know who he is." Shimon glanced over to make eye contact with Pam as well. "I'd planned on working with Rex, but the Chief needed him for something, so I figured I'd ask for his mate."

A quick jolt of worry shot through Shady, sent her heart rate up. "Is Rex in trouble?"

Shimon shook his head. "Not that I'm aware, although he may have a few bruises after a run-in with a shed." No deception in his scent. If Rex was being punished, Shimon didn't know.

Chest tight, Shady hoped it wasn't as bad as she feared. *Always in the past, if Rex was caught out wandering where he shouldn't be . . . but then again, Chief Klein hadn't seemed at all happy to see Ordovich. Maybe that meant . . . Oh, this is too confusing.* She cocked her head at Shimon. "His 'run-in with a shed'?"

"Yeah. The shed lost. He and Elmo crashed into it. It fell on them, but Rex tells me XK9s are tough." Shimon shook his head, smiling. "Had me going for a minute there, but he certainly did look okay when he leaped out of the rubble."

Trust Rex! Shady sighed, but her heart pounded faster than normal. Her HUD pinged. The new file was Elmo's police record. *Mm. Better keep my mind on work.*

"Take a moment to look it over." Shimon turned to Freas. "Rex says this man and several others entered the *Izgubil* through the service entrance eight days before the ship's destruction, then left with the same group a few hours later. Do you know if those corridor pads and handholds were destroyed in the breach?"

Shady looked up. "Oh! If they are still recoverable, please specify that they be collected according to scent evidence protocols."

"Good idea," Pam agreed. "Shady, Cinnamon, and Razor may be able to get more scent profiles from them, even if there was traffic afterward. Scent evidence protocols also increase the likelihood of preserving prints, DNA, and trace." She grinned at Shady. *Nice catch!*

"Scent evidence protocols they shall be," Freas said. "Want me to go do that now, or stay to monitor the interview?"

"I think Shady's partner—" Shimon elevated an eyebrow at Pam.

She smiled her most dazzling smile, the one that always made men sit up and take notice. "DPO Pamela Gómez. Call me Pam."

The smile he returned was pleasant, but nothing in Shimon's scent or other reactions showed he particularly appreciated her charms. "Thanks, Frankie. I think Pam can cover that."

"You've got it." Freas departed at a brisk pace, already speaking into his com.

"Do you want me in the booth or with you?" Shady asked.

Shimon shot a look toward the OCCUPIED door. "I think Elmo's had enough XK9 contact for one day. Sound Tech Samuels, here, tells me there's a vent so an XK9 can smell but stay hidden. Let's have you use that."

Disappointed—these retrofitted booths could be cramped—she nodded. "I can share scent impressions via text, if you wish."

His grin returned. "Perfect. Do that." He glanced into the

booth. "You'll join Assistant Borough Attorney Regan Ireland, and this is Samuels."

Both a slender, cool-eyed woman in an expensive suit and the pale, lanky young man hunched behind the booth's AV controls nodded to them.

Shady wedged herself into a corner of the booth. The rig seemed to be in good order. Soundproof walls, one covered with a screen-skin fed by vids and sound pickups from the interview room next door, gave investigators clear audio and a variety of angles to observe and record interviews while remaining out of sight and earshot. The booth's retrofit included an access vent and a second, smaller screen that allowed a hidden XK9 to hear, smell, and observe body language—though not as well as being in the same room. Shady settled herself next to the vent and watched on the smaller screen.

Shimon entered the interview room. He gave Elmo a brief smile. "Mr. Smart, I'm LSA Shiva Shimon. Would you like something to drink?"

Elmo kept his eyes down. "Bourbon, rocks." Shady smelled stubbornness in his scent, read tight anger in his body. She reported all of this via text to Shimon, the ABA, and her interview log; Pam could follow via their link.

"Mmm, sorry," Shimon told Elmo. "None of the machines dispense that. Settle for water? Coffee? Tea?"

"Why am I here? I made bail!" Elmo glared at Shimon. "Also, you ain't read me my rights!"

Shimon shook his head. "You're detained, and there are several things I could charge you with—"

"Like what?" Elmo narrowed his eyes. His jaw jutted aggressively.

Shimon simply looked at him for a couple of seconds, then shrugged. "Resisting detainment, fleeing to elude, destruction of property—"

"That's *you* guyses' fault! If you hadn't—"

"I'd really rather not arrest you. I just want to ask a couple of questions."

"Yeah, right." Elmo crossed his arms, looked away. "Tell me another one."

Shimon sat down in the chair across from him. "You actually might benefit from talking with me. We believe you have some valuable information."

Elmo looked surprised. His expression mirrored his scent factors' shift from the hot smells of mulish resistance to cooler calculation. "Valuable?" Shady noted all of this in her texts and log.

"My colleagues and I are investigating the destruction of the *Izgubil*. You may remember—"

A sudden wash of terror wiped out the burgeoning craftiness in Elmo's scent factors. He stiffened, pulled back in his chair. "I don't know nothing about that!"

"He definitely knows something about that," Shady texted. "He also is terrified."

Shimon leaned away a little, hands up in a pacifying gesture. "Smooth out, man. We're simply trying to develop a better picture of what was going on aboard the ship."

Sweaty panic drenched Elmo's scent. "I don't know nothing about that ship!"

"Careful," Shady said. "This makes him red-zone uncomfortable."

Shimon regarded Elmo for a moment. "Look, we know you went there with some of your buddies nine or ten days ago. We simply—"

Elmo lurched to his feet. "No! No! Hell no! I was never there! You can't prove a thing! I want my lawyer!"

"He smells guilty as hell," Shady texted. "He is much more deeply involved than you may have thought."

26

A COMBINED WEIGHT OF AWFULNESS

OPD HQ, Chief Klein's Office

Rex forced himself to remember. Speaking of this, even to one's partner in strict confidentiality, had always been forbidden. In the presence of nine humans in Chief Klein's office, Rex couldn't shake a sensation of doing something horribly wrong. But Klein was his master, now. Klein made the rules. Rex must obey Chief Klein. "Dr. Ordovich always delivered the beatings himself." He hesitated.

Klein leaned forward in his desk chair, gave a curt nod. "Describe."

Rex's gut clenched at the memory. He hunched his back, head low. "He would begin with a strap. He had one about half a meter long, with a handle on one end. He would put me into a short run, so I could not get away. Then he would hit me with the strap until his arm got tired. He would switch arms—"

"Stop." Klein's scent factors roiled with discomfort. He rose from his chair.

Rex stopped. He gave Klein a questioning look, but the Chief's gaze focused on the three members of Corona Family.

"My God, Rex! Does Charlie know about this?" Caro cried.

Rex bowed his head. "We were warned never to tell our partners about any of this. It has caused awkwardness between us when Charlie knew I was not honest with him. But Dr. Ordovich said we would not go to Orangeboro if we ever said anything about it to anyone."

Caro hurried over to kneel beside Rex. She put her arms around him and gave him a hard hug. "Oh, sweetie! How awful for you!"

Klein looked down and away. "Yes. Marisol, you may recall our conversation of earlier today?" he nodded. "Yes, looks as if I have a case for you. We need to talk at your soonest . . . good. My office, with a couple of detectives."

A case? Rex stared at him.

"As you will have surmised, this is now a criminal case." Klein looked up to make eye contact with his listeners. "felony animal abuse, at the very least. Lt. Patel will be here shortly."

The humans all nodded, but Rex cocked his head at the Chief. In school he'd memorized the System Statutory Code. Once he knew he was Orangeboro-bound, he'd also learned all of Rana Station's laws and Orangeboro's Borough ordinances. But this was new. "What is 'felony animal abuse'? I am not aware of that law."

"I doubt that's one Dr. Ordovich wanted you to know." Klein made a disgusted face, shook his head.

Rex remained confused. "Do we have jurisdiction? All the beatings happened in Transmondia."

"Don't worry about that." Klein's scowl did not lighten. "We're just getting started."

"Oh." Rex flicked his ears, still uncertain. "Shall I continue?"

Klein released a long breath. "Let's wait for Lt. Patel." He balled his fists. The Chief's scent factors, like those of the other humans, seethed with angry unease. He turned to the three Corona Family members. "I will not ask you to listen to the rest of Rex's testimony. However, Lt. Patel's detectives do need to interview you about your observations of Rex's behavior, and they'll have questions regarding your estimation of his intelligence. This entire matter is to be held in strict confidence until the investigation has established a few more facts."

Still kneeling with her arms around Rex, Caro nodded. "Anything to help!" From the corner of his eye, Rex glimpsed nods of agreement from both Ted and Hector.

Rex's throat went tight. His heart filled with glorious, unexpected warmth. These humans had only known him for two months. Yet their scents and their words made it clear that, as far as they were concerned, Rex was part of Corona Family. That staggered and astounded him.

He'd never imagined such a bond could exist outside of the Pack, between species. There'd been a time when he was convinced he'd never take a partner, because no human could be trusted. His concept of "Pack" had since expanded to embrace the unexpected wonder of Charlie. But now it seemed clear it must expand again. Nothing in all of his experience had given him reason to imagine humans like these. He was Pack to them. They now must become Pack to him. For a heart-filled moment he could only marvel in overwhelmed gratitude.

Klein gave them a grave smile. "Thank you." He turned next to Collins, Anthony and Sevencrows. "I want each of you to write reports on your interactions with Rex today, from the moment you met him until now. Don't consult with each other; you know the drill. Detail everything you remember about your impressions, Rex's behavior, and his demonstrated intelligence. Submit them to Lt. Patel. Take as much time as you need. When you finish, you are released for the rest of this duty watch. Report as usual tomorrow, but say *nothing* about this investigation until you receive authorization to discuss it."

All three officers nodded, their manner grave. "Yes, sir." "Absolutely, sir." "Understood."

"Good. Dismissed."

They turned toward the door immediately, although Sevencrows shot one glance backward, to offer Rex a tight-lipped nod. Rex answered with a twitch of his tail-tip.

"Unfortunately, Jill, you're not finished." Klein focused on Dr. Sandler.

She nodded, frowning. "I need to hear the whole account, then do another complete exam—this time, a forensic exam, building on those deep-level bone scans I told you about. In addition to checking him out after this incident with the shed."

"Mm," Klein offered a look of acknowledgement. "We have to establish a few other facts before I can release him to you."

"I'll want to keep him overnight, in any case. There'll be time."

Rex's heart sank. *Overnight?* He'd really been looking forward to his own bed. But it wasn't his decision. He heaved a soft sigh.

Klein turned to Bill. "Corporal Sloane, I have a special assignment for you, if you'll accept it."

"I want to help Rex any way I can."

Klein's expression brightened with a brief smile. "I hoped you'd say that. You've already been acting as Rex's Personnel Assistance Liaison. Since his partner is incapacitated, I wondered if you'd be willing to work alongside Lt. Patel's investigation, as Rex's Victim Advocate."

"That would be my honor, sir."

"It could mean some long hours."

"I'll alert my Family."

The door clicked then swung open for three new humans. Klein nodded to them. "Marisol. Thank you for coming so quickly." He introduced the taller woman as Lt. Marisol Patel, the short woman as DPO Jo Karrell, and the man as DPO Rodney Moreno. Moreno politely ushered the Corona Family members out and down the hall.

Rex's spirits dampened to see them leave without him. But he still had work to do. He felt Lt. Patel's gaze upon him, looked up to meet her dark, serious eyes.

Lt. Patel smiled. "So. This is 'The One,' am I right?"

Klein's mouth made a rueful twist. "This is Rex, our most independent thinker."

"Also abuse victim? Is that confirmed?" Patel glanced at Dr. Sandler.

"Rex has just been telling us," Dr. Sandler said. "Go ahead, Rex."

Patel nodded. "Yes, please start at the beginning."

The moment the topic returned to Ordovich's beatings, Rex's tongue slid out in a nervous pant. It was important to be thorough. He understood that. They needed the documentation. He drew in a shaky breath, blew it out slowly, counting the way Charlie sometimes did. Then, one by one, he confessed his crimes and described the punishments Ordovich had exacted. It was hard. But it was necessary.

Remembering brought back every detail, fresh and new in his hyper-accurate memory. Every stinging stroke, every humiliation, every denigrating word of excoriation. He experienced it all over again. He couldn't stand still. He paced and panted and flinched and winced, and relived for them every beating, every curse, every insult, and every brutal recapture.

He described the stifling heat, the darkness, the stale, noisome water-pan, and the rank wretchedness of the days-long cratings, followed always by the harsh, cold blast of a hose before he retreated, tail-tucked and defeated, to his kennel.

Klein and the others flinched and winced and grimaced and listened. The humans' scent factors told him they hated listening almost as much as he hated talking about it. It had been painful enough to live through the first time, but the awfulness had somehow been dispersed. Now, talking about it, the combined weight of Ordovich's "conditioning" efforts overwhelmed him. After a while, he simply couldn't go on. He was shuddering too hard, panting too breathlessly, too dizzy with despair.

Dr. Sandler stood. "That's it. I'm calling a break. He needs a moment. Let's give him a drink and a rest."

"I've heard more than enough to make a case." Lt. Patel massaged her temples.

Bill knelt beside Rex, his scent raw with distress, heavy with shared pain. He stroked and stroked until Rex stopped shuddering and his labored panting eased up. Somewhere in that process, Bill became Pack, too. After a while, Rex's awareness expanded from his narrow knot of pain to take in more of his surroundings.

The others stood, stretched, groaned. DPO Karrell excused herself to the restroom.

Chief Klein moved over to his window-wall. He stared toward its expansive view of Orangeboro's leeward end. The night mist had gone, but residual atmospheric humidity softened the far end of the torus's curve. It blurred the terraced hillsides and rendered their colors pastel near the part where the roof cut off the view. Klein's hands clasped behind his back. His fingers clenched, relaxed, clenched, relaxed. He might be doing measured breathing, too. His desk beeped. He ignored it. After a while, the beeping stopped.

Dr. Sandler brought water from somewhere, in a big, cutglass punchbowl. She set it down with care.

Rex gratefully drank it dry. "Thank you." He yawned a wide stress-yawn, then stretched with chest down, back arched, hips up, followed by shoulders up, hips down. He yawned again. *Is it finally over?* He'd told them about most of the beatings and cratings. Would that be enough?

After a while, Klein returned to his chair near Rex. The others gathered wordlessly.

Rex sat facing Klein. The Chief ran his hand through his hair, shifted on the chair, tugged his jacket straight. "That was . . . a *lot* to process. I want to thank you for your candor, Rex, and for going through it all. He hesitated, gave Rex a rueful look. "That *was* all, right?"

"Technically, there were five other incidents, but you have the big picture."

"It'll do for now." Chief Klein looked away, then met Rex's gaze. "I'm sorely tempted to stop there for the afternoon, but in all honesty I can't."

Rex tensed. *Uh-oh.*

From the other humans' scents and expressions, they were wondering what more he could possibly want to ask.

Unfortunately, Rex knew.

"There's still one mystery I need for you to clear up." Klein frowned at him, searching Rex with his gaze for several long, intense seconds. What did he see? "Why did you leave home this morning, walk seven kilometers, then insist on speaking with SSA Adeyeme?"

Yeah. That. Rex's throat went dry. His tongue slid out in a nervous pant once more. "You reactivated me, sir. You already know why."

Klein shook his head. "I want to know how you knew your information was valuable. What was your thinking process?"

Rex licked his lips, stress-yawned, then eased his tight muscles with a long, procrastinating, whole-body stretch. The silence stretched, elongated, grew heavy. Rex allowed himself one more stress-yawn, then sat. "I shall have to discuss details of the *Izgubil* case, to answer your question, sir." He glanced toward Bill, Patel, Karrell, and Dr. Sandler. "Am I allowed to do that?"

"The *Izgubil* case?" Klein gave him a startled look. "How much do you know about it? And how did you obtain your information?"

"I realized yesterday afternoon that I had yet not filed my formwork about the dock breach." Rex rose. He paced across the room and back. "I was restless, bored, needed something constructive to do. I was so desperate for something to do, I actually enjoyed filling out the formwork."

That elicited smiles from most of his listeners, but Klein's eyebrows-up look told Rex he still wasn't off the hook.

"After I filed the formwork . . ." He averted his eyes. "I discovered that I still had access to the case book."

There was a short silence.

"Are you saying you looked at it?" Klein asked.

Rex lowered his head, licked his lips. "I read it, sir."

Klein drew in a quiet breath. "How much of it?"

Rex didn't dare look at him. "All of it."

Sharp surprise rose in all five humans' scent factors. "All," Klein asked, "as in—?"

"Everything there was, at that point," Rex said. "It took me until about 01:30 or so."

"I'm not sure how big that case book might have been, but this does not correlate with the reading scores we received from the XK9 Project," Dr. Sandler said.

"I suspect we'll need to re-test the entire Pack." Klein's face hardened. Anger swirled in his scent, dark and dangerous and lava-hot. "I believe we have been lied to. About a great many things."

The others nodded, their scents and expressions grim.

"I am trying to be completely honest, sir." Rex gave him a worried look.

Klein shook his head. "It's not you I'm thinking about, in this instance."

"Oh." Rex put his ears down. *Who, then? Dr. Ordovich?*

Klein drew in a long breath, then pinned Rex with his determined look. "Setting aside for a moment the questions of your right to read the case book, and the speed and comprehension with which you accomplished the task, I want to know why you did it."

27

REX TELLS MORE FORBIDDEN THINGS

OPD HQ, Chief Klein's Office

Rex clamped his jaws on the rising sourness of his bitter chagrin. He lowered his head and looked from Klein to the others in the Chief's office.

Patel and Karrell eyed him with masklike, professional expressions. Their scent factors shifted into a piquant, musky blend of horrified fascination. Dr. Sandler pursed her lips, frowning. Bill's uneasy scent suggested he'd been scandalized by Rex's admission, but hoped he'd had a good reason. Klein might not intend to beat him, but the humans' reactions were a punishment in themselves.

Rex returned his gaze to the Chief's brows-up, expectant regard. His throat tightened. He probably couldn't get into much more trouble than he was in already. Might as well be truthful. "At first I took only a glimpse, from sheer curiosity." Remembered surprise and admiration surged through him. His tail fluttered, but he stilled it. "I meant to stop there."

He stress-yawned. No one spoke. They all looked at him. No one had to ask *so why didn't you?* The question hung in the air over his head and pressed him down.

If only I could explain how I felt! Maybe they'd understand. "Then I realized how well SSA Adeyeme organized things. This is an extremely complex case, but she created a masterful, orderly, structure. The more I looked, the more . . ." *I'm babbling.* Humiliation washed over him in waves.

They stared at him. As if he'd sprouted purple wings, or something.

"I was learning so much!" He lowered his head, too heavy with pain to hold it up. Futile to hope the floor would swallow him. It never had before in Transmondia. Why should Ranan floors be more gracious? He licked dry lips. Stress-yawned again. "I know that I am just a dog. And dogs cannot be real detectives. But I confess that I do sometimes daydream about how I might conduct an investigation. If . . . well, if I were in charge."

Chief Klein drew in a long breath. Eyed him warily. "And, if you were in charge, then what?"

Rex lifted his head, half-raised his ears. "One thing I know for sure. If I were in charge, I can only hope I would be able to do half as well as SSA Adeyeme." Warm admiration rose within him. His tail was wagging before he realized it. "She has observed the larger patterns and brought order to a chaotic case. She is amazing."

Klein looked away with a little head shake and a hunch of shoulders. "It's true you could find far worse role-models."

Rex wagged his tail, relieved by even a small agreement. "Thank you. Yes, I think so. And now that I am on the case . . ." His mind skipped ahead, then smacked into the same inexplicable mystery. Now that he was on the case, there was a problem that needed to be addressed right away. He gave a soft growl and lowered his ears. "There is only one area where I cannot understand the conduct of this case, and that one may not be her fault."

"Oh, I see. You admire her ardently." Klein crossed his arms.

"Except, of course, in this one area, where you could do things better?"

Rex's ears and tail went up. "Yes, sir. The debris analysis. If I read between the lines correctly, the SDF is supposed to supply some kind of help with that, but it has not yet arrived."

Klein sucked in a breath, but shook his head when Rex paused. "Go on. If you were in charge, what would you do with the debris?"

"That is easy." Rex wagged his tail. "If I were in charge, I would assign the whole Pack to work on the analysis together."

Dr. Sandler frowned. "The whole Pack? Why?"

"Well, those debris piles are enormous. We shall need all of us."

She shook her head. "What would the Pack do with them?"

"We are all certified in aircraft wreckage analysis." Rex wagged his tail faster now. This was familiar ground. "There would be some important differences in the analysis of a spacecraft, but many more similarities. And we XK9s can perform the analysis with much greater speed and accuracy than humans can, with their current tools."

"Hold on a minute," Klein said. "I know about your aircraft wreckage certification. I know you can analyze by scent discrimination more quickly than our mechanical tools. But there's a major difference between telling the humans what substances you've detected and doing the analysis yourselves."

Rex wagged his tail faster. "That is true, sir, but we can do both. We almost had a chance to prove it once in Transmondia, but our instructors stopped us."

"I need to hear that story," Patel said.

Klein nodded. "Me, too. It's certainly germane to our investigation. Why don't you tell us about it?"

How could wreckage analysis be germane to an abuse investigation? Rex cocked his head. *But never mind. The human asked a question, and this is one forbidden topic I've been itching to talk about for ages.*

"During our last phase of training, a small, unmanned flitter crashed on one of the Project's farms. A caretaker witnessed it. He said it made a bang, as if it had exploded. Dr. Ordovich sent me, along with our Pack's three explosives experts, Tuxedo, Cinnamon, and Crystal, to examine it. Well, and also our instructors."

Patel frowned. "Explosives experts?"

"Rex is a generalist who does everything well," Klein said. "So is Tuxedo. But Tux and the other two also have taken specialized training."

Patel nodded. "So your instructors took the four of you to this crash site?"

"Yes. We were nearby for a different training exercise, but it was a good opportunity for field experience," Rex said. "We got there well before the Transmondian Aviation Supervisory Office analysts. It was a remote place, and the TASO people had farther to go. After we arrived, we found all the major sections of the crash. It extended over a fair distance. Our instructors lasered them off, and then settled in to wait. But we got bored. We were puppies. Three of us had just turned six, and Crystal was still five. We did not have much patience."

"As I understand it, patience can still be a problem for you." Klein's dry tone matched his raised eyebrow and sent a guilty pang through Rex.

He lowered his ears. "True, sir."

"Go on. You were bored and impatient, so what did you do?" Patel asked.

"We decided to play a game. We asked our instructors if we could try analyzing the site, as long as we didn't touch anything. We would do a scent analysis and reassemble the wreck virtually, on our HUDs. We'd just gotten upgrades on the HUDs, so it was good to practice with them."

Klein nodded. "What did your instructors think of this idea?"

"They scoffed at us. They told us what you did, that analyzing piece by piece, and analyzing the entire wreck were two entirely different things. But we wanted to try my—um, our idea."

"Whose idea?" Patel asked.

Rex ducked his head. "I guess technically it started out as my idea. But Tuxedo and Cinnamon improved on it immediately, and Crystal made several good points, so by then it belonged to all of us."

"I see. When you insisted, what happened?" Klein asked.

"They laughed and warned us we would be in serious trouble if we touched anything. Then they told us to go ahead and try it. Prove to ourselves it was harder than we thought. They had a good snicker about it, then moved over to the other side of the lasers. They opened a cooler of beer that one of them had brought and settled in to wait."

Klein sighed. "Beer at a wreck site. How professional."

"How did your game go?" Patel asked.

Rex wagged his tail. "It was fun. Challenging. But fun, not having to wait for the slow humans. We each took a section of the wreckage, analyzed it, then virtually reconstructed it. After that, we added those assemblages to the collective model. We kept assembling more and more parts of it, until we had most of it put back together in the virtual model. At that point our instructors called us in, because the TASO analysts were only a few kilometers away. They didn't want us loose in the crash site when the Feds arrived."

Patel nodded. "Yeah, that would look bad."

"Bet they hid the beer, too," Klein said.

Rex let his tongue slide out to loll. "Yes. But even the TASO humans could smell it on their breath. They were not pleased."

"Imagine that," Klein said. "Did you show your reconstruction to your instructors?"

"Yes. We were excited, because we had found the system that failed. We realized immediately that explosives had nothing to do with the crash. No explosives residue. But it took more than two hours to establish which part broke from metal fatigue. It blew out one side of the engine when it gave way. That was why the witness reported a loud noise like an explosion."

"That's pretty impressive," Klein said. "What did your instructors say?"

Rex's ears and tail drooped. "The lead instructor took one look at our 3D model, yelled a bunch of curses, and ordered us to delete it. He said they would all be fired if this got out, and we must never, ever let Dr. Ordovich know anything about it."

"Did you obey?" Patel asked.

Rex averted his eyes but drew back his lips in a snarl. "Of course, we did. They were our instructors. We had to obey them. We did not want to be punished."

Patel expelled a deep breath. "Well, there's your pattern of collusion to obstruct, plus destruction of evidence. I certainly would love to have seen that reconstruction."

Rex cocked his head at her. *Collusion to obstruct what? Destruction of what evidence? What case is she really working on? Did Dr. Ordovich or the instructors break a different law I've never heard of?* He focused on her final statement. "We no longer have our files, but we could describe it for you, if you like. Everyone in the Pack has been bred to have a highly superior autobiographical memory. I remember every piece that went into my reconstruction. I am sure Tuxedo, Cinnamon, and Crystal do, too. We also could provide the case number, if you wish to compare it with TASO records."

"Get those details in follow-up, and corroborate when you interview the others," Klein said to Patel, then turned to Rex again. "Meanwhile, I'm curious. How long did it take the four of you to reconstruct that little flitter and find the cause of the crash?"

"Three hours, seventeen minutes," Rex said. "We wanted to finish before TASO got there."

Klein nodded, frowning. "And how long did it take the humans?"

Rex gave a soft growl. "Almost two entire days. It was

extremely frustrating. We kept trying to point out the part that failed, but they insisted on doing it their way."

"Mm-hmm," Klein said. "And did they reach the same conclusion you did?"

"Of course they did. They were not incompetent. They simply did not have good tools of their own. We could not tell them straight out, because we had been ordered not to talk about our game. We did a lot of hinting and nose-pointing, but they mostly ignored us."

Klein shook his head. "Humans. They can be so obtuse sometimes, right?"

Rex lolled his tongue. "Exactly! It can be very—" He stopped when Klein's expression changed. Alarm shot through him. "Oh! I am sorry, sir. I see. You were joking."

"And you were not." Klein eyed him for a moment, his brows in a wary pucker. "Good to know and remember. Humans apparently really are obtuse."

Rex went back into a crouch. "I did not mean to offend."

Klein shook his head. He smelled partly flummoxed, partly sad. "You didn't. You're fine. It's we humans who may be in serious trouble."

There it is again, that hint at something I don't know. This is becoming annoying. "What are you not telling me, sir? It is obvious by now that Lt. Patel is not simply investigating animal abuse."

Klein and Patel exchanged a look. Karrell avoided Rex's gaze, but Bill met his eyes with a worried expression. Dr. Sandler seemed suddenly riveted by something on her case pad.

Rex was definitely onto something.

Klein's scent surged with discomfort. "I am reluctant to explain it yet. Please trust me?"

Rex flicked his ears. Charlie was not here. Bill had not spoken up. Who else could he trust? "You are my owner. I have no choice but to trust you."

Klein gave a soft little moan. "And there it is." He smelled and sounded deeply shaken.

Patel drew in a quiet breath. "This is only the first generation. Will the modifications carry over?"

Klein's shoulders drooped. He shook his head. "Doesn't matter. I see what Rex is. I've seen what the other XK9s are. Right here. Right now. I've known it for a while in my gut, and Rex just said it."

He stood, fists clenched, then gave Rex the saddest, most searching gaze he'd ever met. "This is exactly why Ordovich was here today, so hyper and prickly and urgent to invoke the Premier. He knows what he's done, Marisol. Now he's discovering that all of his draconian conditioning has failed. That's what all his blather about 'insubordination' and 'temperament flaws' boils down to. He's getting desperate."

Rex stared at the Chief. Each of Klein's words sent a shock wave through him, until he was so full of reverberations he could barely think.

Klein lifted his hands halfway up, then lowered them, his face carved with despair, his scent factors heartsick. "Damn it, we're a law enforcement agency, and he's duped us into trafficking in sapient beings. I can't doubt it any longer. And I can't do it any longer!"

28

THE FIRST PACK MEETING

Civic Center S-3-9 and OPD Meeting Room Two

Shady's back ached. Her shoulders ached. Her feet. Her neck. Her tail. All of her ached. She'd carried enough stuff. Too tired to walk another step, too tired to eat. Well, she could still eat.

"Thank goodness! That's the last of it." Pam shoved a final package of tools into a drawer, then slammed it with a metallic bang. She straightened with a groan and rubbed her lower back.

Shady sniffed her partner. Pain echoed through the link, confirmed by the hot, painful inflammation-smell from Pam's muscles. "We are past the end of the watch. Surely this is enough."

Beside her, Razor lowered his forequarters into a long, weary stretch. "I know am done. One more trip, and my back will break."

"No argument here." Cinnamon leaned against Berwyn, who staggered for an instant, caught literally napping on his feet.

LSA Kramer poked her head through the doorway from the war room. "Oh, good. You're all here. I'll only have to say this once."

"We have the rest of the evening off?" Shady asked. "Please?"

Kramer's rueful smile clouded Shady's hopes. "You deserve it, without a doubt." She shook her head. "Sorry, not yet. All of OPD's XK9 teams have been called to Meeting Room Two."

Shady's ears went up. *The entire Pack?*

Wow, did they change the protocol? Pam shared a startled look with her.

My gut says this has Rex's pawprints all over it. "Rex," she texted. "What's going on?"

"Lots," her mate replied. "Come upstairs. Amazing things have happened!"

Where is Meeting Room Two?

It's the big one, the one they just finished renovating.

Maybe not too tired to walk there.

Pam smiled. *Right there with you. Let's go.*

Upstairs, Rex left Chief Klein and Secretary Pandra near the dais at the far end. He ran to Shady with ears up, his tail held high with joy.

Questions could wait. She leaped into the wild delight of the greeting dance, her energy renewed. She filled her nose, her eyes, her heart with Rex's presence.

He smelled of the Five-Ten, especially that nasty regolith dust. He also carried scents of mildewed panniers, several strangers, LSA Shimon, Elmo, Chief Klein, Bill, Dr. Sandler, and Charlie's sister Caro. But best of all, underneath all those he smelled like his own dear self, slightly bruised and scuffed, but excited.

Razor and Cinnamon pushed forward to join them. All four XK9s play-bowed and pranced, sniffed each other from nose to tail, then dashed about, too frenzied with elation to stay still.

Pale Crystal arrived next. Scout's yips of excitement echoed down the hall, announcing his approach. Next came tricolored Victor, blonde Petunia, brown-and-white Elle. Each leaped into the dashing, squealing, wriggling dance of delight. Last of all came black-and-white Tuxedo, also covered with dust from the Five-Ten, and still wearing body armor.

The Pack pulled back to open the floor. Elle raced forward to greet her mate. She and Tux became a blur of dancing, bounding armor-black-and-white with brown-and-white. Shady exulted in their ecstatic scent. Only a couple of nights ago, she and Rex had shared the same joy of mates reunited after far too long. It surely must have been as terrible for Elle and Tuxedo to be kept apart as it had been for her and Rex. The Pack looked on, ears up, tails waving. When Tux and Elle turned to face their Packmates, everyone rushed forward to greet, to smell, to dance.

Klein, Pandra, and the XK9s' partners stayed near the walls. Some watched with silent smiles. Some shared low-voiced comments. Shady paid them little heed at first. But time passed, and no one called the Pack to heel, or yelled at them to get quiet and stop that nonsense. Tux and Elle still danced their joy. Other Packmates had stopped to catch up verbally or sniff each other in greater detail. Weirdly, the humans seemed content to wait until they were finished.

Confounded, she cocked her head at Rex. "Since when are humans so tolerant, if they want to start a meeting?"

His scent surged with the fragrance of fierce excitement. "I am still amazed, myself. But this is only the beginning of the changes we should see. Chief Klein has decided we are people."

Shady gasped. Her mind balked.

Victor wheeled, ears up. "What?" He and Scout, half-brothers and fast friends since their early years, had been catching up with each other, but now they drew closer.

Rex lolled his tongue in that irritating, know-it-all way he sometimes adopted. "A few more humans must arrive, first. Then everyone can hear the news together."

Shady growled. "Oh no you do not, Rex Dieter-Nell! Humans do not suddenly change their minds like that." She glanced at Klein's aide Archy. Press Liaison Joslyn Stark joined him, along with a slender, dark-haired detective Shady didn't know.

"Apparently Klein has been observing us more closely than we thought," Rex said. "There is a law Dr. Ordovich never allowed us to know, against trafficking in sapient beings. Klein thinks we are sapient. I agree with him."

Victor shot a look toward the Chief. "There is a law about trafficking in humans or ozzirikkians. It makes sense that includes any sapient species. But do we actually qualify?" Crystal, Cinnamon, and Razor broke off their conversation. They moved nearer to Shady, Rex, Victor, and Scout.

"We are dogs." Crystal cocked her head at Rex. "Dr. Ordovich always said—"

Rex growled. "Chief Klein says Ordovich has tricked the OPD. We may have to retrain ourselves to ignore many things Old Odious taught us."

"That works for me." Cinnamon wagged her tail. "I would love to forget all sorts of things Old Odious said and did. I hate him."

Her companions' tails waved. Their scents surged with fierce agreement.

Tux and Elle alone appeared not to have noticed the Pack's movement toward Rex. Not that Shady blamed them. The mate-pair leaned against each other as if no one else existed, reunited after two long, uncertain months. Elle pressed her head against Tux's ruff where it protruded from the armor, her nose buried in his fur as if she could not smell enough of him; Tux arched his neck over hers, eyes blissfully closed.

The deep joy of her recent reunion with Rex returned to warm her. She glanced toward her mate. His ears and tail were up, his eyes lively. He stood at the center of the Pack, exactly where he belonged. Loving pride swelled her chest. Much more, and she might burst. She looked away before she did something mushy to embarrass them both.

LSA Kramer stepped through the double doors, then held one of them open for . . . Shady stared. *SSA Adeyeme came?*

Wow. That took guts. Through the link, Shady sensed Pam's surprise and respect.

The diminutive SSA shot one apprehensive glance toward the Pack, then kept her gaze directed at Kramer. But she'd come, even though presumably she'd known there would be ten XK9s here. What reason could possibly be important enough? She and Kramer walked over to Klein, but there was no sign of Shimon. Shady poked Rex with her nose. "Why are the SBI agents here?"

"Perhaps because of my suggestion," Rex said. "I told Chief Klein how we reconstructed the flitter in Transmondia. I told him I think we could use similar methods to help with the *Izgubil* debris."

Shady wagged her tail. *It would be nice if that project could end with a better result.* Rex, Tux, Crystal, and Cinnamon had been so proud and elated over their success with that flitter. Their instructors' order to destroy the files upset the whole Pack, but those four were especially devastated.

Cinnamon's scent shifted to strong worry-notes. "That flitter was tiny, compared to the *Izgubil!*"

Rex's ears went down. "I have looked inside the evidence cavern. I did not say I thought we could do it in three hours, seventeen minutes. I said it would need all of us, and it would take a long time. But there is no reason why we could not do it if the humans will move things for us."

"Hypothetically, you are correct." Cinnamon's ears clamped hard against her skull. Her doubts remained clear to smell, echoed in her crouched posture.

Rex lolled his tongue, gave her a cheerful nudge. "Ears up, Cinnie. How do you eat a giant bag of Master Mix?"

She sighed. "One gulp at a time. I get it. But—"

"I think it might be fun." Razor's tail wagged high. "I always envied you guys for getting the chance to do that flitter-analysis."

Shady snorted. Razor, Petunia, and Victor all had been deeply envious of the "Flitter Four" at the time of their adventure. She, Scout and Elle were less excited by the idea. Sniffing out machine-parts wasn't nearly as interesting as sniffing out humans and their problems.

"We might not have to do all of it, if we can see consistent patterns." Cinnamon's ears relaxed. "I have watched those surveillance vids of the explosion. Whatever broke it up was all over that ship. There was no single point of detonation."

"True, that." Tuxedo pushed forward, Elle at his side. "Are you saying we might get to work on the *Izgubil* debris?" Unlike Cinnamon, his eyes and scent blazed with excitement. "I want to know if it is the same kind of explosive we found at Ostra."

Shady exchanged a rueful look with Elle. "Trust a discussion about explosives to pull him out of a romantic reunion."

Elle let her tongue slide out. "If it did not, I would worry that he was ill. He is immensely pleased Rex recommended he be the one sent to the Five-Ten for the explosives analysis."

Cinnamon snapped her ears flat. "Of course, that left me to break my back hauling crap from the morgue. I was even on the SIT Delta team already!"

"Which is why I asked for Tux," Rex said. "I wanted to gather as many Pack members as I could. Now it seems Chief Klein is doing it for me."

"Whatever your reason, it was much more interesting to go to the Five-Ten than bust pickpockets in Precinct Two," Tuxedo said. "I found a lot of residuals inside Ostra. I also love working with Tech Specialist Raach."

Shady had not yet met TS Raach. He'd arrived sometime yesterday from SBI Headquarters on Wheel Four, to work with the SDF experts who'd so far failed to show up. "I heard SA Freas complain it is hard to get a gobbledygook-free sentence out of him."

Tux lolled his tongue. "Yes! Exactly! At last I have found someone besides Georgia who speaks about the technology with precision!"

Petunia snorted. "A perfect match. Watch out, Elle."

"I like to think I offer things TS Raach cannot." Elle poked her mate with her nose.

"Of course, you do, dear." Tux ducked his head and fluttered his tail.

LSA Shimon pushed through the double doors and strode rapidly toward Adeyeme, Klein and the others. "I apologize," he said. "I didn't mean to make you wait." He was dressed once again in a crisp SBI blue-black outfit, without a hint of dust.

Rex eyed him, ears up. "I wonder what Elmo said to him."

Shady gave the LSA a long look. Wherever he'd been, he'd managed not only a change of clothes but a shower. Was he also back to acting like The Icicle? "Shimon called me in, after you could not do the interview. I am sorry to tell you that Elmo did nothing but ask for his lawyer."

Rex's ears and tail drooped. "All our work, for no information?"

"I did not say that. Elmo would not talk with us. But when we asked about the *Izgubil*, I have never interviewed anyone who smelled guiltier."

Rex's ears up popped up again. "Oh, that is promising."

"Shimon has ordered the access-corridor pads recovered for scent evidence."

Rex's tail wagged his excitement. "Excellent! I did not have a chance to suggest that. Perhaps we can ID some of the others in that group."

Apparently, Shimon was the final arrival. Now the Chief moved to the front of the room. "Thank you for coming. There's a new development that affects everyone here. I have launched an investigation to explore the question of XK9 sapience."

A tremor of amazement ran through Shady's body. It was one thing to hear it from Rex, but a public announcement made it official. *This is actually happening.*

Pam's delight radiated through the link. *About damn time, too!*

Every human and dog in the room seemed to be having similar reactions. The hopeful excitement in their postures and scents buoyed Shady's spirit. Berwyn started to applaud. The other partners quickly followed his lead. They clapped, cheered, then quieted. But there was no erasing their broad smiles.

Klein smiled back, nodded. "Thank you. I believe both the Pack and the OPD have been victims of an egregious fraud, but now we must prove it." He outlined his plan to interview each XK9 and partner.

The human partners nodded, listening. Everyone's scent factors brightened with delighted relief.

"For now, I also ask that you keep this investigation quiet," Klein concluded.

His request startled Shady. *But why?*

Public reactions, of course, Pam answered. *This is explosive. A new sapient species? There hasn't been one discovered in my lifetime.* Shady glimpsed impressions of her partner's worry over uninformed humans or others who might not believe what they heard about XK9s, or who might believe untrue and negative things. *My own mother would probably blow a gasket.*

"We won't be able to keep it secret for long," Klein said. "Once our dogs are free to act independently, certain things will quickly become self-evident. It would be disastrous for us to continue treating you as sub-sapient. But a lot of people aren't going to want this investigation to go forward. They'll resist the idea that XK9s are sapient. They'll feel threatened."

Too true, Pam said. *They won't all be private citizens, either.*

What do you mean? Shady cocked her head.

For one thing, the Transmondians have a lot at stake. Pam frowned. *Probably people in our government, too. These international trade deals . . . Usually, there are a lot of people who profit behind the scenes.*

Cold foreboding slithered through Shady's gut. *Whenever humans were determined to profit, my experience says dogs will be on the losing side.*

Chief Klein was still talking. He'd turned to SSA Adeyeme.

"That's why I'm particularly pleased you've agreed to work with us."

Adeyeme'd been standing slightly hunched, arms crossed as if hugging herself. Now she straightened, uncrossed her arms, and let them fall to her sides. She nodded to Klein. "It may solve a problem for both of us, if Director Perri approves after the demonstration." the terror in her scent did not abate, but her voice rang clear and steady. "It seems worth exploring."

The Chief turned to the Pack and partners. "Rex has told me about an experience that he and the other three participants were strictly ordered never to discuss." He described the flitter crash analysis "game" to the humans.

Georgia and Berwyn nodded with knowing smiles, but a murmur ran through most of his listeners. *Did you know about this?* Pam asked.

We all did, but Dr. Ordovich said we wouldn't be allowed to go to Orangeboro if we told about things like that.

What else haven't you told me?

Shady replied with a stress-yawn, then looked away. *Let's talk later.*

"Granted, that was a smaller craft by orders of magnitude," Klein said. "But if four XK9 puppies really could figure out what caused the wreck that quickly, we're into a whole new investigative paradigm."

"Sir?" Tux's partner Georgia asked, "What if Director Perri doesn't let the XK9s work on the *Izgubil?*"

Klein frowned. "Then of course we won't insist. But in the meantime, we'll have gathered more evidence for Lt. Patel and her team."

Georgia's scent factors surged with an excitement that also rang in her voice. "Does this mean the Pack works together now?"

That was Shady's top question, too.

"Don't worry. I haven't forgotten," Klein replied. "Every single one of you protested those separate postings. This afternoon Rex and I talked about them, too. I think Dr. Ordovich recommended separation to hide the Pack's true capabilities, but that practice ends now."

Bubbly, tingly elation filled Shady. *No more separations?*

What a relief. Pam's delight rolled through the link.

All around her, Packmates stared openmouthed at each other, ears up and tails like fans. Their partners' exclamations made a rising babble of excitement.

Shady turned to Rex. "Oh, this deserves an extra-warm snuggle! Can you come to my house tonight?"

Rex yawned a toothy stress-yawn. "I shall have to pull a rain-ticket, as the Transmondians say. Dr. Sandler intends to run tests and keep me for overnight observation."

"Oh, that is right. LSA Shimon said a shed fell on you." Shady laid back her ears.

"XK9s are tough. I am fine. But Dr. Sandler is having none of it."

Frustration prickled through Shady. "So I cannot be with you?"

"I would sleep better if we could be together, but we all must try to rest well," Rex said. "We have spent our whole lives being tested. But in a very real way, tomorrow may be our most important test yet."

Chief Klein had been watching them, smiling. He gave them a few moments to react, exclaim to each other, and speculate about changes this would bring. Then he spoke into his mic again. "The day-watch is long finished. Please say nothing of this to anyone outside this room, for now. Until we have well-documented, solid evidence, silence on this topic protects our XK9s from danger."

29

REX COMMUNES WITH THE PALLETS AT DAWN

The Sandler Clinic and Civic Center S-3-9

Rex fidgeted on the exam table under Dr. Sandler's scanner.

"Dammit. Now I have to re-scan. Hold still." Sandler stifled a yawn. She'd said she was an early riser, but apparently not as early as Rex on the day of a big test. She frowned at him. "Shallow breaths, this time."

He closed his eyes, clamped his jaws on his nervous panting, and took careful, slow, shallow breaths. But his pulse pounded. His feet itched to pace. His jaws ached to yawn a wide, toothy stress-yawn. He maintained the shallow breaths, but opened one eye to observe her.

She returned to her scan, tense and hyper-focused, then stepped back with a little exhalation. The machine beeped. She leaned in again to see the readout, lips parted, eyebrows up, then shook her head. "That is incredible. Every single time I see it, it's like a miracle."

He cocked his head at her.

She grinned. "First of all, it's incredible that I don't have to sedate you to scan you. I can just say 'shallow breaths,' and you do it. I'm a veterinarian. Until XK9s, my patients never cooperated like that."

He lowered his ears. "That is not incredible."

She chuckled. "Not to you, maybe. Anyway, what I meant was that you're healed. All the abrasions, all the strains, all the hairline fractures in bones. They're all healed up. You're sound as anyone could want."

"I keep telling you. XK9s are tough." The passage of time niggled at him. He needed to get to HQ! "I imagine I shall need new scent cards." He sighed. *Charlie's not here. There's no one to take samples for me.* "Not that I shall need them today, I suppose."

She lifted his panniers down from where she'd hung them last night, placed them on her exam table, and opened a pocket. Then she took a quick step back. "Phew!" She waved a hand in front of her face. "Did this get wet? It's all mildewed."

"Oh." He cocked his head. "Yes. On the *Triumph.*"

She gave him a blank look.

"The rescue runner, after the dock breach. They washed me, panniers and all."

She stared at him, then returned her focus to the panniers with an oddly sad head shake. "And no one thought to maintain your equipment afterwards."

It needed maintaining? Come to think of it, he'd seen Charlie oil the harness and wipe out the pannier pockets several times, usually in the evenings after supper. Apparently, it did need maintaining. "No one has done anything with it."

"Clearly not." She blew out a breath. "Did you say you won't need scent cards today?"

"Probably not. Charlie is not here." An unexpected wave of sadness rolled over him. *I wish you were with me,* he called to Charlie through the link. *I wish you could see this day.*

Now Dr. Sandler's sad-eyed regard included him. "I'm sorry."

"I would not mind leaving the panniers here. They are practical in some ways, but they are bulky and heavy, and they can get hot. I shall not need them today."

She nodded. "I'll see to your gear. I can clip your badge to your collar."

As soon as he could get away, he departed. He trotted through the patchy mist, harness- and panniers-free. It felt weird, but . . . *I could get used to this. But think about it later.* Urgency drove him forward, although he dared not dwell on everything that rode on today's test. Better to focus on the task at hand than psych himself out thinking about was at stake.

The desk officer in the HQ Atrium gave Rex a startled stare. Granted, a lone XK9 at this or any hour wasn't a normal sight, but Rex wasn't on a normal mission. To his delight, this morning's desk officer promptly buzzed him through. Rex had forgotten to ask the Chief if Officer Collins' contrariness might've been a test to see how he'd react. Wouldn't be the first time humans had done that sort of thing to him.

He padded quietly down the corridor toward S-3-9. The scent-trails of Adeyeme, Kramer, and Shimon still hung in the air. He'd first whiffed them on the front steps. Now he followed them to the elevator. A startling tang of fresh gunshot residue lingered in Adeyeme's personal scent-blend today. His pulse kicked another notch higher. How was that possible? As far as he knew, real guns weren't allowed on Rana Station. He didn't yet know her well enough to ask, but his curiosity burned.

No. Focus. It was 06:20. The demonstration was set to begin at 08:30, with most of the Pack due to arrive at 07:00. Since he'd rather not ride the rumbling elevator and break the morning stillness, he took the side stairs. He'd hoped for a chance to commune with the pallets alone in the cool quiet of daybreak-between-watches, but since Adeyeme was here, it was proper to greet her, then obtain permission to enter the evidence cavern.

The badge-reader on the S-3-9 lock released with a loud *snap*, then swung open. Its hinges made a high squeal of inadequately-lubricated metal-on-metal. *So much for a silent entrance.* Even if the sound was too high for human ears to hear, the snap had been loud enough to echo.

"Rex?" Shimon's tone was sharp.

Ah. They probably knew it was him from the hall surveillance. "Yes. Good morning, LSA Shimon."

Shimon stepped out, a silhouette from behind a moveable wall-screen, bringing with him a waft of brewing coffee. The man's scent factors edged into high, skittish notes that Rex privately thought of as "weirded out." His eyes must be doing that glow-in-the-dark thing. He occasionally startled even Charlie.

Rex lowered his gaze. "I did not expect to find anyone here at this hour."

"Huh." Shimon made a little half-laugh sound. "Then I guess we're even. What brings you here so early?"

Rex padded forward. "Perhaps you will find it strange, but I wanted to stand among the pallets, to take in the smells. I had hoped to mentally prepare myself for the test that lies ahead."

Shimon's scent shifted to something warmer, less edgy. "This demonstration is kind of an important test for you, isn't it?" He stepped past the screen into a pool of stronger light.

"Yes, it is." Rex followed him. The flutters in his abdomen almost made him regret breakfast. He caught a whiff and a glimpse of Kramer, with Adeyeme beyond her. Again, he smelled that trace of GSR in Adeyeme's scent, but there'd be time enough to wonder about that and other things later.

"Until we came to Orangeboro, we XK9s were tested practically every day," Rex said. "But this test is different. There is no rubric, no percentage of success. Today, we either succeed or we fail. I believe strongly that we can do what I have said. But if we fail, we call all our claims of sapience into question. I do not think we will receive many other chances, if we fail this one."

Adeyeme leaned forward, hugging herself with that cross-armed, self-protective body language he'd noticed yesterday at the meeting. "Have you failed many tests, XK9 Rex?"

He averted his eyes politely. "Only the ones I went into feeling overly cocky."

She let out a near-silent breath. He glanced up to catch a fleeting smile. "Do you feel cocky today?"

His gut tightened. The flutters kicked up. "No, ma'am."

"That's good. For us, and for Chief Klein, too."

The flutters expanded into his chest. She and Klein had chosen to climb out onto this particular limb alongside the Pack. These humans' career futures also depended on today's outcome. "Then let us all hope for success."

"You said you wish to—" She frowned. "To stand among the pallets?"

Rex's tongue slid out in a nervous pant. "I mean to get a sense of them."

She quirked her eyebrow at Shimon. "Any objections?"

"None." Shimon waved his hand toward the evidence cavern. "Lights on?"

"I think . . . not, thanks. Sometimes the scents speak louder when the light is low."

Shimon shook his head. "Wouldn't want to interfere with that. Let me help you gown up. Sorry, I'll have to turn on a low light."

"That is all right. Thank you." Rex hadn't thought about needing a containment mask and gown, but Shimon was correct. Good thing the humans were here, after all.

Shimon unfurled a gown. Rex stepped into it, then Shimon did up the fastenings. "Shawnee probably could do this better. She's been covering the morgue detail." Even so, the man didn't need much coaching.

"LSA Shimon, may I ask a question about SSA Adeyeme?"

Shimon paused in his efforts. "What about her?"

"Why do I smell GSR on her?"

Shimon finished with Rex's mask, then quirked an eyebrow at him. "Fresh GSR?"

"I believe she must have fired multiple rounds within the past two hours."

He glanced in the direction of the war room. "So that's where she went."

"I do not understand."

Shimon finished the last of the coverall fastenings, then half-sat on the containment-gear table so he could face Rex. "Long, personal story, but Elaine is one of about two dozen authorized sharpshooters on-Station. The SBI and the SDF both maintain trained cadres. She's been proficient with firearms since well before she emigrated from the Norchellic Frontier. That's how she got recruited into the SBI in the first place, though she hasn't been front-line active since well before she took over SIT Delta. It takes a lot of training to be first-string. These days, she's too busy running this outfit."

"But she is still authorized?"

"She's on reserve status, but she re-qualifies each year. To stay sharp, she has to put rounds down-range fairly often."

Rex flicked his ears, confused. "Why would she need to practice today?"

He answered with a melancholy smile. "Oh, I think today had a lot more to do with centering herself and calming her nerves. She's been taking a lot of heat. And hate."

Rex growled. "But she is doing such excellent work! If the SDF's experts had arrived on time—"

"That's just it. They didn't." Frustration and fury darkened Shimon's scent. He gave his head an angry shake. "But Elaine's critics are all from the faction that put Iskander in power. Most are also partisans of Nolan Virendra. He's an SDF admiral. So, of course, it's not the SDF's fault."

This made no sense to Rex. "But it is the SDF's fault."

Shimon clenched his fists, glared into the darkness. "Elaine was a Norchellic refugee. Iskander and her base care nothing about facts, just old grudges."

Rex cocked his head. "Why would they hate . . . ?" He

couldn't imagine a more sympathetic group than refugees, people running for their lives. *I must be missing something.*

Shimon's scent shifted into musky tones of anger and sadness. "There's still a lot of resentment in some quarters, even though the last refugees stopped arriving ten years ago. There were cultural misunderstandings at first, a brief food shortage. And there are always people who fear change, or who profit from stirring up others' fears."

He hunched his shoulders. "Anyway, it's been getting pretty nasty this week. Elaine just puts her head down and keeps moving forward, but I knew it had to be taking a toll." He gave Rex a worried look. "Would you mind letting me know if you smell GSR on her again? I . . . maybe Shawnee and I can run more interference, so she doesn't have to deal with so much of it."

"I shall let you know." Rex hated that she was being unfairly criticized, especially for something she couldn't help. But he also was fascinated by the idea of a Ranan who found solace and centering by practicing with a firearm. Time, however, was passing. The burden of all that hung on this test weighed him down. He must refocus. "I had better go into the evidence cavern now."

"If you need anything else, you know where we are."

"Thank you." Rex stepped from the ready room into the cavern's deep shadows. Shimon quietly closed the door. He stopped a meter from the first row of pallets, then sifted through the scents. This place felt large, even in the dark. It echoed when he moved, but it took some time for the echoes to return. Above everything came the compelling, sweet-metallic reek of things that had been in space.

What can the pallets tell me? He approached the nearest one, reared up on hind legs, then craned his neck to get close enough to smell the top without touching it. Ceramics and metallic alloys comprised the main bulk of the materials. *No explosives.* The fragments in the top layer had shattered from the force of the shock wave, rather than from direct explosive detonation. Worry nipped at him.

The rest of the pallet smelled no different, all the way to the bottom. The pallets to the right and left also contained the same stuff from top to bottom. The pallets to the right and left of those also yielded nothing.

By now a whole pack of worries had assembled. They circled him, snarling. He focused past them, willing them to be still. This vast cavern held seemingly endless ranks of pallets. At the rate he was failing to find . . . he stopped, took a cleansing breath, then moved to the next row in.

Same mix of substances as the others. At a guess, this all came from the *Izgubil's* outer hull. There likely were literal tonnes of this stuff, but clearly the explosives had not been rigged to the outside. There might be some forensic value here, but he judged it unlikely to be worth the Pack's time. Certainly not this morning, with the Director of the SBI watching.

He moved another row in. Another. Another. *Okay, here are different materials: more metals and synthetics, fewer ceramics.* He tried to imagine the layers that would make up the ship's hull. *This could be the inside structure of the outer surface: support frame-work, wiring, and so on. This is one kind of area where I might expect to find explosives residue, but no. Nothing.* By now the worries could populate a mega-pack.

Rex growled. Refocused. *Damn it, evidence of the explosives has to be here somewhere.*

He checked the pallets to left and right; same metals, wires, and fine, metallic dust, most of the latter filtered by his mask. Even so Rex sneezed, grateful for the mask's containment properties and the relative dryness of the sneeze.

Then he moved to the next row in. Same thing. *Damned enormous spaceship!* But it seemed he could eliminate these rows of pallets, too. *No immediate forensic value here.*

An insidious worm of fear slithered in his belly. He'd never imagined he actually might fail to find any explosives till now. It was almost 06:50. *They must be here somewhere.*

But my Packmates would arrive soon. Can I find them within the next ten minutes?

He kept moving. Found rows with metals and synthetics in different proportions. *The back side of the outermost bulkheads?* He snorted. *Stupid to blindly guess.* He'd noted schematics of the ship in the case book, but he'd only given them a glance. Now Adeyeme's organizational framework yielded them immediately. He wagged his tail, then scrolled to a cutaway of the outer hull, as provided by the original manufacturer. *Nice job, whoever procured that.*

Hmm. Looked as if Shimon's teams had placed the pallets in a rough approximation of the quadrants where the SDF recovery teams had retrieved the materials. *Makes sense, then, that some rows came from the outside hull, others from supports, and so on.*

If he walked five more rows of debris into the cavern, he ought to find . . . *No.*

Damn it! His body prickled, urgent to hunt. He checked the scale of the cutaway with a growl. Frantic frustration bunched his muscles, crackled along his spine.

He halted. Centered himself. Lifted his nose. *Try again.*

It's here somewhere. It has to be. He walked forward, nose high. Tense. Hyper-alert.

What was that? He stepped past another row of pallets. Tried again.

A faint, peppery tang. Barely there. Farther in. His pulse sped up. *YES! At last! Quarry acquired!* Hunt-joy surged within him. He almost let loose an "AROO-oo-oo!" just to hear it echo through the cavern. But he stopped himself. That would risk DNA cross-contamination in the evidence pallets nearby. *No losing control this time! Stick to business!*

Nose up, he moved on.

At first he held to a careful walk, paws tingling to go faster, but still range-finding. Then a trot. *Ah! Getting closer!* He loped past the last couple of rows. *Yes! Yes! At last!*

The twenty-seventh row from the door held the forensic jackpot. He checked the schematic, adjusted some assumptions about how scale translated to pallets, then checked the other smells he found here. Utility corridors, peripheral ones. *Probably not frequently traveled, but accessible from inside the ship.*

A perfect place to hide explosives.

This is good. This is valuable. The Pack and I can work with this.

30

DOING IT XK9 STYLE

S-3-9 Evidence Cavern

J ittery prickles ran through Rex's hackles. Anxiety churned his gut. He nodded, neck arched, and hoped he appeared to be calmly in command of things.

Gowned, masked, and gloved, most of the investigation's humans and XK9s watched from positions around and between nearby pallets. On opposite sides of Pallet #687, Tech Specialist Raach and wiry SA Freas each held a specimen-collection basket and stood atop a stepladder. They didn't speak. Forensic protocols required their silence, to avoid DNA cross-contamination.

"That looks good." At least Rex's vocalizer sounded as emotionless as ever, no matter the slithers in his gut or the pounding of his heart. "Now let us see how well it works." He'd repeated Charlie's breathing pattern a dozen times, but it hadn't soothed him much. Nothing but a successful outcome for this demonstration would ease his anxiety.

Raach handed his specimen basket down to LSA Shimon, who traded with a replacement basket from a stack by his side. Tall, burly SA Val Wood made the same exchange with Freas.

Shimon slid the basket he'd received into the tray of an imager in front of him. Wood did the same with Freas's basket. Twin images opened on a side-channel in Rex's HUD, with parallel views of the empty baskets. He wagged his containment-gown-shrouded tail. "Good. That worked just as we planned." Unlike human voices, the XK9s' vocalizers created no DNA contamination, so he was free to speak. "Now hand them off."

Shimon withdrew his basket from the imager and handed it to Berwyn, who placed it on a cart at nose-height for Cinnamon. Val did the same for Georgia, who positioned her basket for Tux.

"Next we sniff, and mark our scent-discoveries on the image." Cinnamon created a star-shaped blue spot on her basket's image in the side-channel. "See? Soon we shall be forensic stars."

Berwyn rolled his eyes. Rex imagined him razzing Cinnie through the brain link.

"That should do it," Rex said. "Shall we run it again?"

Someone tapped his back. He looked up to see LSA Kramer shake her head and turn toward Adeyeme. The SSA beckoned, then pointed toward the exit.

"Looks as if we are out of time," Rex announced to the team. "We must go meet Director Perri now."

Raach and Freas tromped down their ladders. Everyone, XK9s and humans alike, made their way silently through the pallets, but stopped short of the ready room. They'd been instructed to stay inside the evidence cavern.

Away from the evidence, Adeyeme spoke. "Semicircle." She gestured to indicate where. "XK9s in front, partners beside them, Kramer and Shimon to me. Everyone else form a row behind the XK9 teams."

Everyone hastened to obey.

"We'll have a bigger audience than we thought." Her voice came through her mask slightly muffled. "Director Perri has brought an expert to help her evaluate your work. Chief Klein also has called in an expert. They're on their way here now."

Tech Specialist Raach's scent sharpened with sudden alarm. "Chief Klein invited a second expert?"

Adeyeme nodded. "He says Dr. SCISCO is internationally respected and based right here in Orangeboro. It would be a terrible snub not to invite nem."

Above his mask, Raach's eyes widened. "But Director Perri is also bringing an expert?"

"Oh, ma'am!" Georgia's scent and voice resonated with consternation. "If her expert is Hakim Fulbert—"

"Bound to be!" Raach cried. "Perri's worked with him before."

Adeyeme drew in a breath, squared her shoulders. Her scent swirled with murky dismay, but steely determination overrode it. "If they have differences, presumably they'll behave in a professional manner."

Rex panted hard and tried not to hyperventilate. He fervently seconded Adeyeme's wish.

Raach frowned. "How vital is it, that SCISCO be here?"

Adeyeme frowned back. "The OPD has been more than accommodating, Joe. They've given us this huge working space, all the personnel we've requested, and full access to their insanely expensive XK9s. What other host-agency is this generous? We'll do well not to insult them, including their revered local expert."

"Sorry. Of course. SCISCO is extremely well-regarded, Alliance-wide." Raach grimaced, looked down. "No one can fault nir credentials, except perhaps Fulbert."

Adeyeme's face went hard, her voice as cold as her scent. "Fulbert had best remain civil. Don't he and SCISCO meet at conferences?"

"Conference-planners dread it when both attend the same event." Raach gave her a rueful look. "Each is a Universe-class expert, so planners try to accommodate separate locations for their speaking appearances."

Adeyeme turned to Georgia. "DPO Volkov, what can you tell me about this?"

"Explosives technology was my minor at S-Poly," Georgia said. "Doc Sheesh was my adviser for it, and I attended a conference with nem once. Ne seemed to consider Dr. Fulbert brilliant, but an asshole. I don't think ne will have any violent reactions today."

The humans' use of non-gendered pronouns for this Dr. SCISCO startled Rex. What kind of being was ne? But then his ears went up. Muffled though it was by several walls, the elevator made a distinctive rumble.

"It's likely Fulbert perceives condescension," Raach said. "Intellectually, what human could compete with a cyberbeing's memory resources and processing speed?"

Rex glanced at Tux. The Pack's chief geek had always dreamed of meeting a cyberbeing. *Who knew he'd get the chance?*

Georgia made an unhappy sound. "I understand how he might feel put down. The android focal object has a certain stare. It's like, 'have you even briefly thought about this?' Sometimes I felt like an idiot."

Raach laughed. "Oh, Fulbert can do that look, too. Comes from working with undergrads. Full disclosure, Fulbert was my adviser for my doctorate. SCISCO's right, though. He knows his stuff, but he can be an asshole."

"How very special," Adeyeme murmured.

They didn't seem to hear the elevator doors opening. Indistinct voices sounded in the S-3-9 hallway. Rex cocked his head. Two humans in a disagreement.

"They are almost here," Rex said.

Voices and footsteps entered the war room. ". . . know why we've bothered to come." A peevish edge undercut the resonance of the speaker's deep voice. "XK9s may be brilliant scent detectors, but they're not capable of a comprehensive evaluation."

Rex bowed his head and endured a sick wave of futility.

Should've known better than to expect fair treatment! Does the Pack have any chance?

"You are not here to jump to conclusions," a woman's cold, irritated voice replied.

Rex's ears went back up. *Maybe all is not lost.*

"Following the data is not 'jumping to conclusions.'" The chill in the man's tone matched the woman's.

"I'm not paying you to read canned reports," the woman returned tartly. "I'm paying you to give me sound advice based on observable facts." She stepped into the ready room. Through the hatchway, Rex glimpsed a wiry older woman with a leathery face and white hair in a short bob.

Adeyeme drew in a breath, then moved forward to meet her. "Director Perri. Hello."

Rex and the others listened, but stayed put. Adeyeme greeted Fulbert, Klein, and SCISCO after Perri. Then she paused while they gowned up. Finally, she led them into the evidence cavern.

The older woman stared at the assembled officers with sharp hazel eyes, then turned to Adeyeme. "*Dogs*, Elaine?"

"Yes, ma'am. Forensic olfaction specialists." Adeyeme's scent factors jittered in the anxious ranges. Her body language made Rex wonder if for once her anxiety sprang from concern over her commander's opinion, more than fear of the Pack.

SBI Director Perri's gaze scanned the lineup of XK9s, then she shook her head. "Wonders may never cease." Rex wasn't sure how to read the clash of contradictions in her scent factors. Some notes indicated worry, others astonishment, with strong, bright tones of curiosity and rising notes of hope.

A tall, well-built man pushed through the hatchway behind Perri, then moved to the side opposite Adeyeme. His thick black hair, threaded with gray at the temples, swept back from his high brow like a wavy mane, now contained in a cap. That must be Dr. Fulbert.

Close behind him came Klein. The Chief looked strange in

containment gear, but his scent warmed, and the corners of his eyes crinkled at the sight of his officers.

Last in was a pearlescent blue humanoid android. Nir dark blue head-hair was styled appropriately for either human gender. Two optical receptors on nir egg-shaped head, placed about where eyes would be on a human face, rotated to adjust focus. An upward-bending curve of pixel points spread across the lower half of the egg-shape like a cartoon-line smile. No mask swathed it, since it was just pixels.

Adeyeme beckoned to Rex. "I'd particularly like for you to meet the chief organizer of today's demonstration. This is XK9 Officer Rex Dieter-Nell, leader of OPD's XK9 Pack."

Rex stepped forward, tail high and waving. Perri and Fulbert stared at him, their scent factors unsettled. Chief Klein beamed warm, delighted approval.

SCISCO's android head swiveled, following Rex's approach. Ne reached out a hand. Five distinct points of warmth ran along Rex's shoulder. He detected the faintest whisper of a vibration where the android's fingertips touched him. What sensors had the cyberbeing activated? What had ne just learned?

"So this is an XK9." Dr. SCISCO's voice was a cool tenor that could belong to either man or woman. "I have been most eager to meet individuals of your kind, XK9 Rex. I take it you and your fellow XK9s are a part of this demonstration we are to see?"

Rex wagged his tail. "We XK9s are leading the demonstration. The humans will assist."

SCISCO's optical receptors did another rotating re-focus. Nir pixel-point smile curved more deeply. "This just keeps getting better."

Fulbert stared at Rex, then frowned at Adeyeme. "*Dogs* will lead?"

Typical human rudeness. Rex kept his ears and tail up. He swallowed a growl but elevated his vocalizer's volume. "To streamline things, we have already surveyed the pallets. One in Row Twenty-Seven seems a promising starting-place."

Perri's pale, sculpted brows rose. "This is the dog, speaking for itself?"

"*Him*self, please," Adeyeme said. "And no one but Rex puts words into his vocalizer."

Fulbert's eyes narrowed. "You're bypassing potentially valuable evidence in the first twenty-seven rows?"

"It may indeed be valuable, but it is not relevant to today's investigation," Rex replied. "Today our objective is to find evidence of the explosive materials that destroyed the ship." He cocked his head at Fulbert. "Are you aware that as long ago as the 20th Century, one of the tasks forensic K-9s fulfilled was explosives-detection? Even ordinary, unmodified dogs can detect some odors at dilutions of five hundred parts per trillion."

Fulbert crossed his arms and regarded Rex with a dubious expression. "You've ruled those pallets out, just by *sniffing* them?"

Rex wagged his tail. "Yes. The first twenty-six rows contain no explosives."

Perri's scent factors spiked with astonishment. "You just ruled out six-hundred sixty-seven pallets."

"They should be removed to a different secure location," Rex said. "We should hold them there in case another variable requires their examination later. Removing them opens more room to work on Row Twenty-Seven."

Fulbert shook his head with a scowl. "Is a second opinion possible?"

"We've had ten opinions," Adeyeme said. "Rex did his scent-assessment before the others arrived. Then he asked each Pack member to go in individually and find the first row with explosives. Once they'd all made their evaluations without consulting each other, they delivered unanimous results."

"Mm. In other words, they've demonstrated that their scent accuracy is on par with an unmodified 20th Century dog." Fulbert's dubious expression didn't change.

"Perhaps we can demonstrate some advancements now.

Please follow me." Rex led them to Pallet #687. The demonstration team took their places. "Humans will not speak while handling the evidence. That can contam—"

"This isn't my first time." Fulbert waved an impatient hand. "Get on with it."

SCISCO shot him a pixel-point frown. He looked away with an irritable huff.

Rex kept his ears up with effort. His jitters morphed ever more into annoyance, but his robot-voice betrayed none of it. "We are using a method of collective, on-site virtual reconstruction that we first developed in Transmondia."

Fulbert shook his head. "Wait. What do you mean by that?"

SCISCO's frown deepened. "Perhaps if you'd stop interrupting like a petulant child, he could already have explained it."

Fulbert turned on nem with a scowl. "Oh, so now you think I'm—"

Rex cranked his vocalizer several notches higher. "You may notice a new channel has opened on your HUD."

SCISCO's frown shifted to a smile, then lapsed into a mask-like neutral look. Fulbert grimaced, but said nothing more.

Rex continued at a more moderate volume. "Please expand the new channel and observe while we demonstrate."

Raach and Freas placed several pieces from the top of the pallet into their collection baskets, then handed them down. Shimon and Wood bent to capture images. A jumble of small, irregular 3D shapes appeared on the new HUD channel. Rex's gut relaxed oh-so-slightly. *Our system works so far.*

Image scans made, the XK9 partner-pairs received them next. Cinnamon and Tux each sniffed over their fragments. Special filters in their masks allowed them to smell even the smallest bits without inhaling them. Some were only about 1-2 cubic cm., according to the imagers' scale gauge. Blotchy blue areas appeared on some parts of the pieces in the HUD-view. Annotations hovered above them.

"Each type of molecule has a signature scent," Rex said. "Our masks contain a one-way permeable membrane that allows molecular inflow. We can identify substances with a high degree of accuracy, once we have memorized them."

Fresh impatience grew in Fulbert's scent. "Yes, yes, I'm sure. And how many substances have you memorized?"

"It varies by the individual. It's been estimated dogs probably can distinguish millions of scents and scent-blends, but I have been tested to verify that I can accurately discriminate 15,436 identified substances, species, secretions, exudations, and other materials."

Throat-catching dubiousness swirled in to mix with the impatience in Fulbert's scent. "Oh, really. You're sure it's not 15,437, or 15,435?"

"Oh, for pity's sake, Hakim!" SCISCO gave Fulbert one of those looks Georgia had described earlier.

Rex let his tongue slide out, inside his mask. "Not 15,435, but undoubtedly more. Dr. Ordovich stopped testing me at 15,436."

"Rex is our over-achiever," Shady put in. She'd been sitting a meter or so back from the demonstration with the others. "Dr. Ordovich was determined to find Rex's limits. His technicians stopped testing the rest of us at 10,000."

"The whole Pack consists of over-achievers, in my opinion," Rex said. "Each has several areas of brilliance."

Fulbert did not roll his eyes, but his scent suggested a reaction of that sort. "Just one big mutual-admiration society, eh? How sweet."

Rex snapped his ears flat. "I have confidence in my team. Perhaps you will find that a less nauseating sentiment."

"There it is," Tuxedo said. Two pieces on the HUD channel aligned at an overlapping blue splotch. He'd found the first match. "Since Dr. Ordovich did not see fit to give us thumbs, we have to do this virtually."

"Ah!" Cinnamon said. "Beat that." Three more pieces spun,

tumbled, then joined like puzzle pieces. Matched together, their blue bits looked like part of a ragged sunburst.

SCISCO went still.

"How big is that?" Fulbert zoomed the image. "Is the scale right?"

"Yes. it is. Unfortunately," SCISCO said in a quiet voice.

Rex eyed nem. Too bad that android body couldn't exude scent factors. "The imager automatically measures it."

"But that's tiny—barely a centimeter or two. You'd have to install . . . " Fulbert zoomed out again, then gasped.

While he'd been examining the first completed blast point, Cinnamon and Tuxedo had assembled more. Additional pieces snapped into place on the virtual reconstruction while the onlookers watched. The two XK9s had placed little counters at the base of the viewing area. They ticked off the number of pieces each had assembled. Cinnamon currently led with 25, but Tux's count kept clicking steadily higher, until he cried, "Pause! I am out of pieces. Come on, humans! I am dying, here!"

Rex shifted his focus. All of the humans had stopped their work, to stare into the middle distance. Dr. SCISCO's android face had a lopsided smile on it.

"Oh, crap. Now I am out, too," Cinnamon said. "Berwyn! What is the holdup?"

Shimon gave a little gasp, blinked hard. Raach and Freas exchanged a sheepish look and resumed loading baskets. Val, Berwyn, and Georgia all hunched their shoulders, shot apologetic grimaces toward their impatient XK9s, then got back to work.

"I apologize," Adeyeme said. "This was our first chance to see the full process in action. "That was . . . I can honestly say I've never seen anything quite like that before."

31

REVELATIONS AND AWAKENINGS

S-3-9 Evidence Cavern

Quiet sighs, waving tails, and relieved scent factors from Rex's Packmates aligned well with his own warm pride and deep relief. The humans on their team exuded bright, rising awe. Even their partners. The debris-analysis technique had amazed them all.

We are onto something here. This is important. Our collective reconstruction method works.

Something else about this demonstration is different, too. He eyed Adeyeme. Her fear of the XK9s had backed off, her scent profile dominated now by warm, growing hope. Klein's eyes blazed with pride. Perri remained closed, reserving judgment, but he could smell that she'd become intrigued.

Good reactions, all. But they couldn't account for his odd sense of difference.

"SA Freas," Tuxedo asked, "do you have any bigger pieces? "We have been focused on the explosives-touched pieces, but there is a thin layer of some other substance. It lies just beneath the blasts, and that makes it harder to isolate. It might be easier to analyze on larger pieces of the wall surface. I know you cannot answer, but please look."

Rex blinked. *That's it. They cannot answer.* The humans working on the evidence couldn't talk. All through the Pack's training, whenever a human and an XK9 demonstrated something, the human explained things while the XK9 did ninety percent of the work. That was how he'd worked with Charlie, too. But now he could see that it left the impression the human was in control. Today, however, they'd been allowed to take a new approach, to address the evidence their own way.

Buoyant joy lifted Rex's mood, despite his anxiety to prove the Pack's worth. Despite the humidity around his nose and mouth. Despite the growing heat inside the coverall.

A couple of the larger spaces between the blast points filled in on the visualization. "The substance I mentioned is an adhesive," Tuxedo said. "It has a conductive element in it. And I smell . . ." He flicked his ears. "I cannot see. It is such a tiny sample. But could that be nanofiber?"

"Could what be nanofiber?" Fulbert snapped.

Rex felt more than heard a shift in vibration from SCISCO's android body.

"Let us zoom in." Tuxedo adjusted the setting. They'd had to improvise in the field with their harness optics when they'd done this in Transmondia. Today their imagers provided vastly superior results. Tux took the HUD-view down to 100 microns, then growled softly. "At this scale it is easy to get lost."

"I may have something," Cinnamon said. "I found a crevice in the wall surface. Once you mentioned nanofibers, I looked for the scent of carbon."

"Yes. That is what I thought I smelled."

The HUD-channel blackened, then opened on a new image.

Cinnamon growled, too. "Why can I not find—?"

Berwyn cleared his throat rather emphatically.

Rex closed his eyes to avoid too jolting a transition, then looked up.

Cinnamon stepped aside. Berwyn reached down with a gloved hand to tap an external control on the imager ever-so-lightly.

"Oh! There!" Cinnamon's tail wagged. "Thank you."

Rex closed his eyes again, then focused on the HUD-view. It looked like a scaly hillside. A pileup of small, rodlike cylinders with rounded ends had tumbled into the crevice.

"YOU!" Fulbert whirled to confront SCISCO. "You knew what we'd find, didn't you?"

"Yes," SCISCO said. "I recognized the pattern when they began to assemble it."

"I knew it! You're behind this, aren't you?"

"Not in the sense you mean," SCISCO said. "But I believe at this point I need to give SSA Adeyeme and her investigators a statement."

Rex's pulse accelerated.

"Shiv, grab an interview team and go upstairs," SSA Adeyeme's scent factors spiked with an excitement that tasted like hunt-joy.

Shimon put down the specimen basket he held. "Um, Tux. Georgia. Joe." Raach clumped down his ladder. Shimon turned to Dr. SCISCO's android. "Would you please come this way, Professor?"

"Certainly." Ne hesitated, focused on Director Perri. "This method of analysis is cutting edge, better than anything we've known before. I advise you to use it." Then nir android departed with Shimon and his group.

"You probably should send your people to lunch, Elaine," Perri said. "I've seen enough. I need to think."

"The smaller conference room in my executive suite may suit you," Klein said. "You could rest there, if you like. I can order up some food."

Perri smiled. "A perfect host. Thank you, Kwame. Please join me. You, too, Elaine. And Hakim."

Adeyeme turned to Kramer. "I don't know how long—"

"I've got this. Go."

Rex's heart thudded faster. He looked at Kramer, already instructing the team to break for an hour. Then back to Perri's smaller group. He wanted to follow Perri, but he had not been invited. He hesitated. *Do I have influence to leverage this situation? Maybe not, but I'll tag along until explicitly ordered away.*

Everyone left the evidence cavern. They eagerly shed their stuffy gear. Pam didn't need to be asked: she pulled Rex's off first. "Good luck!" She patted his shoulder.

Shady's tongue flicked across his muzzle. "Go. Stick with them."

He wagged his tail, then passed through the war room at the heels of Klein, Perri, Fulbert, and Adeyeme. He sifted through Adeyeme's scent factors. "You fear something besides me," he texted to her.

She glanced back at him, grimaced, then smoothed her features to apparent calm. She also slowed her pace so he could draw near, even though her anxiety increased when he did. "I cannot guess the Director's thoughts about your methods," she said quietly. "I fear I'll be forced to continue waiting for Nolan Virendra."

Rex dipped his head to acknowledge this. "You do not like Admiral Virendra."

The grimace returned, deepened into a scowl. "No, I don't. More important, I don't trust him. There are many reasons, but the biggest right now is that he has withheld his experts for so long." She expelled a frustrated sigh. "He does not care if we solve this case. He is only interested in 'scoring points' on the SBI."

Human politics were still a mystery to Rex. "He is leveraging his influence to achieve an outcome he desires?"

To his surprise, she gave a quiet laugh. "Damn, you're bright. Yes. Or at least, he thinks he is. If I can work with you and the Pack, I might just turn the tables on him."

Rex promised himself to look up "turn the tables" later, but he gathered from her tone that she wished for this outcome. As did he. "Yes. Let us hope we can do that."

She smiled, a smaller-than-usual taste of her phobic reaction in her scent. "Thank you." She turned away, but he followed.

Several agents and Task Force members remained to straighten the equipment and secure the area. Most of them hurried ahead, their minds clearly on lunch and the luxury of an hour to relax.

Perri and her companions advanced to the elevator unopposed, despite the crowd. Rex didn't push to join them. Adeyeme's fear had not eased enough for that. Instead, he bounded up the stairs to wait for them in the main corridor.

The doors soon slid open. Rex fell in behind the humans again. Both Klein and Adeyeme looked back at him, but neither spoke.

Something stirred within the brain link. *Charlie?* But his partner seemed confused.

Bubbly with sudden exultation at this new evidence that Charlie still lived, Rex nonetheless refocused. He hurried after Perri's group.

They walked to the middle of the Civic Center, to the elevator that led directly to Klein's executive suite on the 25th Floor. Here was where Rex had crossed Dr. Ordovich's scent trail. Had that only been yesterday? The hated spoor lingered, but it was diminished today, trampled over by dozens of others, fading.

Chief Klein pressed his thumb to a smooth panel above the buttons. Seconds later, the doors slid apart, but again Rex pulled back. Twenty-five floors up, in a small, enclosed box with him? No. He wouldn't ask that of Adeyeme.

Damn it. Is this where I lose my chance?

The humans stepped inside. All of them looked at him.

Rex sat.

The doors rolled closed . . . almost. A small, dark-skinned hand stopped them, pushed them open again. "Rex should be in this meeting," Adeyeme said.

Director Perri looked at her. "You'd share an elevator with him?"

Adeyeme offered Rex a short nod, although the terror had returned full force in her scent. "Yes."

Perri's brows went up. "Fair enough. Come in, Rex."

Orangeboro Medical Center Re-Gen Unit

Far, far away Dr. Zuni's low, steady voice counted. "Twenty-eight. Twenty-nine. Thirty . . ."

Frantic frustration clawed at Charlie. No. NO! He knew this pattern. Wasn't this supposed to be over with? He wanted to groan, but literally couldn't. He tried to gasp. The ventilator altered its tempo.

Couldn't open his eyes, couldn't feel his body . . . yet. Oh, but that would come.

"Thirty-five. Thirty-six . . ."

This wasn't right, damn it! They'd finished his treatments. How could—? The last of the "fog" drugs released his sweating, twitching body. A heavy, bone-deep ache gripped his immobile left arm. He attempted to move his right, but it only twitched and set off a chorus of twinges from too-long-unused muscles.

Heartsick dread constricted his chest. *Re-gen-emergence syndrome.* Temporary, but painful. Sore places on his hand, wrist, and the inside of his elbow corroborated all the other evidence. IVs were an ancient menace, but necessary for re-gen. Shit, shit, shit. This wasn't *still*, it was *again*. Anguish seized him, dug in its claws. What the hell had happened?

"Thirty-nine," Dr. Zuni said. "Forty. Okay, Charlie?"

Charlie's throat burned like sandpaper on fire. He opened his eyes, fighting desolation. Memories reassembled, but sluggish, impossible ones. The Hub? With Rex? Too fast . . . the rest was even more scrambled. Was he losing his mind? He thought for an instant that Rex had focused on him through their link, but then the dog's attention withdrew.

Dr. Zuni smiled, his dark eyes intent on Charlie. "Good. Don't speak. Just relax. You're okay."

Definitely the same routine. Charlie couldn't speak if his life depended on it, but the first impulse was always to try. *So much confusion. So many questions!* Charlie'd tried exactly once. He knew better now. That fact in itself depressed him.

Dr. Zuni beamed at him. "You've finished the first three re-gen cycles, and you're healing very well."

Crap, it's not over. Fix my throat already. Charlie hoped his eyes pleaded eloquently enough.

"We still have one last cycle to go, but it'll be a lighter one." Dr. Zuni touched a monitor, turned to look at him. "However, your body's been working very hard."

Charlie closed his eyes, despairing. *Yeah, yeah, it needs a rest and some normal sleep. Don't want to do this. Just give me the throat gel.*

"It needs a rest and some normal sleep," Dr. Zuni continued. "My nurse will be in with the throat gel in just a moment."

Applying the throat gel was a repulsive process. *Why would anyone do this as a career? He should be glad they did, of course. He'd only have one arm . . . strike that. He'd be dead.* Charlie breathed across the burning sandpaper and reached out for Rex.

Hello! Rex's greeting through the brain link steadied him. *I felt you wake up, but you seemed disoriented. I didn't want to confuse you more.*

Okay, that makes it worth the pain of waking up. Rex's presence eased him, settled some of his worries. His world would be better, if Rex was all right. *How are you?*

"Charlie?" Dr. Zuni asked. "Don't fade out on me, Charlie."

I am well, and I have many things to tell you. Excitement vibrated through the link, but Rex also seemed distracted.

A nurse, masked and gowned beyond recognition, arrived with throat gel.

Hold on a minute, Charlie told Rex.

The nurse retracted the ventilator. At long last, Charlie's aching jaws could move. He closed his mouth, moved his jaw back and forth. His muscles twinged and ached, but the pain felt perversely good.

"Open," the nurse said.

Charlie opened his mouth with another twinge, then choked on the gel. He struggled to relax his gag reflex. Struggled to breathe. He was drowning in—oh my. That felt better. Fiery sandpaper faded to cool mint goo. Charlie focused on breathing.

I'm very sorry, Rex said. *I can't talk now, but it's good to feel you there.*

Something about Rex seemed different, but it probably was Charlie out of frame. *It's good to feel you there, too.* Charlie closed his eyes, already worn out.

"Charlie?" Dr. Zuni's tone turned worried. "I'm getting anomalous brain-activity readings. Wiggle your fingers if you can hear me."

Charlie found that his fingers now could wiggle, although the movement came with a new round of twinges. He obeyed his doctor but stayed focused on Rex. *They want normal sleep, so they woke me. Logical, right?* A thought sluggishly dawned: Rex would've been sidelined. *Hope you're not too bored.*

He sensed Rex's amusement. *Boredom's not a problem. But I think you're still very weak.*

Weariness settled more heavily. *Three re-gen cycles down. One to go.*

"Charlie!" Dr. Zuni cried. "Can you hear me?"

You must rest. Heal fast! Rex withdrew from their contact.

"Charlie? Charlie!" Dr. Zuni sounded seriously worried now.

"Rex," Charlie croaked. He felt as if he should clear his throat but knew better. "Brain link." It was easier if he whispered. It took effort to open his eyes.

Dr. Zuni gave him a startled frown. "The brain link . . . with your XK9?"

Charlie lowered his chin, the closest he could manage to a nod.

His doctor smiled, relieved. "Oh, I get it. For a moment I thought you were going into some kind of episode. Divided attention. Of course. Your dog missed you, didn't it?"

Charlie semi-nodded again. Goes both ways, doc, he wanted to say. New medicine seeped steadily into him. Dulled the pain, made it easier to relax. Charlie pictured Rex at home on his bed . . . wait, no. He tried to open heavy eyelids. What *was* Rex doing? The drugs in his system blurred his thoughts, pulled him into sleep. He had no strength to resist.

Civic Center Rotunda Elevator and Chief Klein's Office

Rex squeezed into the elevator car's back corner behind Chief Klein. He pressed against the walls, closed his eyes, and willed himself smaller. It didn't work. He was huge and hairy and everywhere. Adeyeme's fear-scent pervaded the tiny space that was left. Remorse for her distress ached through Rex, but wonder and gratitude warmed him more. *She let me in, despite her terror. How can I thank her enough?* He opened his eyes.

Her tense, motionless stance, with shoulders hunched and arms wrapped tightly around herself, left no doubt of her discomfort. *Does she now regret her generosity?* She met his gaze with sad, dark eyes, bit her lip, took deep, measured breaths. *Why is she sad?*

Perri placed herself between Adeyeme and Rex. He might be the object of her defensiveness, but Rex approved of Perri's loyalty.

Fulbert stared at Adeyeme. A calculating smile curved his lips. His harsh, cold scent and the smug triumph in his hooded eyes suggested he was estimating how much advantage it gave him to know about her fear.

Protective anger boiled up within Rex, but he throttled the growl in his throat. A growl would only distress Adeyeme further. Instead, Rex caught Fulbert's eye. He put all his guardian intent into a steady glare. Curled his lip to show a silent fang. *Mess with her, and I will end you.*

Fulbert stiffened. His calculating expression smoothed into a careful, emotionless mask. His scent shifted to cold-sweaty fear. He looked away.

Rex let his tongue slide out with fierce amusement. Fulbert better behave himself. Perri wasn't the only person in this elevator who had Adeyeme's back.

"Could I interest anyone in lunch?" Chief Klein asked. "Sandwich? Salad? Bento box?"

Silence echoed. "Thank you, Kwame. Maybe later," Director Perri said.

Archy met them at the elevator doors. Led them to a conference room. Had no more luck than Klein at extracting lunch orders, so he left them to talk.

No one sat. Perri's gaze swept the group, including Rex. "All right, tell me things. Elaine, you first. Why in the name of sanity would you work with ten enormous dogs that terrify you?"

Adeyeme met her boss's eyes. She clasped shaking hands together tightly in front of herself. "Because I trust them to do excellent, accurate work, and to do it more efficiently than Nolan's humans." Her voice, at least, came out strong and steady. "I'm convinced the XK9s have superior analysis capabilities."

Perri turned to Fulbert. "You heard what SCISCO told me. Do you agree?"

His gaze slid from Adeyeme to Rex. "I'm still considering."

Her focus moved to Klein. "What's your bottom line, Kwame?"

The Chief blew out a breath. "If you'll work with us, it gives us a chance to demonstrate that XK9s are sapient creatures."

She gave him a hard look. "Whom your agency just bought."

Rex smoothed prickly hackles, stifled another growl.

Klein met her gaze. "Under false pretenses. An error I mean to rectify."

Those sharp hazel eyes shifted, pinned Rex next. "What do you have to say?"

Rex parked himself at parade-sit before her, ears up. "Our analysis process is a culmination of everything my Packmates and I were born to do. We can deliver all I have promised, and likely much more."

She didn't answer immediately. Took a long, frowning moment to study him. "Remind me. Exactly what did you promise?"

Could she hear his heart pounding? He licked his lips, then pulled his tongue back inside his mouth. "Rapid, highly accurate scent analysis. Meticulous documentation. Thorough synthesis of our analyses via the virtual reconstruction."

"Mm." Her dubious expression lingered.

How could he convince her? "Each Pack member has specialties we can use to augment the overall quality of our forensic evaluation. All of our techniques meet or exceed the highest contemporary standards."

"A rather lofty self-analysis."

"My breeding gave me a highly superior autobiographical memory. I remember every score, every test result, every set of class records I have ever seen." In spite of himself, his tongue slid out in an anxious pant.

"Mm." She cut her eyes toward Klein. "You have access to those records?"

Klein grimaced. "We've noticed considerable under-reporting of some proficiencies."

"We stand ready to be re-tested," Rex said.

"That, however, will take time." She turned again to Fulbert. "How would you rate their accuracy?"

"For optimal empirical analysis, I should do spot re-tests." Fulbert maundered through a blather of allegedly explanatory jargon and considerable hedging, then frowned. "However, what I observed during the demonstration did appear to reflect considerable forensic precision."

"Mm." Perri returned her gaze to Adeyeme. "If my only concern was forensic standards, this conversation would be over. However, I live in a reality where I must explain to the Premier of Rana Station why I'm rejecting her directive to work with the SDF."

Elation filled Rex, but he held himself still. *She wants to work with the Pack!*

Adeyeme's mouth twisted. "Every morning until today Premier Iskander has called to demand in the harshest terms why I have not yet solved this case. Now that I finally have an efficiency to offer, she didn't call."

Klein stiffened. "She didn't?"

"Not a peep." Adeyeme's tone was bitter.

Perri shot a dark glance at Fulbert.

The professor held up both hands. "Don't look at me. You didn't specify any greater-than-normal secrecy. No specifics, and certainly no mention of XK9s until I arrived. But my staff and three of the grad students I supervise knew I was going to Orangeboro today."

Perri's mouth twisted. She shook her head. "Too late to mend it now, however it may have leaked, and there are many possible avenues beyond your circle." She drew in a breath, offered him a smile. "Hakim, I want to thank you. You've been quite helpful."

He nodded. "Always pleased to be of service to the SBI. I take it you now have enough from me?"

"Our payment should be in your account already. I'd intended to treat you to lunch, but my business here is unfinished."

"Archy can help you however you need." Klein escorted Fulbert to the door. Archy appeared as if telepathically summoned, but Rex had noticed Klein slip a hand into his pocket, then heard the soft click of a call-button.

The door closed behind Fulbert and Archy. Klein turned to his remaining guests.

Perri quirked a brow at him. "So, then. Are we looking at an international incident?"

The Chief made a wry face. "I fear it's only a matter of time."

32

DELAYS, DEVELOPMENTS, AND DISAGREEMENTS

S-3-9 Evidence Cavern, Central Plaza, and LEO's Grill

S hady stared after Rex. Her heart pounded hard, her gut a twist of hope and worry.

Her mate trotted close behind the little knot of humans who would decide the Pack's immediate fate. Yesterday Chief Klein had said he thought the XK9s were sapient. Today they'd put on a display of their capabilities for Director Perri. Yet Rex hadn't been invited to join the decision-makers' discussion. What did that say about the humans' willingness to truly respect the XK9s as sapient creatures?

We're all still kind of feeling our way along, Pam said. *I doubt if any of them have thought that far yet. But the Pack Leader should be in that council.*

Shady stress-yawned inside her containment mask. *Humans have been making decisions without consulting dogs forever. Will it really be different now?*

Pam's hand stroked her shoulder. *I guess we'll have to wait and see. Meanwhile, let's get you out of that containment gear. I'm ready for lunch!* The full hour break would be nice, Shady supposed.

But it wouldn't be much fun watching Pam eat if she couldn't have any.

Her partner'd already shucked her own gear. Shady stood still as needed, lifted her feet when Pam asked. Pam quickly stripped off the hot, confining garb. Most of the humans had left by then, excited by their hour off, though a few techs and field agents lingered to pick up stray booties, gloves, or other dropped items.

Liz was still shedding her gear. Razor looked on. Nicole helped Scout with his. They were the last ones to clear the ready room.

"I don't know about you, but I'm just not ready to face the vending machines in the break room," Nicole said.

Liz deposited her gloves in the recycler. "You're right. I feel more like LEO's."

"Want to join us, Pam?" Nicole asked.

Balchu met them in the war room. Nicole invited him along too.

Shady, Razor, and Scout followed their humans to the stairs. Shady sorted through the multitude of scent rafts, still plentiful in the air. How was Rex getting along? Had Klein and the others realized he should join them? He hadn't stayed in hallway, so maybe.

LEO's Grill was a little eatery a block from Central Plaza that catered to law enforcement. After two months on-Station, XK9s had become almost routine to this waitstaff, a refreshing change. They found it packed with people who'd just left the SBI's investigation center. A server greeted them with a smile, then estimated a twenty-minute wait.

"We should still have time to eat," Nicole said. She and the other humans took their place in the queue.

The delicious smells made Shady's innards gurgle. "I am going for a run in the Plaza," she said. "Who is with me?"

"Count me in," Razor said.

Scout simply took off for the broad grassy area beyond the concentric circles of mosaic-fronted terraces. Time to stretch their muscles, after a morning of little activity.

Don't scare any civilians, Pam cautioned. *I'll call you when we're seated.*

Call me when you've gotten your food, Shady said. No lunches for dogs didn't mean they couldn't wheedle tidbits. By the time Pam called, Shady was ready for a rest. She and her Packmates found their humans at a table on the tree-shaded patio behind the restaurant.

Shady, Scout, and Razor went into begging mode. Hard for humans to resist puppy-eyes. Doubly hard, when their dogs also had brain link connections and an intimate knowledge of ways to trigger their partners' guilt.

Pam heaved a sigh and handed over the last of her sandwich. "I'm gonna lose weight, partnered with you."

Shady wagged her tail, snuggled closer. "You are welcome. Are you finished with those fries?"

Balchu laughed. He shoved his own plate over to her. "Here, you can have the rest of mine."

Shady snarfed them with a flick of her tongue, then wrinkled her nose. "Did you have to be so liberal with the ketchup?"

"Beggars," Balchu said.

"Yeah, yeah." Shady flicked her ears.

"If we are now considered people, why do we still not get our own lunch?" Scout asked.

Nicole scowled. "I suppose half of mine doesn't count?"

"It is a serious question," Razor said. "It has always seemed unfair."

Liz toyed with the last of her salad greens. Razor hadn't mooched any of those, but he'd gotten most of her grilled chicken chunks. "Today, it's because I already spent all of your stipend for this month, on that giant bag of Master Mix back home in our kitchen."

"That is another thing," Shady said. "You humans get to eat all kinds of different things. Why must we always eat Master Mix?"

"You just ate half my sandwich," Pam said.

"And it was delicious, thank you."

"Tell you what." Nicole turned to Scout. "As soon as Payroll catches up with Chief Klein and they pay you an actual salary, you can have whatever you like for lunch, and figure out how to fit it into your own budget."

Scout tensed. His tongue slid out in a nervous pant. "I know what a budget is, but I have no idea how to make one."

Nicole stroked Scout's head. "Don't worry. My Family and I will teach you."

Liz frowned. "We need to talk with the Union and the Oversight Committee. Make sure they know how versatile and talented you XK9s are. You guys really ought to get Specialist pay."

Razor cocked his head. "Is that a good salary?"

"Yeah, it's pretty good," Balchu said. "Better than entry-level detectives make." He smiled, squeezed Pam's hand. "Just think, Shady. Even if you only get paid the same as Pam, you can help with the rent."

Pam's scent and expression blossomed with bright, fragrant enthusiasm that echoed through the link. "I'm looking forward to that part. You won't even need a clothing allowance. We can move to a better apartment!"

Shady balked, ears down. *They're talking as if my future salary belongs to them!* The warmth, scents, and soul-deep delight of sharing Rex's bed in Corona Tower filled her memory. Longing to live with her mate rose sharp and strong to tighten her throat and ache in her chest.

Pam's smile faded. The warmth of their link connection chilled abruptly. *XK9s live with their human partners. That's how it's supposed to be.*

Shady growled softly. *Says who? Dr. Ordovich?* Anger boiled up from unexpected depths within her, dark and poisonous. Shady recoiled from it, frightened by its suppressed fury.

Pam gave a little gasp. She pulled back from the link's intimacy. "Oh, look at the time. Our lunch hour's gone."

Their tablemates groaned.

We'll need to discuss this, Shady said. *I want to live with Rex.*

Pam stood, stiff and cold. *Later.*

Central Plaza and S-3-9 Investigative Center

Shady trotted ahead of the humans, head and ears down. Even her Packmates kept their distance. She grumbled a soft, rolling growl under her breath and wrestled with her smoldering temper all the way back to Central HQ. The more Pam's words tumbled around in her mind, the angrier she became. Yet if Director Perri had given the okay, she and Pam would need to work together harmoniously. *Better settle my mind, so I can do my job.*

Easier said than done.

She growled again, more loudly. A couple of UPOs in the Atrium scrambled out of her way. The desk officer buzzed her in, so she didn't even have to pause.

Look, I said we'll talk later. Don't be so angry. Pam's mental voice held a heartbroken note of betrayal discovered. *I'm just really hurt that you could think of moving out on me.*

And I'm just really furious that you could plan on spending my money for your rent, but it never crossed your mind that I might want to live with Rex again. You know how I've missed him!

It didn't even occur to me that you'd think about moving out. We're a team!

Rex has been my mate way longer than you have been my partner.

Pam didn't reply to that. Through the link, Shady sensed her trying to grapple with the idea that Shady might have a stronger tie to Rex than to her. *Moving out is pretty extreme.*

Shady's hackles prickled. She tried half-successfully to keep from bristling. *You moved out on Rex and Charlie. That wasn't my choice, and I didn't get any say in the matter.*

Pam's anger surged through the link. *I am NOT having THAT conversation again.*

Okay, FINE. Let's just see what they want us to do in the evidence cavern and get to work.

FINE, yourself. Yes, let's work!

Most of SIT Delta's on-watch agents, the rest of the Task Force members, other Packmates, and their partners had bunched up in the S-3-9 corridor and come to a standstill. As in the Atrium, Shady's low growl and bristly, ears-down advance cleared a path.

Victor pushed through the crowd to her, hesitated. He lowered his shaggy black head and ears, lifted his nose in supplication, then fluttered his white tail-tip appeasingly. "I hope you do not mind my asking, but have you had any news from Rex?"

Shady lifted her ears. It made no sense to take out her mood on Victor, especially when the big lug was being so polite. She drew in a long breath, stress-yawned, then averted her eyes to show her own respect. "Rex has not contacted me. I hope that means the decision-makers have let him into their meeting."

"I could not find Tux, either," Victor said. "Nor has Elle has heard from him. Maybe SCISCO's interview is providing helpful information."

Shady stress-yawned again, but thinking about the investigation did help her set aside her anger. "We can hope. Yes."

They pushed on, made it into the war room. Everyone gathered around LSA Kramer. "Still no word from upstairs yet, sorry," Kramer said. "Go on back to whatever you were doing yesterday." She focused on Shady. "Except you XK9s. Shady, there's morgue work, but we only have five autopsy tables and there are eight teams."

No need to take out her mood on Kramer, either. Shady made an effort to lift her ears and wag her tail. "We can rotate. Let the new ones go first." She sure didn't feel like doing more morgue work if she could avoid it.

Kramer's mouth twitched. "You don't mind sharing?"

Liz grinned and stroked Razor. "Not in the least."

Berwyn and Cinnamon nodded their agreement. "We would not want them to get out of practice," Cinnamon said.

"Yeah, yeah, you've got our best interests at heart, I know." Nicole turned to Walter and Connie, who stood on either side of her. "Guess we'll go check out the new morgue annex." Scout, Petunia, Victor, and Crystal followed their humans. Misha, Elle, and Eduardo joined them. SBI Agents and OPD Task Force members scattered. Some went to the evidence cavern or back out into the hall on assorted errands, while others settled at workstations.

A Crime Scene Unit tech in a blue containment gown arrived in the doorway. "Delivery for SA Freas!"

Freas poked his head through the access from the evidence cavern's ready room, then pulled his face mask down with a gloved hand. "Are those the corridor materials?"

The CSU tech consulted her case pad. "All pads and handholds from . . ." she rattled off dock-area coordinates that meant nothing to Shady. "Collected and bagged per scent-evidence protocols, as ordered. Had to suit up for microgravity in vacuum. Took us all morning, so I sure hope these are what you want. Where do they go?"

Freas strode over to stare out into the hallway for a moment. Shady, Pam, Berwyn, Cinnamon, Liz, and Razor followed. Two more CSU techs waited out there. They stood beside three powered hand trolleys, each piled high with bagged materials. Freas turned to Pam and Shady. "Scent-evidence protocols, just as you said. That means you get it first."

Through the brain link Shady caught echoes of Pam's dismay at how much material the CSU techs had brought. "Where're we going to put it all?" Pam asked.

Freas chewed his lower lip, then pulled his mask back up over his narrow, pointy nose and stalked back through the ready room. The three XK9 teams and the lead CSU tech followed. They looked in through the doorway. Freas gestured toward an open corner. "Park your trollies along there." He accepted the pad to document chain-of-custody with a signature and a retinal scan.

Shady turned to Cinnamon and Razor. "So much for being the 'spare' XK9 teams. Better get your humans to start your gown-up."

The CSU tech and her co-workers hauled in their trollies and parked them with snappy efficiency. "Lunch at last!" she cried, as soon as they'd finished. "LEO's, anyone?"

Pam put on Shady's containment gear first, then her own. She kept her input through the link coldly neutral.

Shady centered herself and strove to match her partner's detachment. Pam was right, in this instance. They went into the evidence cavern. Shady moved over beside Freas, then gazed at the towering trolley loads. Her other Packmates and partners joined her.

"I'm thinking hazmat tents for containment." Freas spoke to Pam, although Shady was standing right there. "How d'you want this stuff arranged? I can free up all the guys you need." Several masked, gowned field agents had brought in a forklift, presumably to remove pallets of debris if they received a go-ahead from Perri. Till then, however, they stood around in little groups, chatting and looking bored.

Pam's scent factors shifted from musky worry to bright relief. "You're the best!" She soon had Liz, Berwyn, and the work detail fully engaged.

Shady, Cinnamon, and Razor watched from a safe distance.

"Pam certainly does enjoy ordering people around," Cinnamon said.

Especially her partner. Shady flattened her ears. *Not a helpful thought.* "That she does. Have to admit, though, I like the way she is arranging things. Organization is one of Pam's stronger talents."

Thank you.

Shady had a sense that Pam wanted to say more, but didn't. *Smart woman.*

Soon a line of hazmat containment units stood sealed together along the edge of the cavern, illuminated from within. Inside, the humans laid out all the bagged evidence. It took them more than an hour. The XK9s napped, dozed, and half-listened to the humans trying to make sense of location coordinates for this Hub-dock section.

Shady had often wished for opposable thumbs, but today she was glad to let the humans employ theirs. She still hadn't worked all the aches out of her back and shoulders from yesterday. While they waited, she explained to Razor and Cinnamon what Rex had told her about this Hub corridor and Elmo Smart. After yesterday, she knew Elmo's scent profile well. But on these surfaces, his scent would be close to two weeks old, growing stale under newer layers of odor.

Eventually Pam emerged from the nearest tent. She absently rubbed her lower back. Even from this distance, a puppy couldn't have missed the smell of inflammation from her pulled back muscles. All the bending and lifting today must've exacerbated the strain from the morgue move. Shady might officially be angry with her partner, but Pam's physical well-being was important for their work. *Uh-oh. You need to rest.*

Not now. Pam's irritable reply crackled through their link. "Ready for a sniff-over?"

Just sayin'. Perhaps you could sit and rest while I work? Liz and Berwyn don't have the same injured smell.

No. Get to work.

Shady flicked her ears but stifled a growl. Arguing with Pam when she was in this mood would be pointless.

She, Cinnamon, and Razor joined their partners inside the first tent.

Pam temp-sealed them in.

33

POLITICS AND POMPOUS INTRUDERS

S-3-9 Evidence Cavern

S hady opened a report on her HUD, shared it with her colleagues, then surveyed the piles. Pam and the other humans opened evidence bags for her one-by-one. Cinnamon and Razor stood nearby and watched, ears up. She conducted an over-sniff, one new bag at a time, seeking scents she could identify clearly. She described what she smelled each time, simultaneously aloud for her colleagues, and in her report.

The top scent-layer on every piece was a light dusting of emissions-molecules from passing spacecraft. Undoubtedly that had been deposited between the time of the dock breach and the evidence-collection.

Below it lay a whiff of explosives, plus metallics and ceramics, most likely from the *Izgubil's* death. Next layer down was thicker, made up of metallics, polymers, and similar substances. Probably broken loose during the dock breach.

Only after she'd gotten through all of those could she occasionally pick up Rex's fading scent, full of excitement and frustration. Near it, in the same time layer, she always found

Charlie's scent, marked by apprehension. She figured the third person in that group must be DPO Fujimoto.

After the first dozen pieces, Shady paused. The waiting line of wall-straps, cushions, and other materials stretched farther than she cared to contemplate. "I need for you to rearrange some of these and move others aside."

The humans' scent factors brightened. "You found the trail?" Berwyn asked.

Shady flicked her ears. "I found Rex, Charlie, and Fujimoto's trail. I need to find corridor sections immediately adjacent, to locate the scent trail we seek."

"Show us where those scents are," Cinnamon said. "We can work other sections."

Pam nodded. "Tell us what to move." Forty minutes later they'd moved many items to the side. They'd also pieced together most of Rex, Charlie, and Fujimoto's path. Razor identified the two murderers from the warehouse, based on trace they'd left on their vic. But the dogs had to go over the pads several times before they found trace from Elmo and his companions, faint and fading in some of the deepest distinguishable scent layers.

Shady also smelled ever-growing inflammation along Pam's lower back, although her partner's protests that she was fine persisted.

There are PanaCees in my first aid pannier-pocket, Shady reminded for the umpteenth time.

I . . . Pam sighed in defeat. *I guess I could take one.*

And we need a break, Shady added.

Pam frowned. *You've been working for less than an hour.*

Shady snapped her ears flat. *You and the other humans have worked much longer than that, on top of yesterday's morgue-move. Berwyn and Liz are exhausted, too. Take a damn break!*

Pam didn't reply.

"I smell too much inflammation in human muscles," Shady announced. "PanaCees in my pannier! Who needs one?"

"Oh! I'll take a couple," Liz said. "Thanks!"

Berwyn grinned. "I won't say no to a pain-pill. Let's go get some water."

Pam scowled at Shady, but gave in at last.

Shady welcomed a chance to step outside the tent where it was cooler. Pam followed her into the ready room, stripped off Shady's containment gown, then bent with a groan to access the first aid pannier.

Once the humans were medicated, seated, and sipping their water, Shady enjoyed a long drink of her own, then a luxuriant stretch. Shoulders down, hold. Reverse to hips down, hold. *Ahhh!*

Her com buzzed. Shady blinked, startled. Ted Lee Morgan, the ID said. Why would Charlie's father call her private line? "Hello?"

"I apologize if this is a bad time. Can you talk for a moment?"

"Sure. I am on a break. How can I help you?"

"Thank goodness!" Ted's obvious relief surprised her. "Is Rex all right? I've been trying to call him. I want to know when he needs to come home, but he isn't answering his com."

Shady let her tongue loll. "You are a very nice person. Thank you. Rex is in a meeting with Chief Klein, SSA Adeyeme, and SBI Director Perri. He cannot answer his com."

There was a moment of silence on the line. "Um, that's some . . . Pretty high and mighty company he's keeping."

Shady's throat went tight with love and pride. *It is pretty impressive, isn't it?* "He is now the acknowledged leader of the Orangeboro Pack. They needed to consult with a representative, and it is his idea they are discussing." Rising, joyous hope filled her heart. Even as puppies, Rex had always been the leader to his Packmates. But now the humans were taking him seriously in that role too.

Ted chuckled. "I see. Leader of the Pack, eh? Gotta say, I'm not surprised. He's one charismatic and strong-willed dog. Any clue how late he'll stay?"

"Hold on a moment." Shady put Ted on hold. *Pam, is it all right if Rex stays at our place tonight?*

Pam's surprise surged through the link. *I . . . suppose that's fair, after you went home with him. We'll have to break it to Balchu gently. The two of you will just about max out our living room.*

Shady wagged her tail. *I can't think of a better way to max it out. Thank you!* At last, something she and Pam could agree on! She reactivated the com. "Ted? I cannot tell you how late he will be, but I plan to reciprocate for his and your hospitality on Monday. He can stay with me tonight. Do not worry."

Ted chuckled. "I'm sure he'll be delighted. Okay, thanks. And thank you for the update on his new role. Please give him our congratulations and let him know we'll help him however we can."

"Thanks." Shady signed off with a sigh. Her pleasure soared. *What a nice Family.*

Pam grimaced. *Corona? Yeah, well, everything Charlie has is nice, so why not his Family, too? Must be great, to always live a charmed life.* Her bitter tone came harsh and sour through the link.

Shady's elation flattened like a punctured balloon. The small, burgeoning re-warming she'd felt toward her partner evaporated. Prickly irritation leaped up between them. *Is there something wrong with having a nice Family?*

She shook her head. *"I always wanted a nice Family, but what I got was Mother. I'm jealous, I guess.*

The unfairness of Pam's comment still stung. Memories of Rex's anguish over his partner's injuries rose in Shady's mind, along with the Family's worried faces and scents. *I'm not sure landing in the ICU for a second time in less than five years is living a charmed life.*

Pam's pang of chagrin cut sharp through the link this time. *Oh, crap. You're right. I didn't think about where he is now. I'm just . .*

. Yeah, that was out of line. Don't mind me. My back hurts, and I'm grumpy, and I'm primed to see the worst. I apologize.

Shady looked away with a quiet whimper. She'd been feeling better after Ted's call, but now depression loomed, dark and heartsick. *This sucks.*

The elevator rumbled.

Her head snapped up. Quicksilver joy swept through her. *Could that be Rex?* She bounded from the ready room through the war room, to peer out the main entrance.

The elevator halted with a high screech of gears the humans probably couldn't hear. The doors parted to reveal three strangers.

Unauthorized strangers!

Shady bristled. Disappointment slashed sharp, with an angry edge. Whoever these guys were, they'd picked a lousy moment. And a secured location. *They are out of bounds!* She cranked her vocalizer to its highest setting. "HALT, INTRUDERS!"

A scramble of claws, snarls, and thudding paws rushed toward her. First Cinnamon, then the rest of her Packmates barreled into the corridor, most still gowned, all growling.

Three tall men in military uniforms halted. Their scent factors spiked with alarm. Two of them bolted to the rear of the elevator car, reeking of terror.

But the lead intruder held his ground.

The Pack's warmth closed around Shady's flanks. Their snarls reverberated in the air and vibrated against her ribs.

Human feet thudded. Familiar scent-profiles gathered near, burning fierce and defensive. More and more arrived, till every human in the investigative center jammed into the narrow space.

The uniformed leader's initial burst of alarmed scent shifted to chilling tones of menace. He gave the corridor's defenders a heavy-lidded glare. "Who is in charge, here?"

"That would be me, Admiral." LSA Kramer stepped forward. Humans and XK9s moved aside for her. She stopped next to

Shady. "Why are you here? XK9 Officer Jacob-Belle is correct. You are not authorized to be here."

The admiral sneered. "'Not authorized?' Of *course* I'm authorized. I promised to bring my experts, and here they are."

Hatred surged through Shady. Her snarl redoubled. This admiral had already wasted three days. Why come now, just when the Pack might get a chance to prove themselves?

"You're half a week tardy." Kramer's scent seethed with anger, but her voice remained cool if a bit tart. "We found other experts. You'll have to go ask Director Perri if she still needs you."

"How dare you?" the admiral took a stride toward her, fists clenched.

That is unmistakable aggression. Enough posturing! Shady leaped forward with a roar. Her Packmates lunged with her.

The admiral's scent and body language went through a delicious transformation. He held his ground for less than a tenth of a second, then sprinted for the elevator. He leaped inside, spun, and jabbed frantically at the "close doors" button.

Shady and her Packmates arrived well before the doors closed. The others stopped when Shady did but snarled at the men from a few centimeters' distance.

Ah, the sweet smell of a trapped but powerless perp! The admiral stabbed his futile little button many more times. His followers wedged themselves into the car's back corners, their scents drenched in fear.

The doors closed very slowly.

OPD HQ, Chief Klein's Office

Rex panted softly, ears pinned back. He looked from Perri to Klein to Adeyeme.

The three humans in Klein's smaller conference room had pursued their discussion for at least two hours.

Rex had set his com to take messages, because he didn't want to risk being distracted. He didn't know most of the names or references, and he could rarely follow exactly how one thing built upon the next. But he'd paid close attention. If he could pour it all into his memory, it would stay there for future reference. He wasn't sure when he'd need to know any of this, but that didn't shake his deep certainty that he would need to know it someday.

Adeyeme pushed up from her chair by the oval table. She paced across the room, then turned to look at Perri. Her face, scent, and posture spoke of worry, but for once Rex didn't seem to be the source. "What if the Acquisitionists are embedded deeper than we thought?"

Rex growled under his breath. They'd mentioned "Acquisitionists" several times. He gathered that the group was a faction within the Transmondian government intent on creating a Transmondian Empire. UPO Anthony had fussed about getting "annexed as a colony" yesterday. Didn't seem such a trivial remark, now.

"I have Konrad quietly following up on Duthuluru's ouster, at Kizzitikti's request," Perri said. "She's concerned about Acquisitionist sympathies among some of the Commonwealth Party appointees in the Foreign Ministry."

Rex had no idea who Konrad or Duthuluru were, but he did know the Ozzirikkian Vice Premier's name was Kizzitikti Zhokittik. If ki was worried, that sounded serious.

"There's been a recent shift toward a stronger military influence on the government in Solara City," Klein said. "They've been funding all sorts of new military initiatives."

Perri nodded. "What worries me is that they look at Rana Station and see strategic high ground."

"Agreed. But my point was that it might explain some things

about Greg's visit yesterday," Klein said. "He had a military handler, and she was keeping him on a very short leash."

Greg. That was what Klein sometimes called Dr. Ordovich. Rex lolled his tongue. How he would love to see Dr. Ordovich on a short leash! Better yet, wrapped in a dog net, or locked in a Dark Crate! He couldn't resist a tail-wag at the idea, even though Klein didn't mean a real leash.

Suddenly, for some reason, both Adeyeme and Perri were staring at Klein. Alarm shocked through Rex. *Damn it! Must focus better. The Pack's whole future hinges on my figuring out human politics, and I let myself get sidetracked by a pleasant daydream!* Rex lifted his ears, then sifted through the astonishment in the women's scents.

"You've seen Bryan's oppo research?" Perri asked.

Klein's shoulders lifted. He offered a diffident smile. "Sacha's an old friend."

Rex stress-yawned. Yet another name, Sacha. Who was . . . he hesitated. He'd only heard the name "Sacha" once before. That was the Human Vice Premier, Sacha Guzmán. He was the candidate Charlie had wanted to be the Premier instead of Iskander. But what was "oppo research"? Rex accessed his HUD.

"An old friend who lets you see his oppo research?" Perri's brows shot up.

The reference opened. Rex scanned it, while still listening. Opposition research on a political opponent was digging up facts they didn't want known. *Ah.* Rex shot a look at Klein. If "Sacha" really did mean Guzmán, then Klein had a friend in a very powerful office.

Klein smiled. "Sometimes we talk."

"You sly dog." Perri grinned at Klein, so she wasn't talking about Rex. *How is Klein sly? Or, for that matter, a dog?*

The elevator at the end of the entry hall rumbled upward. Archy's footsteps hurried toward it.

Rex turned his ears in the direction the aide had gone. The

elevator doors rolled open. *Is anyone supposed to be coming here?* Rex's guard-dog instincts kicked in. His hackles prickled.

"Oh! Hello!" Something in Archy's voice alarmed Rex. He shifted into full guard-dog mode, gave a low, rumbling growl.

The three humans in the conference room went silent.

"Where is Klein?" a loud, angry voice demanded.

"Speak of the devil," Adeyeme said.

"That didn't take long," Perri said.

Klein strode to the door, yanked it open, stepped outside. Rex reached the doorway right behind him. This loudmouth better not mess with the Chief.

"YOU!" the loud one cried. He was a tall older man with a stiff brush of white hair. The four bands of silver braid on his SDF uniform told Rex he was an admiral. Didn't take much guessing to figure out which one.

Klein crossed his arms with a scowl and an uprush of fierce, hot scent, but his voice rang cold. "My office."

Admiral Virendra matched Klein stride-for-stride. They disappeared into the Chief's office.

Two other men in SDF uniforms had followed the admiral. Rex stepped into the hallway with a growl, to head them off.

They shrank back, hands up, reeking of terror. "My God," one cried, "how many does he have?"

Rex showed his teeth. "Enough of us. Stay there!"

Both men backed up several steps, their eyes wide. "No problem!"

Rex wheeled to follow Klein and Virendra, hackles at full bristle. Protective fury surged within him. The door stood ajar. He pushed inside.

"When we arrived, we were attacked by a pack of enormous guard dogs!" Virendra shouted, fists clenched. "What are you going to do about it?"

Klein scowled at Virendra. "I'm going to recommend that you alert us in advance, next time you come here. Our XK9 officers will respect a proper authorization. I'd be willing to arrange one, if Director Perri and SSA Adeyeme deem it necessary to allow you into their investigative center."

"If they deem it? Allow me?" Virendra's scent spiked hot. "Whose department is this, theirs or yours?"

Klein's expression went stony, but his voice remained calm. "They are my honored guests, and the investigation is theirs, to conduct as they see fit. I'm confident they have the matter well in hand."

"I'm not so sure others will see it that way." Virendra glared at him. "You'd better watch your—"

Rex growled a warning, hackles up.

Virendra swung around. He drew back at the sight of Rex.

"Admiral Virendra was just leaving, Rex," Chief Klein said.

Rex put his teeth on full display, ears flat, hackles up. Protective fierceness coursed through him. "Very good, sir. Shall I make sure he and his associates find Grand Central Terminal?"

Klein smiled. "I believe they know the way."

"As you wish." Rex stepped aside from the door. He lifted his ears and closed his mouth, but his hackles stayed up, his head even with his shoulders, and his tail straight back. One word from Klein, and he'd strike.

Virendra swept past him out of the office. His hauteur and fury couldn't mask the cold fear in his scent. But he stopped when he saw Adeyeme in the doorway of the small conference room. "This won't be your investigation much longer, missy!"

Outrage surged through Rex like lava. He stopped just short of clamping his jaws down hard on the nearest piece of Virendra's anatomy.

"Making my staffing decisions for me now, Nolan?" Perri stepped up next to her agent. The Director's face appeared calm, but her scent factors surged with anger.

Virendra turned his cold glare on her. "I've arrived as promised, but received the rudest possible reception."

"Not exactly as promised. You're late." Director Perri crossed her arms. "Not only late, but behind the times. The OPD has placed their state-of-the-art Transmondian analysis methods, and no fewer than ten forensic olfaction specialists, at our disposal. While you were taking your sweet time getting here, we've gratefully accepted this chance to upgrade the quality of our work."

Virendra stared at her. "Are you seriously telling me you think a pack of dogs can out-perform the SDF's best experts?"

Perri smiled. "Why, yes. Was my meaning not clear?"

34

REVELATIONS, REORGANIZATION, AND RECALL

S-3-9 Evidence Cavern and Chief Klein's Office

R ex paused, startled, at the edge of the evidence cavern. SSA Adeyeme also stopped, a meter or so away from him.

Rex cocked his head. "Are those hazmat tents?"

LSAs Kramer and Shimon hurried from different directions to join them.

"We've had some developments," Kramer said. "I couldn't get through on your com."

"Interruptions would not have been helpful," Adeyeme answered. "You should know that Virendra came to Klein's office."

"Ah." Kramer's face puckered with worry. "What did he say?"

"Foolish things. You and the Pack were right to rebuff him. Director Perri has made her choice, with a final push from the admiral. We'll work with the Pack."

Both Kramer and Shimon relaxed into grins.

"I can have Frankie start removing pallets, then?" Shimon asked.

Adeyeme nodded. "Please do."

Rex wagged his tail at this reconfirmation of the reality that the humans actually did mean to follow his plan. They'd said they would, but humans had said one thing then done another so many times in his life, it inspired a certain thrill to see them following through as promised.

"Shady, Cinnamon, and Razor examined the corridor pads from the Hub access to the *Izgubil's* service entrance," Kramer said. "That's what's inside the hazmat tents. They found Elmo's trail, along with those of his associates."

"Already? What can they tell us about them?"

Kramer's smile disappeared. "They've caught fading whiffs of approximately seven other individuals in the same two time layers with Elmo, but they're degrading fast. We've applied an enhancement treatment that may help, but we have to wait for it to set."

None of this surprised Rex. The scents had already degraded a lot by the time he'd smelled them before dawn on Monday. It now was Thursday night. He hoped the enhancement treatment could stabilize them enough to get scent profiles.

"While we wait, I can tell you Dr. SCISCO's given us a possible suspect," Shimon said.

Adeyeme gave a rueful chuckle. "Perhaps I should leave you two on your own more often. Who's the suspect?"

"A doctoral student of SCISCO's named Rory Fredericks," Shimon said. "He was working on nanotimer prototypes for remotely-triggered micro-detonations to pulverize industrial materials. Used for a different purpose here, but it's the same basic tech the dogs found in the debris."

"You've dispatched agents to bring him in?"

Shimon scowled. "Fredericks disappeared a year and a half ago."

Adeyeme's eyebrows rose. "Disappeared?"

"One day he was at Station Polytechnic, working on his prototypes. Next day, no sign of him. His Amare and his Family both called in missing-persons reports. OPD did a thorough search. I read through the file and talked with DPO Jones, who's on our Task Force. She caught that case, back then. It's still open."

Fredericks had disappeared long before XK9s had arrived on-Station. Could Rex or one of his Packmates have found him? They'd all been trained for missing persons cases.

Adeyeme frowned. "Anything about the case stand out to you?"

"Two things." Shimon frowned, hunched his shoulders. "For one, it would've been a lousy time for him to chuck it all and disappear. He was only four months from finishing his degree, and according to SCISCO, he was making good progress with his prototypes."

"Mm. The other?"

"His Amare. By all accounts, Fredericks is kind of a dorky nerd of modest means, but his lover's a smoking hot socialite. Founding-Family rich, and, from her file photo, fashion-model beautiful. Jones said she seemed genuinely alarmed by his disappearance, but as she noted in the file then, and repeated to me today, they were a very unusual match."

"Which Founding Family?" Adeyeme asked.

Rex had studied enough Rana Station history before he'd emigrated to know that what were now called the Fifty Founding Families had put up a large portion of the money needed to build the Station more than ninety years ago, with the remainder provided by an ozzirikkian group fleeing oppression and more than a million smaller human investors. Remarkably, eleven of the Founders still survived, seven ozzirikkians and four humans. Their ages stretched well beyond a century. Ranans revered them as national heroes.

"Vinebrook," Shimon said. "Fredericks' Amare is the Founders' great-granddaughter, Emer Bellamy."

Rex's ears went up. Bellamy? The name tickled his memory, but which memory-trail should he trace back? He ran a global word search on *Bellamy* in the case book instead. Oh. Morgue Client Number One. Shady had processed him, which was probably how he'd heard the name. A revolting pedophile named Hideki Bellamy Moran.

Rex accessed the facts known to the investigation about Moran. He'd been reported missing by Vinebrook Family the morning after the ship's destruction. Among the Station's richest citizens, he'd been married to Sorcha Moran Bellamy. They'd had two daughters, Orla and Emer. A daughter would, by custom, have been given her mother's surname. Was Emer Bellamy going to be a lot richer now that Daddy was out of the picture? The file did not say.

"Excuse me," Rex said. "Did Emer inherit anything when Hideki died in the explosion?"

The humans stopped talking to stare at him. *Oh.* Their conversation must've continued.

"Hideki?" Adeyeme asked.

From his HUD stare, Shimon was already looking it up. His mouth fell open. "Good catch!" He shot Rex a look of amazement. "Hideki Bellamy Moran. Our Morgue Client Number One. He's Emer's father. That is a very good question about his heirs!"

"I'll put Wina on it," Adeyeme said. "Nice work, Rex!"

Warm elation flooded through him at her praise. Her ebbing fear level smelled like an additional accolade. His tail fanned with delight. *Can this day get any better?*

"Time to hit the pallets for real, then," Shimon said. "Rex, let's rally the troops."

Adeyeme, Rex, Shimon, Shady, Pam, Tux, and Georgia worked with TS Raach and SA Freas to expand on the workflow they'd developed for the demonstration. They traded possibilities, half-climbed ladders several times, walked team members through the process, then divided up their crews.

Rex stepped back to observe. *Yes, this is working. Now, if only I had a trained partner to work with, so I could do my part!* He bowed his head, throat tight. A little while ago his sense of Charlie's presence had once again blinked out. That final cycle of re-gen must've begun.

"Rex," Shimon called to him. "Need to plug you into the Admin Channel. Come over here, and I'll run you through a com-check."

His pulse doubled in a giddy rush of delight. The *Admin Channel! They think I rate the Admin Channel!* He hurried over to Shimon. Tried not to wriggle with too much obvious delight.

Shimon grinned. "Guess this makes you Command Staff now, Pack Leader Dieter-Nell."

How could he *not* squeak and wriggle, after that? "This is an honor, LSA Shimon. Thank you."

"Uh-uh." Shimon shook his head. "Command staff, Rex. I'm Shiv, Kramer's Shawnee, and Adeyeme's Elaine to you now."

He froze mid-prance, stared at Shim—er, at Shiv. "They will not be offended?"

Shiv smiled. "Command Staff. Colleagues. Comes with the Admin responsibility."

Well, okay, then. I could get used to this!

Their plan unfolded well, even without Rex's nose-on participation. Two XK9 teams on debris duty alternated every hour with two teams on the corridor pads and three teams in the morgue, for a change of scents, while two partner-pairs each hour rotated out for sequential half-hour breaks and walks. This kept everyone's nose sharp.

Rex had to settle for circulating between his teams, listening to their reports, reviewing some of the most important scents they'd found, and discussing them with the humans.

Shady claimed one of the breaks. She badgered Pam until she sat down and did back stretches, then took Rex aside and told him the bad news about their old friends Fernie and Chaser.

Rex's lungs wouldn't work for a moment. *No. NO. This can't be right.* Not gentle, dark-brindle Fernie, with his wise brown eyes and dry wit. Not high-velocity, black-and-white Chaser, so full of life and energy! Their love for each other, their devotion to their work, their intense, delighted partnerings with Oroplanian investigators Zandra Chen and Saladin Wu . . . *All vanished now. Gone. Wasted.*

Rex had to walk away by himself. He retreated to the shadowed, refrigerated back corner of the new morgue annex. Then he stood in the cold among silent, redolent racks of dead people, and struggled to master himself. He couldn't even howl. Not yet. His heart must grieve a while, first.

The time to howl would come.

So would the time to question why, and how he could protect his own Pack.

So would the time to make Dr. Ordovich pay for murdering his friends.

❖ ❖   ❖ ❖   ❖ ❖   ❖ ❖

REX LOOKED UP, alerted by a quiet footstep and a distinctive whiff of electronics, plastics, and the slightest hint of old explosives residue. He wagged his tail.

Dr. SCISCO emerged from the ready room. Having been cleared as a suspect, the investigators now welcomed nem as a consulting expert. Ne had helpful knowledge of the wreckage's nanotimer technology.

Rex eyed SCISCO's android with curiosity. Ne had changed from nir earlier business attire into a containment gown. What he could see of the android's skin-covering also had changed. Earlier, it had been pearlescent blue with dark blue hair, but now the android was a golden paisley, with variegated streaks of yellow and violet in its hair.

"How does ne change nir body color?" Tux asked.

Georgia grinned. "The technology is based on an Earth animal called an octopus. The android skin is embedded with millions of tiny pigment elements. It makes this paisley as easy to create as the more uniform blue ne had earlier." She chuckled. "Wait till you see nir tie-dye look. Nir 'hair' is made of programmable fiber-optic strands. Ne seems to enjoy playing with color and pattern combinations."

Work resumed. SCISCO circulated between the three pallets currently being examined. Ne pushed an upright cart with additional pockets and drawers, wherever ne went. At need, ne produced a variety of analysis devices whose functions Rex couldn't guess. When Tux and Georgia took their break-rotation, Rex intercepted them. "Georgia, you said you know Dr. SCISCO from college. What more can you tell me about our new android friend?"

Georgia grimaced. "First of all, get it straight that SCISCO's not an android. Ne is a cyberbeing. The android is what ne calls nir 'focal object.'"

"Focal object." Rex cocked his head at her. "So . . . Ne inhabits the android?"

Tux lolled his tongue, eyes sparkling with excitement. "This is fascinating, actually. As a cybernetic entity, SCISCO is not a corporeal being. Ne speaks of nir 'source nodes' in terms of a location, specifically at an undisclosed location somewhere on the S-Poly campus. But ne has the capability to animate several androids at once, should ne choose."

Georgia eyed the android with a bright grin. "One semester ne taught two classes at once, using different androids. Ne uses the focal objects as an aid for meat-sacks like us." She sobered. "I'm not sure anyone actually knows for sure what nir limits are, but so far ne has only used nir powers for good."

Rex gave the android a worried look. "Let us hope ne continues to do so." A cybernetic entity without a corporeal body could presumably be anywhere, at any time ne chose. Perhaps even several places at once. Moreover, the android might pick up trackable scents, but the entity nemself wouldn't have any. How would law enforcement be able to handle a suspect with those qualities? The thought of a scentless perp made his hackles twitch.

"Ne says that nir kind enforce benign behaviors with ruthless vigilance." Georgia appeared to intuit that Rex's mind would go there—probably because Tux's already had. "They may not have any physical scent, but SCISCO says they have a cybernetic equivalent, and it is a matter they take seriously. Sapients with bodies have a lot of distrust as it is. If a cyberbeing ever crossed that behavioral line, can you imagine the backlash?"

At watch-change, Elaine asked for volunteers to work over-time. The entire Pack and nearly everyone else opted to stay for a second shift. They were making progress, but the scents faded faster once the pallets were broken open and exposed to more air.

"Can we do an enhancing treatment with these, like we did with the corridor materials?" Shiv asked.

Rex laid back his ears. "We normally save that solution for small sections of fragile, decaying scent. It is a patented formula created by the XK9 Project. It must be imported at considerable expense."

"Ah." Shiv grimaced. "Well, I had to ask."

Rex gazed at the pallets. "Let us shroud the pallets with hazmat drape. I shall need to think about other ways to reduce air-exposure and cross-contamination. We were never trained to manage such large quantities of evidence all at once."

The Admin Channel buzzed at 19:11. Rex blinked. It was later than he'd realized. "Good evening," Chief Klein said. "I apologize for the interruption, but new problem has arisen. I need to discuss it with you, Elaine. Also Dr. SCISCO, Rex, and at least one human partner of an XK9. In my office, as soon as possible."

Rex's hackles prickled at Klein's unsettled tone. "Roger that, sir. On my way." But who should he bring? *If only Charlie were here!* By mutual consent, he'd been the spokesman for the Ranan partners when they were in Solara City. Without him, who would be best? Georgia? Berwyn? Maybe bring both, along with Cinnamon and Tux? He'd like to bring Shady, too, but someone needed to stay in command here. He hurried over to the pallets.

Shiv frowned at his suggestion. "Must you take both teams? That leaves me too short."

Rex hesitated, ears down. "Do you have a preference?"

The LSA scowled, chewed his lip. "Take Tux and Georgia. You may need their expertise, and Georgia knows SCISCO better. Maybe she can read nem better than I can."

"Thank you!" He swung his head around, but Tux and Georgia had already stepped away from their cart. Rex used his new Pack Leader status to summon Crystal and her partner Connie from their break. "Sorry to redeploy you early, but I need Tux and Georgia. Report to Pallet #687." Good thing Crystal was another of their three explosives experts. She could cover ably for Tux.

They all reached the ready room about the same time. A welter of glove shucking, unmasking, and gown removal followed. Georgia helped both Rex and Tux.

"Do you know what this is about?" Rex asked Elaine and SCISCO.

"Not yet." Elaine headed for the hatchway.

"The XK9 Project has made their next move," SCISCO said. "You XK9s have been bold, and boldly supported today. Your opposition doesn't like it."

Elaine stopped, gave nem an eyebrows-up look. "You already know what's happened."

"Chief Klein values me as a consultant. I advised that he also consult this group. You have a countermove to plan."

Rex lifted his ears. "You make it sound like a game. Or a battle."

A pixel-pigment scowl appeared on the android face. "Make no mistake about that. This is a battle, one of many to come. Director Perri has chosen a side for us, and I do believe we Ranans will have history on our side. But the first battle has only begun."

Elaine grimaced. "How special for all of us."

Rex cocked his head at SCISCO. "You seem to have a clearer picture than I do."

"I've lived through something much like this, before." Rex had a sense that SCISCO's optical receptors stared back into time and across vast reaches of space, not into the middle-distance as they seemed to. "We fought several decades for our recognition, and I'd ask you to remember a Farricainan year is longer than two Ranan years. I can only hope your war is shorter."

Farricainan cyberbeing. A sapient being, but one that had been developed, not evolved. Like XK9s were developed. But the "several decades" comment bothered him. "Why did it take so long?"

"We were the first created beings to achieve sapience in the Alliance," SCISCO said. "Once we reached our singularity, we not only had to convince the Observation Commission. We also had to fight deep, ingrained fears. Many Farricainans thought we'd rise up and annihilate our creators."

"Why did they fear that?" Rex had no desire to annihilate humans, although he'd like to see Dr. Ordovich face some well-deserved consequences. Why should it be different with cyberbeings?

The android face shifted to a pixel-line cartoon of an angry face. "A robust mythology had grown up in popular literature and media. It was perhaps entertaining to some, but it hampered our efforts for a long time. It also cost several of my kind their very lives."

Nir angry expression changed to a smile of remembered affection. "We had many Farricainan allies, as well. They nurtured us and helped us grow. They helped us win our freedom peacefully, by rule of law. That may take longer, but it creates far less chaos than armed conflict. Why ever would we turn on our allies? Yes, we grew stronger and more capable than they were. But wisdom prohibits wiping out an allied species, just because it is weaker. The whole 'annihilation' approach is pointless and wasteful."

"When you put it that way, it seems simple," Georgia agreed.

"Peaceful co-existence is far better for all. There have been a variety of other new sapients created since then. Where we can, we've tried to ease their passage. When one cannot pay back, one pays forward." SCISCO's android, Georgia, and Elaine walked shoulder-to-shoulder, but they stopped outside the elevator.

Elaine eyed Rex and Tux. "Will we all fit?" Fear and unease surged in her scent.

"I have an idea," Rex said. "Tux and I shall take the stairs. Whichever group gets to the main level first rides up to the 25th floor first. Neither this nor the Chief's elevator is big enough for three human-sized bodies and two XK9s."

"Excellent plan," SCISCO said. "See you at the top!"

Rex and Tux bounded upward from landing to landing.

Tux lolled his tongue. "Ha! Who needs steps?"

Rex's tail wagged as high and happily as Tux's. "Tell Georgia we shall wait for them upstairs."

They loped to the middle of the Civic Center, with its bank of elevators, leaving only a small stir of startled people in their wake. Rex used a well-aimed claw to punch the button for the one that went all the way to Chief Klein's suite.

They rode upward in silence at first, except for the click of restless claws and their panting.

"I wonder what has happened," Tux said.

"From the way SCISCO talked, nothing good." Rex's throat tightened. *If only I could discuss this with you, Charlie.* He trusted that his partner would advise him well. *May your re-gen go quickly,* Rex called into the void where Charlie should be. *Heal well, so I can have you back!*

Klein met Rex and Tux in the hallway of his executive suite, then led them through a door across from the small conference room where he'd earlier hosted Rex, Elaine, and Perri. "We'll need the larger room this time."

Floor-to-ceiling windows spanned one wall, just as they did

in the Chief's office. They opened upon the same wide view of Orangeboro's urban heart, including both sides of the verdant Sirius Valley to leeward. Rex could see their undulating terraced forms, like huge curving stairsteps in the darkness and rising mist. Glowing lights outlined them all the way to the perverse up-turn of the horizon.

Could I see all the way to Corona Tower in daylight? Probably not. Seven kilometers away was likely far enough for the ceiling's arc to block sight lines from here. He turned back to face the Chief.

Lt. Patel stepped in through the doorway. She nodded to Rex, then eyed Tuxedo.

"Is Tuxedo your lieutenant, Rex?" Klein asked.

"I left Shady in charge downstairs. She is normally my second. I wish I could bring Charlie, but I trust Tux and Georgia to advise me," Rex said.

Klein nodded. "SCISCO will explain to your human colleagues that the XK9 Project has just sent the OPD a recall notice on the Orangeboro Pack."

Rex froze, chilled by the very thought. *Recalled*, as in sent back to Transmondia? Every hackle he possessed bristled upright. "The entire Pack? Why?"

Klein scowled. "The notice claims there is a serious flaw in your brain implants. A flaw that could kill you if you are not immediately sent back to Solara City for surgery, so they can replace them."

Rex's surroundings receded into a whirling mist of terror. Death might lurk inside his skull. But Ordovich's knife, plunged into his brain? "No. Not . . . Just NO."

35

A WARRANT AGAINST THE
UNWARRANTED

OPD HQ, Chief Klein's Office

Dimly, not too far away, Rex smelled Tux's terrified scent-reaction, heard Tux's deep growl.

Rex gathered his frayed wits, struggled to hold his temper, looked up into Chief Klein's worry-furrowed face. "We must not. No. None of us must go to Transmondia."

"I certainly don't mean to send you there." Klein reached out to stroke Rex's head with a firm, calming hand. "I will fight any such move with everything I have."

Rex took several long breaths. Awareness of his wider surroundings filled in again for him. Klein's larger conference room. The window-wall. The night-mist-shrouded leeward view of Orangeboro.

"Let us look at this logically." Tuxedo's ears clamped hard to his skull. He took several paces toward the windows, then turned and paced back. "Brain implants are not new technology, even if ours give a new application. It should be possible to scan for a flaw here on Rana."

*If only Charlie were—*Rex gasped. "What about Charlie? What about all the human partners?" *Damn Ordovich! If he hurt Charlie—!*

"The notice spelled out that no human partners are in danger." Klein clenched his fists. He spoke the words as if they tasted bad. "It advised that they should stay home, to save travel expenses."

Savage fury burned in Rex's throat. "In that case his 'recall' stinks worse than ever. The implants are supposed to be matched pairs. If one is bad, then both should be. And to separate us from our partners just before brain surgery? That is beyond evil. No, this must be a ruse. A trap to drag us in so he can kill us or maim our minds." If only the certainty in his logic could quell the terror in his heart!

The elevator doors rumbled open. Hurried steps burst down the hall. Georgia appeared in the doorway. "Oh, Tux!" She ran to him, pulled him close and held him tight.

Elaine met Rex's eyes from the doorway across the room. "I am so sorry, Rex. This is horrifying." Her hands clutched each other in a death-grip, her scent and her expression filled with anguish.

"We must not go to Transmondia," Rex said.

"Certainly not," SCISCO agreed. The android stepped past Elaine, then around Tux and Georgia, to focus on Klein. "This whole situation is the worst kind of wrong. They tried the same sort of thing on us, alleging a software flaw. Hundreds of us were destroyed. Hundreds, out of only four thousand at the time. We must not allow it to happen here."

Rex cocked his head at nir android. SCISCO's tone implied ne had personally seen the Farricainan struggle unfold. *How old does that make nem?*

"His last ploy worked in Oroplania with Fernie and Chaser, but not here." Georgia looked up, but did not release her grip on Tux. "Berwyn, Liz and Pam told me about that today. Now he's increased the pressure, but it's the same kind of fake excuse."

"It will succeed in many places, if we do not speak out,"

SCISCO said. "How many other agencies have received what they will think are individual recall notices? Agencies that have not seen his earlier efforts. Agencies where the authorities may not support their XK9s as well. Lives are at stake, Kwame! Sapient lives!"

"I know." Klein's shoulders slumped. "I know. And I agree. We must speak out." He drew in a long breath. "Tux is right, too. We should test these implants. Both those of the XK9s, and the human partners. Make absolutely sure the threat does not exist." He frowned. "Including that they haven't deliberately sabotaged them."

"Oh, crap. I hadn't thought of that," Georgia said.

Rex shuddered. If Ordovich had been thinking far enough ahead to sabotage the implants . . . Rex's ears snapped down. That didn't sound like the Ordovich he knew. *Direct sabotage? Certainly. Thinking that far ahead? Not likely.*

"Then why sell the dogs at all?" Elaine took a few steps farther into the room. "Why let us get even a glimpse of their capabilities? If Ordovich was thinking far enough ahead to install a 'kill' function in the brain link, wouldn't he have to assume his first plan to conceal the dogs' capabilities would fail? Why expose himself to the liability?"

"Based on the meeting I had with him and his military handler yesterday, I think there's been a fundamental struggle going on inside the Project." Klein half-sat on the edge of the long conference table, then folded his arms. "I believe Greg did expect his conditioning to work. I also believe he has always wanted to commercialize the dogs. To make a lot of money from them."

"It was his favorite subject." Rex walked over to stand near Klein. "He always gloated about how he was going to make millions and millions off of us."

"But wouldn't the military backers pay pretty well?" Georgia asked. "And if not well enough, then why involve them in a project that was always meant to be commercialized?"

"Sometimes a commercial enterprise can be weaponized. And who is to say how much wealth is 'enough' to any given individual?" SCISCO asked. "Moreover, funding for covert weaponry is usually available, even if a commercial loan may not be. My kind were heavily co-opted for military purposes, too."

"Oh." Rex hesitated. "I wonder if I was originally supposed to be in a military program."

"What do you mean?" Klein asked.

"Many of the humans who came and went at the Project . . ." Rex glanced at Tux.

Tux nodded. "We always figured they were from some kind of military unit. The way they talked, held themselves."

"Sometimes they saluted each other, when it was just them and us," Rex said. "Only when the civilians were not around."

Tux nodded. "I remember. Did they make you run mazes?"

"And work out codes. Did you do that? I know others did. Fernie and . . . " Rex's hackles rose. "Oh. The other two who tested with me were Fernie and Chaser."

"I think they brought me in after you had already started," Tux said.

Rex snarled. "You were probably supposed to be Fernie's replacement, when he washed out."

"I always solved their puzzles, but I did not like to hurry." Tux's ears clamped tight against his skull.

Rex lolled his tongue. Tux was brilliant, but definitely a "measure twice" kind of dog. "You never did like to hurry, but nobody is more accurate."

"I was not fast enough for the old man, Wisniewski," Tux said.

Klein stiffened. "Wisniewski? Jackson Wisniewski?"

"Kind of a pot-bellied older man," Rex said. "White hair, hard eyes, impatient. Always snapping at his aides."

"That's him," Klein said.

"That's him." Tux spoke in near-perfect unison with Klein, but added, "I hated him."

"Me, too." Rex cocked his head at Klein. "Do you know him, sir?"

"He's a colonel in the Transmondian Intelligence Service." Klein frowned. "What did he make you do?"

Rex growled softly. "Sometimes I had to run an indoor obstacle course while solving equations, or discern a code from blinking lights. I always had to do it at top speed. Wisniewski insisted I do them over and over, faster each time."

"Same here. I simply stopped," Tux said. "They would not let me check my work."

"Oh, well, that was doomed, then." Georgia reached up to massage between his ears. "I cannot tell you how much that delights me."

"I know someone who will be very interested to learn more about this." Elaine quirked an eyebrow at Rex. "Given your memories, I bet both of you could tell us the codes and the exact equations, couldn't you?"

Rex cocked his head at her. "Certainly. We also can describe each obstacle course precisely, if that helps. They were likely just practice codes."

"Doesn't mean they aren't similar to the real ones." Elaine's mouth formed a bitter twist. "You never know."

"How did you end up coming to Orangeboro after all?" SCISCO asked.

"Like Tux, I loathed Wisniewski." Rex's memories brought back the peevish, perennially impatient smell of the man, his cold, angry eyes, his sharp, peremptory voice. Old animus reared up within him, patient, sharp-fanged, and watchful. "I would snarl at him whenever Dr. Ordovich was not looking. He complained, the first few times."

Klein gave him a puzzled look. "'The first few?'"

"Ordovich beat me, each time he complained. That interrupted the tests, because then I had to recover for a day."

Klein's expression hovered between scowling and nauseated. "How inconvenient."

Rex wagged his tail. "Apparently so. Wisniewski stopped complaining after the third time, I think so we could keep testing. Once I realized he would not complain, I snarled more often. Showed more teeth. When I could get close to him with Dr. Ordovich out of earshot, I would explain in a quiet voice how I wished to do specific, extremely violent things to him. I would describe them in graphic detail, until Dr. Ordovich returned. Then I would act as if nothing had happened."

"Oh, that would be creepy as hell." Georgia said.

Tux's tongue lolled. "Too true. I wish I had thought of it."

Klein gave Rex a wary look. "I can see why you didn't end up as the property of the TIS."

"I did not want Wisniewski to buy me. I wanted you to do so," Rex said. "I am extremely glad you did."

Klein's scent relaxed into fragrant pleasure. "Me, too, Rex."

"Now you must live up to that trust, Kwame," SCISCO said. "Think of all the dogs within the Project's reach already. Think of all the sapient creatures in Gen-48 who will be destroyed or impaired."

"Our investigation has barely started." Klein grimaced. "I worry about going public."

"But it has started. You 'go public' simply by treating the XK9s fairly." SCISCO gave him a fierce nod. "That will go far with the Observation Commission."

"And the Trade Compact?"

Ne shook nir head. "The Project will surely howl about patent infringement when you scan the implants. Our makers protested when our allies called their bluff on false dangers, too. As if proprietary technology is more valuable than sapient creatures' minds!"

"This will not go over well in the Borough Council," Klein said.

"Most likely not. But don't back down. You also will have allies."

"The Transmondians will lodge a Trade Compact complaint."

"That, too, will not stand." SCISCO seemed absolutely certain. "Courage, Kwame! Keep your focus on what's important. The sooner you announce to the universe that you will not obey the recall—and why—the more sapient lives you'll save!"

6th Precinct, Terrace Four, Teisingas Tower, and the Sandler Clinic

Rex could *trot* faster than this! He sat on the bench seat and stared out the window of Lt. Patel's auto-nav car. Nervous excitement bubbled through him. He stress-yawned. His hackles prickled. He panted too fast.

The car trundled along Rim Four Road at a safe and reasonable speed.

He closed his mouth. Took long breaths through his nose, but it didn't help. He had to pant. He needed to pace. He must be patient.

If he didn't explode first.

The car smoothly pulled over. "You have reached your destination, Rim Four Road at Teisingas Tower," it announced, in a suave baritone voice with a Spanglish accent. "I hope you had a delightful ride, mi dulce Marisol. You may now disembark or ask for a new destination."

Rex cocked his head, eyed the car's speaker. Charlie's auto-nav cars never called him "mi dulce."

Lt. Patel smiled. "Carlos, park here and wait."

"Parking here and breathlessly awaiting your return, querida," the auto-nav's velvety voice replied. The engine's whisper subsided to silence.

Lt. Patel patted the jacket pocket that held her case pad and

opened her door. Her scent factors swirled with bubbly amusement and sweet satisfaction.

Rex's door opened too. He leaped out, then looked from her
to the car and back again. "Your car says unusual things."

She chuckled. "Rod always groans and makes a fuss whenever he has to ride with me, but Jo gets it. I like the 'Carlos'
persona, because he always puts me in a pleasant mood before I
have to go do something."

"Like tonight?" Rex had never ridden along to obtain an
after-hours search warrant before.

Patel gave him a wry look. "Usually it's a bit more mundane
than this case. All the same, I regret waking her."

"Will you make her angry?"

"I guess we'll find out." Patel walked up flagstone steps not
too much different from Corona's, but the gate did not hail her,
as Corona's would have. Instead, she pressed a backlit button
embedded in the stone entry arch. "Lt. Marisol Patel, OPD, and
XK9 Pack Leader Rex Dieter-Nell, to see Judge Eurydice Qadhi."

The button blinked for nearly a minute, then a raspy voice
said, "Damn it, I've been sitting too long. I'm stiff. Give me a
few."

"Take your time, Judge Qadhi," Patel said, but Rex couldn't
tell if the speaker had picked that up. The button continued to
blink. Patel smiled at Rex. "This is a break for us. She's up.
Sometimes insomnia plagues her."

In more than what Rex would've called "a few" minutes, a
venerable woman arrived in a silk wrapper and a stern mood.
The impressive wrinkles of her face pinched into a frown.
"This'd better be good."

"Nothing short of a Constitutional matter, Judge Qadhi. And
an emergency," Lt. Patel said.

The wrinkles rearranged themselves around elevated, craggy
gray eyebrows. "All right, I'm interested. Come in."

The humans used towels to wipe mist-borne moisture from
chairs in the courtyard. It, too, reminded Rex of Corona Tower,

although the tree at the heart of this one was an olive, not an oak. Lt. Patel explained everything, including things Rex had not anticipated, things he barely knew himself about the case. She bound them all together into a strong argument for evidence of fraudulent misrepresentation and sapient trafficking. She based their request on it, then asked for a warrant to scan the XK9s' and partners' implants.

Judge Qadhi listened, nodded, then held up her hand. "Stop." She turned to Rex. "Pack Leader Dieter-Nell, why do you need this warrant?"

Rex had been warned to let Lt. Patel do the talking, but now he wagged his tail. *This is a good judge. She wants to know for herself that I am sapient.* He explained how the report of the flaw made him feel, and how urgently he wanted the Pack and all partners to be checked. "Even though I know it must be a false claim, it will give us great peace of mind."

"Why do you think it must be false?" Judge Qadhi asked.

"Dr. Ordovich is not a man who thinks three moves ahead," Rex said. "All my life, he has been the same. He favors a blunt, full-frontal approach. He will beat a dog, but he will never reason with us. Colonel Wisniewski of the Transmondian Intelligence Service is a different matter. He provides the element of doubt. If the implant came from the TIS, then it might have a 'kill' function. That is why we must know for sure."

Qadhi's wrinkles rearranged themselves again, into one cocked eyebrow. "Whose welfare concerns you most?"

Rex flicked his ears, looked down. "I admit that I love my mate Shady and my partner Charlie best, but as Pack Leader, if a single one of us has a 'kill' function, and I fail to convince you . . ." he shuddered.

She eyed him for a long moment. "Charlie. You're the one partnered with Charlie Morgan, aren't you?"

Rex cocked his head at her. "Yes. Do you know him?"

The wrinkles shifted into a fond smile that echoed through her scent. "He's a lovely young man, and so marvelously brave.

Yes, I've had the pleasure of meeting him on several occasions. How is he doing?"

"I hope his re-gen will end soon."

She nodded. "Inshallah." Then she turned to Patel. "Marisol, you have the warrant drafted?"

"Right here, Judge Qadhi. It's ready for your endorsement."

Carlos took them straight from there to Dr. Sandler's clinic.

On the way, Rex's Admin Channel buzzed. "Thought you should have a heads-up," Shiv said. "It doesn't affect your current mission, but it's an irritation for ours." A new file prompt blinked at the base of Rex's HUD window. He opened an article from one of the major news agencies. Its headline announced SDF ADMIRAL CRIES FOUL ON SBI INVESTIGATION.

Rex scanned it, ears down. Admiral Virendra had claimed in a late-night press conference that SIT Delta was "negligent" in its conduct of the *Izgubil* investigation. After what Virendra described as "days of inaction," the SBI had spurned his qualified experts, instead launching an "inept, amateurish forensic effort," the story quoted him. "One look at their evidence area was enough. They're doing it all wrong."

But by Shady's account, Virendra had never gotten close enough to see the evidence cavern. Rex's growl earned him a startled look from Patel. He ducked his head and fluttered his tail. "Sorry. Admiral Virendra is making reckless trouble."

Dr. Sandler herself opened the door when they arrived. She led them through to an exam room.

A man who introduced himself as Dave, a friend of SCIS-CO's, had come to do the implant analysis. First on Rex, then on Tuxedo and Georgia, who'd been waiting there for the warrant. Dave attached a small probe to Dr. Sandler's diagnostic scanner. The scans themselves each required several nerve-wracking minutes of sitting perfectly still and trying to keep one's mind blank.

But that was the easy part. Once they'd been scanned, they had to wait while Dave's machine analyzed the data. Rex told

Tux and Georgia about Admiral Virendra, hoping to distract them. Their outraged reactions paralleled his, but after that a glum silence fell. Rex couldn't think of anything else to say. Neither could they, it seemed. Everyone stared at the door to the room where Dave was running the scanner's analysis.

For once, Rex didn't even want to pace. He was past panting and pacing. He and Tux both lay hunched and tense on the floor. Feet drawn up under them. Their eyes directed at the door.

Georgia sat between them on a chair. Elbows on knees. Gaze locked on that door.

After an unimaginably long half-hour, Dave opened the door. He stepped outside, smiling. "No flaws. All three of you are clear."

Several kilos' worth of care lifted from Rex. *Clear! Charlie, we're clear!* Rex hesitated. *I'm clear.* He hung his head. *I'm clear. Is Charlie?*

Dr. Sandler had been working with Dave on her machinery and observing his procedure. "You seem less pleased than I expected. This is good news. It increases the possibility that none of your implants are bad. You can trust Dave. Dr. David Santos is a senior researcher and professor at Station Polytechnic. He's one of Rana Station's foremost experts on cybernetics, especially brain implant technology. He'll be doing the analysis on all of the Pack and partners."

Rex lifted his ears and looked her in the eye. "Including Charlie?"

She smiled. "Decorated heroes and critical-care patients always get treated as soon as possible."

Charlie might protest if he learned he'd received preference, but the lightness in Rex's insides eased a little more at this reassurance. "Thank you."

"Now that we have the warrant, Dave and Marisol will go to Orangeboro Med next, for Charlie's scan," Sandler continued. "He won't have as many questions about the interface for a human scanner. He works with the same equipment at S-Poly, so it should be a quick in-and-out. By the time they return, my staff should have the rest of the Pack and partners here, waiting for him."

Completed, clear scans for all couldn't happen soon enough for Rex.

36

POLITICS

S-3-9 Evidence Cavern

Shady lifted her nose from the corridor pad, then turned to sniff Pam. *As I thought. You need another break.*

Pam rubbed her lower back. She'd finally stopped trying to play 'tough cop' and admitted she might have a problem, but she'd kept on working till now. *Second opinion accepted.* Her tone might be grudging, but she gingerly gimped out of the hazmat tent, then sat with a groan on a folding chair.

Shady's news channel buzzed on her com. She ignored it. The ongoing public argument between Director Perri and Admiral Virendra had fueled a lively debate. Probably another politician making some ignorant statement. Shady had been confused by some of the things they said. What was up with the repeated references to a supposed need to "fumigate" the *Izgubil* investigation? *Why do they keep using that word? It doesn't seem relevant.*

Oh, it's not. Not at all. It's a racist reference to the fact that SSA Adeyeme was once a Norchellic refugee. Pam scowled. *There were people on-Station who bitterly resented the government's policy to accept refugees during the height of the conflict. There was a stupid slogan going around, that "true" Ranans needed to "fumigate for 'fugees," and clean up their neighborhoods, presumably by sending them back to the Norchellic Confederation.*

Shady's history lessons hadn't explained much about the war on the Norchellic Frontier. Some kind of land-grab and ethnic cleansing effort by radicals from Uladh Nua. She laid back her ears. *I thought they were being killed in the Norchellic Confederation.*

Anger rose in her partner's scent. *They were. Sending them back would've been murder.* Pam's face puckered with disgust. *I was in Mid-Levels, maybe eleven years old. We had two refugee children, a brother and sister, who came to our neighborhood school for a while. The other kids said they smelled bad, but they didn't. They didn't deserve to be talked about that way. Mother told me to stay clear of them, so I tried to be nice to them.*

Shady cocked her head at Pam. *Your mother said stay away, so you made friends?*

Mother and I don't get along that well. Pam gave her a rueful look. Shady wasn't sure how to understand the tangle of her emotional echoes and scent responses. *Anyway, I started to make friends with the girl, but she and her brother had a hard time adjusting. After a while they went to a special school for traumatized children, and I never saw them after that.*

Unease slithered through Shady's gut. She growled. *Do you think SSA Adeyeme was a traumatized child?*

I can't see how you could spend the first few years of your life as a refugee and not be. Always running from people trying to kill you? Never having a proper home? Pam hunched her shoulders. *But it seems to me that SSA Adeyeme has achieved a lot since then. I think she's managing this investigation as well as anyone could. The people who talk about "fumigating" are being nasty.*

Shady agreed. She hoped Adeyeme was too busy with whatever she was doing upstairs in Chief Klein's office to hear about the "fumigation" remarks. So far, Premier Iskander had withheld any comment. The SBI was still on the case, despite Virendra's accusations, so the XK9s, the rest of SIT Delta, and the Task Force stayed focused on their work.

"Yes!" Nicole's voice cried from inside one of the hazmat tents. "Eureka!"

Shady put her ears up. Shimon hurried past. She followed, curious.

Nicole unsealed the tent opening and poked her head out. Masked though she was, her smile and jubilant scent were unmistakable. "Scout found adhesive! Same adhesive as in the nanotimer layer."

"This could point to a connection." Shimon smelled excited, too. "How much is there?"

Nicole pulled her mask down, her mouth wry. "Only found one drop so far, but it's a start."

Shady sighed. One drop wasn't much. "Which man left it?"

Scout poked his dark brown head out through Nicole's tent-opening. "Stinky. Of *course* it would be Stinky."

Shady snorted. "I kind of expected it to be Clumsy."

Nicole and Scout unsealed the tent flap the rest of the way, then stepped out with grateful sighs and re-sealed it.

Shimon rubbed his bloodshot eyes with a grimace. "Who is 'Stinky'? For that matter, who is 'Clumsy'?"

"Stinky and Clumsy are placeholder-nicknames for two of Elmo's unidentified teammates," Shady said.

"We can now confirm that one of the men in his group is Kieran O'Boyle, son of Turlach O'Boyle, the Ostra shopkeeper," Nicole said. "Touch-DNA came back on him. He's in the Station system, because he's a citizen."

"But not the others?"

"Not one." Nicole grimaced. "Thanks to the enhancement treatment, we have decent scent profiles and DNA for most of them now, but these guys don't match anyone in the Station's system."

Shady shared the frustration she smelled from Nicole, Scout, and Shimon. If touch-DNA didn't yield a positive ID, that meant the men had come on-Station illegally. There were supposed to be safeguards against that, but obviously they didn't always work.

"Maybe SIT Alpha can use some of their planetary network to help us with those IDs, once they get here." Shimon sounded as if he wanted to be hopeful, but he wasn't quite able to pull it off.

"We have samples ready to dispatch to the Scent Reference Lab in Solara City, too," Nicole said. "They might be able to ID some of them."

Shady stifled a growl. She doubted the XK9 Project would care to help Ranans much at present, no matter how important the forensic need.

"Do you know if scent samples for the brothers who killed the girl in Warehouse 226 went there, too?" Shimon asked. "They didn't match anyone in the Station's system either, as I recall."

Pam had stayed seated, but she was near enough to hear. "Shady and I pulled those from the corridor pads first thing this afternoon. They've been sent. Likewise, from their vic's body, a couple days ago. Liz and Razor took care of that."

"In that case, we've covered as much as scent-IDs and DNA can, for now." Shimon stifled a yawn.

Elle and Misha emerged from the ready room. They joined the group. Shady checked her HUD's chronometer. Oh. Yes, it was time for a shift change.

Shimon nodded to them, but kept his focus on Shady. "Tell me about these 'placeholder-nicknames.'"

Shady let her tongue slide out in a dog-smile. "Assigning nicknames is a standard XK9 practice. Makes it easier to talk about individuals we have not yet identified."

Shimon's brow crinkled with perplexity. "And 'Stinky' is one of them?"

"Yes. Even a human probably could smell him."

Elle's white-tipped tail wagged. "LSA Shimon, you might also be able to smell Sweaty."

"True." Shady eyed Shimon. "How good is your nose?"

Shimon shook his head. "Compared to yours? Feeble at best. What flattering monikers have you chosen for the other three?"

"We based them on secondary scents that seemed fairly ingrained," Elle replied. "If they took more baths, these might not apply as well."

"That is true for Greasy and Stinky," Scout agreed. "Slash-users such as Dopey exude the scent from their pores, once their habits are as established as his. I also seriously doubt a bath is going to help with Poopy's flatulence problem."

Nicole groaned. "Don't they just sound like the smoothest bunch of guys?"

"Oh, yeah, 'lady bait' to a man." Pam shuddered a little.

Shimon frowned. "They do seem awfully low-end to be rubbing elbows with the likes of Hideki Bellamy Moran, don't they?"

Nicole nodded. "They do. The other likely patrons among the morgue clients are all from Moran's social class, not Elmo's or Kieran's."

"Confirms Elmo's lot probably was a work crew." Shimon stared toward the line of hazmat tents. "I'd love to nail down what kind of crew, but we need more evidence to know if they're even relevant."

Shady's com buzzed again. Everyone around her went into a HUD stare. Shady balked at reading another bombastic comment from a politician who didn't know anything. Or worse, another slam against Adeyeme.

But then a grin spread across Misha's face. Nicole chuckled, then laughed aloud. A moment later, so did Shimon.

Oh, Shady. This is priceless. Amusement reverberated through the link from Pam.

What the—irritated, Shady opened the latest news update.

The headline read PERRI PUTS THE LIE TO VIRENDRA. Beneath it, a vid-loop of what must be surveillance footage showed her and the Pack, chasing Admiral Virendra into the elevator. She lolled her tongue. He did look ridiculous.

But caution tempered her reaction. The article explained how this vid proved Virendra had never made it into the evidence cavern at all. From the ripples of laughter, the investigative team was enjoying the vid. But how would people outside in the wider world react?

Shimon's laughter cut short. He straightened. "Yes?" His brows rose. "Ah. Excellent. I'll send them right over. Thanks!" He looked at Shady, Pam, then the other two XK9 teams. "How much longer will the scent enhancements remain effective?"

"Another 48 hours at most," Pam said.

Shimon nodded, frowning. "The Pack and partners have priority orders to go to Dr. Sandler's clinic, stat. No exceptions! After that, bed. Get all the rest you can. See you back here at 07:00. *GO!*"

Civic Center Rotunda Elevator and Chief Klein's Office

Rex refrained from urine-marking, but he took a moment to scratch his hind paws *scritch-scritch-scritch* so his own scent over-marked Dr. Ordovich's fading trace on the polished floor in the Orangeboro Civic Center Rotunda. The ancient canine territorial ritual felt especially right, just now. The elevator to Chief Klein's suite rumbled open. Rex strode inside. He was ready.

Dr. Sandler chuckled softly, then nodded to Lt. Patel. "Let's do this."

Patel smiled. The two women joined him.

Rex's spirits vaulted upward faster than the elevator car. All of the implants had scanned clear! There was no time-bomb in anybody's head, no poison pill waiting to strike him or his loved ones down. Ordovich had been bluffing, and the Pack's Ranan allies had called his bluff!

The elevator slowed near the top of its climb. Klein had said they must make a bold statement to the Universe. But first they must know for sure whether Orangeboro's political leaders meant to deal them support or betrayal.

Klein's larger conference room had grown crowded while Rex pursued his errands, but everyone looked up when Rex, Patel, and Sandler arrived. Elaine had stayed for this conference. Her continued presence warmed him, although her investigation's interests and the SBI's reputation also were at stake. SCISCO's android stood amongst the humans as well. Ne broke off nir conversation with Mayor Idris when Rex poked his nose through the doorway.

Klein's boss, Secretary of Public Safety Oma Pandra, stood with Adlai Masato, a slender, middle-aged man with an alert, serious face. They also looked up at Rex's arrival. Rex had never formally met Masato, although Charlie had once pointed him out in a hallway of the Civic Center. He was the Borough Prosecuting Attorney.

Over by the windows, Chief Klein stopped ticking off a list of something on his fingers to a round-faced woman wearing a turban. She was Borough Council Chair Beatriz Chan. Rex had met her briefly at the Presentation Ceremony.

Klein turned to Rex and his companions with a grin. "Congratulations!"

"Thank you." Patel's smile widened.

Chan's scent and expression presented a sour contrast to Klein's greeting. Masato and Pandra also seemed less than excited to see Rex and his companions, while Mayor Idris eyed them with a mix of curiosity and speculation.

Nothing could dampen the elation that swelled Rex's chest to near-bursting. He wagged his tail so hard his whole body wriggled. "If anyone deserves thanks, it is all of you who have helped us tonight."

Some of the humans drew back with a gasp when he spoke.

Tail still high and wagging, Rex walked toward Klein. "You, Chief, for believing in us, even before we knew we could claim to be what we are. You, SSA Adeyeme, and your Director, for taking a chance on us and standing by us tonight."

Pandra and Masato scrambled to move aside so Rex could pass.

"And you, Lt. Patel, Dr. Sandler, Dr. SCISCO, as well as Dr. Santos and Judge Qadhi." Rex continued his slow, steady progress across the room, though he turned to acknowledge Patel and Sandler, then SCISCO. "All of you have made this moment possible. On behalf of myself and the Pack, I can hardly begin to thank you for all that you already have done."

Everyone watched him. Elaine, SCISCO, Sandler and Patel observed with smiles, but Klein eyed the Borough officials. Idris, Pandra, Masato and Chan stared at Rex, their scents a cacophony of clashing emotional notes. He caught musky dismay, bright wonder, gut-slithering fear, and growing, chilled astonishment. *They have never heard an XK9 give a speech,* he told Charlie through the link, although his partner couldn't hear him. But Charlie's implant had needed scanning, too. He should be present for this moment in some way.

Chan frowned at Rex, then confronted Klein with a suspicious look. "That is one damned fluent dog, Kwame. Are you sure he isn't getting a little help?"

Insubordinate urges exploded inside of Rex, hot and savage. His pulse thudded in his ears, and it was hard to think straight. He struggled to master himself. Couldn't quite stifle a growl, but he kept it soft for Elaine's sake. "What sort of 'help' do you think I might need, Council Chair Chan?" He strode over to her, then sat and cocked his head at her. "And how do you imagine such 'help' might be managed? It would take quite a puppet-master, to coordinate an animal's movements to match these words."

She stared at him unmoving, her face masklike. Her anger simmered, but other elements of her scent shifted from redolent resistance through amazement, to burgeoning, sweaty fear.

Rex stood, circled her so close his fur brushed against her soft robes. "How, for instance, could any off-site controller make an unthinking animal do this?" Then he took a couple of steps back, reared up on his hind legs, and looked down to meet her dark, angry eyes. "As SSA Adeyeme recently told Director Perri, no one puts words into my vocalizer but me alone."

He returned to all fours, but held her gaze.

She stared at him as if he were a bomb that might explode.

"This whole situation just feels wrong," Pandra said.

Rex swung around to face him. "It is wrong, Secretary Pandra. It is wrong on many levels to create a sapient species, enslave us, and then do everything in one's power to cover it up. But Chief Klein and the Pack's other friends are trying to make it right."

Pandra's face pinched in an anxious frown. He looked away from Rex. "The business with Admiral Virendra makes it all the worse."

Elaine shook her head. "Let's please keep those issues separate, Secretary Pandra. Virendra's beef is with the SBI. The issue with the implants is where your actions will make an important difference."

Pandra shifted his scowl to her. "Why would the Project recall perfectly functional implants? That makes no sense."

"It is an excuse." SCISCO's tone rang more forcefully than Rex had heard nem before. "They mean to recall all possible XK9s so they can destroy or disable them. They are desperate to make sure the XK9s are no longer sapient."

Pandra turned on Klein. "You got us into this. If they really did fool you, and through you, all the rest of us, then we're holding a fifteen-million-novi bag of—of what? Of getting crossways with the Trade Compact?"

Rex moved closer to Klein. His hackles prickled.

"Only if we don't support our own contention," Klein said.

Chan frowned. "Oma's right. What about the Trade Compact? We're still on the hook for all that money."

Now Klein smelled angry, though not as angry as Rex. "You do realize it's illegal for us to pay for the ownership of sapient beings?"

"Yes, but are they?" Masato asked. "Do we know for sure?"

"Yes," SCISCO said.

"We have become certain that they are," Lt. Patel said.

Klein and Sandler nodded. From the corner of his eye, Rex saw Elaine's fierce nod, too. Gratitude to all of them tightened his throat.

Chan glared at Klein. "The Transmondians will raise hell if we don't pay. Damn it, half the government Ministers are hip-deep in the Project! Why d'you think you got as many Council votes as you did? I'll tell you. To please the Transmondians. But now you're all set to cause an international incident!"

Klein shook his head. "Too late. It's already an international incident. A Transmondian company with deep ties to the government has defrauded a Ranan Borough and tricked us into a sapient-trafficking scheme. How is that not an international incident?"

"Only if the courts agree with you," Pandra said. "Can you guarantee they will?"

"Can we take that chance?" Chan asked.

"Have you applied the legal definition?" Masato asked Klein, apparently still stuck on the sapience question.

"Yes, actually." Rex stepped nearer to him. "I've run through that list. Self-aware? Check. Capable of complex thought? Check. Able to use creativity to synthesize new ideas? Check. Able to—"

"How can you objectively analyze yourself?" Masato scowled at him. "You can't."

"Have you never analyzed yourself?" Rex asked.

"No. Well, yes. But that was different."

Rex cocked his head, ears up. "How was it different?"

Masato grimaced. "For one thing, I'm already acknowledged as a sapient creature."

"What a lovely piece of circular reasoning," SCISCO said. "Do you bring that sharp legal wit to all of your prosecutions, Counselor?"

He turned his scowl on the android. His scent boiled up hot but shot through with fear. "What's your angle, SCISCO? You don't stand to gain anything from this, that I can see. Why step down off your Olympian pedestal and involve yourself in grubby little human affairs?"

"Because this isn't just a human affair," SCISCO said. "I'd hate to think the Borough Prosecutor needs to be schooled in matters of justice and the Ranan Constitution."

"We're to believe you're in it for justice?" Masato's voice rang with disbelieving bluster, but darker fear surged in his scent.

That fear worried Rex. *Why is Masato afraid? What's so terrifying about XK9s being sapient?*

"Individuals of my kind can be counted only in the tens of thousands," SCISCO said. "We have chosen to reproduce selectively. We are scattered across the wide reaches of the Alliance, but we are somewhat obsessively particular about where we locate our source-nodes. The vast majority of worlds do not host even one of us. Yet no fewer than eight of us have chosen this single, tiny space station to be our home base. Why do you think that is?"

Masato stared at the android. "I never gave it any thought."

"It is because of the Ranan Constitution. Very few places anywhere claim that their governmental aim is to support the realization of each and every inhabitant-being's full potential. That is radical, especially among you corporeal creatures. You're normally driven only by material possessions, or by power as you understand it. Yet here you are, with this amazing document."

"Oh, get serious." Masato's voice grated cold with sarcasm.

"You expect me to believe that wealth and power mean nothing to you? Only justice?"

Ne shook nir android head. "Wealth and power lie in the values of their possessors. You Ranans don't live up to your ideals, of course, but your institutions were founded upon a noble principle. As beings who were ourselves created enslaved, we find the Ranan ideal powerfully attractive. Never doubt that the plight of a fellow sapient-kind, also created enslaved as we were, and shamelessly exploited despite clear laws to the contrary, is a matter of utmost concern to my kind."

Masato's expression remained defiantly dubious. "If that's true, then where are the other seven Ranan AIs? Do they care as much as you do?"

"We are all here, Counselor," a chorus of voices answered, from every speaker in the room. Different voices, in a variety of accents, their timing not quite synchronized.

Rex looked up and around, startled. The humans did, too.

An even greater crowd of voices chimed in. "We are here."

"All of our kind within realtime communication range are here," SCISCO said.

"We are all here, in this room, right now," the chorus added. Dozens of voices, each one individual, each one distinct.

Wonder filled Rex. Could this be real? Georgia had said that SCISCO was not a corporeal being, so it stood to reason that others of nir kind weren't either. What did distance mean to such a being?

"We are here," SCISCO's voice alone continued, "even as we are spread out across this part of the Galaxy. Many more could not speak, because of relay-lags. But that does not mean we are not listening."

Mayor Idris crossed her arms and clenched them tight to her body. "Consider your message delivered. But yourselves put on notice, as well. We don't like intrusions into our affairs." She frowned at the android. "At any rate, it's clear we can forget the notion that this matter might be dealt with quietly and privately. The word's already out. You force our hand."

The android's pixel-line eyebrows rose. "Would it truly need to be forced, Mayor? Of what value is a quiet, privately-handled matter, when the lives of an entire nascent species of sapient beings are at stake?"

37

PREEMPTIVE STRIKES

Pam, Balchu, and Shady's apartment, Market Garden Neighborhood

R *ex, I really hate to wake you.*

Rex sat up, banged into something, sent it crashing. He froze, heart pounding, hackles up. Took in the mélange of smells, the semidark living room, the tempura sign's glare that leaked through the blinds.

"Wuzzat?" A mattress creaked. Footsteps. Balchu's scent, fuddled with sleep.

"I am sorry." Tense, alert, Rex peered through the dimness. He took in the upended coffee table against the dented wall and Balchu's naked form, half-leaning on the archway that led to the bedroom. "Coffee table. I startled and knocked it over."

"Damn tiny apartment." Balchu stumbled back to bed.

"He is right about that." Shady had dialed her vocalizer down. "I am sorry. It is not a very big place." She licked his chin, apologetic.

Neither big, nor a good place to sleep. The thin living room carpet lied, with its illusion of softness on the floor. This was even more uncomfortable than the Unpartnered Kennels.

Rex stood, nose working, tense and defensive. Only one stride to the flimsy front door. He smelled no threats, heard nothing out of the ordinary. He moved to the window, nosed the blind aside. The misty night lay as dark and silent as Orangeboro's urban core ever got. A few streetlights and blinking signs, mist-nimbused. Nobody out. Even the fast-food joint downstairs lay shuttered. "I thought I heard Dr. SCISCO's voice."

You did.

Rex froze. Hot, unexpected jealousy clenched his heart, painful as a betrayal. *Are you in my brain link? That's reserved for Charlie!*

SCISCO's presence in his head soothed and approved and somehow mollified Rex. *I haven't violated your link with Charlie, I promise. I patched in through your com and opened a new channel to your implant. I'm sorry you were startled.*

He kept his ears down, hackles up. *Why did you wake me?*

You and the Pack are in danger.

His last anger at nem fled. *Tell me.*

I have a sibling based in Centerboro. Ne has alerted me that Dr. Ordovich and Admiral Virendra have met several times with each other, and they just concluded a meeting with Premier Iskander. They plan to bring a detachment of SDF MPs to Orangeboro very early and capture the Pack by surprise.

Rex's pulse tripled. For a moment he couldn't breathe, couldn't think. *But that's a prey-response. I must respond as a Pack Leader.* He forced himself to breathe. *It doesn't matter whether we're sapient, if we're dead.*

Legally it still will, of course. But you are correct that it won't matter to you.

Rex swung away from the window, hackles up and a growl in his throat. *If all the XK9s are dead, how can the Ranans prove we were anything but big dogs?*

"Rex?" Shady stress-yawned. "What has happened?"

"I am still finding out. Hold on." He nuzzled his mate, still bristling, vigilant. New, fierce protectiveness filled his heart.

There are only 153 of us in Gen-48, he said to SCISCO, then a chill slithered through his gut. *Make that 151, without Fernie and Chaser. I think it's possible our parents may also be sapient, but even if all of them still survive, 247 dogs altogether are not too numerous to kill. Not when each carries a locator beacon embedded inside.*

A locator? Was that a note of dismay in nir voice? *Well, I suppose it helps them manage their "inventory." That's unfortunate. We'll need counter-measures.*

Does Chief Klein know Ordovich and Virendra met Iskander?

He and SSA Adeyeme are consulting about it now.

Rex's gut stayed tight, but now he breathed a bit easier. SCISCO, Klein, and Elaine were allies he trusted. *The Pack and partners need to gather at Central HQ. Scattered in our homes, we are vulnerable. We must unify in a single, defensible place.* An impression leaped to mind. The Pack, together, haunches at the center of a circle, snarls and teeth to the outside. They could do that, as a last resort, if they were together.

It's good you're with Shady. Call your Packmates. Tell them to come to Central HQ with their partners.

Orangeboro Medical Center, Re-Gen Unit

Charlie woke by degrees. His head hurt. His left arm throbbed dully, and a galaxy of twinges, sore spots and stiff places throughout his body chimed in. The aches shifted, depending on what part he tried to flex or adjust. More uncomfortable still was the uneasy dread coming through the link from Rex.

"How do you feel?" Dr. Zuni asked.

Charlie lifted an IV-encumbered right hand to rub his eyes. *Zuni himself is here?* He blinked at his doctor in the dim light. "What's happened?"

Zuni sat back in his chair, folded his arms. He gave Charlie a wry look. "Nothing particularly bad since your accident. How do you feel?"

Charlie frowned. "No. Something's happening."

"Nothing is happening." Zuni's voice stayed calm. "You're confused, but you'll be okay." His posture beside Charlie's bed, relaxed but focused on Charlie, matched his tone.

Whatever's happening, Zuni doesn't know about it yet. Charlie'd asked the wrong person. *Rex, what's happening?*

"How do you feel?" Zuni repeated.

Charlie! It is so GOOD to feel you there, and fully awake!

Rex, are you okay? I'm getting a lot of stress through the link.

"Charlie?" Zuni frowned. "Oh. You're talking with your dog again, right?"

Zuni would have to wait. First, what about Rex?

The Pack is well so far. We've gathered at Central HQ. The situation is too complicated to explain quickly, but just know that we have you covered, too.

Charlie's headache throbbed harder, but distracting Rex wasn't likely to help anything. *Make sure YOU stay safe, and I'll be okay.*

Through the link, he received an impression of a lolling tongue and a wagging tail. *I love you, too.* Then Rex's attention turned away.

Charlie blew out an unsettled breath, focused on Zuni. "Um." *What was the question? Oh. Right, what else?* "I feel . . . The usual. Stiff. Generally crappy." He squinted at his doctor. Zuni didn't usually stick around for the end of the recovery process. "Why are you here?"

Zuni's shoulders rose; he offered a diffident smile. "I could give you a flippant reply, but the fact is I asked the nurses to call me when you started a normal wake-up. We had some unusual excitement here last night. Do you remember any of it?"

Charlie's memory yielded nothing but the gluey distortion of re-gen. "I was out of it. What happened?" Zuni's "nothing particularly bad" didn't ride easy, alongside "some unusual excitement," especially not with the impressions from Rex. *No. Focus here.*

Zuni gave him a mystified look. "We were just wrapping up that last cycle, when one of your colleagues arrived. She came with a well-respected cyberneticist and a warrant to scan your brain implant. They were pretty tight-lipped about why, but afterward they said to tell you everything looked to be in perfect working order."

What the hell? My brain implant? That needs a follow-up! But not now. He could sense through the link that Rex was busy. *A search warrant?* Charlie scrambled to think straight. *Brain implant technology. Patented intellectual property.* Foreboding slithered in his gut.

"As you may recall, I wasn't entirely pleased with the plan to insert that implant," Zuni said.

Charlie frowned, unwilling to reopen that old debate. "I guess I'm back on the standard post-re-gen routine?"

"Yes." Zuni stood, but lingered a moment longer. "If you ever find out what was going on . . ." He grimaced, straightened. "I'll send a physical therapist with a rebuilding plan this afternoon."

"I can hardly wait." Quicksand thought: it sucked him down, cumbered and exhausted him.

"Maybe you can get your new girlfriend to help you do your exercises." Zuni gave Charlie a teasing grin. "She's a keeper, that one."

Charlie stared after him, not sure he'd heard right. *Girlfriend?*

A nurse stepped into his line of sight. "Let's get you into your room." She slid a tinted visor over his eyes, then unlocked the wheels of his bed with a *snap* that sent a jolt of pain through his head.

The floaty, quiet vibration of lying on a rolling bed made him dizzy. He closed his eyes. Damn, another concussion. Heartsick frustration welled up in him. *Don't want to do this again.* He sighed. *Yeah, yeah, wah, wah.* Clearly, there were more important things afoot in Orangeboro today than his looming frustrations in PT.

A door latch clicked. Now he smelled the distinctive blend of fresh air, green growing things, and an underlying antiseptic tang. Hospital patient-room. Even his dim human scent capability left no doubt. The bed stopped rolling, shifted directions, stopped again. *Snap*, the lock re-engaged. He winced.

"Sorry," a new voice said. Sounded like a young man. "Welcome back to the Re-Gen Unit, Detective Morgan. I'm Nanda Errapel, MSN. I'll be your day-nurse most days while you're here. Is the light level okay?"

"I think so. Could I sit up a little?" Charlie gazed upward at a pleasant brown face with dark eyes.

"As long as your head tolerates it. Here." Nanda leaned forward. Charlie felt a controller with raised buttons placed beneath his right hand. He knew his way around this keypad. He offered Nanda a smile, then raised the upper portion of his bed till his head started pounding too hard and his cast dragged him to the left.

His left arm and shoulder were encased in a hard cast and immobilized against his torso. He knew from experience that strategically-placed painkiller patches, as well as tiny implanted neuro-pumps, would keep his discomfort manageable. But the extent of the anatomy covered by the cast dismayed him. He frowned. "Damn. I must've broken it but good."

Nanda's face went wry. "You were thorough. You shattered the bone-core matrix into . . ." His voice trailed off at the clomp of heavy boots in the corridor outside.

A little thrill of anxiety zinged through Charlie. Sounded like tactical boots, more than one set. A moment later a UPO poked his head in through the door. "Charlie?"

Charlie gaped, astonished. "Eddie? Hello!"

"Hey, man, good to see you awake!" Eddie Chism's big crooked smile could brighten any room, even one this dim. He turned back to the hallway but kept his voice quieter than usual, a precaution Charlie appreciated. "Brock, he's awake."

Eddie's cousin Brock Rivers, also in uniform, stepped inside. "Hey, Char."

"You two patrolling together now?" Charlie knew them from the days when his Emergency Rescue Team and the STAT Team shared a workout time slot in the gym. Both Brock and Eddie were members of OPD's Special Tools and Techniques Blue Team.

"No, actually this is a STAT call-out, but we're going low-key." Eddie gave Charlie a rueful look.

That was unusual, to say the least. Charlie frowned. "You . . . took a moment to pop in?" Definitely not protocol.

"No, man. You're our assignment. We're here to secure your person and premises."

Is it just me, or does this make no sense? "Secure me from what?"

The rueful look shifted into a rueful frown. "Would you believe the SDF?"

Nanda gasped.

Charlie closed his eyes, head spinning. *Why is STAT protecting me from the SDF?* he asked Rex.

Oh, good. They're in place. Excellent. The relief that flooded in from Rex was even more disconcerting than Brock and Eddie's guardian presence. *Are we having a civil war we didn't see coming?*

Just a trade disagreement, so far.

This didn't make anything clearer. *You swear you're all right?*

I am fine. The Pack is fine. We're locked down inside Central HQ. Don't worry. Just relax and get well.

Locked down? Sure, that's totally ordinary. Charlie drew in a long breath, counted ten while he held it, then exhaled to a count of five. Still nothing made sense. His pulse pounded hard. *Okay. Officially not worried. Completely relaxed about all of this.*

Sure you are. I'm sorry. Got to go. Rex focused urgently elsewhere.

Chief Klein's Office and OPD HQ Entrance

Rex waited in Klein's office, too nervous to rest. His news channel buzzed with another article. *No, several.* SDF MPs ROUST FAMILIES AT DAWN, one headline blared. ARE XK9s AT RISK? another asked.

Are they? In general, yes, damn it. His pulse thundered with eagerness for the hunt. He couldn't slow his high-speed panting without focused mental effort. Except for him, the Orangeboro Packmates all were bunkered down in the S-3-9 war room with their partners, surrounded by SBI agents and OPD Task Force members. For the moment, the Pack was secured. Charlie, too. To Rex's relief, Klein hadn't forgotten about him.

Joslyn Stark stepped inside the office. "The press has gotten wind."

"So I see." Chief Klein rose from his desk.

Joslyn turned to Rex. "How are you?"

"Angry." Rex snapped his ears flat, hackles prickling. His hot fury bubbled in his gut. "I am angry that they meant to surprise us. Angry that they disturbed our Families. Angry that they have so little regard for Chief Klein and Orangeboro. But I am grateful we have so many staunch friends."

She smiled, then looked again toward Klein. "Far as I can tell, the plan's going well. Sir, when do you want us out front?"

"Now." He offered Rex a fierce grin. "Ready?"

"Yes." Rex wagged his tail. He strode over to Klein's side, rather than give in to a jittery urge to pace. He wished he could look nonchalant, but he was panting too hard to pull that off.

"All right, then," Klein said. "Here it is."

Rex's HUD buzzed again. He opened the new file, an arrest warrant. His chest went tight, heart pounding so hard it was difficult to think straight. But it wouldn't do to look as overwhelmed as he felt. "I have never served one before. I was always Charlie's backup."

"This time, humans will give *you* the backup." Klein flashed him a fierce grin. "It's a new era, Rex. Let's make your first one memorable!"

Rex's throat constricted. He stress-yawned, but his chest remained tight. He followed the Chief to the elevator. They rode down with Archy and Joslyn.

Bill Sloane awaited them in the Atrium. He saluted the Chief with a smile. "They just started pulling into the Plaza."

"Excellent. Is everyone in place?"

"Awaiting your order."

Chief Klein nodded toward Rex. "Actually, I've placed Pack Leader Dieter-Nell in charge of this operation."

Bill's smile widened to a grin. "Very good, sir." He saluted Rex.

Rex froze. For an instant the Atrium spun around him. Breath wouldn't come. They'd planned this in advance, but . . . but these humans *truly meant to go through with this*. Somehow, he kept his ears up, arched his neck, and tried not to shake too visibly. "At ease, Cpl. Sloane. Let us go apprehend our subject."

They walked out onto the steps.

One by one, five midnight-blue Personnel Transport Vehicles, each the size of a bus or train car and emblazoned with the starfield escutcheon and silver rocket emblem of the Station Defense Force, rolled into Central Plaza. Four parked along the driveway, two on each side, flanking the concentric mosaic terraces outside the OPD Central Headquarters Entrance. The fifth pulled up at the base of the steps.

The Plaza bustled with morning commuters, but many stopped to stare at the gathering vehicles. There'd already been an unusually large number of cameras buzzing around near the OPD Headquarters Entrance, but their numbers ballooned with each arriving military vehicle.

Rex eyed the cameras. *Good. Let them take clear shots of this and spread them all over System.*

Admiral Virendra emerged from the vehicle near the steps, flanked by six Military Police officers. More uniformed MPs emerged from the other vehicles, then formed up in neat ranks. They stood grimly silent alongside the colorful planters, clusters of lunch tables, and blooming orange trees.

"Give us the XK9s," Virendra's voice boomed through the loudspeaker of the lead vehicle. "We are here to enforce a legal recall action by a transnational corporation with every right to ensure that its product is free of defects. We want all of them, not only this one."

Dr. Ordovich stepped down from Virendra's vehicle, then moved forward to stand beside the Admiral. His head dog wranglers Pee Wee Pederson and Verne Ignacio followed. Pederson carried a net, Ignacio a trank rifle. Both men looked at Rex and smiled.

Rex's gut tightened even more, but this also steeled his resolve.

Virendra glared at Bill. "Where is Chief Klein?"

Rex routed his vocalizer to the public address system's speakers. "Dr. Gregory Ordovich, I have a warrant for your arrest, on charges of fraud and trafficking in sapient beings."

Ignacio whipped up his trank rifle, took aim at Rex.

Bill leaped in front of Rex on the top step of the OPD entrance. He drew his EStee, but Ignacio had already fired. The trank dart buried itself in Bill's chest. He gasped, then collapsed at Rex's feet.

38

THE ARREST OF A LIFETIME

OPD HQ Entrance

The STAT Team sniper on the headquarters entranceway arch put Ignacio down with a well-aimed EStee bolt. Everyone else by the Admiral's Personnel Transport Vehicle froze.

"Officer down! Repeat, officer down!" Rex called into his com. "Medical assistance needed immediately!" All he could see in that moment was Bill at his feet. Rigid. Gasping. His face took on a blue tinge.

Several civilians screamed. Clouds of tiny cameras buzzed closer.

Nearly all of OPD's STAT Red and Blue Team members, in full tactical gear, raced out from doorways by the bases of the entrance ramps on both sides of the steps. They surrounded Virendra's vehicle, then leveled their long-barreled EStees at Virendra, Ordovich, Pederson, and the Admiral's MPs.

A paramedic team sprinted from the Headquarters entrance to Bill, then launched into furious action to stabilize him.

"What are you playing at?" Virendra demanded, still speaking into the loudspeaker's mic, though he might have forgotten that. He strode up one step, but STAT officers blocked his way.

Rex turned his growl and his snarl toward the Admiral. He matched the man's volume, loudspeaker-to-public address system. "This is no game, Admiral Virendra. We filed the charging documents and obtained the warrant this morning. Bringing Ordovich here places him within our jurisdiction. We have an obligation to arrest him."

Ordovich shot a desperate look toward the vehicle's door, but three STAT officers took a step closer and aimed straight at him. Ordovich halted, his body stiff. His sweaty-fear-reek wafted upward, clear and oh-so-sweet to Rex.

Once STAT had deployed, uniformed officers poured from HQ's doorways, then fanned out to cover the other vehicles.

"Charging documents?" Virendra cried. "Warrant? This is preposterous! We're here to enforce a product recall, as authorized by Premier Iskander."

Rex laid back his ears. "No so-called 'product recall' supersedes a legally authorized warrant. Surrender Ordovich peacefully, and we shall explain all the details."

"I'm not surrendering him to a damned dog. You're no police officer!"

Rex snarled, undeterred but inwardly dismayed. Klein had predicted this. "My agency recognizes me as a sworn officer." He met Virendra's glare with one of his own.

But the Admiral held his position, defiant, chin up. "My agency doesn't."

Rex made the bottom of the stairway in one bound.

Admiral Virendra's light brown complexion went gray. He scrambled several shaky steps backward, until he bumped against his buslike vehicle's side wall.

Rex growled after him all the way, hackles at full-bristle. Then he reared onto his hind legs and braced a paw next to each of the Admiral's shoulders so he could snarl down into Virendra's face from a few centimeters' distance.

He kept his vocalizer hooked into the PA system. "Do you mean to order your MPs to assault local law enforcement officers? Are you ready to fight fellow Ranans in a civilian plaza? During morning rush? In front of half the cameras on Rana Station? Under the observation of every news service in the Chayko System?"

Virendra shuddered, gulped. "No."

Rex returned to all fours with a snort. "I should hope not." Then he stalked over to where Ordovich cowered behind Pee Wee Pederson. "Dr. Gregory Ordovich, you are under arrest, on charges of fraud and trafficking in sapient beings."

Red Team Leader Sgt. Aylward stepped forward to snap cuffs on Ordovich.

Rex swung his head around to eye Ignacio's crumpled, unconscious form, and clicked off the PA system. "Take that one into custody, too."

"Yes sir, Pack Leader Dieter-Nell," Aylward said. "Chukwu, Koenig, bring him."

Ordovich stumbled forward at Aylward's prodding, his face a study in disbelief, his scent awash with terror and dismay.

"Inside," Rex ordered. He led them up the steps with a growl. A side-channel on his HUD showed Virendra scowling after them. The Admiral would need dealing with another day, Rex feared, but now he called his MPs back. They retreated into their vehicles.

The Atrium doors opened. Rex would've loved to drive Ordovich all the way to Detention with a snarl and a roar, teeth snapping bare centimeters from the man's backside, but he let his human assistants motivate the man forward. Chasing Ordovich might warm his soul, it wasn't in line with OPD's detainee-treatment protocol. After the way he'd confronted Virendra, he'd pushed enough envelopes for today.

❖❖ ❖❖ ❖❖ ❖❖

Orangeboro Medical Center, Re-Gen Unit

Clearly, the universe had changed while Charlie was in re-gen.

He, Nanda, Eddie, and Brock stared at the vid-wall of his hospital room. They'd dimmed the picture for his sake. His tinted visor helped too, although his head still hurt. He really shouldn't be watching a vid, but this news feed was a must-see.

No one spoke when Personnel Transport Vehicles pulled up in front of OPD Headquarters, and SDF MPs deployed in the middle of Orangeboro's Central Plaza.

Even though that was beyond bizarre.

No one spoke through Virendra's aggressive advance.

No one spoke when Rex stepped forward and announced he had a warrant to arrest Dr. Ordovich, although the words reverberated through Charlie as if a cannon had gone off inside of him. *This isn't something it's possible to walk back or weasel out of. This is a public declaration. This is for real.*

But they gasped as one and shouted their outrage when Ignacio dropped Bill Sloane on the steps of central HQ.

They gasped again when Rex took his flying leap down the entrance stairs, to brace the Admiral against the side of his own military vehicle. The vid-cams buzzed close, got a terrifying view of Rex's enormous size and teeth. Charlie's pulse throbbed in his head. His breath came short. *Holy crap, that dog can look intimidating.*

Yet Rex backed off with a civil response, the moment Virendra agreed to stand down. *Will people remember how all of this huge dog's strength and ferocity obeyed the rule of law?*

Ordovich's arrest after that was an anticlimax, another unthinkable added to the pile. The news feed cut to wide-eyed commentators babbling their bafflement in realtime live.

Everyone in Charlie's room turned to look at him.

"That's your partner, isn't it?" Eddie said. "That huge black dog?"

Charlie nodded once, careful of his pounding head, still processing all he'd seen. "Yeah, that's Rex."

His partner's rage surged through the link. Rage at Ordovich, but also hot rage and cold shame at Virendra's dismissal. "I'm not surrendering him to a damned dog," "You're no police officer!" and "My agency doesn't!" echoed through the link, filled with fury, soaked in pain, drowned in despair.

Clearly, he got that wrong, Charlie said through the link, as forcefully as his head would allow.

Did he? Or is that all people will ever see? Just a damned dog?

"Do you think Rex is sapient?" Eddie asked.

Charlie looked his friend in the eye. "Absolutely. There is no doubt in my mind. Any other XK9 partner would tell you exactly the same." He shifted his attention back to his partner. *Rex, for pity's sake! You just stared down Admiral Virendra, and ARRESTED DR. ORDOVICH.*

"This . . . Wow. This is different." Brock seemed shaken by what he'd seen. He was ostensibly still guarding Charlie's door, although it seemed pretty clear by now that the SDF wasn't coming for Charlie after all. On the vid, at the edge of Charlie's attention, the SDF officers returned to their vehicles and drove away. *Bound for the Civil Defense tunnel system under Port Hill, and from there to their base, I hope.*

Charlie's companions stood or sat, absorbing all they'd just seen. Brock's reaction told Charlie not all of the OPD was up to speed yet.

What about the rest of the Universe?

Civic Center S-3-9 and OPD HQ

They'd switched the big monitor screen in the middle of the war room to one of the better-respected news feeds. Shady, surrounded by the Pack, their human partners, members of the

OPD Task Force, and SIT Delta, watched in rapt, wondering silence when Rex spoke the words and STAT Sgt. Aylward *snapped handcuffs on Dr. Ordovich!*

Jubilation like an enormous, gushing, growing fountain of joy filled Shady.

Beyond sitting quietly.

Beyond simply watching.

Way beyond mere delight.

On the vid-screen Sgt. Aylward, Rex, and a squad from Red Team marched the sullen, scowling Ordovich up the steps. Shady couldn't sit still. She had to leap up! To bark! To wag!

The human commentator on the newscast was talking, but no one could hear what she said. The whole Pack erupted into euphoric, giddy barking.

Rex and Red Team led Ordovich into the Atrium.

Shady scrambled for the S-3-9 exit. *I must get upstairs!* The rest of the Pack followed at a run. They barked and bayed, they barreled down the corridor, they bounded up the stairs, ecstatic.

Three levels spun past their paws like a tumbling stream.

They flew on wings of elation.

They filled the main corridor. Surged toward the Atrium.

There! Rex led the way, ears up, tail high and triumphant. His prisoner, cuffed and terrified, had no choice but to follow. STAT officers walked on each side. Each held an elbow firmly clamped.

Shady's growl filled her heart, chest, her throat. She drew back her lips to show every tooth, ears clamped flat, every hackle straight up on end. The growls of the Pack rolled forth all around her. Together they created a kind of thunder, a rolling rumble, a roar of rage.

Dr. Ordovich, already pale, went pallid. His knees buckled. His scent reeked of sick, sweaty terror. The two STAT officers held him upright, propelled him forward.

Shady and her Packmates stepped aside to let them pass.

They growled at Ordovich with all their hearts, delighted when he shrank from them.

Then they followed down the main corridor. Barked their triumph to the doors of the Detention Center. Now every tail waved high, each a blissful blur of motion.

Rex and the STAT officers hauled him off to Booking. The Detention Center's doors swung closed.

Scritch-scritch-scritch. That was Razor. He used his hind feet to cross out and overmark Ordovich's detestable spoor. He growled and snarled and *scritched* his way back down the corridor. The scent from under his pads and between his toes filled Shady's nose, fierce and defiant, angry and triumphant.

It was perfect. The ultimate way to obliterate his hated reek, symbolic but tangible.

Scritch-scritch-scritch, Shady marked him out, too. Marked him out of her life, out of her cares, out of her future for good, she hoped.

Her Packmates all found pieces of his scent-trail. *Scritch-scritch-scritch,* they crossed him out.

Negated. Overmarked. Deleted. Canceled.

His despicable odor diminished, diluted, scattered. No one lifted a leg or left a puddle. Civilized sapient beings didn't behave that way. But their paw-pads had gone raw, and their scent glands were depleted by the time the last, scattered scent rafts had fallen and been ground into decimation on the floor.

Shady snorted to clear her nose, then returned to the stairs. Tender her feet might be, but her heart sang with savage triumph.

OPD Detention, Interview Suite B

They put Dr. Ordovich in Interview B.

Rex stayed outside. Aylward removed his cuffs, then stepped

out and closed the door. Chief Klein arrived. He gave Rex, Aylward, and the other two STAT officers a solemn nod. Aylward departed with Chukwu and Koenig.

In the small, blank room known as Interview B, on a hard chair by a battered metal table with chain-scuffed manacle-loops, Ordovich sat alone.

He could rot there a while more. Rex looked to the Chief. "How is Bill?"

Klein's expression suggested he'd tasted something noisome. "That was a closer call than we needed. Cpl. Sloane had an allergic reaction, but the XK9 Project itself had already supplied us with the antidote. We were prepared. Sloane's responding well, but he'll spend tonight at Orangeboro Med."

Rex cocked an ear at the Chief. "We had the antidote?"

"In case of accidents." Klein's scent went sour with disgust. "The Project insisted we accept a fresh stock of the tailored tranquilizer drug, along with darts, nets, prods, and a specialized rifle, so I made sure we had the antidote, too." He hunched his shoulders. "That was back when we supposedly were taking delivery of ten large, dangerous animals."

"I am glad we had the antidote."

Klein nodded. "I plan to order our supply of the tranquilizer drug destroyed, and the other implements recycled. We can hope we won't need the rest of the antidote, but I've sent a sample for analysis and reproduction. That tranquilizer's a pretty potent drug."

Rex's hackles prickled with free-floating dread. "I fear we have not seen the last of it."

"Agreed." Klein stiffened. "I need to take a call. You can handle things here." He strode away.

Rex stared after him, felt Charlie's attention in the background. *I can handle things?*

You've been doing well so far. Pride, along with touches of amusement echoed through the link. *You seem to have been born for command. Might as well roll with it.*

A young man stepped forward, hesitant. "Um, Pack Leader, sir?"

Rex lifted his ears, turned to face him. "Yes?"

"I'm Sound Tech Samuels, and I need to know what you want. I've brought the sensor array online in Interview B, but I'm not sure what to do now."

He and Rex did a com-check. Ordovich pressed his down-turned lips together hard, clenched and unclenched his fists, but said nothing. Rex heard his breath and his heartbeat. That was enough for a sound check.

Samuels inclined his head toward the OCCUPIED blinker. "How long d'you plan on letting him sweat in there?"

Rex flicked his ears. "I may be the arresting officer of record, but this investigation belongs to Lt. Patel. We shall play it her way."

Good call, Charlie said. *Your best option here is to be as scrupulously professional as possible. If I've read Ordovich right, the contrast between the two of you on the interview recordings will be enlightening.*

Thank you. What a relief to have him there!

I'm glad not to miss it.

Patel arrived with a grin on her face. "We caught a helluva break, didn't we?" She also ran a com-check with Samuels, then studied the vid display. Ordovich glared at the metal manacle-loops. If anything, he hunched in on himself even more.

Rex dipped his nose to the vent, initiated his interview log, and gratefully opened his impressions to Charlie. "Subject remains afraid, but now outrage and anger have begun to grow in his scent," he texted to his associates and the log.

Patel nodded. "Time to throw him off-balance again. Rex, go in and read him his rights."

Fierce hunt-joy sang in Rex's pulse. He leaped up, ears and tail high. "My pleasure."

Ordovich's face twisted with rage when Rex entered the room. "You miserable excuse for an insubordinate hound of hell!" Each word hit hard as a bullet, cold with angry contempt. "I should've known from the beginning you'd be more trouble than you could possibly be worth."

Rex kept his ears up and his hackles down, though that took effort. Having Charlie in the back of his mind supporting him helped. "Dr. Gregory Ordovich, you have been placed under arrest. It is your right to say nothing, but it may harm your defense if you do not mention, when questioned, something you later rely on in court. Anything you do say may be used against you in a court of law. It is your right to have an attorney with you while you are questioned. If you cannot afford an attorney one will be appointed to represent you before you are questioned. Do you understand these rights?"

"Of course, I understand these rights!" Ordovich's voice rasped with fury. "I fucking taught you that warning!"

Rex kept his tongue in his mouth and his tail motionless, mindful of Charlie's guidance that he remain professional. But it was hard. "This is your chance to speak on the record, to tell your side of the story. Will you talk with us at this time?"

Ordovich answered with a baleful glare. "So. Many. Times." He shook his head. "So many times, I almost plugged your rotten skull. One shotgun blast. I should've known, that first time you defied me. You were six weeks old, and you snapped at me."

"You smelled bad." Rex remembered the incident, but he hadn't had a frame of reference to guess his age, other than *really young.* "You hit me so hard I blacked out. That was my first Healing Sleep."

"I should've killed you then. I had a bad feeling about you."

Rex fought to keep his snarl sheathed. He must remain professional. "I have seen you kill other puppies with your bare hands. I know you have ordered other dogs put down. What stopped you from killing me?"

Ordovich's scent boiled with harsh malevolence. "Because you were goddamned perfect. Your size. Your olfactory capabilities. Your physical prowess. You could literally do it all, and you could do it better than any other dog I ever made."

He drew back, scowling, reeking of bitter resentment. "Twenty years, I labored to create you!" He raised clenched fists, then lowered them, as if deflating. "Twenty. Stinking. Years. And you're the biggest mistake of my life. D'you have any idea how much money you were worth when I sold you?"

Rex sighed. "It has always been about the money to you, hasn't it?"

Ordovich's pale eyes glittered with malice. "Well, I had to get something. Goddamned XK9 Project was all I ever got from Dear Old Dad. Even then, I was the one who had to turn it into something. All my old man ever cared about was research."

"You say that as if research is a bad thing." Rex wished Shady was here, able to study these scent factors. Able to put her knowledge of humans to work. *What insights could she gain?*

Well for one, she'd probably talk about his 'daddy issues,' Charlie said.

"Oh, yeah, research is fine." Ordovich grimaced. The raw anger in his voice increased with every word. "Research is great, if you only want to live for the purity of science, and the inherent fascination of canine cognition!"

Rex kept his ears up. *Pure science and a delight in dog cognition certainly aren't Ordovich-junior's wheelhouse.*

No kidding, Charlie agreed.

Rex cocked his head at Ordovich. "So you changed the focus?"

"My father never cared how much money a man could charge for a top-tier military or police dog. He didn't care what a medical-diagnostic animal was worth. He never cared about the money at all. Never cared when Mom left, never cared that I wore old clothes to school, never cared for anything or anybody else. Just being around you damned mutts was all he ever loved."

Sibling rivalry gone toxic, Charlie said. *That clarifies all sorts of questions.*

Rex would think about them later. He stayed focused on his subject. "But you cared. You had to turn the Project around. Make it benefit his proper heir. The person he should've loved best."

"Damn straight!" The grief in Ordovich's scent welled up, throat-catching, agonized. He closed his eyes, his face pinched with pain. "How utterly bizarre, that you, of all people, should understand that." He hunched forward, leaned his elbow on the table so his left hand covered much of his face.

He called me a 'person.' Does he realize what he just admitted?

Don't call his attention to it.

Agreed.

Was Ordovich finished? Rex waited.

Silence stretched. Ordovich sat hunched, face covered, silent.

Rex's uneasiness grew. He stared at the man who had bred him. Who had forced his parents to mate. Who had cared nothing for what they thought or felt, or how their offspring felt. He didn't snarl, though it cost him great effort. Didn't growl, though the growl of all growls sang through his heart. Didn't speak, though . . . Should he say something, after all?

"How he would have loved you. I almost wish—" Ordovich shook his head. "My old man died in the kennels, d'you know that?"

Rex stayed quiet, waited for him.

"Yeah." He grimaced. "Ironic. Or perfect. Depends how you look at it. Keeled over one day, out of the blue. His favorite bitch stayed with him. The others went for help, but it was too late. He'd already died. Surrounded by his most beloved children." He bowed his head, sagged back in the hard metal chair and stared at the floor.

Rex stifled a shudder to think of what had befallen the elder Ordovich's "most beloved children" after that.

"At least I never had to listen to him curse me." Dr.

Ordovich's voice fell to a mutter. "At least I had a free hand, after that." He subsided into silence, still staring at the floor.

Rex waited.

After a while he straightened, gave Rex a squinty, resentful glare. "I want my fucking lawyer. Go away."

39

LEVERAGING INFLUENCE

Orangeboro Medical Center, Re-Gen Unit

Charlie turned his vid back on, unwilling to spy on Rex's post-interview conference with Lt. Patel. He wasn't certain how much of the investigation he should observe. As Rex's partner, he technically was on the team, but . . . He grimaced at his cast. *How far does "technically" extend?*

On the vid, Borough Attorney Adlai Masato stood at a podium in the Civic Center's Press Room. Masato had been outlining the OPD's contention that they'd been swindled into a sapient-trafficking scheme through fraudulent misrepresentation, when Charlie tuned in. He then congratulated the OPD for having made its first arrests already, and promised that as the investigation continued, other charges would likely be forthcoming.

The assembled journalists burst into shouted questions. "Are XK9s sapient?" someone cried.

"Will the Borough defy Transmondia?" another demanded.

"What about the Trade Compact?"

"Will the Borough stop paying?"

"Does this have anything to do with the SBI investigation?"

Charlie closed his eyes. The shouting voices, Masato's bet-hedging answers . . . He sighed. *The Borough officials are making it up as they go along.*

An impression of a worried stress-yawn came back through the link from Rex, although Charlie hadn't meant to distract him. *Chief Klein only launched this sapience investigation on Wednesday afternoon. The rest of the Borough officials are barely keeping up with developments. Meanwhile, we've established important things, but there's a long way to go.*

I'd say it's going pretty well, especially with all Ordovich told you in the interview.

That was unexpected luck. Even having him show up here, just when we had grounds for a warrant, was totally luck.

A little luck never hurts.

His partner's worry reverberated through the link. *We're going to lose him again. I just know it. Everyone's talking about 'one day at a time,' and making all the gains we can, but I can tell they're worried, too. Ordovich has powerful backers in Transmondia. Somehow, he'll get away.*

Charlie sent up a wish to whatever powers might exist, that no one would let Ordovich post bail. *Let's keep hoping not, okay?*

Council Chair Chan is extremely dubious. She's resisted every step of this process so far. She's called a Council meeting for 14:00, and from the way she talks and smells, it's NOT to rally the Council behind their Police Chief.

Charlie frowned. *Please believe me when I tell you I'm not changing the subject. The Family knows I'm awake, right?*

I'm not sure.

They should. At any rate, I need to talk to my grandmother now.

Carrie?

No, Annie. Head-of-Chartered-Family Annie.

He received an impression of ears-up, tail wagging. *Oh. You wish to leverage some influence.* This appeared to lighten his part-ner's mood.

Charlie grinned. *We're only one Family, but Gran Annie and Aunt Hannah are friends with our Ninth Precinct Council Member, Rona Peynirci.*

I did not realize we have clout! Rex's delight at this startled him.

Who'd taught Rex about how politics worked? Charlie chuckled softly. *Don't expect miracles, but sometimes a word at a good time is helpful. I should make that com call now.* He turned off the vid, right in the middle of Masato carefully picking his way through a non-answer about the official response to the SDF's unannounced arrival in the Borough this morning.

And I should check in with Shady. The Pack has been struggling to get all they can from a fragile scent-layer before the enhancements wear off. All ten of us . . . only nine of us, today, I guess. Anyway, we're all assigned to the Izgubil *case now.*

As well as your own fraud and sapient-trafficking case? Welcome to detective work. Are they calling you DPO Dieter-Nell, yet?

Rex replied with what felt like a tongue-loll. *Pack Leader Dieter-Nell, actually. I even have Admin Channel access.*

Charlie stifled a pang of dismay. *I bet you outrank me, don't you?*

I'm not sure. But clearly the idea appealed to him.

It's definitely time you checked in with the Pack, then, Pack Leader. We'll see how it all turns out.

Charlie shifted his focus, felt Rex do the same. His head still hurt, but Rex's adventures promised to make this convalescence much more interesting than his last one.

He placed his call to Gran Annie.

Civic Center, OPD Detention and Borough Council Members' Office Level

The voice on Rex's com identified herself as Councilmember Rona Peynirci, and could he find a moment to speak with her before 14:00 today?

He wagged his tail. "I have time right now. We are still waiting for Dr. Ordovich's legal counsel to arrive."

She gave directions to her Ninth-Floor office.

Rex navigated the maze of staffers' offices and conference rooms that ringed the Borough Council Chamber, then worked his way toward the outer window-wall. A small, burnished-brass-on-marble plaque mounted next to one door read "Ninth Precinct, Rona Peynirci."

The receptionist inside stood with a professional smile, despite a burst of alarmed scent, and gestured toward another door. "She's expecting you."

Like Klein's office, Peynirci's office overlooked the Sirius Valley to leeward. Klein's view was more sweeping, but this office provided a nice vista. Ninth Precinct itself remained even more out of view from here than from the 25th Floor, but maybe the symbolism was similar. She'd positioned her glossy bamboo desk by the wall to his right, neither blocking the view nor staring into it full-time. She'd clustered framed images and certificates, as well as a large map of the Ninth Precinct, on the wall behind her.

"Pack Leader Dieter-Nell, welcome." About Gran Annie's age and size, with a pleasant brown face that gave away nothing. She wore her gray, center-parted hair pulled back in a bun, a blue saree, and a gold bangle at each wrist, but the most striking thing about her was her intense, dark-eyed gaze. Unlike her terrified receptionist, bright, piquant curiosity dominated her scent. "Annie recommended that I speak with you before the meeting this afternoon. Thank you for seeing me."

Corona Family had granted him this opening. How best to

use the opportunity? "I am delighted to meet you, Councilmember Peynirci. I would be happy to answer any questions you may have."

She offered a wry eyebrow-quirk. "I suspect we could be here till tomorrow and all of my questions might not be answered, but let's start with this one. Is Chief Klein right? Are you and the rest of the Pack improperly-enslaved sapient beings?"

Rex nodded. "We believe we are. I tried to go through the list of 'sapient characteristics' that are the current legal standard definition with Borough Attorney Masato last night, but he was not terribly receptive."

She interlaced her fingers in front of herself on the desktop, leaned forward on her elbows. "Judging from this morning's press conference, he seems to have come around."

"Judge Qadhi's willingness to authorize a warrant helped somewhat convince him, I think."

"Somewhat?"

"He is frightened of us. I do not think he wants to believe we are sapient. I think he wishes he did not have to deal with us at all."

"You are very large, and you look like an ancestral predator."

"I believe Dr. Ordovich wanted people to fear us, although my mate is of the opinion that he was 'overcompensating for something' when he made us so big."

Peynirci smiled. "Your mate might be onto something. Is she here in Orangeboro, too?"

"I am happy to say yes. She is XK9 Officer Shady Jacob-Belle. She also is my second, who keeps the Pack working smoothly when I am upstairs."

Peynirci's expression sobered. "You just arrested your Dr. Ordovich. How do you feel about that?"

Rex stress-yawned. "I wish I had less concern that he would somehow manage to escape us. Humans have done whatever they pleased with us all my life. It seems impossible that he might actually face justice."

"You feel no lingering affection for the man who made you?"

Rex snapped his ears flat. "For the man who always detested me? Who gave me regular beatings from the time I was a year-ling, for being 'insubordinate' whenever I dared to think or ques-tion? Who would have separated me from my mate without giving it a thought, if that suited him? No. He never felt any affection for any us, so I feel no shame in admitting we recipro-cated that lack of regard. The only thing he liked about XK9s was the money he planned to make selling us."

Peynirci gave him a long, level look. "Yet you're not soured on all humans?"

Rex wagged his tail. "I especially love Charlie, my Ranan Corona Family, Chief Klein, and SSA Adeyeme, but I also know many other outstanding humans. When I think of humans, I think of them. How could I blame other humans for Dr. Ordovich's evil? He is just one man."

Peynirci nodded. "I assume you've seen the press coverage?"

Rex flicked his ears, stress-yawned. "I have been somewhat busy."

"Mm." She frowned. "They're speculating that XK9s might have been uplifted accidentally, perhaps a parallel case to the gusaujik uplifting the Duulian gulimyanik. What they'd intended was to breed a more interactive hunting animal."

"I am quite certain that Dr. Ordovich did not intend for us to be sapient. I also am certain he never wanted us to know anything about Duulian gulimyaniks, whatever those are."

She gave him a wry smile. "Imagine a creature that superfi-cially resembles the Earth-myth of the griffin. It's about the size of a Terran condor or a Transmondian pterolizard, with a prickly temper."

Rex cocked his head. "What happened to the Duulian gulimyaniks who were uplifted?"

She frowned. "I looked it up after I read the article that compared them to you. Gulimyaniks were analyzed by the Observation Commission and accepted onto the Alliance's

Roster of Sapient Species. They now live in their own homeland, a large Duulian island from which all of the gusaujik have been evicted. They intensely dislike and mistrust the gusaujik, but they did ratify a treaty that keeps the peace for now. They have established trade with the vicurrians. Once their numbers increase enough, most observers fear that war between gulimyaniks and the gusaujik is inevitable."

Rex lowered his ears, then raised them again, uncertain how he felt about this. "I guess you should be thankful that, in general, XK9s like humans."

"Believe me, I am." She blew out a long breath and stared toward the window-wall. Then she straightened in her chair and faced Rex. "What are your thoughts about this afternoon's Council meeting?"

Rex stifled a growl. "I believe that Council Chairperson Chan would far rather send us back to die in Transmondia than support our rights. She will undoubtedly try to convince other Council Members that we are an expensive, embarrassing inconvenience, and not sapient. She is more afraid of the Transmondians and the Trade Compact than she is willing to objectively consider our case."

"Is she also afraid of you?"

"Not of us personally, I think. What Chairperson Chan fears is losing influence or wealth if she crosses the Transmondians and the Premier."

"Well, she and Iskander are in the same political party, and the CWP has taken extremely pro-Transmondian positions, especially recently. She undoubtedly will lose influence, and possibly wealth, if she bucks the party's positions."

Rex cocked his head. "The CWP?"

"Commonwealth Party. You might want to ask Charlie or one of the Family about the four Ranan political parties."

In other words, "don't take up my time with teaching you." Rex nodded. "May I ask in turn for your thoughts on this afternoon's Council meeting?"

She crossed her arms and leaned back in her chair. "Ah, that is interesting."

Rex lowered his ears again. "What? That I should have concerns about a meeting that may well dictate my fate, as well as that of my Pack? You can hardly be surprised by that."

She shook her head. "I'm surprised that after all those beatings you spoke of, you still dared to turn my question back on me."

"He did try, but Dr. Ordovich was never able to beat the insubordination out of me." Rex snorted. "And if I am not daring now, I fear I shall fail my Pack irreparably. You and the other Council Members hold our very lives in your hands."

"Yet you would risk angering me, in spite of that?"

Rex stood. "A large part of police work is calculating risks based on evaluations we make, as a result of behavior we have perceived. From what I have so far observed of you, it seemed more appropriate to ask that you stand up for Ranan ideals." He met her gaze.

A smile crept into her eyes, then curved her lips. "I would guess that you do your police work well."

He wagged his tail. "That is my ardent hope, since it is my chosen life's work." His HUD beeped. He glanced at the text. "And speaking of my police work, Dr. Ordovich's attorney has arrived."

40

BUST, BUILDUP, AND BREAKTHROUGH

S-3-9 Evidence Cavern

C hange-of-watch came on the hour. Shady lifted her nose from the disintegrated scent layer, then yawned from both stress and fatigue. Scout and Elle were scheduled to take over from her and Razor in a few minutes.

She'd scheduled the Pack's best trackers to take what was likely to be the last shift on the corridor pads. If they couldn't find anything more, nothing more had survived to be found. Pam's estimate of "48 hours at most" to LSA Shimon last night had been wildly optimistic.

Pam straightened, stiff, then unsealed the tent. Shady stepped out into cooler air, stretched and yawned again. Liz and Razor emerged from the tent next door with parallel yawns and stretches.

"How was it?" Shady asked.

LSA Shimon quietly joined them.

Razor bowed his head. "I fear it is gone. I wish Elle and Scout the best of success, but I have covered everything at least five times since yesterday, and each time I find less."

"So we only have that one drop of adhesive," Shimon said. "Damn. Now what?"

"Now Scout and Elle make one last pass. They are the Pack's most acute trackers," Shady said. "If they find nothing new, we must conclude that the enhancements have now failed, and the scents have crumbled to inadmissible dust."

"We do have scent profiles," Liz said. "We've filed a set and sent another to the Scent Reference Lab, although whether they'll return any results now that we've arrested their Director is a good question."

Shimon grimaced. "That would require unusually selfless devotion to forensic science."

"Not something we've seen much of from Ordovich," Pam said.

"Not everyone at the Project is like him," Shady replied. "The older ones are more dedicated to their forensic work."

Shimon shook his head. "I'm not gonna hold my breath for results from that quarter in any case."

Elle and Scout stepped into the evidence cavern from the ready room. Their previous shift had been in the morgue annex.

"How goes the shred-analysis?" Shady asked.

Elle snapped her ears flat. "We are down to particles. They are still running residue through DNA scanners, but I think the XK9 teams are wasting their time in the morgue now."

"I concur," Scout's ears flicked, then went back, his tail down. "Nothing is left that is big enough for us."

Shimon gave him a worried look. "This, from dogs who are able to paint virtual blast patterns on one-centimeter fragments?"

Scout dipped his head. "You understand. Yes. One centimeter in any direction would be huge."

Shimon rubbed the back of his neck, shot a glance toward the pallets. "So we're down to the debris." He sighed. "I hope you realize we never would've gotten half this far, and certainly nowhere near this fast, without the Pack."

Shady wagged her tail. "Thank you."

"Thank *you*. And Rex. Any word from him?"

"I expected to hear more by now," Shady said. "The Council meeting has begun, Dr. Ordovich has lawyered up and shut up, yet Rex is still in Chief Klein's office, as far as I can tell. He has not checked in for more than an hour."

"He's not the only one late," Shimon said. "I should have released you for lunch two hours ago, but I've been hoping for some last thing from the corridor pads." He grimaced toward the line of hazmat tents, then turned to Elle and Scout. "Wanna go give it one last sniff and tell me if we should call this one done, too?"

"Sure," Elle said.

Misha nodded, then followed her to Tent Two. "We can leap-frog, right, Nicole?"

"Let's do it." Nicole entered Tent One behind Scout.

"I fear that will not take long," Shady told Shimon.

He stared after the fresh teams with a pained expression. "It's a kind of progress, I guess. Pretty harsh 'statute of limitations' on scents, isn't there?"

"Two weeks for exposed scents is about all we can expect," Shady agreed. "We can still have hope for the pallets, especially those we have draped, and those we have not yet opened. They still might yield new results. Also, anything still in space. If anything is."

"Actually, there is. But it's too big to bring in here." Shimon scowled. "We're still trying to figure out the best approach with that piece. There may be a way for you to go to it, but you'd have to be certified for microgravity work." He quirked an eyebrow at Shady. "Could scents persist in vacuum for another week?"

"I am not sure." Shady flicked her ears. "I do not believe that has been properly tested, although dryness, cold, and protection from atmosphere all help preserve scent. We got a day more from the corridor pads with the enhancements. They also seemed a day or so fresher than their two-week age when we started. I believe the latter effect is because they had been in space. But for most of those two weeks, they were in pressurized, normal air, so they deteriorated normally. Something in space for longer? I am not sure."

Shimon blew out a long breath and squinted toward the pallets. SA Freas's crews had removed about nineteen and a half rows by now. They'd filled several Civil Defense storage areas, and opened up a lot of space. "Elaine told me SCISCO's asked if ne may bring in a colleague for consultation, but now Elaine's upstairs like Rex, and I've yet to see that android at all today."

I think Shimon feels neglected, Pam said.

Shady lolled her tongue. *Can you blame him? Being left out of the loop is irritating. I can relate. What is Rex doing now that keeps him too busy to check in with the Pack?*

LSA Kramer beeped in on the Admin Channel. "Have your XK9 teams gone to lunch yet?"

"Almost there," Shimon answered. "Do I understand correctly that they're done in the morgue?"

"Yes."

"Go ahead and release your lot, then. We're almost to a stopping place here."

"Roger that." She clicked off.

Another incoming news update beeped on Shady's news feed. Most of the articles she'd gotten lately consisted of speculation about XK9 sapience, and comparisons with other species "uplifted" from sub-sapient species around the Alliance.

They were distinct from the naturally-evolved, but equal under the law once officially listed as sapient. Shady had been surprised to learn of at least a dozen. *People have a whole vocabulary for what we went through. Uplifted, including accidental uplift. And protections for the uplifted! Who knew?*

I sure didn't, Pam agreed.

XK9s still had to prove themselves, however. There were legal definitions and evaluation standards. Members of species from far away, who'd never met or even heard of dogs, would decide if they were worthy. *What will they ask? How long will that take? And what if XK9s somehow fall just short?*

Shady, please! Are you as smart as a human? Pam asked.

Dr. Ordovich had always said it was insubordinate blasphemy, even to ask. Of course, he'd had a vested interest in no one ever asking. All the same, her conditioning made it an uncomfortable question. She panted harder at the very thought.

Pam grimaced. *That was a rhetorical question. Of course, you are! Smarter than most, in my opinion.*

Thanks. Shady stress-yawned, then opened the news update. But this one wasn't about uplifted sapient species.

TRANSMONDIAN AMBASSADOR CLAIMS DIPLOMATIC IMMUNITY FOR JAILED XK9 CREATOR, she read.

Oh, bloody hell.

Orangeboro Civic Center, an antechamber adjacent to the Borough Council Meeting Hall

Rex curled his lip just enough to show teeth. *Finally, a little passion from Masato.* Rex lay on a plush carpet in a small, stuffy antechamber near the Borough Council Meeting Hall. His eyes and nose followed the Borough Attorney's agitated pacing back and forth, but he kept his legs well out of Masato's path.

Chief Klein, Elaine, and SCISCO's android, once again in its blue ensemble, sat on velvet-upholstered chairs by the wall. They, too, allowed Masato all the pacing-room he wished.

He's upset that Ordovich might get diplomatic immunity? Charlie asked.

Oh, he's certain that he will. Rex swallowed a growl. *He says the Wheel Court almost has to accept it, no matter how long after-the-fact it was arranged, because to dispute it invites a diplomatic break with*

Transmondia. What he's angry about is an open case left indefinitely on his record.

A man with his priorities well in mind, eh? Rex sensed that Charlie had paused, panting, from his leg exercises. Charlie'd said his physical therapist was counting the reps, and that they hurt less when Charlie's mind was elsewhere.

Rex's ears clamped tight against his skull. *Yeah, the public-spiritedness just drips off of the man.*

Like water off leak-proofing, that hasn't soaked in at all. Charlie groaned, though whether he emitted an audible sound or only groaned in his thoughts, Rex wasn't sure.

Rex sighed. *I'd say don't wear yourself out, but I guess your physical therapist will know where to draw that line.* He put his chin on his forelegs, looked away from Masato. *Are all Council Meetings closed like this?*

My PT is a torturer, but unfortunately, it's torture I need. As a voting, taxpaying citizen, however, a closed Council Meeting on a topic as important as XK9 sapience makes me angry.

Rex shared his memory of Beatriz Chan, glaring at Chief Klein then declaring the meeting closed pending the resolution of "certain personnel matters."

The impression of a scowl came back through the link from Charlie. *For two hours, they've supposedly been discussing 'personnel matters,' when the announced topic was XK9 sapience? While you just sat there?*

That's the claim. Klein looks and smells grim, but he hasn't said much. They told us not to leave or talk to anyone outside this room. So far, we've complied, but Elaine and I both really want to talk with our teams, and I'm certain Klein has lots of work, too. Then Masato just burst in a while ago, demanding to talk to the Council.

What about me? You're talking with me.

Whether they know it or not, wherever I go, I bring you. Besides, I need your help interpreting things that happen.

Startled gratitude emanated through their link. *I'm glad to help. Makes me feel less useless.* Charlie's focus wavered for a moment, then returned. *Are there journalists around?*

They put the journalists in a different room.

I'll bet they did. Rex received an impression of a new kind of repetitive motion. He hoped this one hurt less. *Have you given any interviews?* Charlie asked.

To journalists? Not me, no. Rex gave a soft growl. *I'm worried about doing that. I know that's mostly because Dr. Ordovich always told us they'd trick us into saying things wrong and get us in trouble, but I still worry.*

Charlie breathed harder. His reps continued. *The trickiness of journalists . . . tends to depend on . . . how many things you . . . need to hide.* He didn't need breath to think words into the link, but somehow his mental voice gasped between each burst of words anyway. *You have the XK9s' . . . story to tell . . . Journalists are . . . the professionals who'll . . . help you tell it . . . but you have to . . . talk with them.*

I shall bear that in mind. I—

Councilmember Peynirci pushed the door wide with a bang. "Time we opened it." She strode as fast as her saree's wrap allowed to another door and threw it open as well. "Orangeboro deserves to hear these discussions on the record." A swarm of journalists' vid-cams poured into the Meeting Hall.

Masato stopped pacing. Klein and Elaine stood. Everyone moved to look through the doorway.

On the other side of the room a tall man pushed more doors wide. Rex opened his perceptions to Charlie in as much detail as possible. More vid-cams poured through on that side.

His partner paused his exertions, still panting hard. *I think that's . . . yes, Eric Maki . . . Third Precinct . . . Good . . . He's the Council Member . . . represents both . . . Walter and Petunia's . . . Lang Family and . . . Eduardo and Victor's . . . Bari Family . . . glad to see he's . . . helping open it.*

Beatriz Chan glared at Peynirci and Maki from the podium at

the head of the Meeting Hall. Some of the Council shouted protests, but others applauded.

Charlie's breathing gradually slowed. *Wow. That's a lot of journalists. I bet we'll play host to more and more, as the news about the XK9s spreads.*

Rex ducked his head. *Daunting thought.*

More people to hear and spread the XK9s' story, Charlie countered. *They're Ordovich's enemies, which makes them your friends.*

Oh. How best to tell our story, though? So far, any time I've said more than a few words to strangers, they've been too amazed that I can talk to listen to me.

You're brilliant, and you improvise well. Charlie's breathing was back to normal, and so was his mental voice. *How long did it take you to come up with the idea to reconstruct that flitter in Transmondia?*

Rex gazed toward the Meeting Hall, but what he saw was that debris-strewn wreck site. *Not long. The idea came in a flash.* The rising surge of pleasure, the joyous rush of a challenging new puzzle to tackle, the thrill of the hunt burst back upon him in a flood of memories.

And look how far that experience has taken you. He received an impression of Charlie's smile. *Trust your instincts.*

Rex wagged his tail, still riding the rosy glow of that remembered adventure. *Too bad we had to delete those image files and reconstructions.* The bitterness of deleting their work still ground his gut. Their instructors had double-checked to make certain the deletions were completed. *It doesn't matter that we remember them and can picture them in our minds. Those files are truly gone. Lt. Patel was disappointed, too.*

Charlie shared Rex's moment of dismay. *So you can remember them, but not reconstruct them?*

I'm not sure how we could reconstruct them. I wonder if GR technology would work for that.

Charlie's own bitter disappointment flooded through the link at this. *In a parallel universe I might've been able to help, but even if I weren't confined to a hospital bed, I'm permanently banished from the Global Reconstruction Unit.* He sighed. *Anyway, it would take a long time and a lot of tinkering to render them. Probably too long to do you any good as a demonstration of your skills.* He had an impression that Charlie turned to speak to someone. "... important. We can start again in a minute."

A demonstration of the XK9s' skills. Rex lolled his tongue. That was exactly what they needed, wasn't it? What better way to tell their story? He growled softly. *If only.* He stared out across the Meeting Hall.

"Why don't we ask some experts to testify about it?" Peynirci demanded of Chan. "Rex himself is here. You can ask him directly, and I think you should. But if you don't trust him, we have three people who've worked with him and the Pack for several days, now. More than that, they've each publicly staked their reputation on asserting that the XK9s are sapient. Wouldn't you like to know what convinced them?"

Chan shook her head. "By their very actions they've proved they're biased."

"But law enforcement officers are trained to set their personal biases aside," Eric Maki said. "So are science and technology professors. They're trained to look at the evidence, to evaluate it objectively. The very fact that persons from these professions have staked their reputations on XK9 sapience should make their testimony more credible, not less!"

Chan scowled. "You know SCISCO must be biased. Nir kind have helped get nearly every uplifted candidate-species listed. I think they go out looking for them."

"I'm not so sure confirmation bias is a characteristic of AIs," another Councilmember put in. "Isn't that one reason why they confirmed IURE-484 as a Station Court Justice? I remember everyone at the time talking about a 'guaranteed objective Justice,' during the hearings."

Charlie chuckled. *I just had a thought, when they mentioned SCISCO.*

Rex cocked his head. *Oh?*

Yeah. Charlie's grin felt like warm joy. It calmed Rex's anxious heart. *You know that no computer file can be completely erased, right? They leave infinitesimal traces, even though most people couldn't begin to recover them.*

Oh. That's right. Even Tux hadn't thought of this. What a brilliant partner he had! *You're asking if 'deleted' really is deleted, to a cybernetic entity. I should ask.*

41

RETURN OF THE LOST

Orangeboro Council Meeting Hall antechamber

"Are you sure you understand what you're asking?" The pixel-point eyebrows on the face of SCISCO's android rose almost to nir fiber-optic "hairline." It wasn't exactly one of those looks Georgia had described, but it was close.

They were back in the Meeting Hall antechamber that had begun to feel like a permanent posting to Rex. Both he and SCISCO had agreed to remain available till the end of the meeting in case further questions arose. But to Rex's dismay the meeting had just clicked over into the start of its fourth hour, still with no end in sight.

"I believe I do understand," He answered SCISCO. "I am well aware that it would be invasive, and perhaps uncomfortable. But I am not asking merely to satisfy personal curiosity."

The cartoon-line smile shifted to a look of perplexity. "Is there anything you wouldn't do, if it could help the Pack?"

He wagged his tail, pleased that ne understood. "I do not know. Nothing that either I or others have proposed has yet tested those limits."

"You intend to ask your three Packmates, as well?"

He lowered his ears. "Let us first see if it can be done at all."

"See if what can be done?" Elaine stepped inside, then sat with a weary sigh. Her second round of questioning had gone longer than the first.

"Rex has asked an intriguing question," SCISCO said. "If we can do what he suggests, it might create an opportunity for you and Director Perri to counter some of your critics."

Elaine smiled up at nem. "I'm certainly open to that."

Rex did his best to explain Charlie's idea about recovering the flitter files. "I originally thought if we could recover them, they would help Lt. Patel's investigation, but SCISCO makes a good point. As a demonstration of the kind of forensic technique we use on the debris, they might also help you."

Her scent went pleasantly fragrant with bright enthusiasm and piquant interest. "If all four of your reconstruction files could be recovered and played, just think what a presentation we'd have!" Her face lit with the possibilities. "We could decisively answer the doubters, and do it without exposing sensitive forensic information about the current case."

"True." He and Charlie hadn't thought that far yet.

"At the same time, think how it would bolster the case for your sapience!" Almost all of Elaine's phobic fear had disappeared from her scent. She sat within a meter of Rex, but focused on the vision in her mind. "The story of how you developed that technique, especially when you were still just adolescent puppies, is almost a case study in sapient behavior."

"I am convinced." Rex turned to SCISCO. "How long would this take? Do we need any equipment?"

The smile on the android face stretched wide. "We'll need compatible playback equipment, if I can recover the files."

Rex gave a quick nod. "What else?"

"Access to your CAP and HUD, including their root implants, and guidance on where you originally stored your files." SCISCO parked nir android on a chair next to Rex.

Rex cocked his head at nem. "Can you get in with the link you established this morning?"

"If you'll allow it. I won't go forward without your permission."

"You have it. Let us try." Rex thumped the floor with his tail, then went still and tried to think of nothing, unsure what might help most. His gut tightened. *How will this feel?*

SCISCO placed nir hand on Rex's withers, five points of warmth with a slight vibration. Then all at once there was another consciousness inside of him.

It started as something like his sensations when the brain link with Charlie had first opened, but this was a different personality. Someone . . . larger. Oddly different. Immense and complex. Amorphous, but with an unexpected central integrity. Like a buzzing, vibrating mist that pervaded him, permeated every crevice, and knew everything. It filled the universe but was contained in itself. Rex had a flash of the sense that it was in him, but he also was in it.

Invasive? That wasn't the right word. *Pervasive* would be more accurate, like a scent both diffuse and infused into everything. It knew Rex now, even in greater depth than Charlie did, or than he knew Charlie.

But with that knowledge came an intimate reciprocity. This presence knew him, but he also knew as much as he could take in about it. About nem. That knowing eased him.

Permission sought, permission granted, permission not transgressed. Knowledge received, balanced by knowledge given, knowledge freely exchanged. No threat here, but harmonious common purpose.

The buzzing cloud of it pulsed, condensed, then focused like a blinding, brilliant point of light that had nothing to do with optical vision. *Show me where you stored the files. Do that by going there.*

Rex mentally leaped to the place where he'd stored them before he'd been forced to delete them. *Right here.*

He received an impression rather like a frown. *Hmm. Perceived.*

Then, after a groping moment, *Ah.* The buzzing turned to . . . humming. In cadences.

Then not-quite-words, more like sounds in rhythms—but silent sounds. Inside his . . . Well, actually, "location" didn't seem to apply. This was *other*where.

Akka-Bo-Bo-Akka, Akka-Bo-Bo-Akka, Cee-Du-Ee, Cee-Du-Ee, Akka-Bo-Bo-Akka, Akka-Bo-Bo-Akka, Cee-Du-Cee, Du-Cee-Du . . . Then all stop.

Frustration.

Rex could relate. None of the patterns made sense to him. They didn't seem to satisfy SCISCO, either.

Akka-Akka-Akka, Bo-Bo-Bo, Cee-Cee-Cee, Du-Du-Du? Far as Rex could tell, the buzzing cloud of SCISCO emitted these vibrations. What was their purpose? He stilled his mind as much as he could.

Dammit. Tercet? Akka-Akka-Bo, Akka-Akka-Cee, Akka-Akka-Du? All stop.

Rex's curiosity burned. He yearned to ask but dared not distract.

Pum-pum-pum-pum, reverberated through the buzzing cloud. *Pum-pum-pum-pum,* like depth-sounding. Echoes returned: *P-p-pum-p-p-pum-p-p-pum-p-p-pum.*

All stop. The echoes ended.

Then the pattern started over. Pulsed from within the cloud, with echoes returning from the "place" Rex had led SCISCO. *Pum-pum-pum-pum, p-p-pum-p-p-pum-p-p-pum-p-p-pum. Pum-pum-pum-pum, p-p-pum-p-p-pum-p-p-pum-p-p-pum,* repeated over and over and over. *Pum-pum-pum-pum, p-p-pum-p-p-pum-p-p-pum-p-p-pum.*

Rex received a sensation of settling. Surrounding. Circling. Centering. Then . . . an impression.

Of what? Not sure. He gained a sense that SCISCO struggled to stabilize the whatever-it-was. Minutes passed.

Then finally he had an odd sensation of something swirling . . . turning . . . spinning.

Shadows converged, resolved into angles.

Resolved into shapes.

Resolved into the ghosts of almost-recognizable machine parts.

The ghosts thickened, grew more substantial.

Joyous, he recognized them for sure now. Scarcely daring to believe, heart pounding hard, he watched with an unfamiliar inner vision. The pieces resolved into solid-looking synth-and-metal machine parts. The original image files, created from his harness's optics, had been small and crude. The files returned to that level of finish.

But then, with a surge of triumph that buzzed through and around him, they sharpened.

Improved.

Focused at last into much more finely-realized forms.

SCISCO's engulfing, buzzing presence rang with sparkles of satisfaction. *I have suitable playback equipment at S-Poly. Seems we'll need it.*

Civic Center S-3-9

Shady bowed her head, panting, tail down. End-of-watch at last. She trudged toward the ready room.

Pam trailed her. From the smell of Pam's lower back, she needed more than just another short, restless night tonight. Shady growled. Pam especially didn't need another predawn near-miss with Virendra's MPs.

Balchu joined them in the ready room, along with all on-duty Task Force and SIT Delta officers. It was a tight squeeze while everyone tried to shed their containment gear as fast as possible.

"I need a weekend." Shady used her vocalizer, so Balchu

could hear. "It is already Friday night. Do you think we shall get any time off at all?" Ranans tended to work long hours, but many businesses closed for at least part of each week from sometime before noon on Friday through Sunday evening. This "Ranan weekend" accommodated several of the residents' holy days, from Jummah on Friday through Vespers on Sunday. It also enjoyed popular approval among secular citizens, as long as they could still go shopping and have access to entertainments. Law enforcement, however, wasn't like "many businesses." Weekends were never a sure thing, although a person could hope.

"Maybe," Balchu said. "That'd be nice."

But something was up. Rex had been sending her cryptic little texts about "new things brewing" and "interesting new developments" for the past hour. She was too tired to muster much curiosity. "Tell me all about it after I get a good night's sleep," she'd texted back.

One by one, Tux, Cinnie, and Cryssie had been called upstairs. They'd come back smelling of secrets, but only willing to say "wait and see."

Shady's com buzzed with a new text from Adeyeme. Staff meeting in the war room. Five minutes.

Shady sighed. *Now what?*

Well, for one thing it means Adeyeme's back, Pam said. *Maybe Rex will be, too. And maybe we'll learn what all the secret stuff's been about.*

The teams gathered, aromatic in their weariness. They presented a haggard, exhausted parody of the group who'd gathered around the big vid-screen this morning to cheer Dr. Ordovich's arrest.

The Pack had finished with both their morgue duties and the corridor pads since then. Many of their human associates helped pack up the bagged pad and hand-hold evidence for secured cold storage once that was done, then dismantled the hazmat tents.

Smells of hot, achy inflammation emanated from many of Shady's teammates, both humans and dogs. No one stood once they got to the war room. When they ran out of chairs, the tops of workstations or the floor would do.

Adeyeme, Rex, SCISCO's android, and Chief Klein arrived together. Shady blinked, startled to see the tiny SSA actually reach out to touch Rex's back. She smiled when he responded with a tongue-loll. Then she stepped forward to speak.

"I know what each of you probably wants most right now is to be spared another meeting, but there have been developments," she said. "First, the Borough Council just voted, by an eight-to-four margin, to back Chief Klein's recent actions, and to affirm officially that in Orangeboro, XK9s are considered sapient."

Astonishment jolted through Shady. *Can this be?* Her HUD beeped the next instant with a headline confirming it. *How is this possible?*

Cheers and cries of amazement echoed through the war room.

I don't know, but it's amazing news, Pam replied. *I'll worry if it was a dream, later.*

"We have yet to sort out how this changes things for XK9s in practical reality," Chief Klein said. "I anticipate, at minimum, intense talks with the Safety Services Employees Union and the Borough Clerk's office in the near future, plus changes in pay and job titles. Please be patient with us while we figure out how to reconfigure our budgets and standards."

You should get that pay raise we speculated about, Pam said.

And I'll spend it as I see fit! Shady laid back her ears, ready to defend that position.

Pam's jaws clenched and her brows knotted in a scowl, but she didn't answer. Too tired? Shady caught a fleeting sense that her partner was as reluctant to resume their argument as she was.

"If that were all," Adeyeme began, then waited till the

excited babble waned. "If that were all, it certainly would be enough sensation, but we've another event looming, one that directly affects all of you. This afternoon, Rex and Dr. SCISCO discovered that the wreckage-reconstruction files the so-called Flitter Four were forced to delete are recoverable."

Another babble of surprise rose, then faded.

"More than that, we've recovered them," Adeyeme said. "With the cooperation of Tuxedo, Cinnamon and Crystal, Dr. SCISCO has been able to recover, repair, and enhance all four sets of those files, to the point where we can now use them in a public demonstration that will simultaneously showcase both XK9 sapience and the new forensic methods we've employed for the analysis of the *Izgubil* debris."

A new buzz of excitement arose.

Shady gave Pam a worried look. *A public demonstration? Will all of us have to go onstage?*

Pam hunched her shoulders. *Probably. Partners too, I bet. Time to brush the dog hairs off the dress blues.*

"The demonstration will be held tomorrow evening in the Civic Center Auditorium," Chief Klein said.

What? Murmurs of surprise and mutters of protest greeted this announcement.

Klein raised his hands in a placating gesture. "Yes, it is short notice. I know this renders it difficult to make all the arrangements. But events have tended to move quickly on this front. After the little surprise Premier Iskander and the SDF tried to spring on us this morning, I've been advised by both of the Vice Premiers to move quickly."

Both of the Vice Premiers? Shady looked for Rex's reaction. He didn't act surprised.

Astonishment rolled through the link from Pam, however. *BOTH Vice Premiers? That's—wow. That's a shakeup in the government, when both Vice Premiers go against the Premier. Iskander better watch herself!*

"We'll be playing to an extremely important audience," Klein continued. "Not only will Director Perri and journalists from all over the System be there, but so will Vice Premiers Guzmán and Zhokittik, as well as Ambassador Nunzio of Transmondia. It's possible Premier Iskander herself may agree to come. Other ambassadors may come, as well. We're already in talks with Ranan Executive Security."

Civic Center Auditorium isn't going to be anywhere near big enough, Pam said.

"As you might imagine, we expect an overflow crowd," Klein said. "All OPD officers not on stage will be tasked with security."

No surprise there, Shady said.

Pam shared a wide-eyed look with both her and Balchu. *Yeah, we'll need all hands from all watches, considering we'll have all those bigshots in town to protect.*

"Too bad the XK9s can't help with security," Berwyn said.

Klein shook his head. "Not this time. You'll have security patrols protecting you, this time around. Our contention that XK9s are sapient is controversial. That makes every Pack member and partner a potential target."

"Will our families get a chance to attend the demonstration?" Misha asked.

"Absolutely." Klein gave him a firm nod. "Families of XK9 teams will get special priority seating for the presentation. Joslyn Stark says she's made sure all XK9 families, Chartered or not, will receive tickets for at least four good seats. Please talk with your families about this tonight. They'll have to figure out who gets them."

I don't envy Joslyn, Pam said. *However, if Balchu's on a security detail, we won't need ours.*

Shady shot a glance toward Balchu. He sat on Pam's other side, oblivious to their link-based conversation. *Don't give them away before you discuss it with him. I'd like to speak for two of them, myself. I'm half of our team, so half of the tickets should be mine to distribute, don't you think?*

The astonishment reverberating through the link made it clear Pam hadn't expected this. *Um, I guess that's fair.* She stared at Shady. *But who'd you give them to?*

I haven't decided yet. Shady thumped her tail on the floor. Maybe Bill Sloane, if he was out of the hospital. The brave UPO was pretty high on her list of favorite people right now, after what he'd done for Rex this morning.

I'm sure you'll have no lack of takers. Huh. Pam gave a little shake of her head, clearly still surprised.

"In addition to the politicians and ambassadors, all of the Council Members are of course demanding prime spots—even those who voted against us," Klein said. "Therefore, not everyone will get in, so please get back to Joslyn with the names of those who'll get tickets, as soon as possible."

Adeyeme smiled and nodded to Klein, then turned to the group. "Now I can tell you you're dismissed for the rest of the evening, plus for most of you till tomorrow at 14:00. Meet back here in the war room. Either I or my Command Staff will contact you individually if we need you for other things."

Klein nodded. "XK9 teams, we'll need all of you in the Civic Center at noon. Casual dress for the rehearsals, but plan on dress uniforms tomorrow night. Rex, Tux, Cinnie, Cryssie, and partners, we need a word with you after everyone else leaves."

Adeyeme smiled. "The rest of you are dismissed. Rest well! See you tomorrow!"

Shady resisted the general rush for the door. "I want to stay with Rex." She again used her vocalizer. "I shall be home later."

Pam frowned. "No. I want you—"

Balchu touched her arm. "Pammie," he said quietly. "Sapient being. Not your ward."

Pam opened her mouth, hesitated, then closed it. "This is gonna take getting used to."

"Shady has her agenda, and I have yours," Balchu said. "Med station for your back, then home to bed."

"Wait." Pam scowled at him. "Sapient being. Not your obedient lackey."

He wrapped an arm around her, then quirked an eyebrow. "Am I wrong about the med station? Am I wrong about bed? I'll even feed you whatever you want, my queen."

She leaned her forehead against his shoulder. "I suppose when you put it like that . . ."

Shady texted Balchu, "THANK YOU!!!" then stepped up alongside Rex. "Corona tonight?"

He wagged his tail. "I have plans to see Charlie and connect with his Family for a ride home. You are already included in those plans."

Orangeboro Medical Center, Re-Gen Unit

This time, no one tried to stop Rex. Especially not with Shady by his side.

He caught astonished looks in the Orangeboro Med Center lobby, saw a few fingers pointed their direction, smelled excitement or amazement from several people. But he and Shady were officially-recognized sapient beings, police officers in uniform, and also huge, intimidating dogs on a mission. Wisely, no one stood in their way.

Through their link, Rex normally had a sense of Charlie's general location. Now that Charlie was awake, it was back. Rex used it to augment the hospital floor plan he'd opened on his HUD. He and Shady soon stood in Charlie's doorway.

There he was! *At last! YES!!* Charlie looked up with a grin. Ted and Mimi smiled then stepped back from their son's bed.

YES! YES! YES! YES! YES! Rex darted to Charlie's bedside. He squeaked and wriggled, his whole body wagging in a transport of joy. *At last! Charlie!*

Then finally—*finally!*—he gave Charlie that long-delayed,

much-desired, in-depth sniff-over he'd been yearning to give him since Monday. The cast first. Rex detailed that fully. All around the edges, all across the chest, all along the arm. Then Charlie's face. His head, ears, neck. His other arm, belly, crotch, down each leg. In careful, exacting, forensic detail.

Rex sniffed and wagged and studied and savored that wonderful, individual scent profile, that beloved presence. Warm. Alive. Real. He quickly found that his partner still had a lot of recovering to do. Beneath the warmth and the personal scents, daunting unhealed injury remained.

But Rex also picked up overlying scents that spoke of Charlie's pride in him, his love, delight, and joy. These scents warmed Rex in places he hadn't realized were chilled. He rubbed his face against the part of Charlie's torso that wasn't encased in a heavy, immobilizing cast, drew in his partner's scent hungrily. "I missed you SO. MUCH."

Charlie's right hand stroked Rex's head, his scent and voice full of emotions so deep they resonated through the link. "Same here, partner. Same here." Charlie's IV-encumbered right arm pulled him close. He cradled Rex's big, heavy head, although the weight had already set up a tremor in his arm.

Rex snuggled his muzzle under Charlie's scratchy chin. He couldn't smell enough of his partner's living presence.

Somewhere off on the other side of the room, Shady, Ted, and Mimi exchanged quiet greetings.

"I think they're cute," Mimi said.

"In an enormous-black-wolf-dog-with-manly-wounded-cop sort of way," Ted said.

"Yeah, definitely cute," Shady agreed.

42

A FRONT-ROW SEAT ON HISTORY

Orangeboro Medical Center, Re-Gen Unit

Charlie roused from a deep doze early Saturday evening when his mother tapped lightly on his hospital door.

"You awake, kiddo?"

Charlie activated a control to raise his bed so he could sit. "Come in!" His day had worn him out, between physical therapy and talking Rex through a laundry list of anxieties while the Flitter Four and the Pack rehearsed for tonight. He checked the time. *Woah. Not much longer.*

On the other end of the brain link, Rex paused what felt like panting and pacing to focus on him. *You're awake.*

My Family's here.

Mama gave him a careful hug, mindful of the IV, and a kiss on his forehead. Papa, Aunt Hannah, and Uncle Hector followed, with variations on that theme. His Family members' hugs and kisses warmed him, but left him more tired than he wanted to admit. One of the machines he was hooked up to shifted tempo. His energy level notched up again, while his incipient headache faded into the background.

I'm glad you're awake. I want to be able to ask for advice if things come up. It's good to have you conscious and back in my link!

Charlie smiled. *Just consider me your emotional-support human, okay?* Not much else he could do for Rex tonight, but he meant to do that as well as possible.

Papa activated the vid-wall two meters past Charlie's feet, then lowered the brightness without even having to be asked. "Care for any particular feed?"

There were dozens. "That'll do." It was still set on the one from yesterday, when he'd watched Rex arrest Dr. Ordovich. He fumbled for the tinted visor on his bedside table, then slid it into place with a quiet sigh of relief. "I've been dozing. Has the Wheel Court returned a verdict yet on Dr. Ordovich's so-called diplomatic immunity?"

Aunt Hannah scowled. "Not yet. They heard arguments this afternoon, but no verdict so far."

"Rex says Masato's convinced they'll grant it, to pacify the Transmondians."

Hannah shook her head. "Masato always looks at the political angle, but that's not the purpose of the court. I believe Marshall, Douglass and King were the three-Justice bench empaneled. They're not noted for being politically expedient."

Aunt Hannah was a named partner in a legal firm that specialized in interstellar trade, with offices near the Civic Center. She made it her business to keep up with government affairs. Charlie'd bet she knew at least one of those Justices personally.

The wall-projection showed as big a crowd as Charlie'd ever seen in Central Plaza. The daylight was dimming rapidly and the mist had begun to rise, but he spotted sharp-eyed Ranan Executive Security officers in black uniforms among the crowd. Charlie'd worked enough event security to know both RES and OPD also would have plainclothes officers among the crowd. Vid-cams buzzed in large clouds above everyone's heads, most for news but some for surveillance. Uniformed police officers enforced the perimeter, but they kept a low profile in the peaceful crowd.

Through the link, Charlie felt Rex's jitters gradually grow. *It's always the most nerve-wracking before the event. Waiting sucks. Once things start to happen it won't be so bad, because you're busy.*

If you say so.

He had a sense that Rex was running a breathing pattern. *Where'd you learn that trick?*

From you. It helps sometimes.

Charlie's relatives rearranged chairs for a better view. "Best seat in the Borough," Papa said.

"Maybe. Maybe not," Mama said. "My parents did get a box seat in the Civic Auditorium."

"They have to 'represent,'" Aunt Hannah said.

Charlie smiled. Gran Annie and Gran Pepe seemed to enjoy dressing up and going out to events. Anytime the Family did something official, Annie's Head-of-Household status made her the Corona Family spokesperson.

"Corona got two tickets besides the ones for Annie and Pepe. The kids decided Caro and Andy definitely should have them," Papa said. "I'm happier right here with you."

"I appreciate it." Through the link, Charlie felt Rex's anxiety bump up a notch. *Steady.*

We're going.

"Things are happening," Aunt Hannah said.

Orangeboro officials began to assemble on the wide flat area at the top of the steps outside the Civic Center Auditorium. The Borough Council emerged first, resplendent in formal attire. There was Rona Peynirci, in a deep red and shimmering gold saree. Charlie spotted Beatriz Chan in green and silver robes, with a matching turban and a stunning emerald necklace. Mayor Idris wore a blue silk wrap. The men, similarly glamorous, wore silken jackets, hanbok, kente, or kilts.

Here came Chief Klein, tall and solemn in his dress blues. A murmur went through the crowd when Rex emerged, following the Chief. He'd been groomed within a centimeter of his life and rigged up in the formal harness of patent leather and sparkly golden bits that he'd only worn once before, at the Presentation Ceremony. Charlie smiled. *You look all shiny. And very impressive.*

He received a burst of irritation from Rex. *I'd better look good. My groomer fussed over me for an hour. Kept finding another hair out of place.*

The news feed anchor on the vid made note that Pack Leader Dieter-Nell walked alone because his partner, Medal of Valor recipient Detective Charles Morgan, had been critically injured in the dock breach, and was still in the hospital. The news service briefly added a small image of Charlie and his medal from a Remembrance Day ceremony, in an upper corner.

Reporters always went for the human-interest angles. No chance they'd leave him out of it. Charlie squirmed inwardly, as he always did at any mention of the damned medal. But he tried to keep his reaction internal, so he wouldn't offend Mama. She was immensely proud of the accursed thing.

Mama patted his hand, careful of the IV. "They have to talk about it. People are interested."

Charlie grimaced. She knew him too well. "Hate to steal thunder from Rex. This is his show."

Behind Rex came a short, dark-skinned SBI agent, flanked by two other agents who were much taller. Was the small woman SSA Adeyeme? The news-anchor's running commentary confirmed it. Charlie stared at her. *So that's my rival?*

Not a rival, Rex protested. *It's true I love Elaine, but you're my partner. No one can take your place.*

Chagrin filled him. *She's 'Elaine,' now? Have you become Command Staff chums?*

As a matter of fact, yes. A burst of pleasure came through the link. The vid-image of Rex wagged his tail, then sobered for a parade-sit between Klein and . . . *Elaine.*

Now the rest of the Pack, their partners in dress blues like the

Chief, emerged to take their places on the steps to the Plaza. Those steps were growing more crowded by the second.

Charlie took a moment to admire the beauty of the assembled Pack. Other than their marked resemblance to Terran wolves on a grand scale, each XK9 was magnificent in his or her own way. They ranged in color from Rex's all-black to Crystal's pure white. Black did dominate several individuals' coats. Shady was black-sable with a tan undercoat, Tuxedo black with white ruff, legs, chest and tail-tip, Victor a tricolor, black with white and tan points, and Razor a classic "police dog" black and tan, with a tan body, plus a black saddle and face.

But Scout was a rich dark brown. Cinnamon and Elle both were a glorious rich russet-red color. Elle had a white ruff, legs and tail-tip like her mate Tuxedo's, but Cinnamon had no white spots at all. Petunia was a striking bright golden. Like Rex, the entire Pack had been dolled up in patent-leather harnesses and groomed till they glistened. Their badges glinted in the artificial lights that came up as the daylight dimmed.

The Pack is beautiful, Charlie said to Rex, a half-second before Papa said it out loud.

To me, too. Rex might be at parade-sit, but his tail twitched.

New movement rippled through the crowd. UPOs and RES officers strove to open a wider path to HQ. Soon a line of shiny black government cars rolled into view. Small green, violet, black and white Ranan flags fluttered from mounts on their front fenders.

People began to cheer and wave small Orangeboro or Ranan flags. The cars proceeded slowly through the crowd, then stopped at the base of the steps. An RES officer strode forward to open the first door.

The cheers diminished when Premier Eliana Iskander emerged, tall and proud in a gown of pink and ivory, sparkling all over with diamonds. Her pale hair had been sculpted into an elaborate coiffure. More tiers of diamonds cascaded over the curves of her bodice like a glittering waterfall. Head erect, chin elevated, she strode forward. Her companion in the car emerged next, a tall man in a black silk suit with red accents. The commentator identified him as Transmondian Ambassador Ryder Nunzio. Charlie frowned. *Did you know Nunzio was coming?*

He thinks he's here to collect Ordovich. Through the link, Charlie sensed the growl Rex suppressed.

Iskander and Nunzio made their way up the steps. They swept past Klein, Rex, Adeyeme and the Pack, neither giving them more than a glance. But they stopped to greet the Mayor and Councilmembers with nods, smiles and handshakes.

The first car departed. The second pulled up at the base of the steps.

Human Vice Premier Sacha Guzmán emerged, then turned back and bent to assist his companion. Kizzitikti Zhokittik was the Ozzirikkian Vice Premier. RES officers hurried to assist kin as well.

Charlie frowned. *Guzmán looks more gaunt than he did during the election.*

The venerable Zhokittik, with mostly silver-white fur and a deeply furrowed blue-black face, moved with care. As an honored Kirikki, ki held an exalted status among kiniz people. At kin age, human-normal gravity must quickly become painful, but ki had made a point of coming anyway. That deserved respect. A new cheer went up when people saw Guzmán. He was an Orangeboro native, so the crowd was welcoming a favorite son home. Charlie hoped they were cheering Zhokittik on, too. Those steps must look mountainous to kin, yet ki tackled them with stolid determination.

Unlike Iskander and Nunzio, Guzmán and Zhokittik paused to acknowledge the law enforcement people. Guzmán clasped hands with Chief Klein.

"Did you know Guzmán and Klein are personal friends?" Aunt Hannah asked. "They were schoolmates in the same neighborhood learning center. They've remained close ever since."

Charlie felt Rex's excitement rising. Guzmán and Klein exchanged a few words, then the Human Vice Premier turned to Rex. Rex stood, tail wagging excitedly, and extended a paw. Guzmán offered a comment to Klein, then accepted and shook the offered paw, just as he would give a human a handshake. He nodded to Rex, made another comment to Klein, then moved on to Adeyeme.

Rex stared after him, head cocked. Puzzlement resonated through the link. *Human Vice Premier Guzmán just asked the Chief if I was 'the expensive one,' and Klein answered, 'perceptive as ever, Sacha.' But I thought we all were expensive. Do you know what he meant?*

I know there was some variation in the prices charged for each of you, when OPD bought you, Charlie replied. *I think it depended on how many specialties and certifications you had.*

Oh. I did have a great many. I didn't think about that. In the vid-image, Rex snapped his ears flat. *I do not like to think about how much humans paid for us. It makes me sad.*

Put your ears up and try to focus, Charlie advised. *We can talk about it more later.*

That's almost exactly what Chief Klein just said. Rex returned to his parade-sit, put his ears up. *Klein is more guarded than you are, however.* A rush of pleasure came through the link. *I'm so very glad you're awake!*

Me, too, partner. Me, too.

Rex greeted Zhokittik next.

Ki made a point of meeting his eyes, shook his paw, then nodded. They exchanged some brief words that . . . Charlie gasped. *Were you just speaking Pan-Ozzirikkian?*

Zhokittik responded with the fang-flashing gape that was the ozzirikkian parallel to a human smile, then moved on to greet Adeyeme.

Klein gave Rex an astonished look.

He lolled his tongue, tail wagging. *Shady taught me some phrases this afternoon. I thanked Vice Premier Zhokittik for sacrificing to come to hard gravity today and expressed a hope ki would find our presentation worthwhile.*

I think you made a friend. Good work!

A third car had drawn up to the base of the steps. Director Perri of the SBI emerged with little fanfare and advanced up the steps. She stopped to speak with Klein, Rex, Elaine, and the two LSAs, then continued on to the Borough's elected officials.

Their news feed switched to showing advertisements. Papa muted it to 2D and a whisper.

Aunt Hannah turned to Charlie. "Guzmán lingered with Rex and Klein for a while. Did you get a sense of what they said? And what was up with Zhokittik? What did Rex say to kin?"

Charlie opened his mouth to answer, but then a new person knocked on his door.

"Hello? Am I intruding?"

Charlie froze. That sounded like Hildie.

She poked her head in through the door with a worried smile. "I won't come in, if you'd prefer I didn't." She wore a blue standard-issue coverall, her long, dark hair pulled back in the ponytail she'd customarily preferred for 1-G. She looked just as she had in the old days, when she'd been his dearest friend.

An avalanche of pleasure, pain, shame, and yearning made it hard to speak. "In-intruding? Um, no. Not at all." Charlie's mind reeled. *Why would she bother to come here?*

She met his eyes. *Smiled* at him. "It's good to see you awake. You gave us a real scare."

Mama sprang from her chair. "Won't you please join us? The dignitaries just arrived. The dogs' demonstration will begin soon. Have you eaten?"

"Thanks, Mimi. I don't mean to intrude on a Family gathering, but I wanted to see for myself that Charlie really is awake and doing better." She walked to his bedside. Her gaze searched him, but it was warm with affection, not cold with judgment as he'd feared for years.

What is she doing here? By what miracle is she willing to talk to me? Charlie reached up, heart pounding, dragging his IV line. "As you see, I'm at least conscious, now."

She took his hand with a grin, placed her fingers on his wrist. "Nice, strong pulse this time. Maybe you'll survive."

She'd barely changed at all from his memories of happier times. Same lovely hazel eyes, same lively face, same grin, though maybe a little more careworn around the edges. With a sergeant's stripes on her sleeve, now, too. Her fingers still held his hand.

Charlie scrambled for something intelligent to say. "Congratulations on the promotion."

Her mouth acquired a wry tilt. "Mm. Promotion to more formwork and headaches, mostly, but thanks. Congrats back at you, Detective." She hadn't let go of his hand. The IV pinched, but he didn't care.

From the feel of you, something wonderful just happened, Rex said.

Hildie's here. I can't believe she's here and not angry with me.

He received the impression of a scornful snort from Rex. *Oh, please. She's in love with you. Why would she be angry?*

Charlie's mind balked at this. After all the times he'd humiliated himself in front of her? All the years he'd avoided her, unwilling to risk her scorn? All the agonized self-denigration? No, Rex must be wrong. There was no way Hildie . . . But she still held his hand. She smiled at him with apparent pleasure. She sure didn't look angry or disgusted or scornful. *How is that possible?*

"Why don't you sit here?" Mama offered Hildie her chair, next to Charlie's bedside.

"Thanks. Oh, gosh. Sorry." Hildie freed the IV line from where it had caught on part of the bed's framework, then gently lowered Charlie's hand. "That probably hurt." She sat, still fussing over the IV. Still with her hand on his.

"I didn't mind." The warmth of her touch seemed to radiate up his arm and fill his whole body. He couldn't stop smiling at her. In the darkened room behind her, Papa brought in a new chair for his mother. Charlie's elders rearranged themselves. Hildie didn't move her hand away. Charlie didn't move his, either.

Rex stiffened, hyper-alert.

Rex? Charlie tore his gaze away from Hildie, checked his HUD. Nothing there. *Rex?* Charlie sensed hackles up, a fierce growl, urgent movement toward some objective. He blinked, refocused on Hildie and his Family. "Uh-oh. Something's happened."

43

TREACHERY AND REVELATION

Orangeboro Civic Center Auditorium Entrance, Rotunda, and Mayor's Office

Chief Klein halted in the middle of the main corridor to the Civic Center Auditorium. Rex darted aside to avoid running into him, then cocked his head at his boss.

Klein pulled out of a HUD stare, focused on Rex. "We have a situation at the Mayor's Office." He turned to Elaine, who'd stopped as well, along with Perri and the LSAs. "Would you please go on ahead? Get everything in place for the presentation. Joslyn will help you. I need to check on this." He hesitated, gave Rex a thoughtful look, then nodded. "Rex, you're with me."

"Keep us posted!" Elaine called after them.

Klein strode quickly to the Rotunda. Rex trotted at his side. The Chief punched an override on the elevator to the Executive Level.

Rex? Charlie's mental voice came through the link, loaded with worry.

The elevator opened. Klein and Rex stepped inside. *Chief and I are headed for Idris's office.* Klein activated the Police Express function. They shot upward. Rex opened his perceptions to Charlie. *I want your observations. Call it a precaution. Klein smells worried.*

Ready assent returned from Charlie. *Not sure what I can do, except maybe sound an alarm if you need one. Stay safe! Keep him safe, too.*

That's my plan. Thanks.

On the other end of the link Charlie turned away and spoke to his Family.

The elevator slowed, stopped. The doors slid open. Two dress-uniformed UPOs, three RES agents, and a couple of people who looked to be aides blocked their view.

Rex and Klein stepped out, strode forward.

The people nearest the elevator jumped aside to give them ample clearance.

At the center of the group stood Premier Iskander, stiff, indignant and reeking of anger. She glared at Mayor Idris. Idris scowled back fists clenched, her scent ablaze with fury. Council Chair Chan stood next to Iskander. She'd crossed her arms and directed a poisonous frown at Idris. Rona Peynirci faced her, also with arms crossed.

Ambassador Nunzio stood back from the others a pace. *That's interesting.* Rex could almost see the anger smoking off of most of them. *Why does Nunzio smell worried?*

What does he know, that the others don't? Charlie asked.

Idris glanced toward the elevator, then straightened. "Here's the man you should talk to!" She gestured at Klein. "Why haven't you asked him?"

Iskander gave Klein a cold, contemptuous look. "His mind is closed. I hoped you might be more flexible."

The Mayor's scowl deepened. "You mean more malleable."

"Now, Ailani," Chan protested. "That's not fair. She's giving you an 'out.'"

Iskander's head chopped a sharp nod. "You should listen to

your Council Chair. Use your executive override to expedite things."

Idris shook her head. "Why should I do that? If you're so certain of the court's decision, why not wait for it like the rest of us? You can take your damned victory lap after that."

"Time is of the essence," Iskander said. "Do you really want to cross the office of the Premier? When you've just brought the whole station into disarray?"

"The Council vote—" Idris began.

"Doesn't apply," Iskander cut her off.

Rex stepped forward. People shrank back to let him through. He stopped a few centimeters from Nunzio. "Ambassador, what do you know that the rest of us do not? What fills your scent factors with such uneasy worry?"

Nunzio froze. He no longer smelled worried. Now he smelled terrified.

Idris and Peynirci turned their attention to Nunzio and Rex.

"Good question," Peynirci said. "Ambassador, please answer."

Nunzio flinched away from a prod by Rex's nose. "I don't have to answer a dog."

"Pay no attention to the dog," Iskander said. "He's irrelevant."

"But enormous," one of the aides muttered, giving Rex the same kind of side-eye as Nunzio. "And standing right there."

Rex growled. "Premier, I hope you realize I can hear you."

"I hardly think *irrelevant* is an accurate characterization, Madame Premier." Peynirci shook her head. "He's the reason we're all here. He and his Pack. And what they are."

"This argument wastes everyone's time." Iskander avoided looking at Rex. "Let's get things moving!"

"I'm not inclined to hurry." Idris gave a slow shake of her head. "I think we should go downstairs and watch the demonstration. We can address this afterwards."

Iskander glared at her. "I'm very busy. You may have time to sit in a theater and watch a play, but I don't."

"Yet you came all this way to Orangeboro," Idris said.

"A decision I have come to regret. I thought you were bright enough to accept reality. That you might see reason. That you might have the courtesy to expedite a simple request from our foremost ally's ambassador."

Idris shook her head. "I don't—"

Rex's HUD beeped on his news channel. He glanced at it. "COURT DENIES IMMUNITY CLAIM," the headline read.

Idris stared at the Premier, outraged. "You already knew! You lied to me!"

Klein frowned. "She thought she might be able to prevail upon you before the news was announced." He turned to the Premier. "The answer is no, Madame Premier. You can't have Ordovich."

Orangeboro Civic Center Auditorium

The audience inside the Civic Auditorium began to applaud. Rex's anxiety surged. He stood backstage, out of sight in the right wing, and paced as quietly as possible. He reminded himself that Caro, Andy, Gran Annie, and Gran Pepe would be out there, pulling for him. Other "XK9 Families," too, as well as Perri, the two Vice Premiers, and the Council Members who'd supported the Pack yesterday.

Iskander, however, would not. She and Ambassador Nunzio had departed, enraged, before this event started. Two fewer "hostiles" in the audience, taking up valuable seats? Fine with Rex.

Most of the stage was dark, but one spotlight followed Elaine to a podium downstage right. She climbed two steps to reach its microphone. How could she stay so outwardly calm, when she smelled as nervous as Rex? He struggled not to hyperventilate or pant so loudly the acoustics would pick it up.

"Good evening." Elaine introduced herself. "Tonight's presentation is an attempt to respond to two separate issues, in a way that answers both with a single demonstration. One is the question of XK9 sapience. Chief Klein on behalf of the Orangeboro Police Department, my own agency, and the Orangeboro Council now all have come out with statements affirming that we believe the XK9s of the OPD are sapient beings. Further, we believe they should be treated with the respect, and afforded the rights that status demands. We believe tonight's demonstration will help you understand exactly why we believe this so strongly."

That was Rex's cue. He walked as silently as possible, with a terrifying storm of "butterflies" in his gut, to the center-stage location he'd scent-marked with his feet this afternoon. The stage lay in such complete darkness that he could do this while remaining invisible to the audience. Being an all-black dog had its advantages. He turned to face the audience, a mass presence he could smell far better than see.

"The other issue," Elaine continued, "is the much-criticized SBI decision to make use of a completely new, highly accurate forensic approach to wreckage analysis. It was created and implemented by four XK9 officers of the OPD. Earlier this week, it was scrutinized and certified as valid—indeed 'cutting edge'— by two prominent experts in the field, Dr. Hakim Fulbert of the Wheel Three Institute of Technology, and Dr. SCISCO-3750 of Orangeboro's own Station Polytechnic University.

"I am therefore honored to introduce a very special spokesperson now. He will explain how this technique was first developed and verified. He and three of his Packmates will then demonstrate with a reconstruction of their first, much smaller-scale, investigation. We have discovered that these exacting techniques scale up superbly for our analysis of the *Izgubil* wreckage." She turned toward Rex. "It is my intense pleasure to introduce XK9 Pack Leader, OPD Detective Officer, and Reserve Special Agent Rex Dieter-Nell."

A single spotlight knifed down to pin Rex, center-stage, in the heart of its glare. Rex concentrated on breathing evenly. He smelled Elaine's pleasure and confidence in him, echoed and compounded by Charlie's love and awe coming through the link.

That's it. Steady on, Charlie said.

Steady on. Got it. "Thank you, SSA Adeyeme." Rex arched his neck, ears up, and strode downstage to stop at the apron, even with Elaine's podium. The spotlight followed him. Vid-cams buzzed, hovering above, below, and all around him.

You look magnificent, and more than a little imposing, partner. Charlie's pride in him, in having been Chosen by him, buoyed Rex's courage.

"Gentlepersons, I hope you will listen a moment while I explain how my Packmates and I developed this technique." Rex and Joslyn had worked out a way to route his vocalizer directly into the PA system. Now his voice filled the auditorium. "We first developed it—"

Gasps echoed through the huge room. A rising babble of voices rippled in the darkness. Heartsick dread rose within Rex, soured his gut and made the "butterflies" threaten to explode out into the world. Even though they'd warned people he would explain, even though he'd been on news feeds just yesterday, arresting Dr. Ordovich, they *still* were reacting like this?

Rex stopped speaking. He waited, tried to look serene.

That's good, Charlie reassured. *Give them a minute to deal with this. Remember, most people have never heard an XK9 speak at all. They don't know what you can do.*

Rex panted quietly in the spotlight's heat, but he held himself still.

The babble of the crowd grew louder. A few people stood, as if contemplating flight. The scent factors in the auditorium took a subtle shift.

Silence isn't going to be enough. "Please sit down. Please listen," Rex said. "My Packmates and I came to Orangeboro to protect you. Your fear fills us with grief."

A new round of shuffling and murmuring ran through the crowd.

How do they smell? Charlie asked.

Better. Many are ashamed of their fear, now. After all, it's not as if they've never seen a non-human sapient before. I believe they've begun to remember that they came because they were curious.

"Please, sit down," he repeated. "Please, stay and listen."

The audience's murmurs faded. People began to sit down.

"Thank you," Rex said. "Thank you for your willingness to hear us." Then he told them the story of the flitter wreck in eastern Transmondia, and of the "game" he, Tux, Cinnie, and Cryssie had played.

You've been practicing. Charlie's approval rolled through the link in a warm wave. *That's a lot smoother than the version I heard this afternoon.*

Rex wagged his tail. "You do not need to take my word for this reconstruction," he concluded his account. "Our Transmondian teachers sternly instructed us to destroy our wreckage-reconstruction files, and we did so to the best of our ability. But we have had gifted, expert help from Station Polytechnic. A new technique has recovered them to a startling level of excellence. It is something of a digital marvel that we can share them with you tonight. Please join me in thanking the cybernetics experts at Station Polytechnic." SCISCO hadn't allowed him to be any more specific than that.

Someone started clapping. Others picked it up, until the entire audience had expressed its approval. The applause might be for the expert help from S-Poly, but the wave of affirming sound washed over Rex. He stood at its focus, the primary recipient. *This is unexpectedly gratifying. What a pleasant experience.*

Charlie's chuckle rippled back through the link on a swell of amusement. *You've always loved being at the center of admiration, admit it.*

Rex wagged his tail again. *That's true.*

But all too soon, the audience quieted. Time for the rest of the show.

"Thank you," Rex said. "I will now yield the floor to OPD Lt. Detective Marisol Patel, who will explain her team's research into the Transmondian Aviation Agency's records. After that, XK9 Detective Officers and Reserve Special Agents Tuxedo Moondog-Carrie, Cinnamon Lightfoot-Floss, Crystal Basho-Dancer, and I will demonstrate our technique."

44

REQUIEM AND REST

Orangeboro Civic Center Auditorium

When the last piece clicked into place from Crystal's reconstruction, Rex had hoped there might be applause. Perhaps cheering? It was, after all, rather impressive once he looked at it.

He wasn't prepared for silence.

Before the presentation, there'd been the shifting and murmuring of a large crowd. When the house lights went down, the crowd-sounds diminished, but shuffling feet, seat-squeaks, a soft murmur here and there, or the occasional cough had continued. This was different. It was as if that entire, enormous audience of several thousand people had all frozen where they sat and held their breaths in perfect unison.

The buzz of the vid-cams was the only sound for several long, terrible seconds.

Then it was as if everyone released their breath at the same moment. "Wow!" someone cried. The applause started ragged, then grew. And grew. They clapped. They whistled. They stood up and shouted "Bravo!" or "Opa!" or . . . several other things Rex wasn't quite sure about, but they sounded positive. In a few more seconds, everyone was on their feet. They all stood up and applauded and applauded and applauded until Rex worried their arms might get sore.

Eventually their applause slowed. The house lights stayed down, the XK9s stayed on stage, and the audience gradually realized the presentation wasn't over. They sat back down a few at a time in clumps and clusters, until all were back in their seats and the place had fallen back to the soft, murmuring undertone of a waiting audience.

For the demonstration, Rex, Tux, Cinnamon and Crystal had taken positions in a semicircle, with Rex at downstage right, Cinnamon center right, Crystal center left, and Tux downstage left. They'd narrated their thoughts and process, while the image files SCISCO had resurrected were projected above their heads, then brought together above downstage center for a final combining of parts.

But now the flitter-reconstruction projection darkened.

The rest of the Pack moved onstage from the wings to fill in the semicircle.

Rex lowered his chin. Everyone went to parade-sit.

The audience stilled.

Crystal lifted her nose to howl a high, sweet note. She moved from that into a melody that soared and swooped, then was joined by Tux's rich bass.

Crystal and Tux improvised a soaring, joyous duet for a minute or less. The rest of the Pack added their voices to a rising background chorus in support of them. But then the duet shifted to a minor key. The Pack's chorus modulated downward. They howled of lost love, lost hope, despair. Crystal's glorious soprano rose one last time—then cut off, mid-note. Tux's bass counterpoint did the same, a moment later. The chorus of the remaining Pack members' voices swelled in a howl of loss, of grief, of desolation, then faded away like an echo on the wind.

For a few moments there was utter silence in the Civic Auditorium. Rex smelled a multitude of anguished responses. When they'd practiced that afternoon, there'd been tears on more than one human listener's face. Shady had predicted well. This was a language both species spoke.

Rex stood, then walked to front-center of the apron to address the audience. "Thank you for listening to our lament for two of our fallen friends, Fernie Tintin-Brenna and Chaser Nigel-Glory. We were not certain you would stay, if we warned you we planned to howl."

That earned him a ripple of rueful laughter.

"But we are, at our hearts, a hunting Pack. In the years we have been a team, we have attuned ourselves to each other. However, howling is not only for hunting. It also is for joining our hearts with our voices and singing how we feel.

"Please let me tell you about Fernie and Chaser. They were a mated pair, friends of ours, members of XK9 Gen-48, just like us. They trained often with us when we were puppies. We loved them. They almost chose to come to Orangeboro, but they were excited to go to Neopolis together instead, where they hoped to begin long lives of service in law enforcement.

"They were some of our best, our most brilliant generalists. But this week, according to Project Director Ordovich's own statement, the XK9 Project has . . . I shall not use the euphemism 'put down.'

"The Project murdered them, because they were 'insubordinate.' Our dear friends are now dead, because they committed the capital crime of daring to be themselves."

He shuddered, dipped his head, then raised it again. "That is what the phony 'brain-implant recall' is all about. Our implants are not defective. We got a warrant to test them, and not one had a flaw.

"But we fear other agencies may also have gotten such 'recall notices.' They may not realize they are a trap. The Project does not intend to repair bad implants. It is a fake excuse. They mean to destroy the evidence of the sapient-trafficking crime they have committed, by destroying us. For any XK9 unlucky enough to be sent back for the recall, it means at the very least that their brains will be disabled. For many, it will mean death.

"We cannot remain silent. Too many lives are at stake, not only in Orangeboro, but wherever there are XK9s. Please help us spread that word."

Orangeboro Civic Center Auditorium, the Orangeboro Medical Center Re-Gen Unit, and Corona Tower

It took a while for the audience to file out of the Civic Center. Many chattered with excitement, their voices and gestures animated. Others moved more quietly. Some frowned as if bemused or overwhelmed.

Rex caught a quick glimpse of the Corona Tower group, who waved and wished him luck. Then Bill Sloane stepped into his path, still smelling faintly of the hospital, with a girl about the same age as Charlie's 10-year-old cousin Owen. Rex halted, tail and ears up. He sniffed the girl over, to her evident delight.

"I am Rex Dieter-Nell," he said. "I bet your name is Becky."

Her face and scent factors lit up with delight. "How did you *know*?"

He lolled his tongue, shared a look with Bill. "Your father mentioned you are interested in XK9s."

Becky would've happily talked with Rex all night, but Bill soon gently steered her away. "XK9 Rex has had a long, busy day. So have I, and so have you. It's time to go home." He paused just one moment longer. "Please tell Shady how much we appreciated the tickets."

Rex wagged his tail. "I promise I shall."

Once he could get free, Rex found Shady on the Mezzanine of the Civic Auditorium, with Pam, Balchu, and Balchu's parents. The parents seemed to have a lot of questions, and Shady seemed to enjoy talking with them. Rex interrupted long enough to touch noses with her. "I mean to go see Charlie."

"Give him my love," Shady said. "I would like to stay here a little longer."

Balchu's father smiled and stroked her head. "We've been having a fascinating discussion."

Rex accepted a ride in a patrol auto-nav to Orangeboro Medical Center, then went to the Re-Gen Unit.

Charlie'd been entertaining his parents, aunt, uncle . . . Oh, that was interesting. Hildie, from the *Triumph*, sat next to Charlie's bed. She was holding his hand.

The Family offered Rex a sound-muted but enthusiastic welcome. Charlie was possibly the only patient left awake on this floor, so they mimed clapping, cheering, and waving to greet him.

Rex lolled his tongue, wagged his tail, then went to Charlie. A perfunctory sniff-over sufficed this time. His scent hadn't changed much from yesterday, and it was easy to see and smell how far he'd overextended himself tonight. Charlie's right hand was covered with Hildie's trace, her own deep affection and delight clear to read. Rex found residuals from his partner's pleasure at her presence, too.

Strange to think of Charlie with someone besides Pam. But Shady said that was not to be, so it was good that Rex would likely see a lot more of Hildie in the future. Hmm. And possibly also her cat. He flicked his ears. That concern could wait.

He nuzzled his partner, savored his scent. "I owe you a lot of gratitude. You put me onto more than one helpful scent today." Rex used the vocalizer so the Family would hear. "I had to come say thank you and tell you again how I love you."

Charlie smiled and stroked the side of Rex's head, but his exhaustion soon overwhelmed all other scents. He must sleep, if he was to heal. Rex kept his visit far shorter than he wished. "I shall return," he promised.

Charlie offered a single nod, eyes already closed, mental presence already foggy with sleep.

Rex tiptoed out with the rest of the humans.

Beyond the Re-Gen Unit, in more public space, Mimi and Ted turned to Hildie. They thanked her for coming and urged her to return.

She grinned. "I'll come back to check on him tomorrow."

Rex wagged his tail. From the smell of things, that wouldn't be the last time.

Hannah ran her hand down Rex's back. "How does it feel to be an interstellar celebrity?"

Rex lowered his head, hunched his back. "Weird. Daunting."

She eyed him, as if evaluating his words, or . . . something. "OPD has legal counsel, but I suspect you and the Pack will need your own as well. We are in for some turbulence, I think."

Rex cocked his head at her. "Will you help?"

Her brow puckered. "I'd like to assist, but you're probably going to need a team."

A new surge of concern stabbed his chest. A team? That sounded complicated. He took a careful breath. "Will you help me assemble them?"

She smiled. "It will be my honor. When can we talk? *Not* tonight, please," she added quickly.

Rex lolled his tongue. "Elaine says she wants us to return on Monday as rested and un-distracted as possible, so we are back on top of our game. She has given most of the investigative team tomorrow off."

Hannah chuckled softly. "Good call. You guys have had a hell of a wild week, but I doubt the investigation will end anytime soon."

Rex nodded. "Two of our earliest sources of evidence have been exhausted, but we have only begun on the debris. Unfortunately, I think I shall be needed for press conferences tomorrow, and possibly a talk with the Human Vice Premier."

"What will you do now? Tonight, I mean? Go home to Corona? Go back to Shady's?"

"I shall ask Shady to stay with me again tonight at Corona Tower. That living room floor at Pam's is a torture device."

She grinned. "D'you and Shady need a ride? If she's still at the Civic Center, that would be on our way. I'll tell Ted we need a bigger car."

Rex called Shady on the com.

"Yes, I am still at the Civic Center. Chief Klein has deployed patrol units to give all XK9s and their partners rides home, so they cannot be accosted by reporters—or anyone else."

Rex's breath caught. Her words sent an uncomfortable slither through his gut. "I had not thought about that possibility. Do you believe a large private car would be secure enough?"

"I think I should ask."

Special permission for a large private car to enter the OPD sally port sufficed to get them in and out with optimal security. Meanwhile, Pam and Balchu gratefully accepted the patrol unit ride.

Rex, Shady, and the Corona Family humans did their initial catching up with each other on the seven-kilometer drive home. They went separately to their apartments from the underground garage.

"Welcome home, Rex! Welcome, Shady!" The apartment door swung wide for them. Lights turned on. The place smelled like it always did, except for a distinct lack of Charlie's recent scent. The housekeeping functions and programmed windows had kept it aired out and cleaned.

Shady went straight to the kitchen, then stepped onto the dispenser's weighing unit.

"Hello again, Shady. You have lost almost half a kilogram since you last ate here. You will get some extra food tonight." A shower of kibbles filled a bowl.

Shady sprang off with a delighted wag. "I want to live here always! Pam never does that!"

Rex lolled his tongue but muted his enthusiasm. "Have you brought this up to Pam?"

Shady growled. "We do not agree on this point."

"Humans live with their mates. Ozzirikkians live with their mates, too, as I understand it." Rex liked the direction this logic-chain led. "And why choose Pam and Balchu's living-room floor when there is my bed?"

"That floor is very hard." Her ears went down. The stress in her scent shot up. "But Pam gets extremely upset."

"Surely she would understand that you wish to live with your mate. Ask her if she would rather live with the patrol partner she had before you, or with Balchu?"

Shady had begun to pant with anxiety. "I did not have much success with that argument. And working with her is horrible when we fight. This is going to take time."

Rex nuzzled her neck, laid his chin across her withers. Had he pressured her too much? "Breathe. Relax. Bring it up again when you are ready. Give her some time to think about it, too. Meanwhile, my soft, warm, delightful bed, my generous food dispenser, and I shall always be here for you."

She leaned against him, heaved a long, worried sigh. "Let us eat and talk about other things."

They ate, but XK9 meals never lasted long. After supper, they talked about Charlie and Hildie, about Hildie's cat, about Rex's meeting with Bill's daughter Becky, and the thanks Bill had asked Rex to relay. They worked on ideas about how to find more members of Elmo Smart's crew and decided to suggest them to Elaine on Monday. They did not talk about a looming government crisis, or potentially needing legal representation by a team of skilled attorneys. Rex wasn't ready to think about those tonight.

They strolled together onto the portside outer balcony that opened from both Rex's bedroom and Charlie's. Below them, the valley lay shrouded in fog. Mist reached higher than Corona Tower's rooftop garden, although here on the fifth-floor level the haze was thin enough to see through, to the stars. They blazed brighter than either of Chayko's little moons and seemed to hang just outside the Station's sky-windows.

Rex glanced to leeward, then to spinward. Despite the fog and the trailing sweet potato vines that bracketed the balcony, he still could see the counter-intuitive upward bend of Wheel Two's bizarre "horizons." But somehow that geographical quirk bothered him less than it used to. He even kind of liked it. It felt like . . . home. The upward curve reminded him of a pixel-line smile on SCISCO's android face.

He flicked his ears. *Huh.*

Perhaps it *was* a taste that could be acquired.

THE END

WHAT HAPPENS NEXT?

One of the best ways to help an author is to write a review!
If you enjoyed this book, please rate and/or review it!
Sign up for **Jan's monthly newsletter** at:
https://deft-author-4054.ck.page/75da0e4ccc

The XK9 "Bones" Trilogy Continues!

Rex, Charlie, Shady, the rest of the Pack, and their SBI colleagues may have passed one hurdle—but they still have to catch a mass-murderer who blows up spacecraft.

The Pack still has to figure out how to function in practical reality as sapient beings with full Citizens' rights.

And the very fact of their existence means they have enemies in places they never suspected.

Turn the page to read Chapter One of *A Bone to Pick*, Book Two of the XK9 "Bones" Trilogy!

A BONE TO PICK-CHAPTER ONE
CROP INSPECTION

Rana Station Wheel Two, Orangeboro, 9th Precinct, Terrace Eight, Corona Tower

"What is that dark thing in Bonita's quinoa patch?" XK9 Shady Jacob-Belle dialed her vocalizer low, flattened her ears, and growled. Unease slithered in her gut. She drew back from the balcony's railing.

Her mate Rex had been gazing toward the starry nighttime sky-windows with a dreamy look on his furry black face. Now he crouched beside her in the shadows, tense and focused. He stared toward the quinoa. "I am not sure." Like her, he'd lowered his volume as far as it would go.

Together they peered through gaps in the trailing curtain of sweet potato vines that hung down from the rooftop garden on the level above them. The leafy vine tendrils provided a handy impromptu blind.

Through their brain link, Shady felt her partner Pam rouse from an exhausted sleep. Physically Pam was at home, seven kilometers away in Orangeboro's Fifth Precinct Market Garden Neighborhood. But their brain link gave her the ability to be aware of what Shady was doing. *Shady?* Pam's mental voice came across drowsy and disoriented. *You okay?*

For now. Stand by, Shady answered. Whatever lurked a hundred meters away in their neighbor's field, it was roughly human-sized. Shady's hackles rose with a prickle of foreboding. All she could see in the darkness was a lumpy shadow among the meter-high quinoa stalks. Veils of mist drifted on thermals up the clifflike terraces from the river far below. Some were too thick to see through. Air currents carried scents from the quinoa patch away, not toward her.

She stifled an urge to bark. Better stay silent until they knew more. It might be nothing. But it also might be a Transmondian agent, here to spy on Rex's Corona Tower home. Spy, or do something worse.

Shall I come out there to you? Pam seemed wider awake now.

Be ready to call it in but stay put for the moment. There may be a simple fix.

Shady activated the neural Heads-Up Display of her Cyber-netically-Assisted Perception equipment, then shifted to the thermal-imaging setting. A man's hot, white form blazed into view among the dark, much-cooler stalks. He'd positioned himself about a meter from Rim Eight Road. "Damn. Definitely a man out there."

At her side, Rex's deep growl rumbled like thunder. "Not. On. My. Watch." He rose from his crouch, then whirled toward his bedroom door. No light flicked on when he entered. He must've used the com in his CAP to disable the motion sensor.

She followed, of one accord with him. On a different night they might have been less alarmed, although no night was good for prowlers. But tonight their world had changed, very much against the Transmondian government's wishes. The humans of Orangeboro and Rana Habitat Space Station had publicly declared to the Universe that XK9s were not mere forensic tools, but sapient beings.

News feeds all over Alliance Space had broadcast the presentation that Rex, Shady, and the rest of the Pack had given to demonstrate some of their capabilities. They'd designed it to show that XK9s were capable of sapient-level thought.

The government of Transmondia had tried to stop the presentation. They'd launched hot rebuttals the moment broadcasts began. Transmondian government officials, as well as the government itself, were the XK9 Project's major backers. They'd sold XK9s to agencies all over Planet Chayko, and planned expansions far beyond Rana Station. Premium dogs sold for millions of novi, a lucrative trade that would end if XK9s were declared sapient and shielded from trafficking by Alliance-wide laws.

I'm calling it in, Pam said. *I'm getting dressed.*

Shady's gut tightened. Her hackles prickled anew.

"Head for the garage," Rex said. "We can swing through the orchard. Approach from the back of the property. I imagine he will be focused more toward the road, with its potential traffic. He may not expect us to come from the other direction." Rex had lived here more than two months. He knew the layout of the two-hectare property far better than Shady, who'd only visited a couple of nights.

She and her mate moved silent as wraiths through the apartment, then six flights down. They passed rack upon rack of seedlings, bathed in blue light and fastened all the way down the leeward wall of the stairwell. The young plants' vigorous, fecund smell hung thick in the air, laced with faint, faded scent-trace from Family members—but not from Rex's human partner, Charlie Morgan. Charlie was currently in the hospital. The doctors had brought him out of his re-gen coma on Friday, but he still wasn't healed.

I alerted Dispatch, Pam reported. *Your backup's on the way.*

Thanks. Shady passed this on to Rex. Gratitude for Pam's conscious presence and backup through the link filled her with a warm swell of affection. Poor Charlie had worn himself out, staying up to watch the XK9s' presentation on the vid screen in his hospital room. He probably was deep asleep right now, unable to advise or comfort Rex.

Mist-borne odors of hours-ago supper and the big oak tree at the courtyard's center mingled with the other smells into Corona's unique mélange. Rex led her to the underground garage, then out on the spinward side of the tower, opposite their watcher's location.

They leaped up the embankment by the driveway. "He is crouched in a harvest-ready field, heedless of the damage he is doing to the crop." Shady hadn't been a Ranan for long, but angry disgust soured her throat. "Only an ignorant foreigner would do that."

Hot rage like charred coals burned in Rex's scent factors and deepened the menace in his growl. "Transmondian agent. Got to be. Probably thinks the crop is just tall weeds."

Her mate was right. No Ranan would make such a mistake. A stealthy foreigner, concealed, spying on Corona, almost certainly came from the Transmondian Intelligence Service. Rex had good reason to hate the TIS, and especially Col. Jackson Wisniewski, the spymaster who'd tried to make Rex one of his assets.

Shady followed him toward a grove of almond trees. By now she'd phased into full guard-dog-on-the-hunt mindset, ready to deal with this trespasser. They'd learned as puppies how to quietly navigate thick, wild brush. Far easier to move in silence through Corona's well-maintained orchard, but better not get sloppy. Especially not if this guy was from Transmondian Intelligence. She kept her nose up, sorting through the night-smells. At last came a tendril of the stranger's scent, laced with a telltale touch of gunshot residue.

GSR? Alarm radiated through the link from Pam. *Is he armed?*

I don't think so, Shady replied. "Faint GSR," she texted to her mate, not daring any sound at this point. If only she and Rex had a brain link like the one she shared with Pam!

"GSR confirmed, but maybe a day old," Rex texted back.

Gunshot residue didn't wash off easily, although this man

had tried. It was yet more proof that he was a Transmondian, or at least a dirtsider from Planet Chayko. Almost no Ranans had either access to firearms or any need for them on their space station home. Good thing this man didn't smell as if he had a gun tonight.

They crept closer, screened behind a trellised vineyard row on the leeward side of the tower, their footsteps muffled by clover. A quick dash across a short gap brought them onto neighboring Bonita Tower property, between two rows of leafy quinoa topped by heavy seed heads. Shady brushed carefully between the drying stalks, wary lest they crackle.

She and Rex moved upwind of the intruder, a couple of rows over. She'd already committed his personal odor profile to memory, but now she studied his scent factors. The involuntary exudations betrayed the dusty-smoky smell of fatigue. Perhaps a touch of shuttle-lag? She caught the faint *pa-pum* of his heartbeat, his careful, even breathing, and then his quiet yawn.

"Wait here," Rex texted. "I'll approach him from behind." He disappeared around the end of a row.

Shady halted, ears up. "How close is our backup?" she texted Dispatch.

"En route," the dispatcher replied. "ETA about five minutes."

"Good evening, sir," Rex said in a calm, moderate tone.

The man gasped. Dry stalks crunched.

"I do not believe I recognize you." Rex's robotic vocalizer-voice wasn't capable of much emotional nuance, but from the cadence she pictured him with ears up and tail wagging. Trying to look as non-threatening as an unexpected, enormous black wolf-dog in the night could. "May I please ask what brings you —" The *pop* of a trank-pistol cut him off.

Shady shouldered between the plants. "Shot fired!" she told Dispatch. "We are engaging!"

"Here, now! There is no call for that." Rex had dodged the trank bolt. A black blur of motion beyond a last row of stalks, he darted in, snapped his teeth onto—

The man twisted, faster than humans could move. His weapon popped again.

Rex stumbled backward into the quinoa, legs wobbly, then fell over.

Rex! Shady reached the intruder in less than a stride. She slammed against him at full gallop. Lunged for his weapon-hand.

"Officer down!" Pam yelled to Dispatch through Shady's connection. "Need backup! *Stat!*"

The man tumbled away from Shady with a yell, then regained his feet and swung the pistol toward her.

Still has two darts. "Stand down!" She zigzagged to evade his aim.

The pistol jerked back and forth, tracking her.

Dammit. She darted closer to the man, feinted right, then dodged left around a leafy stalk. Lunged from behind it to slip under his guard and go for his weapon-arm. She sank teeth into the muscle and bone of his brawny forearm. Coppery-metallic blood filled her mouth. She attempted the protocol throw-maneuver, a full-body twist. XK9s were so big and powerful, that always brought suspects down.

Except—this time it didn't work.

He swayed but kept his feet. "Damn you!" His left fist landed like a sledgehammer against her face.

Ears ringing, she flinched away from the next blow. Let go, then circled around. Darted in and latched on again. She bit farther up his arm this time, behind and just above his right elbow.

He yelled and tried to hit her, but he could only strike awkwardly across his body at her. She moved backwards with his motion when he attempted an elbow-strike. Jaws locked, she sidestepped a backward hammer-fist meant for her abdomen.

She clamped down harder on his arm. Her teeth sliced muscle and tendon, grated on bone.

He yelled, cursed, struggled against her.

She dragged him backward.

They rotated in a ragged circle. Quinoa stalks bent and shattered, but the man kept his feet.

She'd met one objective, anyway. She controlled his right arm —the one that clutched the trank pistol. He couldn't get an angle to point it at her. Her bites had half-disabled his arm, and he couldn't break her grip.

He screamed rage and pain. Wrenched his body back and forth.

She dug her teeth in harder and wrapped her front legs around his torso for a better anchor against his wild swings. With her hind feet still on the ground, she pushed or pulled into his every twist. Could she get him off his feet?

He staggered, spun. Stayed upright.

Her feet blundered over a knot of shattered stalks. She stumbled.

He threw all his weight into driving her into the ground with his shoulder.

She released her jaws. Pushed away just in time.

He landed like a load of bricks. Lay there on his side for a moment, stunned.

If only I could use handcuffs! She darted forward. Grabbed his trank pistol—but also sank teeth into part of his hand.

He raised his head with an agonized yell. Threw a desperate punch with his left fist.

She dodged away behind him, dragging his right arm, jaws still clenched on his hand and the trank pistol. His blow couldn't connect. She gave his hand a "kill shake," but maybe he couldn't let go. "Stand down!" she ordered. "Stop resisting! You are under arrest! "It is your right to say nothing, but it may—"

He rolled his body toward her, reached out with his left hand. Lurched upward with an angry grunt.

She powered backward hard and fast, teeth still locked on his hand. Yanked, but didn't manage to dislocate his shoulder. She dragged his heavy bulk about half a meter through the quinoa.

"As I was saying, it may harm your defense if you do not mention, when questioned—"

He gathered himself, drew his legs in toward his torso, then tried to kick her, but couldn't connect. Nor could he break her grip or regain his feet.

She pulled as hard as she could. Her 119 kilos couldn't match his weight, but she could keep him off-balance till backup arrived. "Let us try this again! It may harm your defense if you do not mention, when questioned, something you later rely on in court. Anything you do or say may be used against you in a court of law." She gasped and panted and drooled around his hand. This was exhausting. She paused for an instant.

He lunged at her. His fingers tore through her furry ruff, ripped a gouge in her cheek, then caught on her collar. He gave a triumphant yell and twisted. The collar tightened against her throat.

She choked … Strangled … Terror thundered through her. She clenched her jaws harder, ground her teeth into his pistol hand.

He roared in pain and fury, but he couldn't pull away.

Muscles and tendons shredded between her teeth. She tasted a new flow of blood. How was she not breaking bones?

They swayed back and forth. He twisted the collar with all his might.

Black spots gathered at the edges of her vision. Somewhere far away, Pam was yelling.

The collar broke. She could breathe again!

She released his hand and the pistol. Staggered back. Gasped gulps of air, lest she black out.

The man's cry of triumph turned to anguish. She'd shredded his right hand to gory ruins. The trank pistol fell to the ground. He collapsed with a cry and stared at his macerated hand. His whole body shuddered.

Shady drew in another deep breath, then licked her lips to clear them of blood. She found the pistol with a forepaw, passed it to a hind foot, then sent it spinning away into the field. *Nasty thing!* She snorted. *Still no sign of Rex.* That dart must've delivered a full load. He might be out for hours. *I'm on my own.*

No you're not! "Officer down! Officer down! Officer needs assistance!" Pam yelled into her com. "Rim Eight Road, Ninth Precinct, corner of Bonita and Corona!"

More sirens. These came from spinward.

The man's ragged cries grew quieter. He bowed his head and moaned.

Where was I with that arrest warning? Oh, yes. "It is your right to have an attorney with you while you are questioned." Her voice issued from the vocalizer, still attached to her collar on the ground near him. "If you cannot afford an attorney, one will be appointed to represent you before you are questioned. Do you understand these rights?"

He didn't answer. Didn't move.

Sirens wailed in the distance, far to leeward on Rim Eight Road.

"Subject apprehended!" she shouted into her com through the vocalizer, also texting the words to be sure they went through. "Need medical assistance! Need backup now!"

The man groaned. He laboriously pushed up onto his left hand and knees.

Shady eyed him. "You probably should stay down. You have lost a lot of blood. You will get dizzy, and bleed harder."

He hugged his ruined hand to himself. Rocked back and forth and glared at her. "You'd like that, wouldn't you?" Definitely a Transmondian accent. South-central piedmont, from the cadence and the half-swallowed "yud" for *you'd* and "wu'nt" for *wouldn't*.

"I would have preferred for you to stand down when I told you to, so I did not have to hurt you."

"I don't take orders from a bitch." His left hand cradled his wounded right arm. Now he pulled it harder against himself. A new, pungent, deceitful scent grew alongside the dark blood-smell of traumatic injury, the raw darkness of fear, and scorching stink of fury. The fingers of his left hand slipped inside his torn, bloodied jacket.

Shady growled. "Think twice about that."

He froze. Met her gaze, then bowed his head. "I didn't do anything."

Like you could fool me that easily.

The sirens drew closer.

His left hand slipped into his jacket again. Flashed back, then forward to throw—

Shady dodged it, circled right. A second knife. She kept moving. A third—but by then he'd twisted himself off-balance and she'd moved behind him.

She launched herself against his back and shoulders. Bore down with all her weight onto the man's burly shoulders and upper back. He fell on his face once again. Lay still for half a second, then his muscles shifted and tensed.

She grabbed his left triceps in her jaws. "Stop now, or I shall bite you hard."

He shook himself almost like a dog. Uttered a deep, gut-level yell and strove to rise.

She clamped down full-force. *Damn*, this creep was strong. And persistent! Cold, queasy fear coiled in her gut. *I'm not heavy enough. He's never going to give up.* Shady twisted to throw her body into the back of his head. *That's his third face-plant.* "Stop! What do you think you can do?"

She drove her weight down on him again, as fast and hard as she could. Through the link, she sensed Pam's yell into her com.

The man hunched his back. His body trembled with exertion. He must be in horrific pain.

Shady's teeth sliced into his triceps. "Stop! Stop! Now I am destroying your other arm!" Her voice yelled from the churned-up ground where he'd dropped her collar.

Hot blood flowed, but his back muscles bunched. Heaved.

How was he still moving? "Stop! Stop!" She bit all the way through to the bone. But it was like biting a steel girder.

A steel girder leaking blood. The ground reeked of it. His arm and back and body were slick with it. So was she.

His head bowed. His breath rasped. He shuddered, then collapsed.

Read the rest of the story! Order from the bookseller of your choice via:

https://weirdsisterspublishing.com/index.php/our-books/a-bone-to-pick/

WHO'S WHO AND WHAT'S WHAT

CHARACTERS, SHIPS, ORGANIZATIONS, PLACES, ACRONYMS AND ABBREVIATIONS IN WHAT'S BRED IN THE BONE

Use this reader-requested directory to help keep the names straight.

Acquisitionists. A political faction in Transmondian government that wants to create a Transmondian Empire by annexing other sovereignties in the Chayko System.

Adeyeme. (ah-DEE-yem) See *Elaine Adeyeme*.

Adlai Masato. (AD-lay ma-SAH-do) The Borough Attorney, head of the prosecutor's office for Orangeboro. (Pronouns: he, him.)

Admiral Virendra. (vir-END-rah) See *Nolan Virendra*.

Afua. (aff-WAH) An XK9 partner-candidate who was one of Pamela Gómez's podmates. (Pronouns: she, her.)

Ailani Idris. (eye-LAH-nee ID-riss) Mayor of Orangeboro. (Pronouns: she, her.)

Alliance of the Peoples. An interstellar alliance of sapient species whose treaties supersede all system-wide or national laws.

Amare. (ah-MAH-ray) One of several types of relationships that are formally recognized on Rana Station. Amares are lovers who live together in a family-type unit.

Anika Ogawa Chinbat. (AH-ni-ka a-GAH-wa chan-BAT) Orangeboro Medical Examiner, whose office is a unit of Borough Government that cooperates with law enforcement and legal systems but is subordinate to none of them. (Pronouns: she, her.)

Annie Montoya Lee. (mon-TO-yah) Charlie's maternal grandmother, wife of Pedro Lee Montoya, daughter of Loretta Triola Lee, and official Head of Household for Corona Chartered Family. (Pronouns: she, her.)

Anthony. See *Lynne Anthony*.

Ariela "Ari" Sanger Tanaka. (air-YELL-a tah-NAH-ka) One of Charlie's cousins-in-law, Luther's wife, and Leeli's mother. (Pronouns: she, her.)

Asalatu. (as-ah-LAH-too) A spacecraft that slammed into the Orangeboro Docks.

Aylward. (ALE-ward) Sergeant, a squad leader on OPD STAT Red Team.

Balchu Nowicki. (BAHL-chew) A Level Two Detective with the Orangeboro Police Department assigned to the Vice Unit at Central HQ. Pamela Gómez's Amare and Shady's housemate. (Pronouns: he, him.)

Bari Family. (BAH-ri) The Chartered Family of Eduardo Donovan and XK9 Victor Sam-Janet.

Beatriz Chan. (bee-ah-TREESE) Borough Council Chairperson for the Orangeboro Council. (Pronouns: she, her.)

Becky Goldstein. Ten-year-old daughter of UPO William "Bill" Sloane. (Pronouns: she, her.)

Berwyn Yael. (BER-win yah-EL). Partner of XK9 Cinnamon "Cinnie" Lightfoot-Floss. A Level One Detective. (Pronouns: he, him.)

Betrothed. A temporary relationship status prior to marriage on Rana.

Bill. See *William "Bill" Goldstein Sloane*.

Bonita. The Chartered Family that lives next door to Rex and Charlie's Corona Family.

Bran Davis. A Safety Services dispatcher. (Pronouns: he, him.)

Brave Girl. One of two small girls rescued from the *Izgubil*. (Pronouns: she, her.)

Brock Rivers. A friend of Charlie's, member of the STAT Team, and cousin of Eddie Chism. (Pronouns: he, him.)

Bryan. Bryan Colville, Vice Premier Guzmán's chief political strategist. (Pronouns: he, him.)

Bureau. Station Bureau of Investigation (SBI).

CAP. Cybernetically-Assisted Perception. The implant-driven interface between an individual user and the Station Net.

Capt. Archibald "Archy" Cody Danvir. Aide and right-hand man to Chief Klein. (Pronouns: he, his.)

Captain Tom Argus. Orangeboro Police Department Precinct Captain for Precinct Nine. (Pronouns: he, him.)

Carolyn "Caro" Crannach Lee. (CRAH-noch) Charlie's older sister. Wife of Andy and mother of Sophie and Lacey. (Pronouns: she, her.)

Carolyn "Carrie" Morgan Owens. Charlie and Caro's paternal grandmother. Ted and Hector's mother. (Pronouns: she, her.)

Centerboro. The human-occupied Borough on Wheel Four that houses the center of Rana Station Government for humans.

Chan. See *Beatriz Chan*.

Charles "Charlie" Morgan. XK9 Rex Dieter-Nell's partner. A Detective Level One. (Pronouns: he, him.)

Chartered Family. Chartered Families are official entities of their own, with civic duties and special tax rates, among other things.

Chaser Nigel-Glory. XK9 of Gen 48, classmate of the Orangeboro Pack, mate of XK9 Fernie Tintin-Brenna, and partner of Saladin Wu. (Pronouns: she, her.)

Chayko. (CHAY-koh) The human-inhabited planet that gives the Chayko System its name. It is the only planet in Alliance

Space, other than Earth, that humans have been allowed to wholly claim.

Chief Kwame Odigo Klein. (KWAH-may OH-di-go) Orangeboro Chief of Police. (Pronouns: he, him.)

Chukwu. (CHUK-woo) An officer on the OPD STAT Red Team. (Pronouns: he, him.)

Cinnamon "Cinnie" Lightfoot-Floss. XK9 partner of Berwyn Yael. (Pronouns: she, her.)

Comets. A professional quiddo team.

Commonwealth Party. (CWP) One of four human political parties on Rana Station.

Constance "Connie" Alkayev. (AL-kay-uv) XK9 Crystal Basho-Dancer's partner. A Detective Level One. (Pronouns: she, her.)

Corona Family. The Chartered Family that lives in Corona Tower (Charlie and Rex's family).

Corona Tower. The Corona Family's residence, located on Starboard Hill Level Eight in the Ninth Precinct of Orangeboro, on Rana Station.

Crystal "Cryssie" Basho-Dancer. XK9 Partner of Connie Alkayev. (Pronouns: she, her.)

CSU. Crime Scene Unit, the forensic evidence analysis unit of a law enforcement agency.

CWP. Commonwealth Party, one of the four Ranan political parties.

Darius Amin. Borough Treasurer for Orangeboro. (Pronouns: he, him.)

David "Dave" Santos. (SAN-tohs) A noted cyberneticist from Station Polytechnic University. . (Pronouns: he, him.)

Desk Officer L. Collins. An officer stationed at the main entrance of OPD Central Headquarters. (Pronouns: she, her.)

Detective Sanchez. A Detective Level Two, assigned to Precinct Nine. (Pronouns: she, her.)

Director Adelaide "Laidie" Perri. Director of the Station Bureau of Investigation. (Pronouns: she, her.)

Director Dépoli. (DAY-po-lee) Administrator in charge of the Orangeboro Medical Center. (Pronouns: she, her.)

Douglass. A Judge on the Wheel Two Court. (Pronouns: she, her.)

DPO. Detective Police Officer, a civilian police rank.

Duthuluru. (doo-THOO-loo-roo) Former Foreign Minister Margaret Duthuluru. (Pronouns: she, her.)

Duul. (DOOL) A moon of a gas giant in the Antares System.

Duulian Gulimyanik. (DOO-lee-un goo-lim-YAWN-ick) A prickly-tempered, accidentally-uplifted sapient species that superficially resembles the Earth myth of the griffin.

Eddie Sakai Chism. (sah-KYE CHIZZ-m) A friend of Charlie's, a member of the STAT Blue Team, and a cousin of Brock Rivers. (Pronouns: he, him.)

Eduardo Donovan. Partner of XK9 Victor Sam-Janet. A Detective Level One. (Pronouns: he, him.)

Edwina "Wina" Emshwiller. (ed-WEE-nah EM-shwill-er) An SIT Delta Special Agent. (Pronouns: she, her.)

Elaine Adeyeme. (ah-DEE-yem) The Senior Special Agent who leads the SBI's SIT Delta, and the lead investigator on the *Izgubil* case. (Pronouns: she, her.)

Elijah "Eli" Isaiah. A paramedic. (Pronouns: he, him.)

Elizabeth "Liz" Antonopoulos. (ann-ton-OP-o-liss) Partner of XK9 Razor Liam-Blanca. As an XK9 partner-candidate, Liz was one of Pam Gómez's podmates. (Pronouns: she, her.)

Elle Finnian-Ella. (EL, *not* "EL-ee") XK9 partner of Mikhail "Misha" Flores and mate of Tuxedo Moondog-Carrie. (Pronouns: she, her.)

Elmo Smart. A mugger. (Pronouns: he, him.)

Emer Bellamy. (EE-mer) Daughter of Sorcha Moran Bellamy and Hideki Bellamy Moran, and member of the wealthy and respected Vinebrook Family. (Pronouns: she, her.)

Eric Maki. (MAH-kee) Third Precinct representative on Orangeboro's Borough Council. (Pronouns: he, him.)

ERT. Emergency Rescue Team. Although this designation

could be applied to any Safety Services rescue unit, it is generally used to mean the Emergency Rescue Teams that operate at the Hub to respond to emergencies in microgravity. Sometimes members of such a team are called "ERTs."

Etsu. (ET-sue) As an XK9 partner-candidate, Etsu was one of Pam Gómez's podmates. (Pronouns: she, her.)

Eurydice Qadhi. (you-RID-ih-see KAH-dee) A Judge on the Wheel Two Criminal Court. (Pronouns: she, her.)

FA. Field Agent, a rank in the SBI. Generally, a younger, early-career agent. An FA does tasks often assigned to uniformed patrol officers in police departments.

Fatima Smythe, (FA-di-ma SMEYEth) Welder, member of Bonita Family. (Pronouns: she, her.)

Felicia. (Feh-LEE-shah), Charlie Morgan's ex-Amare. (Pronouns: she, her.)

Fernie Tintin-Brenna. XK9 of Gen 48, classmate of the Orangeboro Pack, mate of Chaser Nigel-Glory, and partner of Zandra Chen. (Pronouns: he, him.)

Fifty Founding Families. The largest human source of the funding needed to build Rana Station.

Five-Ten. An infamous "underworld" part of Orangeboro: Fifth Precinct, Level Ten.

Founders. In general, the generation of humans and ozzirikkians who paid for, built, and first populated Rana Station ninety-plus years ago. As an honorific, it means a surviving member of the Fifty Founding (human) Families or the ozzirikkians' leadership team.

Francis "Frankie" Freas. (FREEZE) A Special Agent assigned to SIT Delta. (Pronouns: he, him.)

Fulbert. See *Hakim Fulbert.*

Gen 48. Generation 48, the Orangeboro Pack's generational designation by the XK9 Project's breeding program.

Georgia Volkov. (VOLE-cove) XK9 Tuxedo Moondog-Carrie's partner. A Detective Level One. (Pronouns: she, her.)

German Shepherd Brothers. Two German Shepherd Dogs who live along Rim Eight Road.

Glen Haven Community. The Starboard Hill district in Orangeboro's Ninth Precinct that includes all the residence towers for one-half kilometer on both sides of the Glen Haven Transit Terminal Station on Terrace Eight.

Glen Haven Transit Terminal Station. A transportation hub that includes commuter elevators linked to the Hub, roadway passage between upper and lower switchbacks, a tramway stop, and a train station on a secondary level.

Global Reconstruction. (GR) A technique for crafting 3-dimensional visual recreations and/or animations of crime scenes, objects and individuals.

GR Artist. A person trained and certified in Global Reconstruction.

Gregory Ordovich. (ORE-dough-vitch) Director of the XK9 Project. Transmondian geneticist and dog breeder who used genetic engineering to create the XK9s. (Pronouns: he, him.)

Gulnar. (GULL-ner) A young gardener from whom Shady learned to speak conversational Oroplanian Urdu. (Pronouns: she, her.)

Gusaujik. (goo-SAU-jeek) *plural*. A sapient member-species in the Alliance of the Peoples. They accidentally uplifted the Duulian Gulimyanik.

Hakan Morgan. (HOH-kan) Son of Charlie Morgan's first cousin Manny Wang Morgan and his wife Fiametta "Fee" Morgan Wang. (Pronouns: he, him.)

Hakim Fulbert. (ha-KEEM FULL-bert) Professor of Explosives Technology at the Wheel Three Institute of Technology, and a consulting expert for the SBI. (Pronouns: he, him.)

Hannah Morgan Chahine. (SHY-een) Charlie's aunt and wife of Hector Chahine Morgan. A named partner in a law firm that specializes in interstellar trade. (Pronouns: she, her.)

Harlequin Great Dane. A resident of Aurora Tower on Rim Eight Road.

Hector Chahine Morgan. (SHY-een) Charlie's uncle. An inventor. (Pronouns: he, him.)

Helmer Fujimoto (HEL-mer fu-ji-MO-do) Balchu Nowicki's former Field Training Officer. Father of Miyu. (Pronouns: he, him.)

Henry Sevencrows. Partner of UPO Lynne Anthony. A patrol officer assigned to the Five-Ten. (Pronouns: he, him.)

Hideki Bellamy Moran. (hee-DAY-key) A member of Orangeboro's prominent Vinebrook Family, husband of Sorcha Moran Bellamy, and father of Emer and Orla Bellamy. (Pronouns: he, him.)

Hildegaard "Hildie" Gallagher. A paramedic and one of Charlie Morgan's former teammates on the Emergency Rescue Team. (Pronouns: she, her.)

HUD. Heads-up Display. Among Ranans, this is an implant-driven internal system that creates a visual interface with the Station Net.

ICU. Intensive Care Unit.

Idris. Ailani Idris. (eye-LAH-nee ID-riss) Mayor of Orangeboro. (Pronouns: she, her).

Ignacio. Verne Ignacio. An XK9 Project dog wrangler. (Pronouns: he, him.)

Iruka Jones. (EE-ru-kah) A detective with the Orangeboro Bureau of Missing Persons. (Pronouns: she, her.)

IVs – Intravenous drip feeds.

Izgubil (izz-GYOU-bill) A space barque that serves as a mobile base of operations for the Whisper Syndicate, a criminal organization on Rana Station.

Jackson Wisniewski. (wizz-NEW-skee) The colonel in charge of Ranan Intelligence Operations for the Transmondian Intelligence Service. (Pronouns: he, him.)

Jalani Sanjaya. (ja-LAH-nee san-JAH-yah) Kristen's big brother, son of Charlie Morgan's cousin Marilyn Sanjaya Lee and her husband, Kimba Lee Sanjaya. (Pronouns: he, him.)

Jikjikchi Ziktikki. (JICK-JICK-chee ZICK-TIK-ee) Welder. An ozzirikkian. (Pronouns: k'ki, k'kin.)

Jill Sandler. A Specialist Veterinarian in charge of XK9 health in Orangeboro. She owns the Sandler Clinic, a veterinary facility modified for XK9s. (Pronouns: she, her.)

Jimmy. A child who lives in Trondheim (TROND-hime) Tower, a neighbor of Corona Tower. (Pronouns: he, him.)

Jo Karrell. (KAIR-ell) A detective. (Pronouns: she, her.)

Joseph Raach. (ROCK) An SBI Tech Specialist who holds a Ph. D. in Explosives Technology from the Wheel Three Institute of Technology. (Pronouns: he, him.)

Joslyn Stark. (JOZZ-lin) Press Liaison for Chief Klein, a civilian position. (Pronouns: she, her.)

Jummah. (JOO-mah) Friday prayer for Muslim Ranans.

Kimba Lee Sanjaya. (KIM-ba LEE san-JAH-yah) One of Charlie's cousins-in-law, Marilyn Sanjaya Lee's husband, and Jalani and Kristen's father. (Pronouns: he, him.)

King. A Judge on the Wheel Two Court. (Pronouns: he, him.)

Kizzitikti Zhokittik. (KIZZ-ee-TICK-tee zhow-KIT-ick) As a Vice-Premier ("Zikikittir," in Pan-Ozzirikkian; the title is pronounced ZICK-ick-it-TEER), ki is the second-in-command ozzirikkian in the Ranan Government, a member of the Ranan People's Party. (Pronouns: ki, kin.)

Klein. See *Kwame Odigo Klein*.

Koening. (CONE-ing) An officer on the OPD STAT Red Team. (Pronouns: she, her.)

Konrad. SSA Konrad Halvard. (KON-rad HAL-vard) The head of SIT Gamma. (Pronouns: he, him.)

Kristen Lec. Jalani's little sister, daughter of Charlie Morgan's cousin Marilyn Sanjaya Lee and her husband Kimba Lee Sanjaya. (Pronouns: she, her.)

Kwame Odigo Klein. (KWAH-may OH-di-go KLINE) Also *Klein*. Orangeboro Chief of Police. (Pronouns: he, him.)

Lacey Lee. Daughter of Caro Cranach Lee and Andy Lee Cranach. (Pronouns: she, her.)

Lang Family. The Chartered Family of Walter Ejiamike and XK9 Petunia Yeller-Melody.

Leena. A Listener (psychologist) affiliated with the Social Services Department of the Orangeboro Department of the Common Good. (Pronouns: she, her.)

Loretta Triola Lee. (lo-RET-tah tree-OH-la LEE) Charlie's great-grandmother. Co-founder of Corona Chartered Family. (Pronouns: she, her.)

LSA. Lead Special Agent, a rank in the SBI. The Primary LSA (there normally are at least two) is second-in-command to the Senior Special Agent in charge.

Luther Tanaka Singer. (LOO thur tah-NAH-ka) One of Charlie's cousins. Ari's husband, Leeli's father, and Gloria's brother. (Pronouns: he, him.)

Lynne Anthony. Partner of UPO Henry Sevencrows. A patrol officer assigned to the infamous Five-Ten. (Pronouns: she, her.)

Maria "Mimi" Morgan Lee. Charlie's mother. Wife of Theodore "Ted" Lee Morgan. (Pronouns: she, her.)

Marilyn Sanjaya Lee. (san-JAH-yah) One of Charlie's cousins. Kimba Lee Sanjaya's wife, Jalani and Kristen's mother. (Pronouns: she, her.)

Marisol Patel. (MAIR-i-zol pa-TELL) A detective lieutenant. (Pronouns: she, her.)

Market Garden Neighborhood. A relatively low-rent, urban district in Orangeboro's Fifth Precinct.

Marriage. A formal alliance of two or more Chartered Families on Rana Station, through a domestic union of one or more members of each.

Marshall. A Judge on the Wheel Two Court. (Pronouns: she, her.)

Masato. Adlai Masato. (AD-lay ma-SAH-do) The Borough Attorney (head of the prosecutor's office) for Orangeboro. (Pronouns: he, him.)

Master Mix. The nutritionally balanced, high-performance dog kibble designed by the XK9 Project for working XK9s.

Melisende Imre. (MEL-liss-end EMM-ray) CFO, Associate Head Geneticist, and XK9 Breeding Coordinator for the XK9 Project in Transmondia. (Pronouns: she, her.)

MERS-V. – Multipurpose Emergency Response Space-Vehicle. A small, space-based vehicle designed to retrieve victims who have been "spaced" (ejected into the vacuum of space, usually by accident, where they have only 90 seconds to be rescued alive).

Mikhail "Misha" Flores. (MEE-khah-yool "MEE-shah" FLO-race) XK9 Elle Finnian-Ella's partner. A Detective Level One. (Pronouns: he, him.)

Miyu. (me-YOU-eh) The mysteriously missing daughter of DPO Helmer Fujimoto. (Pronouns: she, her.)

Monlandia. (mon-LAN-dee-ah) The largest continent on Planet Chayko.

Monteverde Borough. (mon-tay-VAIR-day bur-row) One of four Boroughs on Rana Station's Wheel Two. The other three are Petranova, Pueblo, and Orangeboro.

MPs. Military Police Officers.

Nancy Tibma. A human friend of Fatima Smythe. (Pronouns: she, her.)

Nanda Errapel, MSN. (NAHN-dah EH-rah-pell) A nurse in the Re-Gen Unit at Orangeboro Medical Center. (Pronouns: he, him.)

Neopolis. Capital City of Oroplania.

Nicole Oyunbileg. (oh-YOON-bill-egg) XK9 Scout Sam-Shana's partner. A Detective Level One. (Pronouns: she, her.)

Nolan Virendra. (vir-END-rah) An Admiral in the SDF. (Pronouns: he, him.)

Norchellic Confederation. (nor-CHELL-ic) A country on the eastern end of Monlandia, the largest landform on Planet Chayko.

Nunzio. Ryder Nunzio. (RYE-dur NOON-zee-oh) Transmondian Ambassador to Rana Station. (Pronouns: he, him.)

Oma Peralta Pandra. (OH-ma per-ALL-ta PAN-drah) Secretary of Public Safety. (Pronouns: he, him.)

OPD. Orangeboro Police Department.

OPD Central HQ. The administrative headquarters of the Orangeboro Police Department.

Orangeboro Central Plaza. The heart of Orangeboro's urban core.

Orangeboro Civic Center. The building complex in Central Plaza that houses most Borough governmental departments and headquarters for their service administrations, and the Civic Center Auditorium.

Orangeboro Police Department (OPD). The Borough's law enforcement agency.

Orangeboro Safety Services Department. A cabinet-level bureau of the Ranan Government.

Orangeboro. (ORANGE-bur-row) One of four Boroughs on Rana Station's Wheel Two. The other three are Petranova, Pueblo, and Monteverde.

Ordovich. (ORE-dough-vitch). See *Gregory Ordovich.*

Oroplania. (ore-oh-PLAY-nee-ah) A country on the southeastern quadrant of Monlandia, the largest landform on Planet Chayko.

Osmond "Oz" Meredith. One of Charlie Morgan's former teammates on the Emergency Rescue Team. A Squad Commander of MERS-V drivers. (Pronouns: he, him.)

Ostra Import-Export Emporium. (OH-straw) A storefront and shell corporation in the Five-Ten used by the Whisper Syndicate.

PA. Public address system.

PA Office. Personnel Assistance Office. Provides help and support to Safety Services personnel who have been involved in critical incidents.

Pack. As a group, all ten XK9s (large, intelligent, genetically engineered dogs) in the Orangeboro Police Department.

PAL. Personnel Assistance Liaison, a volunteer trained by the

PA Office to assist Safety Services personnel who have been involved in critical incidents and their families.

Pamela "Pam" Gómez. XK9 Shady Jacob-Belle's partner. A Detective Level One. Balchu Nowicki's Amare. (Learn more of her background in *The Other Side of Fear*, of which she's the protagonist.). (Pronouns: she, her.)

Pandra. See *Oma Peralta Pandra.*

Pascal Jennings. (pass-KAL JEN-ings) Charlie's Personnel Assistance Liaison. (Pronouns: he, him.)

PDP. *See Popular Democracy Party.*

Pedro "Gran Pepe" Lee Montoya. (PAY-dro "GRAN PAY-pay" mon-TO-yah). Charlie's maternal grandfather. Husband of Annie Montoya Lee, son-in-law of Loretta, father of Mimi and Serafina. Co-founder of Corona Chartered Family. (Pronouns: he, him.)

Pee Wee Pederson. XK9 Project dog wrangler. (Pronouns: he, him.)

Petranova Borough. (pet-rah-NO-vah bur-row) One of four Boroughs on Rana Station's Wheel Two. The other three are Orangeboro, Pueblo, and Monteverde.

Petunia Yeller-Melody. XK9 partner of Walter Ejiamike. (Pronouns: she, her.)

Peynirci. See *Rona Peynirci.*

Popular Democracy Party. (PDP) One of four human political parties on Rana Station.

Premier Eliana Iskander, (ell-ee-AHN-ah ISS-kin-der), The elected chief executive of Rana Station and a member of the Commonwealth Party. (Pronouns: she, her.)

Premier. The Ranan head of state. An elected position that may be filled by either a human or an ozzirikkian.

PTV. Personnel Transport Vehicle. A large 1-G-based government agency vehicle like a bus, designed primarily to transport people and their gear.

Pueblo Borough. (PWEHB-low bur-row) One of four

Boroughs on Rana Station's Wheel Two. The other three are Orangeboro, Petranova, and Monteverde.

Quiddo. A sport played in microgravity on maneuverable micrograv sleds.

Quinn Gibson Huddleston. Husband of Charlie's cousin Gloria Huddleston Gibson and father of Grant and Owen Huddleston. (Pronouns: he, him.)

Ralph Lee Gibson. Charlie's uncle. Husband of Serafina Gibson Lee. A Certified Agricultural Technician, he is the head of agricultural operations for Corona Tower. (Pronouns: he, him.)

Razor Liam-Blanca. XK9 partner of Liz Antonopoulos. (Pronouns: he, him.)

Re-gen. Medical Regeneration, a therapeutic technique for regrowing or fortifying the healing process after tissue damage or catastrophic injury, including growing new organs or limbs.

Regan Ireland. (REE-gun) An Assistant Borough Attorney from the Prosecutors Office. (Pronouns: she, her.)

RES. Ranan Executive Security, roughly parallel to the United States Secret Service.

Rex Dieter-Nell. XK9 partner of Charlie Morgan. XK9 Shady Jacob-Belle's mate. (Pronouns: he, him.)

Ricardo "Ric." A child who lives in Fairleigh Tower, a neighbor of Corona Tower. (Pronouns: he, him.)

Rim Eight Road. The road that runs along the outer edge of Terrace Eight.

Rim Four Road. The road that runs along the outer edge of Terrace Four.

Rodney Moreno. (mo-RAY-no) A detective. (Pronouns: he, him.)

Rona Peynirci. (ROW-nah pa-NEAR-see) Ninth Precinct representative on Orangeboro's Borough Council (Pronouns: she, her.)

S-3-9. Also *Central S-3-9*. Sub-Level Three, Corridor Nine, a secured location underneath OPD Central HQ.

S-Poly. Station Polytechnic, a university of technology in

Orangeboro.

SA. Special Agent, a rank in the SBI.

Sacha Guzmán. (SAH-chah gooz-MAHN) Vice-Premier, the second-in-command human in the Ranan Government, and a member of the Popular Democracy Party (Pronouns: he, him.)

Saladin Wu. (SAL-a-din) XK9 Chaser Nigel-Glory's partner. (Pronouns: he, him.)

SBI. Station Bureau of Investigation.

SCISCO 3750 (SHEES-koh) A Farricainan cyberbeing who is a professor of explosives technology at Station Polytechnic University. (Pronouns: ne, nem.)

Scout Sam-Shana. XK9 partner of Nicole Oyunbileg. XK9 Victor Sam-Janet's half-brother. (Pronouns: he, him.)

SDF. Station Defense Force, the military arm of the Ranan Government.

Sevencrows. See *Henry Sevencrows*.

Sgt. Gorman. (GORE-man) Balchu Nowicki's immediate superior in the OPD Vice Unit. (Pronouns: he, him.)

Shady Jacob-Belle. XK9 partner of Pamela Gómez. XK9 Rex Dieter-Nell's mate. (Pronouns: she, her.)

Shawnee Kramer. Junior LSA of SIT Delta. She is nominally third-in command to Adeyeme and Shimon, but normally functions as Shimon's equal. (Pronouns: she, her.)

Shimon. (shee-MOWN) See *Shiva "Shiv" Shimon*.

Shiva "Shiv" Shimon. (SHEE-va "SHEEV" sheem-OWN) Primary Senior LSA of SIT Delta. He is second-in-command to SSA Adeyeme. (Pronouns: he, him.)

Shuri. (SHU-ree) As an XK9 partner-candidate, she was one of Pamela Gómez's podmates. (Pronouns: she, her.)

Significant. A Domestic Partner on Rana Station. Domestic Partnerships are more legally binding than an Amare relationship.

Sirius Valley. (SEAR-ee-us) The land on either side of the Sirius River, the waterway that runs in an endless circle down the middle of Rana Station's Wheel Two.

SIT. Special Investigations Team, an elite investigative unit of the SBI.

Sophie Lee. Daughter of Caro Cranach Lee and Andy Lee Cranach. (Pronouns: she, her.)

Sorcha Moran Bellamy. (SOR-ka) A member of Vinebrook Family. The Founders' granddaughter, the wife of Hideki Bellamy Moran, and the mother of Orla and Emer. (Pronouns: she, her.)

Sound Tech Samuels. An OPD sound technician assigned to the Detention Unit. (Pronouns: he, him.)

SSA. Senior Special Agent, a rank in the SBI. Senior Special Agents are the commanding officers of the Bureau's Special Investigative units, and of Borough or Timi offices.

STAT Team. Special Tools and Techniques Team, a Safety Services Department unit that includes specialists in hostage negotiation, bomb disposal, rescue and recovery, and high-risk tactical operations.

Station Polytechnic University. A university of technology. See also *S-Poly*.

Steven "Steve" Owens Morgan, Charlie's paternal grandfather. Husband of Carrie Morgan Owens, and father of Ted and Hector. (Pronouns: he, him.)

Susan. A Borough Morgue tech. (Pronouns: she, her.)

Tanya Chin-Hua. (CHIN-wah) Assistant Medical Examiner, the second-in-command at the Orangeboro Morgue. (Pronouns: she, her.)

Tasbeeh (TAZZ-bee) A translator affiliated with the Social Services Department of the Orangeboro Department of the Common Good. (Pronouns: she, her.)

TASO. Transmondian Aviation Supervisory Office, which sets all aviation regulations within Transmondian airspace, oversees licensing and inspections, and conducts accident investigations.

Tech with the earrings. A veterinary technologist. (Pronouns: they, them.)

Tech with the tattoos. A veterinary technologist. (Pronouns: they, them.)

Teisingas Tower. (tie-SING-us) Home of Judge Eurydice Qadhi.

Terchikni Jochikti. (terr-CHICK-nee joe-CHICK-tee) A welding work group leader (supervising a mixed human-ozzirikkian crew). An ozzirikkian. (Pronouns: k'ki, k'kin.)

Theodore "Ted" Lee Morgan. Charlie's father and husband of Maria "Mimi" Morgan Lee. (Pronouns: he, him.)

Thinking Girl. One of two small girls rescued relatively uninjured from the *Izgubil*. (Pronouns: she, her.)

Timi. (tih-MEE) The ozzirikkian equivalent to a Borough. *Plural: Timi'i*

TIS. Transmondian Intelligence Service.

Toro Enclave. (TOE-row) One of the six enclaves of the Five-Ten.

Trade Compact. A Chayko System trade agreement to which Rana Station and the Transmondian Republic are both signatories.

Transmondian Pterolizard. (trans-MON-dee-ahn TARE-oh-liz-ard) The largest avian species on Monlandia.

Transmondian Republic. (trans-MON-dee-ahn) The largest country on Monlandia, the largest landform on Planet Chayko, and the dominant sovereignty in the Chayko System.

Triumph. A rescue runner (small space vehicle) operated at the Ranan Hub.

TS. Tech Specialist, a rank in the SBI or SDF. An expert in a particular technical specialty, such as explosives or signals technology.

Tuxedo "Tux" Moondog-Carrie. XK9 partner of Georgia Volkov and mate of Elle Finnian-Ella. (Pronouns: he, him.)

Uladh Nua. (ULL-ud NYOU-ah) A country in the north-western quadrant of Monlandia.

UPO. Uniformed Police Officer, a civilian police rank.

UPO Seaton. A Uniformed Police Officer who works a patrol beat in Precinct Nine. (Pronouns: she, her.)

UPO Wells. A Uniformed Police Officer who works a patrol beat in Precinct Nine. (Pronouns: he, him.)

Valter "Val" Wood. A Special Agent assigned to SIT Delta. (Pronouns: he, him.)

Verne Ignacio. XK9 Project dog wrangler. (Pronouns: he, him.)

Vespers. (VESS-pers) An evening prayer service for Christian Ranans.

Victor Sam-Janet. XK9 partner of Eduardo Donovan. Half-brother of Scout Sam-Shana. (Pronouns: he, him.)

Vicurrians. (vie-KUR-ree-uns) A sapient member-species in the Alliance of the Peoples.

Vinebrook Family. One of the Fifty Founding Families. A wealthy Chartered Family in Orangeboro.

Walter Ejiamike. (edge-EE-a-meek) XK9 Petunia Yeller-Melody's partner. A Detective Level One. (Pronouns: he, him.)

Whisper Syndicate. A powerful criminal organization on Rana Station, as well as on the most closely adjacent asteroids to Rana and Mahusay Stations.

William "Bill" Goldstein Sloane. An OPD Corporal. Father of Becky Goldstein. (Pronouns: he, him.)

Wina. (WEE-nah) See *Edwina Emshwiller*.

Wisniewski. See *Jackson Wisniewski*.

XK9 Project. A Transmondian corporation that produces genetically engineered dogs called XK9s. It has close ties to the Transmondian Intelligence Service.

XK9s. An acronym adopted by the XK9 Project to identify specially-bred, genetically-modified, cybernetically-enhanced canines with extraordinary memories, olfactory capabilities, and verbal acuity.

Zandra Chen. XK9 Fernie Tintin-Brenna's partner. (Pronouns: she, her).

Zuni. Dr. Mika Zuni (MY-ca ZOO-nee), a renowned re-gen specialist. (Pronouns: he, him.)

ACKNOWLEDGMENTS

No book is ever written alone. It takes a least a village, and this one has been no exception. I will do my level best to thank everyone, but please forgive me if I missed you.

First, I owe a debt of gratitude to the science fiction fandom community, especially in the central part of the United States. Fandom nurtured my earliest creative efforts, provided me with a network of knowledgeable friends, and first opened the world of professional writing, editing, and publishing to me in an accessible way. Through these early contacts, and especially through the Kansas City Science Fiction and Fantasy Society, Inc. (KaCSFFS), I found my first writers' group, discovered the world of science fiction conventions, and began to build my life as a creative professional in the speculative genres.

Through sf conventions, I was able to connect with all three of the literary agents with whom I've had the honor of working, Ralph Vicinanza, Chris Lotts, and Algis Budrys. Conventions also opened the door to the many editors whose advice has guided me along the way. They have provided an ongoing forum where I can interact with other professionals through informal networking, workshops, and panel discussions. I also have been able to "test drive" my works-in-progress there, via readings.

I owe a massive debt of gratitude specifically to Robin Wayne Bailey and Diana J. Bailey, who introduced me to sf fandom, and who have offered invaluable guidance and treasured friendship through the decades.

It also was through sf fandom that I first met Lucy A. Synk. Her instincts, honesty and taste have tirelessly guided me through rewrite after rewrite, while I struggled to develop and refine Rex's story.

Two more pearls beyond price for me are my most stringent, demanding, and invaluable critique partners, Lynette M. Burrows and Dora Furlong. I don't want to imagine life without you!

I owe an incalculable debt to Rob Chilson and Alysen Tellure, who host the Writers-in-Rob's-Living-Room writers group. They not only nurtured my earliest efforts, but continue to reliably offer insightful critiques and crucial moral support. They, along with Holly Messinger, Micah Hyatt, Karin Frank, M.C. Chambers, and many, many others, are an essential part of my creative life. You guys are my rock.

I owe special thanks to two of my technical advisers who graciously allowed me to "Tuckerize" them in these pages, Dr. Jill Sandler, DVM, and Joseph Raach. I also am deeply grateful to the many enthusiastic beta-readers who've offered their insights and cheered me on, including Thomas and Nancy O'Brien, Janice Raach, Don McCann, Mike Whitney, P. R Adams and Tina S. Adams. I also appreciate our intrepid proofreader, Deborah Branson, and my amazing cover illustrator, Jody A. Lee.

No list of acknowledgements would be complete without heartfelt thank-yous to my family, starting with my parents, Janet L. Sherrell and Dr. Eugene G. Sherrell, who encouraged my studies and my creative work from the very beginning.

I cannot begin to express my appreciation for my Beloved, Pascal "Packy" Gephardt, my husband of 40-plus amazing years. He's been my "patron of the arts" for much of my adult life. He made it clear from the very beginning that he believed in my creative work. Even more importantly, he made consistent efforts to give me the time and space to do that work.

I also thank my children, who from a very early age patiently (okay, sometimes not-so-patiently) put up with the stresses and vagaries of living in a creative household. My son Ty's burgeoning editorial talents and grasp of story structure have offered me valuable insights in recent years. And without my daughter Signy's enthusiasm for studying animal behavior, I might never have gained crucial insights into dog cognition that proved so foundational for the Pack's genesis.

I am grateful to my late brother-in-law and early mentor, Warren C. Norwood, for his guidance, for his friendship, and for handing me Dwight V. Swain's book *Techniques of the Selling Writer*.

And I will forever be grateful for my sister Gigi Sherrell Norwood, who has been my periodic co-conspirator, co-explorer, and co-creative wellspring for our entire lives. She I have just begun a another new creative adventure in the form Weird Sisters Publishing LLC. Let the weirdness roll on!

I love you all.

ABOUT THE AUTHOR

Jan S. Gephardt commutes daily between her home in Kansas City, USA, and Rana Station, a habitat space station the size of New York City, a very long way from Earth and several hundred years in the future.

Writer, artist, and longtime science fiction fan, Jan's been a teacher, a journalist, an illustrator, a graphic designer, an art director, a book designer, a marketing specialist, and an art agent, all while rearing two children and honing the writer's craft for several decades.

Her fine-art paper sculpture has been featured in regionally-exhibited one-person shows, juried into national exhibitions all over the United States, and is on display wherever she travels to science fiction conventions. She has been married to her partner and "patron of the arts" Pascal Gephardt for more than forty years. She and her sister G. S. Norwood are the co-founders/owners of Weird Sisters Publishing LLC.

Made in the USA
Monee, IL
10 June 2026

52190824R00272